ACCIDENTAL DEATH
IN BIARRITZ

A Novel

David Robert

ISBN: 1483986810
ISBN-13: 9781483986814
Moonlight Books
PO Box 184
Chapel Hill, NC 27514-0184
Fax: 919-967-6666
Email: drdeadmule@gmail.com

This book is dedicated to Jerry Leath Mills.

*Celebrated teacher, inspirational mentor, legendary
Dead Mule authority, and friend nonpareil.*

CHAPTER ONE

The grey schnauzer strained at the leash, its front feet clawing at the air and only occasionally touching the pavement. The dog had the mischievous face typical of the breed with drooping, almost human whiskers and bright darting eyes surmounted by wild, wispy eyebrows. He panted against the choke of the collar, his wet tongue dripping thin, glistening strings of saliva. Attached to the other end of the leash was a man in his late seventies named Jean Haraout, a pensioner who lived nearby on the rue d'Albarade. He shuffled along the sidewalk using short, quick steps, his espadrilles rarely rising more than two inches above the pavement. He wore a large black beret that partially obscured a shrewd, inquisitive face, a face with a hint of mischief not unlike that of his eager canine companion. As he walked along, he admonished the dog with what had become a familiar litany of remonstrations and punctuated each one with a short jab of his old Basque cane.

When the old man reached the corner of the rue Million and the upper coast road, called simply La Perspective, he reined in the dog just as its front feet touched the curb. At that instant, a small sports car came screaming around the corner, passed them in a flash of red and fled down the hill towards the center of Biarritz.

"Marcel! Arrête! You will have us both killed one of these days."

At the mention of his name, or perhaps because of the sudden jerk on the leash, the dog turned briefly to eye his master. He then

1

gave out two insistent barks and resumed his tug of war with the old man.

"Marcel! What did I tell you? Arrête!" Old Haraout carefully surveyed the road for traffic. After waiting for another speeding car to pass, he led the dog across to the macadam apron overlooking the cliffside park. At the edge of this tongue of pavement were four green benches facing the ocean. On the bench nearest the park's entrance sat a middle-aged man in a brown tweed Kangol cap that was cocked low over his forehead. He had pulled the collar of his blue English windbreaker up around his neck so that Haraout could barely make out the features of his swarthy face. As the old pensioner walked past the seated man he tipped his beret and wished him a customary 'Bonjour, M'sieu'. The younger man grunted an unintelligible reply and quickly turned his head. Haraout entered the park, muttering to himself about the lack of civility displayed by the country's younger generation. He took several steps down the macadam path then stopped to unhook the leash from the dog's collar. For the first time all morning, Marcel stood still and patiently waited for his master to unfasten the clasp. This quickly accomplished, the old man sent the dog on his way with a paternal slap on the rump.

"Go on then, you rascal. Do your business."

Nose down, the dog ran ahead and soon left the pathway to explore the bordering undergrowth. Haraout slowly followed his small companion, shuffling along in his peculiar way, swinging his makhila with jaunty precision.

The macadam path crisscrossed the south-to-west facing cliff face in a pattern of acute angles, interrupted at irregular intervals by rock buttressed landings that offered clear views of the ocean and coastline. The old man knew the park well and, depending on weather and wind, would take different routes down to the lower coast road, grandly named the Boulevard du Prince de Galles. There was very little wind today, even at the top of the cliff, and the sun had already broken through the early morning cloud cover. It promised to be a glorious fall day. Haraout began humming an old Edith Piaf tune, 'Je ne regrette rien', softly singing to himself the title's refrain. He had just reached the path's first switchback when he heard the dog begin barking. It was not his usual playful voice but an insistent, furious barking. His hearing was not especially good, but he thought he also heard raised voices. What he heard next there was no mistaking: it was the distressed yelping of an injured animal. He hastened his pace while calling out to Marcel to return immediately. He was halfway down the second leg of the path when the dog arrived at a run. Haraout took the leash from his coat pocket. The dog had stopped four or five paces in front of him. Haraout noticed that the animal was trembling.

"Marcel, what is wrong? Come here to me." He jabbed his cane in the air as he spoke.

The shivering dog looked up at the old man but did not move.

"Marcel, I tell you, come here this instant." He took two steps toward the animal who seemed to take his movement as a cue. The dog barked several times and took off in the direction from which it had come. Cursing to himself, Haraout followed the barking dog down the path. Marcel waited for him at the base of a large semi-circular landing that jutted out from the cliff face. He was whimpering in an almost plaintive way now. Next to the dog was a body.

Haraout slowly approached the motionless form. The supine body was that of a young man with long, sun-bleached blond hair and a ruddy complexion. It rested in an almost dramatically arranged position, the left arm angled behind the head, which was cocked to the right so that half of the face was hidden. On the left side of the neck was a two- inch bloody mark that vaguely resembled the letter 'J', a 'J' with part of the bottom hook cut off.

Haraout bent down and gingerly touched the young man's right wrist. It was still warm. For a moment, he entertained the thought that the young man might still be alive, in spite of the chilling rictus of panic that had frozen the boy's features. While Haraout was checking for a pulse, Marcel worked up the courage to approach the body. The dog tentatively sniffed at the left hand then farther up the sleeve where a red stain was just beginning to be visible. He began to whimper. The old man looked over at the blood-soaked sleeve. He began to feel slightly sick. He stood up and reached in his pocket for the leash and gently spoke to the dog.

"Marcel, come. We must go."

CHAPTER TWO

It was mid-afternoon when Peter Ellis finally finished the article. It was a freelance feature, devoted to the special gastronomic attractions of Paris in the fall. It was not his usual fare but it was a welcome change. His previous project had been an investigation into a Corsican mafia attempt, nearly successful, to compromise one of the most prestigious mustard firms in Dijon so as to force it into a money laundering partnership. During his investigation into the mob's activities, he had received several threats against his life. Celebrating the pleasures of fresh belon oysters, regional wild game and Beaujolais nouveau had proved a timely and pleasurable diversion. So what if the hoopla surrounding the midnight tapping of the nouveau wine casks was nothing more than a monumentally clever promotion gimmick. It was certainly preferable to receiving grossly tortured dolls in the mail, his name written across the mutilated plastic bodies.

He left his office at the European News Bureau and walked down to the Café du Gave. It was a small, old-fashioned café with an ancient pock-marked zinc bar. The owner, M. Hustet, was washing glasses when he arrived. Looking up as Peter Ellis approached, he smiled, dried his right hand on a bar towel and offered it to the journalist.

"Bonjour, Pierre. How are things going?"

"Bonjour, M. Hustet. Going fine. And with you?"

The man behind the counter shrugged. "You know, Pierre, an espresso here, a glass of wine there. Nothing changes. You will take something?"

"A demi-pression, please."

Peter Ellis unfolded a copy of the <u>International</u> <u>Herald</u> <u>Tribune</u> and found the page with the book review and the comics. He folded the length of the page in half, in the fashion of New York train commuters. M. Hustet, in a well-practiced gesture, flicked a coaster on the bar for the frothing glass of beer.

"Eh bien, Pierre, what scandals have you been pursuing today?" Ever since the owner had discovered that his regular American customer was an investigative journalist, he had treated him like a minor celebrity. And wanting to impress his other regulars with <u>his</u> closeness to fame, he had taken to quizzing Peter Ellis on his work.

"The scandal of tourism."

The old man gave him a knowing look and gestured with both arms. "Just so! My wife Marie's Aunt Eugenie took a package tour of England last year. Quelle catastrophe!"

Peter Ellis stopped him before he could go into the details of his aunt's English catastrophe and explained the nature of his article. The journalist was giving his opinion on the current crop of Oleron oysters when M. Hustet excused himself to serve two customers at the other end of the bar. "Yes, the season is upon us. You will excuse me, please, Pierre?"

Peter Ellis sipped the cold Alsatian beer and started reading the newspaper. He began with the comics, saving "Calvin and Hobbs" for last. There was usually a small, hard nugget of wisdom wrapped in the semi-sweet chocolate of its humor. After the sports section, he ordered another demi-pression and turned to the op-ed page. The Safire column was, as usual, nicely written and, as usual, clearly slanted to the right. He respected the columnist's opinions, though Peter Ellis sometimes wished that Mr. Safire would stick to writing about language. He finished his beer with the business section and motioned to M. Hustet, who was arguing with one of his regulars about a recent ministerial appointment.

"Eh bien, Pierre, another?"

"No thank-you, M. Hustet. I am in need of a long walk. I have been sitting all day. Please give my regards to Mme. Hustet."

"Of course." The bar owner started to say something else, but thought better of it. "A demain, Pierre."

"A demain, M. Hustet."

Peter Ellis caught the bar owner's slip. He was about to say something like "And give my regards to Mlle. Burke", but then had remembered that the woman he liked to call "la belle Americaine" was no longer in Paris, was no longer with Peter Ellis. La belle Americaine, indeed.

Peter Ellis strode out to join the late afternoon bustle of the rue d'Artois. He followed the Avenue Franklin Roosevelt down to the Champs-Elysees and turned onto the famous tree-lined boulevard toward the Place de la Concorde. Rust-brown leaves, tired and brittle, covered the ground and crackled under his feet. He reflected that he would have to find another project soon, one that demanded his full attention and one that, ideally, would remove him from the city where shared memories with Burke seemed to lurk around every corner. He thought of something he had read earlier in the <u>Herald Tribune</u>. It was one of the news briefs to which he rarely paid much attention. The headline of this one, however, had mentioned Biarritz. Another "B", another love affair, this one dating back more than twenty years to his first visit to the southwest coast of France. Though this old love affair had nothing to do with a woman, a woman was responsible for it, specifically a young Bardot-like blond busting out of a blue bikini on the cover of <u>Surfer</u> magazine. Whether it was the blond or the pictures of the big French surf, he soon made what would turn out to be a fateful decision. It was a decision he had never regretted. After his first visit to Biarritz in the summer of sixty-six, he was in love. And it wasn't with the girl on the cover.

He reached the Place Clemenceau and waited for the light to change. As in almost every city in France, there was also a Place Clemenceau in the center of Biarritz. In the old days, Peter Ellis went there every day except Sunday to buy a copy of the <u>International</u>

<u>Herald Tribune</u> at a bookstore on the corner of the Place and the Avenue Victor Hugo. More often than not, he would then install himself in one of the comfortable wicker chairs of the Café Royalty across the street and leisurely read the paper over a café crème and croissant. He was picturing that other Place Clemenceau when the light changed. As he moved toward the Jardin de Paris, he thought again about the article in the paper. The headline had read: 'Death in Biarritz Ruled Accidental.' In spite of its scant detail, the short article had made a curious impression on him. As he walked along the wide pedestrian boulevard, he opened the paper and re-read the article:

"The death last week of an American, Mr. Kevin Duffy, aged 23 has been ruled an accident by the police in Biarritz. Authorities have concluded that the victim had climbed onto the railing of a scenic overlook in the cliffside park above the Plage Côte des Basques and lost his footing. A thorough investigation and autopsy have uncovered no evidence of foul play, according to Chief Inspector Jacques LeClerc, who has suggested to town officials that warnings be posted to prevent a re-occurrence of the tragedy."

Peter Ellis knew well both the beach at Côte des Basques and the cliffside park overlooking it. When he had finally moved to Biarritz in the early seventies, he had rented an apartment across the street from the entrance to the park. Perhaps that explained the frisson he had felt when he had first read about the death of Kevin Duffy. But the more he tried to picture the accident, the more bizarre it seemed. He was intimately familiar with the paths that traversed the cliff face down to the lower coast road bordering the beach. For a year he had walked them almost daily. As best he could remember, there was no reason to climb the railing of any of the overlooks—every one gave a clear view of the coastline. He decided to telephone his old friend, Maurice Claverie-Laporte, who lived in Anglet, a small town on the coast just north of Biarritz. Although Maurice had retired from the investigative arm of the Brigade Financière a year earlier, he retained certain discreet contacts in various branches of the French police bureaucracy. If there was anything peculiar about the case, he would either know it or be able to find out. More to the point, Maurice would know if there was the potential for a story. Peter Ellis was aware of the cold-blooded turn his thoughts had taken, but he badly needed something to take him away from Paris. If that something took him to Biarritz, all the better.

He walked through the Jardin de Tuileries to the Louvre's large courtyard, past I.M. Pei's famous (or infamous, depending on your aesthetic bent) steel and glass pyramids. He, for one, found them beautiful, though he really couldn't say why. They certainly seemed to light, and lighten, that massive enclosed space. He followed the Quai du Louvre down to the Pont Neuf, past the Taverne Henri IV overlooking the prow-like tip of the Ile de la Cité over to the Left Bank. He crossed the Quai des Grandes Augustins, turned left and walked down to Number 15. He stopped in at L'Ecluse, a small bar on the ground floor of his building, to collect his mail. He thumbed through the short stack of letters: three bills, two responses from magazine editors and a statement from his stock broker. He wasn't really expecting to see a letter addressed in Burke's familiar neat script. She had said she thought it would be easier for both of them if they didn't communicate for a while. Didn't he agree? Yes, he supposed he did. What did she expect him to say? He ordered a demi-pression and opened the statement from the brokerage house. After a quick confirmation of his transactions and ending balance, he opened the two letters from the magazine editors. One was an enthusiastic rejection and the other was a muted acceptance with an attached list of 'suggested' changes he might consider making to his article. The list of changes did not surprise him—this particular editor always 'suggested' copious changes, knowing full well that most of them would be ignored.

Peter Ellis finished his beer and walked up the three flights of stairs to his apartment. The curving staircase was narrow, dark and uncommonly steep. The apartment was small even by Left Bank standards: a miniscule bathroom, what passed for a kitchen on one wall and a combination living room/bedroom, the total space not more than forty meters square. This smallness, however, did not bother Peter Ellis. The apartment had something that was much more important to him, something that more than made up for its minis-cule size: It had a view, a spectacular view, of the river Seine.

He threw the mail on his desk and walked over and opened the two large windows. The sun was beginning to set and the early autumnal light suffused the city with a warm glow. He looked down at the river's mustard green water flowing in swirls past the stone embankment of the Ile de la Cité. And suddenly, like in a movie flashback, he had a momentary vision of Burke. He went to his desk and pushed the rewind button on his answering machine. The ending click came in a matter of seconds. There were two messages, neither of which he felt immediately impelled to answer. If Burke wasn't going to write, she certainly was not going to call. If she had changed her mind about 'not communicating', she would write him a letter. Her preference for the written word was one of the many things he had loved about her.

Peter Ellis took out his address book and looked up Maurice Claverie-Laporte's number. His old friend answered on the third ring. Peter Ellis detected the slightest trace of impatience in his voice. He remembered how much Maurice shared his own distaste for the telephone.

"Monsieur Claverie-Laporte?'

"Oui."

"You have just won a trip for two to Martinique. Congratulations!"

There was a slight pause. Then a distinctive laugh. "Pierre? Is that you, Pierre? How extraordinary!"

"Extraordinary, Maurice? I think you exaggerate. The telephone is not that new, even in France. And knowing how much you like receiving calls, I thought…" Before he finished his sentence, his old friend had interrupted.

"You misunderstand, Pierre. It is extraordinary because I intended to call *you* tonight."

"Was your call going to concern the accidental death of a young American named Kevin Duffy in the park below my former apartment on La Perspective in Biarritz?"

"Again, extraordinary! How did you know?"

"There was a short article in today's <u>Herald</u> <u>Tribune</u>."

"But no! That is not what I mean. I mean, how did you know that my call would concern the unfortunate death of this young American, M. Duffy?"

"I knew because it is the same reason I am calling you, Maurice. Tell me, what do you know about this so-called accident?"

"Eh bien, that,just as you suspect, it may not have been an accident at all. It seems that M. Duffy had become involved with a local girl, a serveuse at the Patisserie Dodin. It also seems that at least one person, a certain M. Jean-Claude Duchon, did not approve of this alliance."

"You think he may have murdered the Duffy boy?"

"I do not know. I am not even sure that M. Duffy was murdered. However I am presently expecting a call from my friend, Inspector Rectoran, later this evening. Among other things, he is going to check the autopsy report. I understand there was a peculiar wound on the body."

"But the newspaper said that the autopsy revealed no evidence of foul play."

"I know."

"Will you call me after you hear from your friend?"

"That was my intention, Pierre."

Peter Ellis replaced the receiver in the cradle and walked to the open windows. The sun had set and its radiant afterglow bathed in warm light the slender turrets of the Conciergerie. He contemplated the sun-streaked skyline, letting his thoughts wander aimlessly as evening settled like a veil over the city. An approaching bateau mouche, its blinding spotlights working their way down the embankment, brought him abruptly back to earth. He suddenly realized that he was very hungry.

At the Brasserie de L'Ile St. Louis, he ordered the choucroute garni, a specialty of the house, and a large mug of Mutzig beer. Within minutes, the waiter delivered a huge steaming plate of ham, corned beef, saucisson and frankfurters piled over a mound of pungent sauerkraut laced with large black peppercorns. He spooned a liberal dollop of hot Dijon mustard onto the side of the plate and enthusiastically began to eat. By the time he left the restaurant, his sinuses were clear and his head was soaked with perspiration.

He walked across the Pont St. Louis to the Ile de la Cité, then down the Quai aux Fleurs and the Quai de Corse to the Taverne Henri IV. Once there, he ordered a chilled glass of Poire William. The Henri IV closed relatively early and the owner and his long-time barman were busying themselves with end-of-the-night chores. Peter Ellis stood at the narrow, polished brass counter exchanging small talk with the two men and savoring the sweet pear aroma of the Alsatian eau-de-vie. When he had finished with his closing duties, the owner joined the journalist for a nightcap to celebrate his recovery from a recent case of grippe.

Peter Ellis returned to his apartment just after ten. He went directly to the answering machine and re-wound the tape. The first message was from a colleague trying to arrange a tennis match. The second was from Maurice. He listened to it closely, re-set the machine and began to pack his suitcase.

CHAPTER THREE

The waitress had not seen the man arrive. She was placing a fresh batch of fruit tartes in the pastry display case. Something -perhaps the sound of a chair leg scraping the floor, she wasn't sure what -had caused her to look up from the neatly arranged rows of pastries. And there he was, seated at a small table by the window, meticulously combing the few strands of grey hair on his very large, very round head. Even seated, it was apparent that he was not a tall man, though 'small' certainly would never be used to describe him, not with his wide shoulders and torso the size and shape of a wine cask. He wore a grey Harris tweed sports coat with a yellow silk pocket handkerchief over a light blue Oxford shirt open at the neck and almost passed for a retired English military man. However, there was something unmistakably Gallic about his facial features, some-thing that recalled Flaubert in his later, corpulent years,though this comparison would have been lost on the striking, raven-haired girl who was now approaching the man's table, a small gold menu in her hand. Her familiarity with the great author was limited to a television broadcast of a film adaption of <u>Madame Bovary</u>. The waitress placed the menu on the table in front of Maurice Claverie-Laporte.

"You would like something to drink, monsieur?"

Maurice looked up and briefly studied the girl's face. She had not looked at him when she spoke. And he noticed that her gaze now seemed to be trained on something far removed from the mundane scene visible through the shop's large, plate-glass window. His lack of reply finally caused her to look down at him. Maurice smiled his best disarming smile.

"You have Earl Grey tea, mademoiselle?"

"Oui, monsieur. Is that all?"

"I just noticed you putting out some fruit tarts. I believe I saw some strawberry ones among them, did I not?"

"Oui, monsieur. The patissier just now finished making them."

"Excellent. Even though I shouldn't," he patted his ample stomach, "I shall sample one of your strawberry tarts with my tea."

"Very good, monsieur. Merci."

While she took his order, the girl had her head bowed as though in prayer. She did not once look up from her order pad. Maurice, in his turn, did not take his eyes from the girl's face, carefully studying each feature. It most definitely was not an unattractive face to study: magnificent hazel eyes (it had only taken a single glance to notice them), a strong aquiline nose, prominent cheek bones and a high, smooth forehead. Only her mouth kept her from having the face of a covergirl. Relative to her other features, it was small and the lips were thin; however, it seemed appropriate, Maurice mused, for her seemingly taciturn nature. She was a tall girl and had the long, shapely legs of a dancer. Even in her black skirt, prim white blouse and light blue apron, it was apparent she had the kind of figure that would turn heads on the Grand Plage. Maurice had no trouble imagining how the American boy, Kevin Duffy, could have had his judgment impaired by such a girl.

The subject of his musings returned to the table with a laden silver tray. This time Maurice made a point of keeping his head lowered while she went about her business. Only after she had placed before him the bright red, gelatinous strawberry tart and poured his tea did he look directly at her.

"You are Chantal Clairac, are you not?" His question took her by surprise. He detected a reddening of her cheeks. "Permit me to introduce myself." He reached into his inside coat pocket and produced a black, lizard skin wallet. In a practiced gesture, he flipped it open to reveal an official-looking identity card. In the picture, he wore a severe expression. He held the card up for the girl's inspection, though he doubted whether she even had the presence of mind to read his name. "I am Inspector Maurice Claverie-Laporte of the Brigade-Financière." He conveniently left out the word 'former' before 'Inspector'. He did not want to confuse the girl, who now seemed on the verge of tears.

"Please. Do not upset yourself. I have only come to see if we might have a little talk after work today."

"A little talk?" She looked at him, evidently puzzled.

"About your poor friend, Monsieur Duffy. I realize how difficult it has been for you these last days. I assure you it will only take a few minutes."

"But I have already talked with the man from Inspector LeClerc's office. He said that there would be no more questions."

Maurice saw there was now moisture in her eyes. "Yes, I am sure he did. He did not realize, however, that we must file a separate report with the American embassy. It has been requested by Monsieur Duffy's family." He paused to allow his reference to the boy's family to register. "So please. For them. A few minutes of your time this afternoon when you have finished work? We could meet just down the street. Do you know the Player's bar?"

"Yes. I have seen it."

"You are finished when?"

"Usually by six-thirty."

"Then I shall meet you there sometime after six-thirty, agreed? It will be much appreciated by Monsieur's family."

She slowly nodded her head in assent and whispered something. Maurice lightly touched her wrist.

"Thank-you Mademoiselle Clairac. Thank-you very much."

CHAPTER FOUR

Peter Ellis left Paris shortly after eight o'clock under an October sky overcast and heavy with moisture. He took a local train to Versailles then a cab to the garage where he stored both his car and his surfboard. By ten-thirty, he was speeding south on the autoroute L'Aquitaine, his head suddenly light with the twin sensations of escape and blind anticipation. Between Tours and Poitiers, the horizon began to clear; by the time he reached Bordeaux, only soft white brushstrokes of cirrus marred a pristine, cerulean sky. He barely noticed the vast, green Landes pine barrens, his mind's eye already picturing the rocky headlands and exploding surf of the Côte Basque.

When he reached Biarritz, he drove directly to the Hotel-Restaurant Les Flots Bleus, where he had stayed, on and off, for the last twenty years. Located on the coast road, La Perspective de la Côte, the hotel commanded, from its vantage point one hundred and fifty feet above the beach, a spectacular view of the Bay of Biscay and the mountainous northern coast of Spain. It also overlooked, coincidentally, the cliffside park where the young American, Kevin Duffy, had somehow fallen to his death.

A pixie-faced Moroccan girl led him to a modern efficiency apartment on the second floor of an austere, turn-of-the-century, beige stone house with a Mansard roof. Called 'Mar y Montes', the house was situated next door to the hotel proper, at the corner of La Perspective and the rue Million. His apartment was on the western side of the building, where a set of French windows gave onto a small stone balcony with a black, wrought iron railing and afforded a view not only of the "sea and mountains" but also of a modern, character-less eight story apartment building.

He set up his portable cassette player on a heavy Basque-styled oak table and inserted a John Hiatt tape. He unpacked his two suit-cases, then showered and shaved. He dressed informally, choosing a clean pair of black jeans and a drab olive canvas shirt. He telephoned Maurice and left a message confirming their 8:30 dinner engagement and spoke with his friend, Marc Dufau, and arranged to meet him in the morning for some surfing. Finally, Peter Ellis took his holstered Colt 45 automatic and placed it and some extra money under the plastic lining of his bedroom's waste basket. They would be the only things he would put in the basket during his stay at Les Flots Bleus.

It was early evening when he left his apartment. He crossed the upper coast road to the sidewalk and short shell and concrete fence that bordered the cliffside park. To his left, the purple sky was slowly deepening to black above the flickering lights of the northern Spanish coast. Below him, long lines of surf pounded relentlessly against the large boulders that buttressed the seawall protecting the lower coast road. The wind had picked up and gusted wildly around him, the sea air washing away the last grimy vestiges of city life. He began walking along La Perspective, down the southwest side of the Pointe Atalaye, in the direction of the Vieux Port.

At the bottom of La Perspective, the road took a sharp, one hundred and eighty degree turn around a ten-story concrete-and-glass box that had once, he recalled, been a fashionable hotel. Below the road, rising above the contorted rock of the wave-battered point like some freakish growth, stood the fantastic Villa Belza. The decrepit house was the result of a forced architectural marriage: the half facing east was a four story, no nonsense Basque farmhouse formed by the intersection of two large rectangles and capped by two A-framed, orange tiled roofs; the half facing west was a six story, multi-faceted Béarnaise tower, featuring a small, cantilevered turret on one corner and a steep, slate roof. For several minutes, Peter Ellis studied the crumbling building from his roofline vantage point. The Villa Belza, he mused, had once also been a fashionable residence. Now, against the moonlit background of crashing surf and gusting wind, the formerly proud aristocrat was merely a fenced-in prisoner of its buffeted situation.

He continued down the hill to the Sentier de la Baleine, a steep series of steps leading to the Vieux Port and the Santa Maria bar. A stone vaulted room barely thirty feet long cut directly into the cliff face, the bar and its small terrace overlooked the protected, horseshoe-shaped beach that, centuries before, had been the town's original port. He ordered a Kronenbourg 1664 from a tall, freckled girl with short, blond hair. As he drank the cold beer, he tried to imagine what it would be like to live in the Villa Belza. He decided to send Burke a postcard of the place and ask her what she thought of the idea. He figured the chances of it happening were about equal to those of Burke coming back. It was the first time he had accepted the truth of their situation. It was probably not a coincidence that this acceptance should surface in Biarritz.

Maurice was talking with a red-haired woman seated in the far left corner of the restaurant in front of a television with the sound turned down. When she saw Peter Ellis, she smiled broadly.

"Monsieur Pierre! How have you been?"

He leaned down to kiss her on both cheeks. "Very well, thank-you, Mamie. And you?"

She pursed her lips and motioned with her hand the familiar gesture of 'comme ci, comme ca'. "You know how it is, M. Pierre. One is not getting any younger. You are staying with us long?"

"I am not sure, Mamie. I have come to help my friend Maurice with his investigation of the death of the young American."

Mamie shuddered. "My Lord but it was terrible. And right here in front of the hotel. Old Haraout and his Marcel found the body. I am surprised he did not have a heart attack. He and his Marcel have not been the same since that horrible accident."

"You know M. Haraout well, Mamie?"

"But of course, Pierre. He is a regular customer here. He lives just around the corner on the rue D'Albarade."

"I should very much like to speak with him tomorrow. Do you know how to reach him?"

"Certainly. I'll have Arlette call him after dinner."

"Perfect. And now," he indicated Maurice, who was eyeing the food that had just been delivered to an adjoining table, "I believe it is feeding time for my old friend here."

Arlette, Mamie's daughter, seated them at a table near the restaurant's glassed-in front entrance that offered a view of the glittering sweep of coastline. She suggested the <u>moules marinières</u> and the <u>gigot d'agneau avec flageolets</u>. Peter Ellis ordered a half bottle of dry Jurançon for the mussels and a bottle of Madiran to drink with the lamb. She thanked them for their order and said that a waitress would return shortly with their wine.

"So Maurice, what have you discovered about the death of the young Mr. Kevin Duffy?"

The older man leaned forward in his chair and clasped his hands, prayer-like, on the table. He spoke in a deliberate, low voice.

"Well, to begin, that it is highly improbable that his death was <u>purely</u> accidental."

"What do you mean?"

"I mean that according to my source in the department, the wounds of which I spoke on the telephone last night were almost certainly caused by a knife. And it is impossible that they were self-inflicted."

"What do the police think?"

"Ha! What do the police think indeed! I'll tell you what they think: nothing at all. Because, you see, there is no mention of the knife wounds in the final autopsy report, even though the attending doctor assured my friend that he had mentioned them, though not as the cause of death."

"And that was?"

"A sharp blow to the head. Which does not surprise me. You will understand when you see where the young man fell. I am sure old

Haraout will show you the exact spot tomorrow. He is very proud of his memory. When do you intend to see him?"

"Early in the morning before I go to Chambre d'Amour. There seems to be a good swell building, according to my friend, Marc Dufau. I'm to meet him there at nine for some surfing. By the way, you didn't mention on the telephone that the Duffy boy was a surfer."

"But why do you suppose that I thought of calling you immediately, Pierre. I was certain you would be interested—and particularly suited to help me."

Their waitress arrived with the chilled half bottle of Jurançon and a large tureen of steaming mussels. The shiny blue-black shells were almost an inch and a half long and simmered in a rich wine broth of parsley, onions, shallots and garlic. Peter Ellis watched as his friend, with characteristic gusto, began eating. In the local fashion, he used the shell of one mussel as a pincer to remove the succulent bright orange flesh.

"What have you discovered about the girl? What is her name?"

"Chantal. Chantal Clairac. A very attractive girl, which may be unfortunate for her."

"How do you mean?"

"I will tell you. I met with her earlier this evening." He stopped to dab a trickle of broth from his chin. "She is a very simple girl, very naïve in a peasant kind of way. Like many girls who work in shops here that cater to the rich, she has learned how to look sophisticated, but I fear she is greatly lacking in sophistication when it comes to the judgment of others. Jean-Claude Duchon is a perfect example."

"He is the spurned lover?"

"That is exact. And a charming one he appears to be."

"Do you think he could have been involved in the boy's death?"

"My friend, that is precisely what we must attempt to discover. I have yet to meet this Duchon, but from what I have heard of him, it would not surprise me." The former inspector stopped to sample the straw-colored wine, nodded his head with approval, then continued. "Duchon works for a restaurant food distributor in Bayonne. Apparently, he services most of the restaurants, cafes and bars between Biarritz and St. Jean-de-Luz. After the death of Kevin Duffy, my friend Mme. Haizart called me and asked for my assistance. You may know her establishment?"

'Very well. It is not far up the street on the rue Gambetta. An excellent, traditional Basque restaurant."

"Exactly. As you may recall, she also has several small rooms that she rents, mainly to surfers and other young travelers. Kevin Duffy had been living there for two months at the time of his death. It seems he had become very close to Mme. Haizart's son, Michel. That is how I came to discover that Duchon had tried to coerce the boy to break off his relations with Chantal Clairac.

"It seems Duchon's first attempt was to leave a letter under the boy's apartment door, which warned him that he had prior claim to Chantal and informed him, by innuendo, that she was not the fine, honest, working girl that she appeared to be. M. Duffy apparently did not believe a word and, initially, did not mention the letter to anyone. A week later, the boy was stopped by a man in the street outside his apartment building. You will guess that the man was none other than our jilted lover, Duchon."

As if to accentuate his point, Maurice Claverie-Laporte broke off a large piece of baguette. He began mopping up the broth left in the bottom of his bowl. Only when he had finished did he continue his story.

"Duchon told the boy that he was an old friend of Chantal and wanted to show him something. He handed him an envelope of photographs and said that they were very special because they showed Chantal for what she really was: a prostitute. Monsieur Duffy closely studied the Polaroid snapshots. They were indeed of Chantal and she was in various stages of undress. But the boy noticed that there was something peculiar about the angle from which they were taken and something unusual about her facial expression. He also noticed that they had all been taken at relatively long distance. In none of them did she seem to be posing for the camera."

"In other words, the girl did not know that she was being photographed."

"That is what I have been thinking."

"This Jean-Claude Duchon seems the kind of friend one could do without."

"Just wait, Pierre, until you have heard the rest. Even while the Duffy boy was looking at the nude photographs of his girlfriend, Duchon began explaining that he was only doing this for Chantal's own good. He said that she had severe emotional problems, though she was very clever and had learned to hide them behind a gay exterior. It was only through his efforts that she was no longer a prostitute. She was presently going through a difficult transition period and he was begging the boy, on behalf of Chantal's mother, an old friend, to terminate all relations with her. He understood that this would be difficult—she was a very beautiful girl—but it was for her own good, if not survival. He said he was appealing to the young man's sense of decency."

"Well, at the mention of the word 'decency,' Monsieur Duffy lost his composure. He began screaming at Duchon—he could not remember what exactly—and tearing up the photographs. As he left, he pushed a startled Duchon roughly out of the way. It was after this confrontation that he went to my friend Madame Haizart and told her what had happened. Three days later, he was dead."

"Did Madame Haizart explain all of this to the police?"

"Of course. But it seems that Chief Inspector LeClerc and Duchon are old friends. LeClerc apparently just shrugged it off as petty jealousy and pointed out that, in any case, Duchon was in a café in Bayonne at the time of the accident. There are at least ten witnesses."

"So what do you plan to do?"

"I shall tell you after we deal with another pressing matter?"

"Another pressing matter? What else could there be, Maurice?"

"Why, a fine gigot d'agneau, of course!"

As if on cue, the waitress appeared and removed their empty dishes and the spent mussel shells. She replaced them with two warm plates and a large platter of sliced, rare lamb surrounded by flageolets. She opened the bottle of Madiran and filled their glasses. The lamb was exceptionally tender and the beans, in a savory garlic and onion butter sauce, were firm, not mushy. The wine was a rich garnet and, though young, had a fine, fruity nose and clean, dry finish. The retired inspector and the journalist ate and drank and did not speak again of the events surrounding the death of the young American surfer, Kevin Duffy, until their plates had been cleared and cheese ordered.

"So Maurice, do you have a plan?"

"I do, but I must frankly admit that it is a dubious one. And perhaps a dangerous one where you are concerned. Before I get into it, though, let me complete the background for you.

"You see, there is a local mobster named Gambia, who I pursued for years while I was still active in the Brigade."

"That is a very unusual name, Maurice."

"His real name is Gandia. For some reason he changed it to Gambia after his first stint in prison when he was still a teenager."

"How amusing, to name yourself after a country in Africa. So, Maurice, tell me about this M. Gambia."

"Well, he has his hands in everything from prostitution and gambling to forgery and drugs. It seems that Duchon has been doing a little work on the side for Gambia."

"What sort of work?"

"As you recall, Pierre, our friend Duchon works for a restaurant food distributor. In the course of his rounds, he regularly visits most of the establishments in the area. When new girls come to work in these establishments, he makes a point to meet them immediately. He observes them for several weeks to decide which ones seem vulnerable to drugs, alcohol or men with money. Along the way, he drops hints about knowing all of the local nightclub owners and how he can arrange free admission if they ever want to go. Eventually some of them succumb to the temptation. Duchon directs them to one of the clubs owned by Gambia and, according to my sources, receives a handsome commission for his efforts."

"And Gambia does what he can to recruit them for another kind of work."

"Precisely."

"Did you question Madame Haizart about this practice?"

"Yes. She said that she had heard rumors and that it would not surprise her if they were true. She thought complaints had been filed against him by at least two other restaurants. By her own admission, she did not care for Duchon even before this business with the Duffy boy. In fact, she said she made it a practice to warn her new girls about him."

"What about the girlfriend, Chantal Clairac? When you saw her this evening, did you ask her about Duchon's other activities?"

"Not exactly. It was not possible."

"Not possible?"

"You must see her to understand what I mean. She reminded me of a stray dog who has been so often kicked by people that it flinches at the least movement of a person."

"What <u>did</u> you talk about?"

"I asked her to tell me about her relationship with the Duffy boy."

"That's all?"

"Easy, my friend. Easy. You do not know how much gentle persuasion it required to extract the few answers that I did manage."

"I'm sorry Maurice. Please continue."

"She told me pretty much the same story that Madame Haizart had told, with one glaring exception."

"Duchon?"

"Yes, Duchon."

"Did you ask her about him?"

"Oh yes. I asked her if she knew that Duchon had spoken to her friend several days before he died. Needless to say, she did not. I then told her that M. Duffy had left a journal. I mentioned that I was concerned about several recent entries and wanted to discuss them with Duchon tomorrow."

"This story about the journal is not true, is it?"

"Of course not. It was a way of sending a little message to Duchon. And of seeing how much Mlle. Chantal knew of her American friend's habits."

"Do you think she believed you about the journal?"

"I am sure of it. When I mentioned it, she made an excuse to leave. The girl is a very poor liar."

"You mentioned nothing of the knife wounds?"

"No, we can not be certain at this time who knows about them. With the exception, of course, of certain policemen. I think it best we save that information for later use."

Peter Ellis nodded in agreement. The waitress had come to remove their cheese plates. She asked if they cared for anything else.

"Maurice, a little Armagnac perhaps?"

"I shouldn't, but for the occasion of your arrival."

"Excellent! Two Armagnacs please, mademoiselle." The waitress left and Peter Ellis looked back to his friend. "So Maurice, tell me about your plan."

CHAPTER FIVE

J ean-Claude Duchon was standing at the end of the bar near the door. He had been standing there for almost an hour. For most of that time, his gaze had been fixed on the modern, white apartment building directly across the street from the small, neighborhood, café. In fact, his eyes had only left the building on the three occasions he had turned to order another drink. He decided he would give her ten more minutes. He turned and gestured to the barman with his empty glass.

"Another Ricard, M. Duchon?"

"Please, Achille."

"Mlle. Chantal had to work late?"

"Yes, too late."

He did not try to hide the impatience in his voice, nor the fact that he was more than a little upset.

When the barman had replaced his glass, Duchon added water from a small pitcher. He tasted the dull, cloudy drink then returned his attention to the white apartment building.

He was a small-framed man of medium height, with thinning, gun-metal grey hair. He was very sensitive about his increasing baldness and made a point of combing the triangular patch of hair above his forehead straight back to cover what he could of his naked pate. He had a narrow, angular face whose features shared one noticeable common characteristic: everything was marked by an incredible thinness: the small mouth had razor thin lips; the long nose was sharp and pointed; and, the dull blue, furtive eyes were strangely set off by wispy, grey eyebrows that had the appearance of being shaved.

Jean-Claude Duchon's narrow features underscored an equally narrow sense of humor, and that only on his best days. Today was far from one of his best. It had taken five calls to the patisserie to reach Chantal. Then she had tried putting him off again. It was too soon after the accident. He had nearly reminded her that more than two weeks had passed since the boy's death. In the end, he resorted to pointing out that he still paid half the rent on her apartment and, as the lease was coming due, they needed to discuss future arrangements. He had assured her that the meeting would not take long and had even suggested a drink afterwards, like in the old days. And this was the thanks he received. What if she did not show up at all? No, that thought he could not support. It was not his fault that the American boy was dead. He hadn't told him to jump.

He took another sip of his drink and lit another cigarette. The anisette was beginning to kick in, flooding his mind with thoughts of the recent unexpected events. He had certainly wanted the boy to leave Biarritz. He could not deny that. But he had not meant for him to leave in a coffin. He had explicitly told Gambia what he wanted. Frighten the boy into leaving. Frighten him, not kill him. Gambia had assured him that's all his boys had tried to do. Maybe Carlos had not used his best judgement with the knife. But how could they have predicted that the American boy would go crazy? They had tried to stop him. Still, there was no reason to panic, Gambia had said. LeClerc had taken care of the autopsy. The copy received by the press had no mention of knife wounds. And once the papers deemed it "tragic and accidental," that made it official as far as anyone was concerned. Duchon had to agree with Gambia on that one. Which brought him back to the one remaining problem. Chantal. She had not been herself since the accident. He needed to be sure it was only the shock of the boy's death. What if she had been told of his previous encounter with the American boy? That was another reason he needed to speak with her: to lay to rest his lingering suspicions. And the sooner, the better.

So where was she? Was she making him wait on purpose? Was there something she was afraid to tell him? He began to think what he would do if she did not show up at all. Just the thought made him furious. Dead boy or no, he would certainly give her cause to regret <u>that</u> decision. It was at this moment that he recognized the long-legged figure of Chantal approaching the apartment building.

Duchon finished his drink in one gulp. He quickly crossed the street and waited for Chantal at the entrance to her building. He did not respond to her subdued, almost whispered greeting. He purposely waited until she had closed the door behind them and placed her small bag of groceries on the kitchen table before he began to speak. He could play the waiting game too.

"I am happy to see you could finally find time to see me."

"You are angry with me, Jean-Claude." It was not a question but an admission. She was standing at the entrance to her kitchen and seemed to be studying the space of floor that separated them. Duchon walked over to her and grasped her upper arm, forcing her to look up at him.

"Look at me when you speak. I have been waiting for almost an hour and a half for you in that damned café. The least you can do is to look at me when you speak!"

"Yes, Jean-Claude."

"So where have you been?"

"I needed some bread and a few things at the grocery." Her voice barely rose above a whisper.

"It takes you now an hour and a half to buy a baguette?" Duchon tightened his grip on her arm as if to punctuate the question.

"I had to meet with the inspector about the accident. Please, Jean-Claude." She looked at him, tears visible in the corner of her eyes.

Duchon released his hold on her arm. He turned his back to her and took several steps into the small living room, feeling the need for movement to dissipate his growing anger.

"Why didn't you tell me you were meeting with LeClerc's man? What did he want?"

"It was not the man from Inspector LeClerc's office. It was another man. He showed me his identification card. I can't remember his name. It was one with two names."

The news caused Duchon to stop abruptly and turn back towards the girl.

"Why didn't you tell me? What did he want?

"He said he was checking on details for the American Embassy, for Kevin's parents. He said there were some unanswered questions, that the Embassy had asked him to confirm that it was really an accident. It was just an accident, wasn't it Jean-Claude?"

"Of course it was an accident! You have spoken with Inspector LeClerc's men. Do you think the police would lie to you?"

"No, Jean-Claude."

"And you saw the story in the newspaper. Do you think the newspaper would say it was an accident if it was not an accident?"

"No, Jean-Claude."

"Did your mystery inspector say it was not an accident?"

"No, Jean-Claude. He said there were some details that had not been explained. And he asked me about you. Please, don't be angry with me, Jean-Claude. I didn't know what to do."

Duchon suddenly felt sick. He <u>knew</u> there was going to be trouble because of that American bastard's death. He had told Gambia there was going to be trouble.

"Why did he ask about me? I had nothing to do with your damned American friend's death. Everyone knows I was in Bayonne when it happened. I hope you at least had the sense to tell him that."

I tried to Jean-Claude, but he said you had spoken to Kevin before he died. Is that true, Jean-Claude?"

"I saw him once on the street and spoke to him briefly. It was of no importance. He refused to listen to me."

"You spoke to Kevin? What did you say to him?"

"Nothing! I have just told you. It was of no importance."

"Why didn't you tell me?"

"Chantal, have you become hard of hearing too? It was of **no importance**." He had walked over to her and now he grasped both of her arms and squeezed them. "Now forget about my talk with your little friend and try to remember what else this inspector asked about me." He released his grip on her arms, shoving her brusquely away from him.

"He said he wanted to speak to you tomorrow after work. He said he would call you."

"Speak with me? About what?"

"He said Kevin had left a journal."

"Oh shit!

Jean-Claude Duchon could barely believe what he was hearing. The little bastard had left a journal. And when Chantal's mystery inspector read it, he would probably discover the details of their meeting. He thought about the pictures he had taken of Chantal last year at Gambia's apartment. What if the boy had written about them? And, if so, what if this inspector asked Chantal about them? How would he be able to explain that to her? The existence of a journal introduced an ugly world of possibilities to consider. And he would not know where to begin until he had talked with this inspector with no name.

"Jean-Claude, is something wrong?"

Duchon had almost forgotten that Chantal was in the room.

"Jean-Claude, will you meet with the inspector tomorrow?"

"Of course. Perhaps I shall be lucky enough to discover his name. I must go. I shall be late for dinner."

But food was the last thing on Jean-Claude Duchon's mind at that moment. He would tell his wife to eat without him, and if she complained, then be damned. He needed to speak with Gambia immediately.

CHAPTER SIX

———————

Peter Ellis had left a wake-up call for six-thirty. He quickly dressed—shorts, a T-shirt, tennis shoes and a University of North Carolina sweatshirt Burke had given him—and walked down the narrow service road to the hotel's rear entrance. The dining room was empty except for Arlette and her husband. He joined them for a small breakfast of strong café au lait, croissants and mineral water. They talked of an up-coming surf fishing trip to Morocco that the family was planning. By seven o'clock, he was seated on one of the green benches overlooking the beach of Côtes des Basques.

It was a cool, clear morning with only a few high wisps of cloud in the sky. The mountainous coast of Spain, normally obscured by mist or fog, stretched out to his left as far as the eye could see. A strong offshore wind was blowing and from what he could tell from his vantage point—his view was partially cut off by the untrimmed cedar hedges bordering the cliffside park—a good-sized swell was rolling in from the Bay of Biscay. It looked as though the surf gods were smiling on him at least.

He had only been waiting five minutes when he heard a voice behind him. He turned in time to see the bundled-up figure of old Haraout being pulled across the street by a panting grey schnauzer. As he stood to meet the old man, he found himself smiling at the mock-gruff way Haraout chastised his insistent small companion. He felt certain that the scene played itself out in nearly identical fashion every morning.

"I have the pleasure of making the acquaintance of Monsieur Jean Haraout, I believe?"

"What remains of him after seventy-six years." He offered a small, bony hand. "And you are Mme. Mamie's American friend, the journalist."

"Peter Ellis."

The two men shook hands. The dog, sensing an additional delay to his morning constitutional, gave out two high-pitched barks. The old man jerked lightly on the leash.

"M. Ellis, this young truant is Marcel. I must apologize for his behaviour. He is intolerable in the mornings before his walk." They began following the dog towards the entrance to the park. "Eh bien, so you have come about the accident with the poor young American. Did you say on the phone that you knew his family?"

"Not exactly. A friend asked me to look into some inconsistencies in the final police report. You can imagine what a shock the death was to the boy's family. The police report was so impersonal. The accident itself seems so improbable, so hard to understand. The parents wanted someone unofficial to look into the circumstances of the boy's death. To help them come to terms with it."

"I understand completely. For my part, I shall tell you all that I can, which I fear is not much. I must say, I do not envy you your undertaking, M. Ellis."

They had reached the entrance to the park. The old man bent down and unleashed the dog.

"Go do your business, you rascal."

The dog raced down the black macadam path. Haraout slowly straightened up, carefully folded the leash and placed it in his pocket.

"So, M. Ellis, I presume you would like to see where I, or more precisely, Marcel, found the body?"

"If you would be so kind. May I ask you a few questions about that morning?"

"But certainly!"

The two men began descending the sloping pathway past the spindly cedar bushes that served the dual purpose of border and ground stabilizer. There was no sign of the schnauzer.

"Did you see anyone in the park that morning before you discovered the body?"

"No. There was no one on the path. There rarely is at this hour. Of course, as I told the police, there was the rude man above, on the bench."

"Excuse me, M. Haraout, I do not understand you. A rude man where?"

"Why, above." He turned and pointed with his cane. "On the same bench where you were sitting. I told the inspector, but he did not seem very interested."

"What was his name?"

"The man? I have no idea. I only know he was very rude when I wished him 'Bonjour'. It is typical of the young in France these days, I fear. They are ignorant of even the most basic etiquette. I can assure you, things were much different when I was a youth."

"I am sure they were, M. Haraout; however, I see I have not made myself clear. It was not the name of your rude man that I wanted, but rather, the name of the uninterested inspector."

"Oh well, that I can tell you: Chief Inspector LeClerc."

"Thank-you. Now, with regard to the rude man, can you describe him for me?"

"It was difficult to make out his features, you understand, because of the way he was dressed. He wore one of those Scottish tweed caps pulled down over his eyes. The collar of his windbreaker was up around his chin; the coat was dark blue, I believe. Though I could barely see his face, it seemed to be of a dark complexion."

"How old would you make him to be?"

"That, I can only guess. He was not a teenager, to be sure, but he was what I, at least, would call young. One thing of which I am certain, M. Ellis, he displayed the uncivil behavior of youth."

"I am sure you are right. So after seeing this man, you continued on you way?"

"That is exact. Marcel was especially intolerable that morning."

They had reached the first of the many switchbacks that criss-crossed, at acute angles, the terraced cliff face. To their right, the ground dropped off sharply to the section of pathway immediately below them. They walked towards the first landing that offered a clear view of the ocean and coastline. The old pensioner shuffled along in his distinctive, jerky fashion, tapping the pavement occasionally with his ancient Basque cane. Peter Ellis carefully measured his gait to keep pace.

"So, M. Haraout, would you please describe to me the events of that morning from the time you entered the park?"

"I shall do my best, monsieur." The old man paused, then called out: "Marcel, where have you gotten to? Marcel! Come here this instant!"

By the time the two men reached the base of the large semi-circular lookout that jutted from the cliff face, Haraout had finished recounting the story of his discovery of Kevin Duffy's body. By this time also, Marcel had returned from his morning duties and was now exploring the undergrowth at the edge of the pavement.

"So this is where you found the body?"

They were standing on a narrow concrete apron that fanned out from the short, stone planter that formed the base of the lookout. Haraout pointed to a spot midway between a green wooden bench and the planter.

"It was just there. I believe you can still discern a small blood stain." He pointed with his cane.

"You must excuse me, I know this may sound morbid, but was there anything peculiar about the body? Any wounds that you could see? I realize, given the circumstances, that these are not the kind of details one might remember."

"On the contrary, M. Ellis. The body lay in such a strange posi-tion, it is something I shall remember for the rest of my life. It was as though someone had dropped a dummy from up there." He pointed with his cane to the top of the slanting, rocky structure. "The body lay in a completely unnatural way. When I checked it for a pulse, I noticed something else, something, upon reflection, I find very unusual."

Peter Ellis looked closely at the old man's shrewd, lined face. "What was that, M. Haraout?"

"Just here," he pointed to the left side of his neck, "just here there was what looked like a small knife wound in the form of the letter 'J'. What I now find strange is how the boy could have come by it in the fall. It was here," he pointed again, "**under** the jaw."

"You are very observant, M. Haraout. Did you mention this wound to the police?"

"Of course I did. The inspector said he probably cut himself shaving. I believe he takes me for an old fool. I am certainly not young, but all the same, I have retained some of my senses."

"M. Haraout, I am coming to think that it may be the inspector whose judgement is suspect. May I ask you just a few more questions?"

"Certainly."

Peter Ellis turned toward the ocean and pointed to the coast road that ran along the south side of the Pointe Atalye. "You see those people fishing along the coast road down toward the Villa Belza? Do you recall seeing anyone on the morning of the accident?"

"Alas, monsieur, I do not recall looking down there on the morning of which you speak. However, in principle, there are people fishing there on most mornings, weather and tide permitting."

"Excellent. That is what I thought. Now, do you recall seeing the man on the bench when you returned from finding the body?"

"You mean the rude one in the Scottish cap?"

"Precisely."

"I can tell you for certain that he was not there. I mentioned this as well to the police inspector but, again, he did not seem concerned. I found his attitude somewhat bizarre, and not a little rude as well."

"I believe you had good reason to find it so. For my part, I find it more than a little bizarre. You can be sure it is something I intend to explore. But now, I must take my leave of you and Marcel. You have been very helpful, and I thank you not only for myself, but also on behalf of the family of the unfortunate M. Duffy."

"I am happy I could be of a little service to you, M. Ellis. If you have any further questions, you have my number. Good luck." The old man touched his cane to his beret and started shuffling his way up the path. "Marcel, come along you little rascal. It is time to go home and have our breakfast."

Peter Ellis studied the scene of the accident for several minutes. The curved, rock wall of the overlook rose above him some twenty to twenty-five feet to a narrow ledge eighteen to twenty-four inches wide. Above the ledge, the wall continued up another twenty feet at an angle fifteen to twenty degrees off vertical. The top of the overlook resembled the parapet of a medieval castle with large stone teeth connected by green steel piping that served as a kind of railing. If the Duffy boy had fallen, or been pushed from the top of that wall, it was not difficult to imagine how, given the angle of incline, he would likely land in an unusual manner. But old Haraout made a good point regarding the cut below the boy's jaw. Given the circumstances, it was difficult to explain without the presence of another party. He decided to walk down to the coast road and see how the fish were biting.

The first two fishermen he talked to were tourists who had only arrived in Biarritz the day before; however, the third man was a local and had been fishing there with a friend on the day of the accident. In fact, he had been fishing that day in almost the same spot as today. Peter Ellis pointed out the large, semicircular rock and asked whether he or his friend had happened to notice anyone up there on the morning in question. From where they stood, they had a clear view of the turret-like structure. Much to Peter Ellis's surprise, the man said that both he and his friend had, in fact, been surprised to see four people there that early in the morning. Four people? Was he sure? He was positive. His friend could confirm it. But they didn't stay for more than two or three minutes, nor did he or his friend see them leave. They just seemed to disappear. Peter Ellis thanked him for the information and wished him luck with his fishing. As he walked back to the hotel, he had to admit that, so far, he certainly couldn't complain about his own luck. And, given the size of the swell and the wind direction at the Côte des Basques, he felt there was no reason to believe it wouldn't continue with the surf at Chambre d'Amour.

CHAPTER SEVEN

When Peter Ellis pulled into the large parking lot overlooking the beach at Chambre d'Amour, he was not disappointed. Two hundred yards out to sea, long, green glassy lines of surf were breaking with angled precision. A strong wind was blowing directly offshore, hollowing out the six-to-eight foot tubes, holding the wave faces veritical until the very last moment when they pitched forward and collapsed in an explosion of foamy turbulence. Peter Ellis rolled down his car window and sat for several minutes, watching the thundering surf. It was a sight that never failed to make his heart beat faster.

He locked his car and started walking south along the wide concrete sidewalk bordering the beach. The scene reminded him of a carnival. He passed small groups of surfers surveying the waves and following the action of the riders in the water. Some had already changed into their black or brightly colored wetsuits, while others stood in motley denim uniforms and zap-art canvas loafers. He reached the southern end of the walkway where, perpendicular to the bench, a jetty of large, green-black granite rocks extended a hundred yards out into the ocean. He turned his back to the gusting offshore wind and stood facing the booming surf. He watched a surfer drop down the face of a breaking wave and turn sharply at the bottom, carving out a graceful roostertail of white seaspray. His back to the wave, the rider sliced across the dull, gray-green surface just ahead of the crashing water. In the last instant before the wave closed out, he knifed sharply through the collapsing lip. This surfer was very good, Peter Ellis thought, and, at least on this wave, very lucky as well.

He was startled by the high-pitched bleating of a horn directly behind him. He instinctively turned and recognized, through the windshield of a small, blue station wagon, the grinning face of his old surfing friend, Marc Dufau. When Peter Ellis reached the car and extended his hand, he too was smiling.

"I should have known."

"I saw your car and board and knew you couldn't be far. I have ordered some pretty waves for you today, don't you think?" He gestured with a sweep of his arm toward the ocean.

"That is certain, my friend. Now if you could just do something about the temperature of the water."

"Did I not recommend a good wetsuit?"

"Yes, you did. It is a great improvement on my last one. Still, you know how I like warm water. It comes from growing up in Florida."

"Well, you're in France now and the waves are almost perfect. I suggest we stop yapping and go surfing."

While the two friends changed into their lycra shirts and wetsuits, they exchanged bits of personal news. Peter Ellis had known Marc Dufau for almost sixteen years. When they had first met, in 1972, Marc was an apprentice chef at Les Flots Bleus. He was from a small village in the Béarn, not far from Pau. He had discovered surfing as a teenager on holiday in Biarritz. He had moved to the coast as soon as he had finished restaurant school.

Marc Dufau was short but wide-shouldered, with a torso that bespoke the benefits of constant surfboard paddling. He had straight black hair that was beginning to grey at the temples, a large Charles deGaulle nose and brilliant blue eyes that were rarely without the glint of humor. It was his sense of humor and uncharacteristic (for a Frenchman) openness that had first appealed to Peter Ellis. Later, he found that they not only shared a passion for surfing but also an enthusiasm for wine, spirits and all things gastronomic. Ten years ago, Marc had opened his own small establishment near the Vieux Port in

Biarritz. Today, Peter Ellis counted him among his oldest and truest friends.

Since he had told his friend about Burke's leaving when they last spoke on the telephone, he was prepared for his first question.

"So, you have still heard nothing from America?"

"No. She has been true to her promise of silence."

"Things have been hard for you, I think."

'Well, I won't pretend that I have not been thinking about her, especially when I'm not working. You know, it is not often that you find a woman like Burke. I keep asking myself what I did wrong. Or what I didn't do right."

"Perhaps it has nothing to do with you. Perhaps it has something to do with Mlle. Burke. You often spoke of the difference in age."

"Yes, there was that; but I had a feeling that it was becoming less of a factor."

"Maybe it was the nature of your work. Your last investigation could not have been easy for her. You yourself said that you wondered toward the end, when you were receiving the mutilated dolls and the death threats, whether it was all worth it. Think how Burke must have felt."

"Of course, you have a point. But I offered to give it up after that piece. And I was serious about giving it up. Hell, the idea was even beginning to appeal to me. I _can_ write about other things, you know."

"I'm sure you can. But would you be happy doing it?"

"I think I would be happy if Burke were still with me."

"Excuse me, Pierre, happy is not the right word, though I think you know what I mean. I am sure Mlle. Burke would understand my meaning. Don't you think?"

"She could at least call me. Tell me how she's doing."

"Maybe she's afraid to."

The two friends had finished changing. Marc had already removed his board from the back of the station wagon and had begun waxing it. Peter Ellis went to unstrap his board from the old set of rusting roof racks that he had owned almost as long as the car itself. His friend looked up from his work and pointed to the racks.

"Well, it's reassuring to know at least some things don't change. If those racks last much longer you'll be able to sell them as antiques. Do you need any wax?"

Marc Dufau tossed him the block of paraffin. When Peter Ellis had finished waxing his board, he and his friend walked over to the old concrete ramp that led down to the beach proper, which was ten feet below the rock-buttressed boardwalk. He knew the water would be cold. It always was in Biarritz, except for a couple of months in late summer and early autumn. Still, the initial shock of the icy surf as it washed over his head and down into the miniscule openings of his wetsuit took his breath away. He began paddling hard. He knew from years of experience that the water temperature would only be a minor inconvenience once he had paddled for a few minutes. But, Christ Almighty, it sure felt cold now every time he had to duck under the churning walls of whitewater.

There were no easy ways to get out at Chambre d'Amour, no channels deep enough to lessen the rigors of paddling through the power-sapping whitewater of a succession of broken waves. He and his friend had scouted the inside for a place with a mild riptide that would aid them in getting out past the breakline. What they had settled on was not as forgiving as Peter Ellis had hoped. After five minutes of hard paddling, he had totally forgotten about the coldness of the water. His arms were beginning to ache and he was breathing heavily. Marc had already reached the line-up and was sitting on his sharp-nosed, seven-foot-two red thruster looking out to sea, trying to pick out the next set. Peter Ellis reached him just as the set's first wave was coming through. He watched as his friend stroked into the third wave, a solid seven footer by any but Hawaiian standards. He dropped down the face, disappearing for a moment, then reappeared after making a bottom turn that brought him into the barrel. From his position outside, Peter Ellis could not follow all of his friend's ride, but he could see enough to know it had been a good one.

He waited through the entire set, giving himself time to recover from paddling out and time to study the way the waves were lining up. On the second wave of the next set, he misjudged his take-off and had to bail out. He dove under the breaking wave, his ankle leash pulling him violently as his board got caught in the whitewater. While he was paddling back into the line-up, he saw Marc catch another good wave.

On his next wave, he again took off too late but managed to make the steep drop only to catch the rail of his board on his bottom turn. The collapsing wave buried him, so that for an instant—though it seemed to him like minutes—he became disoriented, not knowing which way was up, which way down. When he finally reached the surface, his heart was pounding and he was gasping for air.

He paddled back out and spent the next set studying the take-offs of some of the other surfers. He made a smooth entry on his next wave, carved a conservative, sweeping bottom turn and, after a short ride, managed a clean kick-out. After several more uneventful but confidence building rides, he dropped into a wave that was easily two feet overhead. He nailed a solid bottom turn and managed to position himself in the deepest part of the tube. He sliced across the glistening, green surface, his face just inches from the wave, his right hand trailing a white gash of seaspray in the glassy water. When he finally kicked-out, he was trembling with exhilaration that he only experienced when surfing. It was a feeling he had never been able to describe: it was like sex in the sense of being agreeably spent and somehow purified, yet it was in other ways a totally different sensation. He had often tried to explain it to Burke, but ultimately always gave up in frustration. He had seen a bumper sticker at a beach in North Carolina once that summed up the futility of describing the feeling, even if it did reinforce a certain brand of surf snobbism: "Surfing: If you haven't done it, you can't know." All he knew was that after a wave like the one he had just ridden, his skin felt electric and his senses were suffused with a kind of euphoric clarity.

He overcame the temptation to paddle out and catch one more wave. He guessed that he had been out for over an hour, which was not bad for a first day back after four weeks of city life. He also realized that his aching arms were probably not up to another struggle through the break. He caught Marc's eye and indicated that he was going in. Then he stroked into an onrushing wall of whitewater and, laying prone on his board, leisurely rode it all the way to the gravelly beach.

He had figured to finish before Marc and they had agreed to meet in one of the small, ground floor cafés in the string of three story buildings that lined the beach parking lot. While he was changing, he saw Marc take off on one of the biggest waves of the day, make a perfect snap turn at the bottom, carve a sweeping, inverted 'S' across the green translucence of the face, cut back to stay close to the pocket, then try to power through a collapsing section, getting covered up then hammered by the crashing wall of water. Both rider and board disappeared momentarily, then the surfboard popped out of the water into the air, fluttering like a leaf in the strong, offshore wind. Two seconds later, Marc appeared, holding one arm over his head as protection against the loose board. The wipeout didn't seem to bother him, and he immediately began paddling back out. Peter Ellis just shook his head and smiled to himself.

He finished changing and strapped his board to the old surf racks on his car. Since his arrival an hour and a half earlier, the parking lot had filled considerably. All down the concrete boardwalk, surfers and their companions huddled in small groups discussing the wave conditions, occasionally pointing to other riders in the water. Several were making their final preparations before going out, waxing their boards, checking the knots of their ankle leashes to make sure they were securely fastened to the boards. Among those he passed who were changing into their wetsuits, he couldn't help but stare furtively at a tall, athletic French woman with short, straight blond hair and small, youthful breasts, whose pink button nipples stood erect against the chill wind. Although there was only a hint of resemblance between this woman and Burke, and that more to do with a kind of shared innocent sensuality, he immediately began thinking of his former companion and lover. By the time he reached the small café, he had worked himself into a state which, had he analyzed it objectively, he would have discovered to be equal parts self-pity and misguided sexual excitement. But, of late, objectivity rarely governed his thoughts concerning Burke.

After he had seated himself at a small, white, square table facing the parking lot and ocean, he suddenly became aware that his morning's workout had given him an appetite for something more mundane but, certainly, more attainable than that which he had just been contemplating. When the young long-haired waiter arrived, he ordered a baguette sandwich of jambon de Bayonne, a bowl of café au lait and a bottle of sparkling mineral water. He had plans to meet Maurice for lunch at the restaurant of Mme. Haizart to finalize their plans and to interview the owner and her son; but that rendez-vous was two hours away. He felt sure that he would be hungry again by that time.

Maurice had given him two earlier editions of the local paper, **Sud-Ouest,** that detailed the accident and reported the official findings of the police, amply quoting Chief Inspector Jacques LeClerc. According to Inspector LeClerc, it was a clear-cut case of accidental death. The young man had apparently been standing on the stone railing of the overlook and had lost his footing. His death was caused by a crushing blow to the side of the head. There were no witnesses, as far as the police knew. The body was discovered by the pensioner, Jean Haraout, while he was walking his dog in the park overlooking the beach of Côte des Basques. It was certainly a tragedy, a man snatched from life at such a young age and he, Inspector LeClerc, had personally sent condolences to M. Duffy's family in America.

From what he had discovered only this morning, Peter Ellis had to wonder just how hard Inspector LeClerc had tried to find witnesses to Kevin Duffy's death. And was his lack of effort primarily due to laziness or to something more malevolent and self-serving. Maurice had promised to complete his background briefing at lunch. He was especially looking forward to what Maurice had to say about LeClerc. From the little information he had already received, the self-described thorough inspector hardly resembled the inspector who seemed primarily interested in closing the case as quickly as possible.

The waiter arrived with the sandwich and drinks, arranged them neatly on the small table and wished him 'bon appétit.' Peter Ellis broke a sugar cube in half and stirred it into the milk-lightened coffee. He took a long swallow of the cold, effervescent mineral water to wash the taste of salt from his mouth. He figured he had drunk at least a glass of sea water while he was in the surf. He had gulped half a glass on his first wipeout alone. He sipped from the large bowl of coffee; it was slightly bitter and still very hot. He began eating the sandwich of jambon de Bayonne, noting with appreciation the crispy freshness of the baguette and the liberal portion of the wonderful local ham.

As he ate, he studied the small café. It was an open, cheerful space accented in tropical greens and yellows, with a rattan ceiling, white tables and matching white chairs with wicker seats. In one corner sat a large German shepherd, taking in the scene with alert eyes and pricked-up ears. In another was a white cage with two green cockatoos. When he arrived, someone on tape was singing an old song which he thought was called 'My Buddy'. Now, the same someone was spiritedly advising his listeners to 'Accentuate the Positive'. It was rather incongruous advice, Peter Ellis thought, given his present state of mind.

In the time since he had taken his seat in the café, two groups of shivering, wet-haired surfers and their windswept companions had arrived. One group, at a table close-by, he quickly recognized as Australians. They ordered hot chocolate and croissants in a Down Under franglais that made him smile. At least they were making an effort to speak the language, unlike many Americans he encountered. Burke and he had often discussed this lingual laziness to the point that it had become a kind of inside joke, when they overheard a guilty party, they had only to look at each other to trigger a shared, smiling response.

He suddenly thought of the dead boy, Kevin Duffy. What had <u>he</u> been like? He realized he knew almost nothing about him. He surfed. He seemed to like France and the French. He thought enough of a serveuse in a pastry shop to risk threats to his physical well-being.

As recently as two and a half weeks ago, he could have been one of the surfers sitting in this same café warming himself with coffee or hot chocolate after a morning of surfing the cold waters of Chambre d'Amour. But he had somehow managed to fall from a lookout with a three foot protective wall and crack his skull. And, with apparently remarkable efficiency, the police, under the personal guidance of Chief Inspector Jacques LeClerc, had concluded that the death had been an accident. Peter Ellis was, in that instant, struck with a strange feeling of kinship with the dead boy. It washed over him like a winter wave that momentarily takes your breath away and leaves you shuddering. He realized, all at once, that he did know something about Kevin Duffy; in fact, he knew a great deal. That the knowledge was, at present, hidden in a kind of shared past didn't bother him. Instead, it filled him with the quiet excitement and determination that accompany the first clear perception of why one commits to certain dangerous undertakings.

He was on his second bowl of café au lait when Marc Dufau entered the café. He waved acknowledgement, gesturing that he would join him in a few minutes. He stopped at several tables to greet friends and talk about the day's surf. Peter Ellis recalled seeing two of them in the water while he had been out, though he couldn't remember anything about their surfing. Marc finally joined him at the small, white table, but only after he had passed by the bar to shake the barman's hand in that singular, typically French fashion.

"It is sympathetic, this little bistro, don't you think?" He gave a short wave of the hand to indicate the surroundings.

"It is very cheerful. And my ham sandwich was excellent."

"How did you find the surf?"

"Let's just say I survived it. Though I did have one good ride at the end. That's to say good for me. I am going to need several days to get back into surfing shape."

"The conditions today are ideal, though, don't you think?"

"They are, except for the water temperature."

"Remember Pierre, this is France, not Florida or Costa Rica. You are spoiled. Today the water was just a little chilly. Wait until January. Then you will know the meaning of cold water!"

"Not spoiled, Marc, just getting old. And the older I get, the more I dislike cold water. But you are right about the waves today. It is hard to imagine them being much better. You had some very nice rides, I might add."

"Merci. I had one very long wave that was superb."

"You mean the one that closed-out at the end and buried you?"

'Exactly! It was fantastic. I almost made that last section. Still, it was a beautiful wave. The next time, I'll make it through that section." He laughed. "Either that or bust my ass again."

The waiter arrived with a bowl of steaming coffee and a large croissant. He collected the empty plates and confirmed that they did not need anything else. Marc Dufau put two large lumps of sugar in his coffee then began eating the croissant. The two men did not talk for several minutes. From the stereo speakers came the distinctive, sensuous growl of Louis Armstrong explaining what goes on 'When It's Sleepy Time Down South'. Peter Ellis remembered how a musician friend had once described his unique vocal phrasing as coming from the way he played trumpet, and how it was revolutionary at the time. Whatever the case, the man could certainly sing. Marc Dufau seemed to be listening to the song too, because he didn't begin speaking until it was over.

"He was formidable, don't you think? What a voice!"

"Louis Armstrong? He was a genius. One of the great American masters. And that song is one of my favorites."

"It is a classic." He paused, then looked his friend squarely in the eye. "But I believe there is something besides music that you want to discuss with me."

"Yes, Marc, that is so. I am here to help my friend Maurice Claverie-LaPorte investigate the death of a young American surfer named Kevin Duffy."

"But I read in the paper that the police had concluded it was an accident. Something about him standing on the railing of an overlook in the park above Côte des Basques."

"Yes, that is what they have concluded. Maurice, however, believes there was more to it than that."

"You mean that someone killed him?"

"Not exactly."

"But why?"

"Easy, Marc, not so fast. I'll explain everything I know; but first, I'd like to ask you a few questions. Okay?"

"Certainly. Go on. Though I doubt if I can help you very much."

"Did you know Kevin Duffy?"

"I knew him only slightly. Some surfers I know brought him to my restaurant a couple of months ago. They introduced me. He seemed very nice, a little shy. He said he was trying to learn French. At the time, he had only been in Biarritz a few months, I think. He seemed to be making good progress, though his accent was very American. Afterwards, I often saw him here and at the other surf breaks. We always said 'hello'. For someone so tall, he was a very good surfer. Very aggressive. Not afraid to take chances. Perhaps that explains his walking on that rock railing."

"That is possible, but I think improbable for reasons I shall explain later. Did he return to your restaurant after that first visit?"

"In fact, he did. Two times, I believe."

"Was he with anyone?"

"He was with a local girl. Chantal. Chantal Clairac. She works at Dodin with a sister of Edith, one of my waitresses. Apparently Yvette, the sister, is one of the only friends she has there."

"That seems a bit unusual. Do you know any reason for it?"

"I am not exactly sure, but I have my suspicions. She does not have the best of reputations. It could simply be a case of jealousy. She is certainly a strikingly attractive girl."

"So you knew of her bad reputation before she came to the restaurant?"

"Biarritz is still a small town in many ways, my friend, in the winter especially. People have little else to do but talk."

"Do you know anything of the origin of Mlle. Clairac's bad reputation?"

"I understand it mainly has to do with a food salesman named Jean-Claude Duchon."

"Yes, Maurice has spoken of him."

"Before she started seeing the American, Kevin Duffy, it seems that she was Duchon's lover."

"That is hardly cause for blackening someone's reputation, especially in this country. Unless, of course, she flaunted the affair in public so as to embarrass M. Duchon's wife. Was that the case, then?"

"No, not at all. According to Edith, Mlle. Chantal was obsessed with discretion. She even refused to discuss the affair with Yvette, her best friend at the patisserie. No, the problem had to do with Duchon himself. It seems he has friends in the local mafia for whom he provides certain services."

"Such as introducing them to young girls who have come to Biarritz to work in the restaurant industry. Only, his friends in the mob have other plans for them."

"So you are already aware of his work on the side?"

"My old friend, Maurice, gave me a little background on M. Duchon last night, which you have just confirmed."

"You must understand, Pierre, what I am telling you is based on hearsay. I can provide no proof for these accusations, though I can assure you that they figure prominently in Mlle. Chantal's questionable reputation."

"Guilt by association, you mean?"

"Precisely. Also, the fact that in both appearance and personality, Jean-Claude Duchon is a weasel of a man. No one could understand what Chantal saw in him, or perhaps more to the point, what accounted for the undeniable hold he had on her. That is, until the young American, Kevin Duffy, arrived on the scene."

"Marc, surely you have learned from your own experience that one of the greatest mysteries in the world is why a particular someone is attracted to a particular someone else. I, for one, don't understand it and doubt that I ever shall. As for exercising control over someone— having a hold on them as you put it—that is an entirely different matter. That situation usually exists in cases where the attraction is one-sided and is an attempt to force the other party to act <u>as though</u> there was mutual attraction. How someone arrives at being able to exert this control is a question with many answers, none of which are usually very pretty. My God, listen to me! I sound like one of my former college professors, whose defining talent was his ability, at all times, to state the obvious."

Marc Dufau was smiling. "Sometimes, Pierre, it is not such a bad thing to state the obvious, especially when it is done with such passion. But, what you are saying makes sense. I, like you, believe there is an explanation, other than that of attraction, for the hold Duchon had on Chantal Clairac. I wonder how Kevin Duffy was able to break that hold?"

"Yes, that is something I was wondering myself. Of course, it is possible that he just came along at the right time. That, whatever it was, Chantal had been able to overcome it herself and was simply waiting for someone to come along, someone to whom she was genuinely attracted."

Marc Dufau sat silent for several minutes, slowly turning his coffee cup in the saucer. He had the faraway stare of someone lost in reflection. Suddenly he spoke.

"You know, Pierre, I think you may be right. I can't believe I forgot to tell you this earlier. After Chantal's first visit to my place with Kevin Duffy, Edith remarked that Chantal seemed finally to be getting over her big loss. When I asked her if she meant Duchon, she sort of laughed and said 'not exactly'. Then, she apologized for laughing and said that was because of my reference to Duchon. When I asked her to explain why that would strike her as funny, she didn't answer but stared at her feet in the manner of a child who is being scolded. Then, to my surprise, I noticed that tears were beginning to run down her cheeks. When I tried to comfort her, she threw her arms around my neck and began bawling. While I was trying to calm her, she kept repeating the same phrase: 'La pauvre petite'."

"What do you think she meant?"

"I'm not sure but there is one more thing that might interest you about Chantal that I learned later from Edith. About six months ago, Chantal disappeared for two days. It was a weekend, so she didn't miss work but she did miss an outing to San Sebastian with Edith and Yvette that had been planned for several weeks. When she returned to work on Monday morning, she acted like a zombie, according to Edith's sister, and not only refused to answer questions about the previous two days but seemed genuinely unable to do so. Apparently, it was another two weeks before she began acting anything like her normal self. I don't know if this has any bearing on your investigation, Pierre, but I'd be surprised if Duchon didn't have something to do with Chantal's 'lost weekend'."

"So would I. And I intend to find out exactly what he had to do with it. I thank you, my friend, for all the information. I think it would be best, for you, not to mention this conversation to anyone. If anyone asks you about me, just say we are old surfing buddies and that, as far as you know, I am here to write a feature on surfing. Which I might just do when I finish with this Duchon affair."

"Do you have time to go back out for a few more waves?"

"No, I've a luncheon date with Maurice in a little over an hour. But I'll call you tonight about going tomorrow morning. Good luck!"

"And you, also. Be careful. There are more sharks on the land here than in the water."

From the parking lot of Chambre d'Amour, Peter Ellis turned on to the narrow coast road and followed it up and around the promontory of Pointe St. Martin. There, though still two-laned, it became the Avenue de L'Imperatrice and began its long, nominally-imperial descent into Biarritz. He drove slowly, re-acquainting himself with the familiar landscape while noting the inevitable changes. Among the latter were two new highrise construction projects. In the twenty-odd years that he had been visiting this corner of France, these angular, looming structures had been slowly but inexorably taking over

Biarritz and her adjacent neighbors. He quickly decided that it was too beautiful a day to dwell on such depressing prospects; moreover, his interviews with old Haraout and Marc Dufau had provided him with enough depressing news for one morning.

He passed the elegant, though shuttered, Hotel du Palais, hibernating behind locked iron gates after another summer's extravagant exertions. Other familiar sights came in quick succession: the mustard-colored city administration building; the curving, white-columned arcade of the Café des Colonnes; the dilapidated, art deco Casino Municipal, which continued to shadow the Grande Plage like a tattered gambler who has fallen on hard times.

A short block beyond the Café Royalty, with its distinctive green awning and old wicker chairs, he veered left and drove up the rue Gambetta past Les Halles. At the top of the hill, he turned right on the rue Million. He parked at the end of the street next to the building called 'Mar y Montes', the annex to the Hotel Les Flots Bleus. The sea, the mountains, the blue waves—the location had them all, he thought, and now it could add 'accidental' death to the list.

He crossed the rue La Perspective and, standing next to a short wall made of shells and cement, he looked across at the southwestern face of the Pointe Atalye. At its base, just above the narrow beach road, were several abandoned German artillery bunkers, gaping reminders that death was not such a stranger to this cliffside park after all.

Turning his gaze to the green, undulating water that stretched to the horizon, he tried to picture the young American who, not so many days earlier, had come to survey the same expanse of ocean and coastline. He wondered what the weather had been like that morning? Since the two fishermen down on the beach road had clearly seen four men on the overlook below, he presumed there had been little morning fog. Nor had the fisherman he interviewed mentioned rain. He wondered whether Kevin Duffy had taken time to appreciate the majestic beauty of the mountainous Spanish coast. Or was he in a hurry to get down to the water and check on the surf. He thought of the many mornings he himself had spent here, years before, doing the same thing. He remembered the mixed feelings of exhilaration and fear when he awoke to the unmistakable thunder of a big swell and knew, just from the sound, that La Barre was breaking. And as he stood there, high above the sparkling waves breaking over the rocks of Côtes des Basques, Peter Ellis began to understand why the death of a young American surfer, whom he had never even met, had taken such a hold on him.

CHAPTER EIGHT

Peter Ellis arrived at the Hotel-Restaurant Haizart on the rue Gambetta a few minutes before one o'clock. He was greeted at the door by a handsome Basque woman in her late forties. She was of medium height with wide hips and full breasts. Her hair was dark brown and was cut so short that it barely covered the nape of her neck. She wore a pleated, knee-length wool skirt of green and blue Tartan design and a perfectly pressed, cream white cotton blouse with large breast pockets.

"A table for one, Monsieur?"

"For two please, Madame. I am meeting a friend whom I believe you know. M. Chaverie-Laporte."

"Of course, you are Maurice's journalist friend from Paris. It is M. Ellis, is it not?"

"At you service, Mme. Haizart." He extended a hand for her to shake. She took his hand firmly and held it for several seconds while closely studying his face.

"Have I not met you before, M. Ellis?"

"You have a very good memory, Mme. Haizart. It has been at least five years. I was with my friend, Marc Dufau."

"So you know M. Marc?"

"Very well. We have been surfing together here for, let's see, sixteen years. When we first met, he was a young apprentice chef at Les Flots Bleus. He had just bought his first surfboard."

"You have known Biarritz for a long time, M. Ellis."

"Twenty-two years. I first came in the summer of sixty-six when I was still a teenager."

"It has changed much since that time."

"I fear you are correct. I much preferred it in the old days, though I am sure all the development is good for businesses like yours."

"Sometimes I wonder, M. Ellis. Sometimes I wonder." She led him to a discreet table at the back of the restaurant, saying it was Maurice's favorite. "Would you care for an aperitif while you are waiting for the inspector?"

"You have Kronenbourg 1664?"

"Yes, monsieur."

"Perfect. And may I please have a menu to look at while I wait for Maurice."

"One beer and one menu for monsieur. Thank you."

In less than a minute, a young waitress arrived and handed him an opened menu. She poured the beer into a stemmed glass embossed with the company logo. Like Mme. Haizart, her dress was impeccable: a starched, white cotton blouse and a simple, red peasant skirt with green trim. Peter Ellis thanked her and received a demure smile in response. He had almost finished his beer when Maurice finally arrived.

"Please excuse my tardiness, Pierre. I was not paying attention to the time; this case has taken over my thoughts."

"It is no problem, Maurice. It has given me the chance to enjoy a cold beer and try to make sense of the information I have gathered this morning."

"You must tell me all about it. But first, let us order. I am dying of hunger."

"There are several things on the menu that tempt me. What do you recommend?"

The older man perused the menu quickly. "You are familiar with Ttoro, the local fish soup?"

"Yes, of course."

"Well then, to begin, I suggest the Ttoro and, afterwards, the poulet Basquaise. It is the best in Biarritz."

"If you say so, then I know it must be true. And to drink?"

"The red Irouleguy?"

"That sounds perfect to me."

Maurice placed their orders with Mme. Haizart and then asked Peter Ellis about his morning's interviews. The journalist told him about his meeting with Haraout and about his lucky encounter with the fisherman. He then recounted what Marc Dufau had told him of Chantal and about her so-called 'lost weekend' . When he had finished, he saw Maurice nod his head in assent but noticed that the expression he wore was one of deep disapproval.

"Excellent, Pierre. We are already beginning to make progress in this dirty affair. Old Haraout, he seems to be very observant."

"Yes he is and he also seems to have a reliable memory. Do you think he is in any danger?"

"No. He has already been interviewed by the police and, from what I understand, they treated him like a child. They did not even take a written statement. As far as they are concerned, apparently, his only contribution to the case was that he just happened to discover the body. And I believe it would be wise for us to let them continue thinking just that. If we must call on him to testify later, we can take appropriate steps to protect him at the time."

"Good. So what else have you discovered?"

Before Maurice could begin, the shy, young waitress arrived with the fish soup and bottle of wine. The two men silently observed while she served the wine and filled their soup bowls from a silver tureen which she then placed in the middle of the table. She went about her job with the quiet efficiency of a worker who has been well-trained. After being assured that the two gentlemen needed nothing else, she wished them 'bon appétit' and left as discreetly as she had come. Maurice sampled the soup.

"Ah-h-h. Now this is the real Ttoro." He motioned to his friend with his spoon. "Please. You must taste it. The very essence of the sea."

While Peter Ellis sampled the fish soup, Maurice began telling him what he had found out about Gambia and his friends.

"You will recall from last night that I mentioned a Corsican, Joseph Gambia, nicknamed 'Jojo', who is the leader of the criminal syndicate which controls most of the south-west of France." Peter Ellis, his mouth full of hot soup, nodded. "Well, when I first came across his name while still an inspector for the Brigade, I thought he was just another small-time thug. But, the more I looked into his affairs, the more I realized that I had very much underestimated him. I also noticed that little fish soon disappeared when the big fish, Gambia, moved into their waters. Before long, I was able to put together a clear picture of his operation. And I can assure you, it is a large and lucrative one. With headquarters in Biarritz, his territory stretches all the way from Tarbes, in the east, to Bordeaux in the north. You can imagine my surprise when my initial report on Gambia was dismissed by the national police as the work of a too lively imagination. Three months later, it was suggested by my superiors that I take early retirement for 'health reasons'. Health reasons! Can you believe it?"

He snorted and took a large gulp of wine. From the silver tureen, he ladled more soup into his bowl.

"You will take more soup, Pierre?"

"No, thank-you Maurice. Though, as usual, you are right, it is delicious."

"Well, since my retirement in May, I have continued to pursue my investigation of Gambia for, shall we say, personal reasons. Little by little, with the help of two or three old friends at the gendarmerie and in the local force, I have begun to understand why my report was dismissed without the least attempt of verification."

"You think some of the local authorities are involved with Gambia?"

"Yes, I am certain of it. And not just the locals. Oh no! Gambia's web reaches all the way to Paris."

"You suspect Duchon's friend, the chief inspector?"

"Oh,yes!. I would be very much surprised if Chief Inspector Jacques LeClerc is not up to his ears in Gambia business. But, to prove it- that is another matter. He has many powerful friends here and in Paris."

"So it is not just Gambia that you're after?"

"I want the whole rotten lot of them."

"What about the death of Kevin Duffy?"

"It may sound heartless, but his death is serving a good cause. He can not be brought back to life. But, if we are successful, his death, at least, will not have been in vain."

He broke off a piece of bread from the baguette and mopped the inside of his soup bowl. He washed the bread down with a swallow of wine, wiped his mouth and continued. "Now, let me tell you of my morning. I am sure you will find the story interesting."

"Everything you have said so far, Maurice, I have found interesting. I am just wondering how you plan on trapping this little group of gangsters?"

"Be patient, my friend, be patient. I am coming to that."

"Forgive me, Maurice. Please continue."

"You will understand, Pierre, there are still some small-time crooks who owe me favors from my days with the Brigade. This morning, I paid a visit to one, who lives in Anglet. His name is Pioche and he has a great weakness for gambling, which has caused him, at times, some inconveniences at the hands of the local mob enforcers. Now, Pioche may be a bit of a scoundrel, but he is not really a bad sort and perhaps, through necessity, has an amusing sense of humor. He is also very perceptive and can tell you more about the illegal goings-on in Biarritz than anyone I know.

"I went to Pioche under the guise of trying to substantiate a rumor concerning a new gambling and prostitute operation that Gambia has opened outside of Guétary. It is called 'Le Gentleman' and is advertised as a nightclub de luxe, which is what Pioche initially swore it was. However, after a little persuasion, he admitted he had heard 'some stories' about some private rooms in the back and about a fancy house next door. He informed me that the nominal owner was a woman named Janine Destin, but that he was absolutely certain that she was in partnership with Gambia. I then asked if he was aware of any new enforcers in town. He said there were three young Corsicans who had recently arrived to work at 'Le Gentle-man'. He only knew the name of one, a certain Carlos, whose short temper he had witnessed on a recent night at the club.

"Finally, I asked Pioche about Duchon. He laughed and wanted to know if I was looking for a poule to soften my old age. I told him what I had heard about the food salesman. He confirmed that my information was true and added that it was his understanding that Gambia not only paid Duchon a finder's fee but also allowed him, now and then, a free sample of the merchandise. So what do you think Pierre?"

"With your information and Kevin Duffy's 'diary', I am looking forward to our meeting with Duchon this afternoon. It should prove to be amusing in a sadistic sort of way."

"That is precisely what I was thinking. I hope he does not disappoint us and fail to appear."

While Maurice was finishing his story, the waitress had come and cleared the table of their bowls. She returned with a large platter of chicken in a savory tomato, pepper and onion sauce and a dish of steaming rice.

"My God, does that smell good."

"As I told you Pierre, it is the best poulet Basquaise in Biarritz and not just because of the sauce. Wait until you taste the chicken. It comes from the farm of Mme. Haizart's brother in Hasparren." As he spoke, the inspector, with practiced expertise, served their plates from the large platter. "I suggest we give this beautiful bird our undivided attention. I shall tell you of my plan when we have finished."

So, the two men ate and drank and spoke of the glories of good food and well-made wine. Afterwards, the waitress replaced the empty chicken platter with a cheese tray of Camembert, tome de Pyrenees and various shapes, sizes and styles of chevre, from dry, chalk squares to creamy, straw-colored cylinders. Only after the espresso was ordered and Maurice had pushed his chair back from the table and lit a Gauloise did he begin to outline his plan for bringing down Joseph Gambia and his associates. As Peter Ellis suspected, it was a plan that depended far too much on how well they could manipulate a certain food salesman from Bayonne without getting either him or themselves 'accidently' killed.

CHAPTER NINE

When Joseph Gambia arrived at Le Fronton, a nondescript, roadside bistro in Bidart, he found Jean-Claude Duchon waiting at a table in the restaurant's back room. A half-drunk glass of Ricard was not far from his right hand, which held a freshly-lit cigarette. An ashtray held two extinguished butts.

"You are early, I believe, Jean-Claude." Gambia made a show of glancing at the elaborate Rolex on his hairy left wrist.

"I finished my morning rounds early." Duchon took a nervous gulp of his drink. "I have been a wreck since last night. I hardly slept at all. What are we going to do, Jojo? What if my old lady finds out about Chantal? She'll take me for everything. I won't be left with a sou."

The words gushed out. He took another swig of Ricard. "What are we going to do?" He looked imploringly at Gambia, who had remained standing during Duchon's outburst.

"First, you are going to calm yourself and stop acting like an old woman." Gambia took a seat across the table from Duchon. "Secondly, I am going to order a drink, since it appears, from your state, that I'll need one. And thirdly, you are going to collect your thoughts and tell me everything you learned yesterday."

"The little bastard kept a diary. He apparently wrote…" Gambia raised his hand and stopped him in mid-sentence as a young waitress, wearing a short skirt and too much make-up, approached the table. She handed them menus and took their drink order. When she walked away from the table, both men watched the exaggerated movement beneath the skin-tight skirt.

"Not bad. Not bad at all. I may have to see about that one." He turned to face Duchon. "You may continue now, Jean-Claude, but please, try to calm yourself. I'm sure this is something we can deal with. Have a little faith in me. Have I ever let you down before?"

"No, Jojo. But I wish Carlos and his buddies had not killed that damned American kid."

Gambia slapped the table top with the palms of his hands. "Now listen, imbecile, this is the last time I'm telling you, so get it into your little bald head: Carlos and the boys did <u>not</u> kill that stupid American kid. He jumped. He didn't have to, but he did. It was his choice. They were not going to kill him, just teach him a little lesson. Which, if I recall correctly, is what you wanted. I <u>am</u> right in thinking this, am I not? That <u>is</u> what you asked me to do so you could reclaim your little Chantal? Am I right? Answer me. Have you lost your voice? It certainly was working well when I came in a few minutes ago."

Duchon rubbed his face with his left hand and sighed. "I am sorry, Jojo. Of course you are right. I am not myself today. I had no sleep. The old lady was furious because I missed dinner waiting for Chantal. I know it was an accident. I don't know what I was thinking. You have been a good friend, Jojo. I owe you a lot."

"No, you owe it to yourself not to worry. This is not the first problem we have had to solve together, Jean-Claude." The comforting tone had magically returned to Gambia's voice. "Look, here come our drinks. Watch this, I'll show you the famous Gambia touch." He winked at Duchon.

The young waitress placed the two Ricards and a small carafe of water on the table. At close range, it was evident why she wore so much make-up: she was still at that age where acne is a daily problem. Gambia had put his hand on her forearm.

"Mademoiselle, I have bet my friend the price of lunch that a girl as pretty as you is bound to have an equally appealing name. Would you be kind enough to tell us your name?" As he said this, he released his hold on her arm.

"I am called Chantal, sir."

Duchon, who had just tasted his drink to see if the mixture was satisfactory, coughed violently. Gambia smiled broadly at him, showing a full set of newly capped teeth.

"See, I told you so, Jean-Claude. Chantal. Like a song. Are you alright, my friend?"

"Fine." His voice was a raspy wheeze. "My drink went down the wrong way is all."

"Well, I think you must agree that I have won our little wager, isn't that so?"

Duchon nodded. He had regained his composure. "Absolutely. It will be my pleasure to buy your lunch."

The two men placed their orders.

"That will be all, sirs?" She glanced furtively at Gambia.

"Almost. I desire just one thing more. I feel I owe you a favor since, thanks to you, I am eating free today."

"Sir?" The young waitress looked puzzled.

"Do you like to dance, Mlle. Chantal? You know, in the clubs?"

"Yes, sir. Very much."

"Do you know Club Le Gentle-man?"

"I have heard people speak of it. They say it is very exclusive."

"Yes, we try very hard to attract the right kind of clientele."

"It is yours, Le Gentle-man?" The girl spoke with the enthusiasm of a child for a new toy.

"Yes, one could say that it is mine, mademoiselle. And since you have, after a fashion, bought me lunch, I would like to provide you with a little token of appreciation." He reached in his coat pocket and took out a black, lizard-skin billfold and a black and gold Mont Blanc pen. He extracted a gold-embossed card and wrote a few words on the back, signed it and handed it to the star-struck girl. "With my compliments, Mlle. Chantal. This will cover your admission and whatever you care to drink. Should you care to bring a girlfriend, it will cover her as well."

"But I can't accept this, monsieur. It is too much."

"It is nothing. I insist."

The girl hesitated, then tucked the card in her notepad. "You are too generous, monsieur. Thank-you very much. I had better see about your order."

"Mlle. Chantal."

"Yes, monsieur?"

He ran a forefinger lightly down the side of her skirt. He felt no panty line. "I look forward to seeing you soon at Le Gentle-man."

As soon as the waitress was gone, Gambia took his glass and clicked it against Duchon's. "You see, Jean-Claude, it is the golden touch. I shall have that little tartine within the month." He took a large swallow of Ricard. "Now, tell me exactly what _your_ Mlle. Chantal said that has so un-nerved you."

Duchon proceeded to recount Chantal's meeting with the mystery inspector, her discovery that her American friend had kept a diary and her new-found suspicions about his death.

"And this inspector with no name now wants to question _me_ at six this afternoon at the Player's Bar. What did that little bastard write about me? I can't believe all this is happening!" He drained the rest of his drink.

"There is only one course of action, Jean-Claude."

"What is that?"

"You must meet him, of course."

"But why? What if he tries to make a scandal? I would lose my job, everything. You know, I have already had a warning about the girls. I…"

"Calm yourself, Jean-Claude, please. Let me explain: You must meet this mystery inspector, first, so we can discover his name and who sent him. Then I can have LeClerc check on him, maybe even have a word with him or with his superiors. Second, you must talk to him to discover what is in the boy's diary. I suspect you have nothing to worry about, but it would be wise to find out. It is not your meetings with the boy that concern me. It is whether Chantal told him about that unfortunate weekend. I can't imagine that she would have, that she even remembers, but we need to be sure. For everyone's sake. Do you not agree?"

"Of course I agree."

"If he questions you about the meetings, simply explain that it was a misguided case of jealousy. You certainly meant no harm to the boy."

"Well, that's true."

"If you say so Jean-Claude. But, at all costs, don't let him upset you. Be reasonable. There is no way they can tie you to the boy's death—enough people saw you in Bayonne that morning. And, as far as a scandal is concerned, he will need more than a dead boy's diary to take any action."

"Yes, I suppose you are right, Jojo."

For the first time since his meeting with Chantal the previous evening, Jean-Claude Duchon felt the knots in his stomach loosen. He was even beginning to feel a little pang of hunger. He should have known he could count on his friend, Jojo. They may have had an occasional disagreement—Jojo's Corsican blood could get the better of him at times, causing him to say and do things he regretted—but things always worked out in the end. This little problem would be no different.

"You can be sure I am right." Gambia interrupted Duchon's brief reverie. "And, if it will make you feel any better, I'll be waiting for you across the street at Les Colonnes. I may even try to catch a glimpse of your mystery inspector. But enough of this business, it is time to eat. Here is our new friend, Mlle. Chantal, with our food!"

The young waitress smiled coquettishly at Joseph Gambia as she carefully set down a plate overflowing with steak frites. "Will that be all, monsieur?"

"For the moment, Mlle. Chantal." He ran a finger down the length of her pale forearm. "For the moment."

CHAPTER TEN

After lunch, Peter Ellis and Maurice Claverie-LaPorte briefly
visited the site of Kevin Duffy's death to confirm certain
logistical suppositions. When they parted, they agreed to
meet at the Player's Bar fifteen minutes before six. Peter Ellis decided
he had just enough time to drive over to the neighboring Landais
village of St. Martin de Hinx and pay a surprise visit to his old friend
Olga van Cijs. And so, thirty minutes later, he found himself on the
outskirts of Bayonne, heading west on the route nationale 10.

He had chosen the old road over the recently completed autoroute strictly for its nostalgia value. When he had rented a room from
Olga and her artist husband, Roger, in the summer of 1972, he had
driven the road almost daily on his way to one of the many surf spots
around Biarritz. With the exception of Oloron and one or two other
places, the road was not especially interesting or scenic, unless you
considered the miles of evenly spaced trees bordering it an attraction; however, it was an old friend, and Peter Ellis had a particular
weakness for old friends. Especially of late. Anyway, he concluded,
as he slowed for a lumbering cattle truck, it was a glorious, sun-
drenched fall afternoon, so why rush.

The old grange that Olga and her late husband had converted
into a combination art studio-residence was on a narrow, roughly
paved road a kilometer or so outside the miniscule village of St.
Martin de Hinx. As he carefully navigated the potholes, Peter Ellis

noted with pleasure that almost all of the old farms were still intact. At the sight of "La Grange", he felt a chill suffuse his body. He wondered whether he was getting sentimental in his old age. He passed the small pasture that had previously held the two van Cijs daughters' horses. He turned into the familiar driveway that skirted the left side of the house and parked next to the small pond in the center of the circular turn-around. He had barely stepped from his car and lazily stretched when Olga appeared from the opposite side of the house, adjusting her bathing suit top.

She was a tall, big-boned woman in her late fifties, with large breasts, still shapely legs and an attractive round face, whose defining features were a set of full lips and slightly plump cheeks, both naturally red. When she recognized her visitor, she put her hand to her mouth in mock surprise.

"I cannot believe it. It is really you, Peter."

"In the flesh, Olga."

They embraced warmly. Then Olga held him at arm's length and carefully looked him up and down. Ever since they had become friends, it was the way she greeted him after an extended absence.

"Well, you seem to be taking care of yourself," she gently patted his stomach, "though I see you have not given up your beer."

"You know better than that, Olga."

"Yes, I suppose I do. But tell me Peter, do they have no sun anymore in Paris. I cannot recall seeing you with less of a tan."

"There's been very little sun of any kind where I've been during the last month, I'm afraid. I may as well have been in jail. However, I plan to remedy that situation while I am here."

Olga clutched him lightly by the arm. "Come, I have someone special for you to meet. She arrived from Amsterdam just last night on the train."

Peter Ellis immediately thought that one of Olga's two daughters had come to visit. He had not seen either of them since his last trip to Amsterdam. He was preparing a feigned dramatic scene as they turned the corner of the old barn. The surprise that registered on his face was both apparent and genuine, for the extremely attractive young woman covering herself loosely with a brightly-colored shirt was neither Gradje nor Andrea van Cijs. Olga had begun laughing.

"I have you good this time." She broke into another fit of laughter. "You thought it was one of my girls, and you were very smug about it too."

"I am guilty on all counts, Olga. But, watch out, I shall get you for this."

"Whatever you do, I am sure it will have been worth it." She turned from Peter Ellis to the nearly naked women on the chaise-lounge. "My dear, meet an old, dear friend of the family and famous journalist, Peter Ellis."

She held out a hand with long, delicate fingers. "How do you do, M. Ellis. I'm Anya."

"And I'm Peter—please don't make me feel any older than I am."

She smiled. "I'm sorry. I guess it's just a habit from work."

"Well, I believe this calls for a drink of celebration. White wine, Anya?"

"That would be very nice, Olga."

"You may be in luck, Peter. I believe I even have some Kronenbourg in the fridge."

"You will spoil me yet, Olga."

"Stop it Peter. Why don't you tell Anya about yourself, and try not to exaggerate too much. I'll be right back."

Anya had let the shirt fall, so that it barely covered her pubic hair. Peter Ellis pulled up a lawn chair next to the two chaise-lounges, removed his t-shirt and tried not to stare at Olga's very blond friend. Which was not an easy thing to do because Anya had a downright wonderful body, one she obviously took good care of, he thought, for he guessed her to be in her late thirties. She looked to be of medium height, though she had long, sinewy dancer's legs. Her hair was extremely blond and straight, cut to a length just above her shoulders. It framed a pleasing oval face with a small pert nose, thin, rose-colored lips and pale blue eyes. Also rose-colored were the large aureolas on her full, slightly pendulous breasts.

"I hope you'll forgive my wanton appearance, but the weather has been terrible recently in Amsterdam. This is the first I've seen of the sun in two weeks, I think."

"You are totally forgiven. I know how you feel. It has not been much better in Paris."

"You have only just arrived in the region yourself?"

"I drove down yesterday."

"It is for business or pleasure, your trip?"

"A little of both. And you? You are on holiday?"

"Yes, for two weeks."

"Do you intend to spend all of your time here?"

"I'm not sure, at the moment. I was thinking about passing a few days in Spain. But I shall think on that later. Right now, I am so content to be out of the city, I cannot think of anything."

Peter Ellis had been doing his best at keeping his eyes on hers and not on the rest of her. But it was a struggle. In making a slight adjustment in her seating position, she had caused the brightly colored shirt to slip to the side, revealing a thin patch of silky blond hair. Upon seeing it, he felt himself harden. He shifted nervously in his chair. He hoped his thoughts were not as apparent as they seemed to be to him. What was it she had been talking about?

"Yes, I know the feeling well. I can't tell you how happy I am to be out of Paris for awhile."

"How long are you going to be in the region?"

"That depends on the project I am working on. At least two weeks, for sure."

"You are staying where?"

"At the hotel of some old friends in Biarritz. It is called Les Flots Bleus and has what I consider to be the most spectacular view in the entire town. You must come over and see it one of these days. I would be happy to drive you there."

"That would be very nice."

"As for Spain, I would be happy to give you the names of some of my favorite places. Depending upon your schedule and my work, the three of us could even take a day trip there. I know Olga loves the Spanish Basque country. We used to go there often in the old days."

"You have known her long?"

"Almost sixteen years. I lived here in the summer of '72, not long after she and Roger bought the farm. At that time, they were still renovating the building."

"It was so sad about Roger. He was just beginning to get the recognition and prices he deserved."

"So you knew Roger well?"

"I am not sure I would say that. I was his student."

"You're an artist?"

"Actually, I'm a banker."

"Don't let her kid you, Peter. She's a painter, and a very good one. She has been wasting her talent at the bank."

Neither Anya nor Peter Ellis had seen Olga arrive. At the sound of her voice, they turned their heads in unison. She was carrying a tray with two glasses of white wine, a bottle of beer and a frosted mug. She distributed the drinks, leaned the tray against the wall, undressed and lay on the chaise-lounge next to Anya. She raised the large, tulip-shaped glass by the stem and dipped it in their direction.

"To good friends. One can never have enough."

Peter Ellis raised his glass in response. "I'll certainly drink to that."

"And I as well." Anya clinked her glass against his.

"So, Peter, tell me, have you come down just to surf or are you working on an article?"

"There is the possibility of an article, Olga."

Peter Ellis then proceeded to tell them about the 'accidental' death of Kevin Duffy and the peculiar circumstances surrounding it and about Jean-Claude Duchon and his relationship with Joseph Gambia.

"My friend, Maurice, thinks there is a connection between the death and the mobster and that if he can uncover it, he may finally be able to nail Gambia. It is something he has been trying to do for years. You might say it's his personal grail."

"Why did he ask you to come down?" It was Anya who spoke.

"Well, in my work, I have developed certain small skills in digging up seemingly unimportant bits of information that, more often than not, fit together at some point like pieces of a puzzle. In addition to this, shall we say, research, Maurice thinks I may be helpful in convincing Duchon to implicate Gambia, since national publicity is the last thing a person in his compromised postion wants. Of course, for the time being, I only have hearsay to go on, so I shall have to convince Duchon with what I like to think of as 'facts of the imagination'. Finally, Maurice thought my surfing knowledge and connections would be helpful in this case. As for my interest in the affair, you could say it is somewhat autobiographical. Anyway, I was looking for an excuse to leave Paris."

"Do you not think you will be in any danger?" Anya looked at him with what was, to Peter Ellis's mind, an appealing air of concern.

"There is always that possibility. It comes with the territory, I'm afraid. I can assure you, it is not something I am seeking out."

"Enough of this distasteful business, Peter. I'm sure you'll work everything out; you always have in the past."

"Not always, Olga, though I appreciate the vote of confidence."

"Well, Maurice is not the only one here who requires your assistance. As it happens, so do I."

"Olga, you know if it's something I am capable of doing, all you have to do is ask."

"This is something I am sure you are capable of, Peter." She paused for effect and took a slow, deliberate sip of wine. "In fact, it is something I don't think you will find unappealing."

"So are you going to tell me what it is or do I have to guess?"

"I would like you to make time in your busy schedule to show Anya some of the more charming little villages of the region. Places that might appeal to the artist's eye."

"Olga, really! That is not necessary. Your friend sounds like he is going to be much too occupied with his investigation to waste time driving around the countryside with me."

"I would be delighted to show Mlle. Anya some of my favorite places, Olga. In fact, I was in the way of suggesting it when you arrived with the drinks." He turned to Anya. "Do you have plans for tomorrow?"

"No."

"Good. I suggest we go to Sauveterre-de-Béarn for lunch. Then, if you see something you want to paint, I can take a walk around town or down by the river. What do you think?"

"If you are sure it won't disrupt your work, I would love to."

"I am sure." He thought to himself that he would gladly drop the whole damn thing in Maurice's lap if it came down to a choice between spending time with Anya and nailing Gambia. "I am surfing in the morning with my friend, Marc, but we'll be finished certainly by ten. Let's say I pick you up by noon. Will you join us, Olga?"

"Another time, Peter. I made plans some time ago to dine with friends in Hossegor. But, thank-you for thinking of me." She caught his eye and winked.

Peter Ellis left La Grange at four-thirty. He hardly noticed the countryside on the return drive to Biarritz, his mind's eye fixed on topography of a distinctly different nature.

CHAPTER ELEVEN

Maurice was waiting for Peter Ellis at a table in the back next to the large plate glass window that overlooked the Grande Plage.

"So, my young friend, how was your afternoon? I trust Mme. Olga is doing well?"

"She is, as is her beautiful visitor from Amderstam."

"A beautiful visitor from Amsterdam, Pierre? Perhaps you can be more specific?"

Peter Ellis gave him a brief description of Anya, leaving out most of the graphic details.

"Eh bien, Pierre, it seems that you may finally be getting over your American friend, Mlle. Burke."

"I wouldn't say that I'm getting over her so much as discovering someone new, who happens to be beautiful and, apparently, very talented."

"Well, I am happy for you. I can vaguely remember what it feels like, that first <u>frisson</u>. It has been a long time." He paused and lit a cigarette. "A few words of advice. You are still very vulnerable. Take things slowly."

"I'll do my best. I can tell you it won't be easy with this woman."

"It never is, Pierre. It never is." He took a long draw on the cigarette. "So, do you remember how we are going to play this little drama with M. Duchon?"

"Yes. Do you really think he will come?"

"Yes, if for no other reason, out of curiosity. He will want to know what is in the boy's diary. And, he will want to find out who this inspector is who has come to ask questions about what has been ruled an accidental death, for I am sure Mlle. Chantal was not able to give him my name. I am confident he will call Gambia or LeClerc as soon as he leaves us. By tomorrow, I shall be expecting an official reprimand for misrepresenting myself to the girl and to him."

The waiter arrived with their drinks, vermouth on the rocks for Maurice and a beer for Peter Ellis. A few minutes later, a ferret-faced man with thinning gray hair walked in and said something to the barman, who turned and indicated their table. When Duchon reached them, they were both standing. From his expression, it was obvious that there were many other places he would rather be.

"Monsieur Jean-Claude Duchon?" Maurice extended his hand.

"Yes!" He snapped off the reply. The anger in his voice was palpable.

"It is a pleasure to meet you. I am Inspector Maurice Claverie-LaPorte and this is Monsieur Peter Ellis from the United States."

Duchon took their hands in turn and gave them a quick, cursory shake.

"Inspector, you have some identification I presume?"

"Of course. Please forgive me."

He reached into his breast pocket and produced a well-worn billfold. He flicked it open and handed it to Duchon, who studied the photo I.D. for nearly half a minute.

"Since when did the Brigade Financière become interested in dead American tourists? That is why you are here, is it not?" He spoke rapidly.

"Yes. And, you have reason to question the Brigade's involvement, since, strictly speaking, there is none. I was asked to look into the boy's death by a friend at the American Embassy. I am acting, shall we say, in an unofficial capacity." Maurice smiled benignly at Duchon.

"Looking into the boy's death? What is there to look into? He was standing on the railing, for God knows what reason, and fell. It was an accident. The police have closed the case."

"So they have, so they have. Perhaps M. Ellis can better explain our interest. M. Ellis?"

"I would be happy to, Inspector." He nodded at Maurice and addressed Duchon in a calm, hard voice. "Monsieur, I was very close to Kevin Duffy. He was like a son to me. I even taught him to surf. In fact, it was I who suggested he come here, since I myself had visited Biarritz as a young man.When I was informed of his death by his parents, I told them I would come immediately and make the necessary arrangements. I reasoned that no good could come from their visiting the scene of Kevin's death. They protested at first; but, I reminded them, among other things, of my familiarity with the region and the language and they soon agreed that it made more sense that I should be the one to make the trip. Of course, there were other reasons I felt I should come, not the least of which was guilt for suggesting that Kevin visit this area in the first place.

"It was my initial intention to stay in Biarritz only as long as it took to settle Kevin's affairs and file the appropriate documents. But, upon arrival, I began to discover certain discrepancies, certain troubling bits of information concerning the death of my young friend. So, I called the American Embassy and asked for their assistance in resolving the problem to my satisfaction. As fate would have it, the official I spoke with is a friend of Inspector Claverie-LaPorte here."

The barman arrived with a glass of Ricard and a small pitcher of water. Peter Ellis paused to take a sip a beer. He glanced briefly at Maurice, who was leaning back in his chair, hands folded on his ample stomach, impassively taking in his little performance. Duchon filled his glass with water and took a noisy gulp.

"M. Duchon, perhaps you are aware of some of the discrepancies of which I speak?"

The question seemed to startle him. He came close to knocking over his glass.

"I have no idea what you are speaking of. If there is something of importance you want to discuss with me, please get to the point." He pulled back his left sleeve and made an exaggerated show of checking the time. "I have one final appointment this evening before dinner. My wife is very strict about eating on time."

The vaguest, almost imperceptible smile crossed Maurice's face. Peter Ellis fixed Duchon with a steely cold stare.

"I shall be as brief as possible, M. Duchon. I certainly do not want to cause you any problems with your wife. However, it is important that you hear what I have to say. Very important, I think.

"You see, when Kevin's parents told me of his death, they said only that it was an accident, that he had lost his balance and fallen on some rocks. It was only when I arrived here and spoke with Inspector LeClerc that I discovered the details. At my request, he accompanied me to the park above the beach of Côte des Basques and showed me exactly where they, or perhaps I should say where the old man, Haraout, found the body. He told me his theory of how Kevin came to fall and said that unless the autopsy uncovered information to the contrary, accidental death was the only conclusion that made sense. As you well know, the autopsy discovered nothing unusual, according to Inspector LeClerc. So, Kevin's death was ruled an accident and the case was closed."

"Excuse me, M. Ellis, but I fail to see your problem with this conclusion." A certain confidence was creeping into Duchon's voice. The nervousness evident on his arrival had all but disappeared. He took a large swallow of his drink.

"I will tell you my problem with the conclusion, M. Duchon. And I am sure it will interest you. It is like this:

"After I met with the appropriate officials and signed their various forms, I went to Kevin's apartment to pack what few things I thought necessary to send back to his parents. You may be interested to know, M. Duchon, that my young friend had aspirations of being a writer. At my suggestion, he began, three years ago, to keep a diary. When I found it among his things, I felt compelled to read the last entries he made before his death. He wrote a great deal about the girl he was seeing, Chantal Clairac. He thought he was in love with her; but, it seems someone else also thought they were in love with her. Can you guess who that someone might be, M. Duchon?"

"I do not know what you're talking about, monsieur. This is a complete waste of my time."

"Don't play the imbecile with me, M. Duchon. Chantal Clairac was your mistress, at least until she started seeing my young friend. Perhaps there are other things that would upset your wife even more than your being late for dinner. What do you think? Am I still wasting your time, or would you like me to continue?"

"Continue, please." The color had suddenly drained from his face. His voice was a whisper.

"Very good. I promise you, the story gets better. Would you care for another drink?"

He nodded his head. After Peter Ellis had ordered, he continued:

"Well, it seems that someone very closely resembling you tried to convince Kevin that he should stop seeing Chantal. Someone who told him that she was not the nice girl she appeared to be. That someone even produced some very peculiar, nasty photographs of her. I must say, my poor, young friend did give a surprisingly accurate description of you. Which is not to say that you would agree with it, M. Duchon."

"Listen, monsieur, I admit I was jealous. It is a normal reaction. You must understand that. But, I had nothing to do with the death of your friend. Everyone knows I was in Bayonne when it happened."

"Yes, M. Duchon, you had many witnesses in Bayonne that morning. That is one of the other things that bothers me. It was almost as though you went to that particular bar on purpose that morning. Let me ask you an interesting question: Do you know where your friend, Joseph Gambia, was on that same morning? Is it possible that he was in the vicinity of the park overlooking the Côte des Basques beach? And please, M. Duchon, don't tell me you don't know who I am talking about. The inspector and I, we have done our homework. We know about your little business arrangement with him. Is it possible you even tried to get Chantal to work for him?"

"You are crazy, monsieur. I am in love with Chantal. It is I who saved her last year. As for M. Gambia, if you want to know where he was that morning, why don't you ask him? Since you have done your 'homework' so well, I am confident you will know how to get in touch with him. I will tell you and your inspector friend one more time, I had nothing to do with the boy's death. It is perhaps true that I wanted him out of town. For a man in my position, that was natural. It is also perhaps true that I used certain unfortunate photographs in my possession to persuade him to leave Chantal. But that is all!"

"Are you telling me you did not threaten him? From what is in his diary, it sounds as though you made it plain that staying with Chantal might be dangerous."

"We all say regrettable things in the heat of passion. Everyone does. I will not pretend to be different from any other man."

"Oh, but I think you are, M. Duchon, because the person you threatened, my friend, Kevin Duffy, 22 years old, died in a mysterious way shortly after you warned him to leave town. I will tell you frankly, M. Duchon, that bothers me a great deal. Now, I am not saying you had him killed. As revolting as I find you, you do not impress me as a killer. But I do think you have certain information about the death of my friend that you are not telling me, information I intend to find out one way or another. Do you understand?"

"Are you threatening to blackmail me? Because, if you are, you will have to answer to Inspector LeClerc."

"Take it how you will. Anyway, I have several things to say to Chief Inspector LeClerc that I am sure he will not want to hear. As for your friend, M. Gambia, you can tell him that we know that my young friend was not alone on the overlook the morning he died."

"What do you mean, 'not alone'?"

"Exactly what I said. He was not alone. He had company. And I think your friend might know who that company was, in fact, might have been part of it."

"This is all preposterous. How come the police could find no evidence of others being there?"

"Perhaps they were not looking hard enough. For whatever reason."

"You really are crazy, M. Ellis. Now you are accusing our police of lying about the cause of your friend's death. If I were to tell Chief Inspector LeClerc, he would not like that. He would not like that at all."

"That is very true, M. Duchon. But the evidence Inspector Claverie-LaPorte and I have found leaves me no other conclusion."

"What evidence? There is no other evidence. Inspector LeClerc said so."

"So he did; however, he was mistaken. Either that, or he was saving it for some reason of his own."

"What reason would that be? It makes no sense."

"Oh, I would not go that far, M. Duchon. Maybe you should ask him. At the moment, Inspector LeClerc's apparent lack of professionalism does not concern me. What <u>does</u> concern me is the information <u>you</u> are hiding. So this is what I suggest: You go home tonight to your wife. I am sure you will be punctual. You don't want to upset her at the beginning of the weekend. For the next two days, you think about everything I have said. Think about it very carefully, M. Duchon. Then, if you decide there are other things you have forgotten to tell me, leave a message for Peter Ellis at Les Flots Bleus—you know the place?"

"Of course. What do you think?"

"Good. You leave me a message telling me when and where we might rendez-vous on Monday. As much as you disgust me, I mean you no harm. Unless, of course, you did mean for Kevin to be attacked. I am only interested in knowing how he came to fall, or jump, from that overlook above Côtes des Basques." Peter Ellis held up his hand to keep Duchon from speaking. "Don't tell me again that it was purely an accident. It may have been, shall we say, an assisted accident—those involved may not have meant for him to die—but he did die and there were others with him at the time of his death. I intend on staying in Biarritz until I find out who is responsible. Do you understand? If that means making myself into your worst nightmare, then so be it. That does not have to happen. As soon as I think you have told me everything you know, I shall see to it that certain entries in Kevin's diary are destroyed and that the remainder is preserved for his family and friends. As they say in tennis, M. Duchon, the ball is your court. Have an enjoyable weekend."

Duchon rose to leave. Peter Ellis stood and made to shake his hand. The food salesman merely shot him an icy look and scowled.

"You are a real bastard, do you know that?"

He turned abruptly and strode out of the bar, the bald crown of his head glistening under the neon light of a beer sign by the door.

Peter Ellis turned to Maurice, who wore a mischievous expression. "So, what do you think, Inspector?"

"Your performance was worthy of the stage. Even I was impressed by some of your fabrications. I fear, however, that our friend was not equally amused."

"What do you think he will do?"

"I wish I knew. As you said, we have put the ball in his court. We must wait and see how he plays it."

CHAPTER TWELVE

J oseph Gambia was waiting for Jean-Claude Duchon at an outside table across the street at the Café Les Colonnes.

"So, how did your little conference go?" His voice was pleasant, almost playful.

"This is not a matter to laugh at. That American friend of the boy, he has the kid's diary. The kid wrote about me _and_ about the pictures. The American guy as much as said he would go to my wife and tell her about everything."

"Well, then you would be rid of her. You keep saying that is what you want. And Chantal is certainly free now." He smiled broadly at his agitated friend.

"Please, Jojo. This is not a joke. This American bastard—his name is Peter Ellis by the way—thinks both you _and_ I had something to do with the boy's death. It is absurd. I had nothing to do with it. I was in Bayonne. Everyone knows it."

"Jean-Claude, save your lies for someone else. You forget who you are talking to. If you are trying to convince yourself that you had nothing to do with it, go right ahead. But, don't waste my time with such foolishness. Did you say anything about me to them?"

"Of course not, Jojo. Not a word."

"Good. Now, let's see what we are dealing with. First of all, who is this 'mystery inspector' and where is he from?"

"His name is Maurice Claverie-LaPorte. He works with the Brigade Financière."

Gambia responded to his friend's information with a howl of laughter. Duchon looked at him dumbfounded.

"Evidently, I am missing something. Would you please tell me what is so funny?"

Gambia let out another burst of laughter. He began shaking his head. "Oh putain, Jean-Claude: This is rich. This is truly rich. You have been meeting with the old, fat one!"

"You know him?" Duchon sounded incredulous.

Gambia had begun laughing again. "After a fashion, my friend, after a fashion."

"So what is his story? Is he on our side?"

"He most definitely is not on our side. Oh no, not the upright Inspector Claverie-LaPorte."

"Then what do you find so amusing?"

"Simply this, my friend. You have been meeting for the last half hour with the former Inspector Maurice Claverie-LaPorte."

"Former?"

"Exactly! He was forced into retirement several months ago. He had begun looking into certain matters that were none of his business. Certain, shall we say, very delicate matters where some of my friends at the Commisariat also have an interest. They spoke to his superiors, who decided he needed a physical and sent him to one of their doctors. This decision was made easier by his prolific eating habits. Anyway, the doctor, aided by a suggestion from one of the more powerful commissioners, came to the conclusion that the old inspector was in poor health and should take early retirement. It seems the inspector did not agree with their conclusion and made quite a scene of leaving the department. Why look," he pointed across the street, "here comes our rotund old friend now. I am almost tempted to wave."

"Please, Jojo, I am in no mood for jokes. At any rate, it was the American friend of the boy who did all the talking, the man named Ellis."

"And where is he?"

"He must have decided to have another drink. With all his damned talking, he probably needs one. I will point him out when he leaves."

"You do that. While we are waiting, why don't you tell me what he said to make you upset, Jean-Claude?"

Duchon recounted their conversation. By the time he was finished, he had worked himself into a state of renewed agitation.

"What am I going to do, Jojo?" I believe he is serious about showing my old lady the diary. And what other evidence can he have? Do you think someone saw Carlos and the boys?"

"Jean-Claude, calm yourself! Please! No one saw Carlos and the others. You forget, I was there. The only other person there was the old one with the dog. LeClerc has taken care of him. Even if he decided he could recognize me now, who would believe him. As for other so-called 'evidence', I think this American, this M. Ellis, is bluffing. LeClerc made sure the mention of knife wounds was deleted from the autopsy. What else could there be? Unless your little friend, Chantal, has been talking out of school. That would be very unfortunate for all concerned, Jean-Claude. If I were you, I would make sure, as soon as possible, that she has not said anything about that unfortunate incident last year. And, I would advise her, in the strongest possible terms, to keep her distance from the fat inspector and his American buddy."

"I have already thought of that. I am going to pay her a little surprise visit tonight after she gets off work. Don't worry about Chantal. I know how to deal with her."

"You had better, Jean-Claude. LeClerc would be very upset if any bad publicity came of all this. You certainly understand that?"

"Of course, Jojo."

"Okay. You take care of the girl, I'll talk to LeClerc about dealing with former Inspector Claverie-Laporte. As for this American, M.Ellis, where did you say he is staying?"

"At the Hotel Les Flots Bleus."

"Fine. Don't worry about him and the diary. I'll deal with that problem myself. Next week at this time, you will be thinking how foolish you were to get so upset over such a silly threat."

"I hope you are right, Jojo."

"Of course I am right. Let's talk no more about these imbeciles. Will you have another Ricard, Jean-Claude?"

"Please."

Gambia caught the eye of waiter, pointed to his glass and held up two fingers. When their drinks arrived, he clicked his against Duchon's.

"Here's to putting this little affair behind us once and for all."

"I will happily drink to that."

"And to getting rid of the two old women in our lives."

"Now, you are joking. Why would you want to get rid of Janine? She is just your business partner now. You are free to do as you like with other women."

Gambia took a large swallow of this drink, smiled thinly at Duchon and said nothing.

***

An hour later, Joseph Gambia was in the apartment of his official partner and former lover, Janine Destin, preparing drinks for her and for his unofficial partner and friend, Chief Inspector Jacques 'Jacky' LeClerc. Janine's top floor penthouse was in an angular, modern building in the center of town, overlooking La Grande Plage. It commanded a panoramic view of the ocean and coastline from Pointe St. Martin and the Biarritz lighthouse south to Pointe Atalye and the Rocher de la Vierge. LeClerc and Janine Destin were on the oceanfront balcony, discussing the merits of a new Italian restaurant when Gambia delivered their drinks, Pernod for him, bourbon and Coke for her.

"I do not understand how you can drink that horrible American concoction, Janine."

"And I, Jacky, have never understood this universal French attraction for anisette. I think there must be some secret ingredient that makes it addictive. One certainly does not drink it for the taste."

She took an appreciative sip of her drink. "Ah-h-h, now that's good!"

She was a full-figured woman in her late thirties, which is to say that she had grown a bottom to match her upper body, an upper body that still turned heads when she walked down the street in a tight sweater. She had dark, brownish-red hair, cut in a fashionable short style, round, brown eyes, a slightly curved, narrow nose, strong cheekbones and the kind of full-lipped, round mouth that makes men think of sex. When she was younger, she had caused more than one fight between suitors. Now, in early middle age, she was still lusted after by most of her male counterparts, including one Inspector Jacques LeClerc.

Much to his dismay, however, Janine Destin had rebuffed his advances, saying that it had nothing to do with his having a wife but everything to do with their business partnership. This did not mean he had given up trying. As he was fond of saying, both to himself and to his cronies, what Jacques LeClerc wants, Jacques LeClerc gets. Janine was taking more time to tame than usual, but he was sure that one day, in the not-too-distant future, he would feel those magnificent monsters slapping against this eager face. As if to assure himself, he stole a furtive look at Janine's chest, seductively exposed above a low-cut, emerald green sweater.

Just because he had not convinced Janine Destin to give in to him did not mean that the chief inspector was practicing abstinence. His position of official power and his discreet partnership with Gambia and Janine coupled with his relative good looks gave him ample opportunity to indulge his sexual appetites. Yes, it had to be said, even by his detractors, that he was not a bad-looking man, even with the extra weight he had put on since retiring from the Bayonne Rugby Club five years ago. Almost six feet two with wide shoulders and a big torso, LeClerc had been able to hide his added girth until recently. Even he had to admit, though, invariably on those mornings when he was trying to overcome the effects of a previous night's over-indulgence and, catching a glimpse of his large, naked body in the full-length bathroom mirror, that the good life he had become accustomed to was taking its toll. His face, for the most part, still retained the rugged, if somewhat simian, good looks of his youth: a wide, narrow forehead, heavy, black eyebrows over small, darting brown eyes, a flat nose under which grew a thick, black mustache, and a solid, square jaw in which was set an expansive, full-lipped mouth. Yes, he would think, later on those same hangover mornings, as he studied himself in the small shaving mirror, his gut safely hidden from view, this face was not too bad to look at, not bad at all.

"You like my sweater, Jacky." Janine gave him a knowing smile.

"Yes, I was thinking how perfectly it complements your hair color." He stared straight into her eyes, trying to keep his voice matter-of-fact for Gambia's sake. He knew it didn't fool Janine.

"What in the hell are you two talking about? I thought we came here to discuss business, not fashion. And since when did you become interested in women's clothes, Jacky, apart from your interest in trying to remove them." He looked smugly at the inspector.

"There you go again, Jojo, everything must have something to do with sex. More and more, I think you have a problem with your dick."

"You know better than that, Janine. Of all people."

"Is that so? I wouldn't be so sure if I were you."

"I have never heard any complaints from any of my women."

"Perhaps, like me, they were trying to be nice and not bruise that fragile male ego."

"Ha! That's a good one. Are you now telling me I didn't always satisfy you?"

"Think what you will."

The inspector had been listening to their verbal sparring with a bemused expression. But, their conversion had taken what was, for him, an irritating turn. Imagining Gambia in bed with Janine soured his fantasies for her. Hearing them talk like this was worse.

"That's enough, you two. I didn't come up here to hear about your past sex life. I thought you said we had business to discuss, Jojo."

"Please forgive me, Jacky." Janine squeezed his hand. Of course, you are right. I should know better. He's just trying to get me started."

"Me? Who started this whole thing in the first place?"

"I said 'enough'! Okay?"

They both looked at him and nodded.

"Janine, why don't you start? How are things at the club?"

She reached in the large Hermés handbag, which lay on the seat next to her, and removed two long, bulging envelopes. She handed one to LeClerc and threw the other in Gambia's direction.

"Here's your cut for last month. It's a little less than the previous one, but that's to be expected in view of the season. I don't think either of you will be disappointed."

"How are the two new girls working out?"

"Not bad, especially Dany. I think she's a natural. She's already selling more champagne than any of the others. And, she must be doing other things right, because most of her customers seem to come back."

"A nice way to put it, Janine." Gambia tipped his glass at her. She looked briefly in his direction, shook her head and continued.

"The other one, Marie-Thérèse, would do much better I think, if our new Romeo, M. Carlos, would leave her alone once in a while. He barely gives her a chance to hustle the paying customers. Sometimes I wonder where you find these stupid gorillas, Jojo. You need to have another talk with him."

"My God, Janine, give the boy a break. He and the others have only been here a few weeks. They'll come around. Anyway, I just talked to him yesterday."

"I must say, Jojo, I agree with Janine on this one. I have serious doubts about this Carlos. Apart from his temper, he seems to have much too high an opinion of himself. I really don't know if it would be wise to keep him. Look at the mess he got us into with the American kid."

"The kid <u>jumped</u>, Jacky. You yourself questioned the other two. There was nothing they could do."

"I'm not so sure about that, Jojo, the more I think about it. And, what was he doing holding the knife against the kid's throat. Do you think that was smart <u>or</u> necessary?"

"Okay, he made a mistake. He knows he made a mistake. I guarantee that!"

"Just tell him to leave the girls alone during business hours Jojo, if he wants to keep his job."

"Hey, I thought we <u>all</u> voted on these kinds of things, Janine."

"I agree with Janine this time, Jojo. Either Carlos shows some marked improvement in his behavior, and shows it immediately, or I say we send him back to Marseille. Make an example of him."

"Okay, that's enough! I get the message." Gambia took a swallow of his drink, then exhaled audibly. "Well, while we are on the topic of Carlos, I might as well tell you who our friend Duchon just finished meeting with."

"Don't tell me it has to do with the death of the American kid. I thought my last press release put that case to rest."

"You're going to love this, Jacky. Our old friend, Maurice Claverie-LaPorte has involved himself in the affair."

"You mean the old fart who used to be with the Brigade Financière?"

"The very one. And you know what that means—it means he's trying to tie me to the kid's death."

"You say Duchon met with him today?"

"Duchon today, Chantal Clairac yesterday. He showed both of them his ID and said he was still with the Brigade."

"I'll have his fat ass this time. He's finally gone too far."

"Jean-Claude said he was with the American who came over to deal with the boy's funeral arrangements and the paperwork. A Peter something."

"It must be the boy's uncle. I met with him. I don't recall his name, but he seemed satisfied that it was a case of accidental death. He seemed mainly concerned with concluding the whole process as quickly and painlessly as possible. He was greatly worried over the effect it had had on the boy's parents."

"Well, I can tell you that, according to Duchon, the uncle, if that's who this American guy is, is definitely not satisfied with your official findings now. He apparently has the boy's diary and is threatening to blackmail Duchon with it. He also mentioned that he had certain 'evidence' to back up his suspicions. He wants Duchon to get back in touch with him by Monday."

"How in the hell did he get up with Claverie-LaPorte?"

"They told Duchon a fairytale about someone at the American Embassy, who knew the old fart, asking him to assist the boy's uncle with the arrangements. But I don't buy that. I think Claverie-LaPorte, himself, got in touch with the American through that Haizart woman. You know, her son was a friend of the Duffy boy. My guess is the American kid told her about Jean-Claude's little visit and the pictures, so that, when she hears about the accident, she decides to call our buddy, Claverie-LaPorte. As much as he likes food, he's probably a client of her restaurant. However the two of them got together, we need to do something to put an end to their snooping around."

"I certainly agree with you there. What do you think we should do?"

"This ought to be good." Janine snorted, and finished the remainder of her drink.

"Janine, if you would listen for once in your life, you just might learn something of value."

"From you? You must be joking. You forget, Jojo, I know what head you think with."

"Enough, you two! Let's figure out how to put an end to this business once and for all. So Jojo, what's your plan?"

"I presume that impersonating an officer is still a crime?"

"Of course it is."

"Well I thought you might have a talk with Claverie-LaPorte. Tell him you've had a complaint. Tell him you're willing not to file any charges if he'll forget about the death of this American kid and start minding his own business."

"I can do that; in fact, I had already planned to. But what about the uncle and the diary?"

"I thought I might send Carlos and the boys over to his apartment. Make it look like robbery. Take the diary but also take any money or valuables they find."

"Maybe Carlos can make the uncle jump out the window and kill himself too. Really, Jojo, you can't be serious about using Carlos again. Jacky, tell him." She looked over at the inspector and gestured with an upturned palm at Gambia.

LeClerc did not immediately reply. He seemed to be weighing something in his head.

"Jacky? Are you still with us?"

"Yes, Janine, my dear. I was just thinking. I believe Jojo is right this time. And, if he'll be kind enough to get us another drink, I'll explain why."

"Thank you, Jacky." Gambia cast Janine Destin a smug look. "Satisfied?"

"Just get me another drink, Jojo. And put more bourbon in this one. If I'd only wanted a Coke, I would have asked for one." She turned to LeClerc. "Okay, Jacky, I'm listening."

∗∗∗

While Joseph Gambia was in Janine Destin's apartment meeting with his two associates, Jean-Claude Duchon was talking with Achille, the barman at <u>Le Sportif</u>, waiting for Chantal to come home from work. He was in a much better mood than on the previous day and had already bought the barman a drink. They had been discussing an upcoming rugby match. Achille had played when he was young and was a great enthusiast.

"Did you ever play, M. Duchon?"

"Rugby? Are you kidding? You rugby players are too crazy for me. Why, didn't someone bite off an opponent's ear several years ago in England?"

"He just took a small piece of it," Achille laughed, "but everyone knows, the English are not civilized. Just think about what they eat."

"I'll drink to that." Duchon raised his glass.

He was not sure why, but after talking with Gambia, he suddenly had the feeling that everything was going to work out all right. In this new-found mood of optimism, he had stopped by a wine store and bought a bottle of Spanish champagne. He had asked Achille to keep it cold for him. The barman had given him a conspiratorial wink.

"A little surprise for Mlle. Chantal?"

"And a big one to follow, Achille, if you know what I mean." He gave the barman a wolfish grin. "A bit of dessert before the old lady's cooking."

Yes, he definitely felt that his fortunes with Chantal were also about to change. And not a minute too soon. He couldn't remember the last time he'd had sex. He only did it with his wife on the two or three occasions a year when she drank too much, which meant that he had to be blind drunk himself. He started getting hard thinking about Chantal spreading those long legs.

He was on his second Ricard when she turned the corner and crossed the street to the little bar. He rushed to open the door for her, flashing what he took to be his most endearing smile, and quickly kissed her on both cheeks.

"Achille, a glass of your best white wine for the most beautiful girl in Biarritz!"

"With pleasure, M. Duchon. Bonjour, Mlle. Chantal. Everything going well?"

"Yes, thank-you, Achille."

"Very good. I'll be right back with your wine."

When the barman had gone, Duchon took Chantal by the hand and began to trace a line up the length of her forearm with his middle finger.

"So, how were the blue hairs today, my little one?"

"Not too bad, except for old Mme. Chambon. With her, it is always something. Today, the crust on her tarte aux pommes was too hard."

"You had no visits from fat former inspectors, I trust. Or their rude American friends?"

"Former inspectors? I don't understand what you mean, Jean-Claude."

"Your friend from yesterday, with whom I met not long ago. He lied to you. He <u>used</u> to be with the <u>Brigade</u> <u>Financière</u>, but they retired him many months ago. I saw Jojo afterwards. He knows of him. He told me the whole story."

He paused while Achille placed a small napkin on the bar followed by a glass of straw-colored wine. "M. Duchon, another for you?"

"In a minute, Achille. Thank-you."

"With pleasure." Observing that they were in a private conversation, the barman moved a discreet distance down the bar. Duchon turned back toward Chantal Clairac.

"Why didn't you mention yesterday that the inspector had an American friend with him, Chantal?"

"An American friend? I have no idea what you are speaking of, Jean-Claude."

He studied her face. It held a look of evident consternation. "You did not meet this man, Peter Ellis, when he came to make the arrangements for your unfortunate friend?"

"It was his uncle who came to make the arrangements for Kevin, at least he said he was his uncle. I thought his name was Paul, but I could be mistaken."

"And you have not seen this uncle since when?"

"Since the day of the service here."

"Where was he staying, this uncle? Do you know?"

"In Kevin's room chez Mme. Haizart."

"Well, it seems he is still here, but he's now staying in an apartment at Hotel Les Flots Bleus on the Perspective."

"What is he still doing here? It is very strange."

"I'll tell you what he'sdoing here at the moment: he's trying to make trouble for me. But not for long."

"Make trouble for you? Why?"

"The damned diary of your friend. This Claverie-LaPorte, the former inspector, has it in for Jojo, and thinks I can help him. So, he has put all sorts of crazy ideas about your friend's death into the uncle's head."

"What kind of crazy ideas?"

"Just crazy ideas to make him use the diary against me. This idiot uncle, Peter Ellis, even threatened me this afternoon. Can you believe it? He as much as said if I didn't decide to help them by Monday, he would show my wife the part about us, what your friend apparently wrote about my little conversation with him that day."

"But what does this have to do with Kevin's death?"

"That is just my point, Chantal. It has nothing to do with it. LeClerc assured the uncle that the death was an accident; but then, this former inspector, Claverie-LaPorte, seeing an opportunity to use me to get to Jojo, started filling his head with speculations that maybe it wasn't an accident. He's even made the uncle believe that Jojo may have had something to do with it."

"Do you think he did, Jean-Claude?" She looked at him plaintively. "You didn't ask M. Gambia to do anything to Kevin, did you?"

"Of course, I didn't. My God, what do you take me for? All I did was talk to your friend one damned time. And that was because I missed seeing you. Is that such a terrible reason for talking to him?"

"No, Jean-Claude. I'm sorry."

Duchon took her hand in both of his. He had obviously made a wrong turn in the conversation. The way he was going, he would never get her into bed. It was time to change course.

"Chantal, my dear," he squeezed her hand, "I did not mean to upset you with this conversation. To the contrary, I am only trying to protect your feelings by telling you the truth of what the old former inspector is up to so that, should he or the uncle ask you to help them, you will know what they are really after. For my sake, as well as Jojo's, it would be best if you say nothing more to them. If they persist in bothering you, call me or Inspector LeClerc. Claverie-Laporte is already in trouble for pretending to still be a policeman. Will you promise me you'll do that, Chantal?"

"Yes, Jean-Claude, I promise." Her voice was a whisper.

"You will not regret it. When I told Jojo I would be seeing you, he said to make sure you know how much he appreciates your being on our side against these troublemakers. He also mentioned that he intended to reward your loyalty in a very generous way when this little inconvenience has been resolved to his satisfaction. I was not to tell you this, but I felt you should know." He squeezed her hand again to emphasize his point. "So, if you see Jojo in the next few days, please don't let on that you know what he plans to do. He wants it to be a surprise. Okay?"

"Okay, Jean-Claude."

"But Jojo's not the only one with a surprise for Mlle. Chantal." He caught Jojo eye and gave her a little wink. "Achille, if you please! Will you bring my bill and the package you have so kindly been holding for me?"

"Right away, M. Duchon."

Duchon paid the bill and made a show of leaving Achille an uncharacteristically generous <u>pourboire</u>. Then, cradling the wrapped bottle in his right arm like a baby, he crossed the street with Chantal. While waiting for her to locate her key and unlock the door, he began whistling the theme song to a Sergio Leone spaghetti western. He followed her into the small kitchen, a distinct spring in his step. Chantal began putting away her few purchases.

"Chantal, please! I am sure all that can wait. Look what I have brought."

She turned in time to see him ceremoniously remove the bottle from its decorative box.

"Just like the old days, n'est-ce pas?"

She stood as still and lifeless as a statue. Duchon attributed her speechlessness to the overwhelming surprise his gift had engendered. Now things were moving in the intended direction, he thought. And, with the thought, he stepped close to Chantal and held her lightly by the shoulders. He forced her to make eye-contact.

"It has been much too long, my dear Chantal." He moved his hands down her back and pressed his mouth on hers. Her closed lips were rigid and unmoving. He tried to part them with his tongue, but she held her mouth tightly closed. And, all at once, Jean-Claude Duchon realized the hopelessness of the situation, the enormity of his self-deception. He pushed her brusquely away.

"So, this is the thanks I get for all that I have done for you?"

"I am truly sorry, Jean-Claude, I cannot do anything now. It just does not feel right."

"It certainly felt right before that young American kid arrived. Perhaps you think you are too good for me now. That you can take your old friends for granted, is that it?"

"No, Jean-Claude. I swear. It is not that; I don't know what it is. I only know that it is stronger than me, this feeling."

He pointed a thin, menacing finger an inch from her face. She cringed like a small dog, expecting to be hit.

"Well, I suggest you work on coming to your senses, and quickly. Things cannot continue like this. I will not have it. There are plenty of girls who would jump at what I am doing for you. And would be only too happy to show their appreciation in the expected ways. You understand?"

"Yes, Jean-Claude."

"And don't forget what I told you about the old fart, Claverie-LaPorte, and your little friend's uncle. If you so much as say two words to them without talking to me or LeClerc first, you will learn the real meaning of something stronger than you. This is a very serious matter. Do I make myself perfectly clear?" He jabbed his finger roughly against her upper chest.

"Please, Jean-Claude."

"Don't worry, I'm not going to hurt the poor young widow. But I suggest she think very carefully about what I have said. I will not be this nice forever. And, while she is at it, she might just remind herself of those other things I have done for her in the past year."

Jean-Claude Duchon took the unopened bottle of Spanish champagne, dropped it loudly back into the gift box and left the apartment without saying another word.

CHAPTER THIRTEEN

When Maurice left the Player's Bar after the meeting with Duchon, Peter Ellis moved from their table to the polished brass counter at the front of the room and ordered another Kronenbourg 1664. The barman, Philippe, an old acquaintance, was a great <u>amateur</u> of local potables, especially Armagnac and the regional <u>eaux-de-vie</u>. Peter Ellis always looked forward to their conversations. The barman said he had recently discovered an especially good Poire William from St. Jean Pied-de-Port and promised to bring in a bottle the following day.

"I look forward to tasting your new find, Philippe. As I think you know, <u>poire</u> is my favorite <u>eau-de-vie</u>; however, I am not certain that I can make it tomorrow. You see, I have promised to take a new friend to Sauveterre-de-Béarn."

"Ah yes, Sauveterre. A charming little town indeed! I presume we are talking about a new female friend?"

"Yes, and a very attractive one at that. She is from Amsterdam and is staying with my old friend, Olga, at her farm near St. Martin-de-Hinx."

"I see." The barman whistled lightly and rolled his eyes, shaking his down-turned right hand sideways in the well-known Gallic gesture. "May you have good luck!"

"It is not at all like that, Philippe. She is very nice <u>and</u> very intelligent. In fact, according to Olga, she is an extremely talented artist."

"Well then, I wish you even greater luck."

"If things work out—and I don't mean in the way you imply, Philippe—I'll certainly bring her by sometime this weekend."

"I look forward to meeting her. You've always had excellent taste." He immediately realized his gaffe. "I'm sorry, Pierre, I didn't mean to bring up a sore subject."

"Don't be ridiculous, Philippe. It is all over between Mlle. Burke and me. Some things just aren't meant to be. And now, I must be on my way. I don't want to miss the last of the sunset. I'll see you sometime this weekend." The two men shook hands.

"Au revoir, Pierre. See you soon!"

Unlike Maurice, Peter Ellis, upon exiting the bar, turned left on the rue Gardéres in the direction of the Grande Plage. By so deciding to take the coast road back to his apartment, he avoided the scrutiny of Joseph Gambia, who was still sitting with Jean-Claude Duchon at one of Les Colonnes' sidewalk tables that commanded an unobstructed view of the intersection of the rue Gardéres and the avenue Edouard VII. His decision would prove to be a fortuitous one, though this fact was presently lost on him as he strolled leisurely past the Casino Municipal toward the south end of the Grand Plage. For, as it happened, he had decided to take this longer way home for purely aesthetic reasons.

When he reached the beach promenade, he turned left on the road that curved around the Casino Bellevue and began his ascent of the Pointe Atalye. On his right, he passed a path that led to the small, rocky, turret-like island called Le Basta. The swell was still strong and waves exploded in the hollows that had been cut out of the jagged rock by the constant motion of the sea. In the narrow space between the mainland and the isolated mass of rock that had once been a part of it, the white water roiled with a turbulence that sent sheets of salt spray high into the air, so that clouds of fine mist drifted over the pathway, settling on the clothes and exposed skin of passers-by. Perhaps it was the smell of the salt air, perhaps it was the booming sound that the waves made when they exploded in the subterranean caverns that undermined the cliff face, maybe it was the combination of the two, but, all at once, Peter Ellis was transported to a scene that had played itself out in this very location the previous spring.

He had been seeing Burke for about six months. He had talked often of Biarritz and had promised to take her there as soon as the weather turned warmer. It was a Thursday, he remembered. He had just finished an extremely depressing piece about the spread of AIDS among the Parisian prostitute population and was walking home in a light spring rain. Suddenly he had the idea to surprise Burke with the trip and decided to celebrate the event with a bottle of Veuve Cliquot. With Burke watching with a kind of amused curiosity, he popped open the bottle, poured them both a glass and, with a flourish, announced that tomorrow they were leaving for a short holiday in the southwest of France. He added that she should not even think of protesting, for it would do no good. Tomorrow, he was taking her to Biarritz.

Burke fell in love with the region immediately. The weather was glorious and she seemed to find something to photograph around every corner. On their second evening, after dinner, he took her to the Player's Bar for drinks. Afterwards, he decided, like today, to take the coast road back to the apartment. When they reached the turn to Le Basta he suggested they go out to one of its benches and contemplate the splendor of the evening sky.

"Are you sure that contemplation is all you have in mind, Monsieur Ellis? I do have my honor to protect."

"On my word as a gentleman, mademoiselle, I would not dream of compromising the honor of an innocent young woman such as yourself!"

"In that case, I shall allow you to take my hand and lead me across this perilous chasm. You are certain it is safe, the bridge I mean?"

"Absolutely!"

And so they had crossed to Le Basta and sat on a bench looking across the breaking surf at the illuminated façade of the Hotel du Palais and, beyond, at the revolving beam atop the lighthouse rising above the Pointe St. Martin. She sat close to him, her head leaning against his shoulder. Even now, he remembered vividly the unique, sensuous scent of her hair. He couldn't recall how the conversation had started—probably something corny, like about how nice it was to be able to share the kind of experience they were having. (For someone who made his living choosing words properly and imaginatively, he had a distinct talent for verbal maladroitness when it came to describing his own feelings to someone.) What he had been trying to tell Burke that night, what he wanted her to begin considering, was the possibility of a future together. His initial intention, he recalled, was to see how she reacted to a joking, seemingly spontaneous remark. Instead, he immediately found himself knee-deep in an earnest, over-analytical testimonial guaranteed to scare off even the most committed heart. When he realized, by her silence and the way she had instinctively stiffened, that he was on the verge of ruining a wonderful night, he kissed her lightly on the cheek and abruptly suggested they walk down to the Port Vieux for a nightcap.

Now, six months later, he found himself on the same coast road, approaching the Place Eugenie, trying to decide if what he had just said to Philippe, the barman, about it being all over between him and Burke, was actually true or was he merely trying to clear the emotional decks in preparation for tomorrow's date with Anya.

When he reached the Port des Pecheurs, he turned right on the pathway down to the small harbor. The tide was rising—he estimated it to be midway between low and high—but most of the small armada of pleasure craft and fishing boats lay at the angle of their hulls, still aground. A thick concrete breakwater, at least twenty feet high, protected the port to the north and several couples were walking along its ramparts, keeping well away from the ocean side, where waves thundered against the wall, pushing sheets of whitewater within two meters of the top outer edge. He stopped briefly in front of Albert's famous restaurant and watched two waiters put the finishing touches on an enormous, tantalizing display of fruits de mer: oysters from Arcachon and Oleron, local langoustines and mussels, clams of various shapes and sizes, squid and crab legs and shrimp that he guessed were from Spain by way of the boats of St. Jean-de-Luz. He had never taken Burke to Chez Albert, he thought, which gave him the idea to take Anya there for their first meal in Biarritz. There would be no memories to haunt their evening. And besides, it was one of the best places in town.

From the Port des Pecheurs, he abandoned the coast road, choosing instead to take a short cut over the rocky hump at the neck of the Point Atalye that brought him into the Place du Vieux Port. From there, he followed the rue La Perspective around the Eurotel and up the south facing slope of the point. To his right, the sky was darkening over the mountainous Spanish coast, an uneven, layered wash of copper, green and purple. To his left, several large residences stood in mute majesty, seeming to survey the chaotic world below them. As he passed, Peter Ellis studied each one in turn: #23, Iruzki Azpian, a sprawling Basque-styled mansion; #25 Hegoa, white and modern; #29 Villa Maria Elena, an imposing spinster hidden behind a tall, protective wall; #31 Villa Marthe-Marie, its hard rectangular lines softened by an ivy covering; #33 Les Corsaires, a pink modern apartment building, its rounded lines following the elbow curve of the road. It was strange, he thought, as he approached his apartment. In all the years he had stayed at the Hotel Les Flots Bleus, he could not recall seeing a single person enter or leave any of the residences he had just passed. It was as though they were inhabited by ghosts.

He stopped in at the hotel to see if there were any messages and to order a beer to bring to his rooms. In his apartment, he put an old Van Morrison tape in the boom box and took out a yellow legal pad and a gold Cross pen. With Van singing in the background about what was going on down at the Kingdom Hall, he sat at the large oak table in the vestibule and began to record all of the information he had gathered so far, including detailed accounts of his meetings with Haraout, the fishermen, Marc Dufau, Maurice, Mme. Haizart and, finally, the weasel, Duchon. It took him all of one cassette recording and half of another to finish his summary of what he had discovered during the past twenty-four hours concerning the death of Kevin Duffy. He then showered, shaved and changed into a cotton Oxford shirt with burgundy pinstripes, pressed, black Levis and black Yves St. Laurent boots.

He entered the restaurant by the back door and stopped at the kitchen entrance to wish Thierry, the cook, a good evening. He was in the mood for something simple and hearty, so he ordered an entrecote au poivre with frites and a side dish of haricots verts. With his meal, he drank a half bottle of Madiran that was only satisfactory, the light garnet wine tasting of tobacco, leather and slightly bitter currents. The steak, however, was perfectly cooked, the fries were crispy and the large plate of green beans could not have been better. Afterwards, he drank a glass of Bas Armagnac with two of the traveling salesmen who accounted for more than half of the hotel's daily clientele. On a hunch, he asked them if they had heard of a relatively new nightclub called 'Le Gentle-man'. One of the men laughed and wagged a finger in his direction.

"Someone is looking to get into some trouble, I think."

"What do you mean, monsieur? I feel I am missing something."

"Truly, you are not pulling my leg, M. Ellis? You do not know what goes on at this so-called club?"

"No, only that a friend in Paris said I might find it amusing."

"Well, your friend has a great gift for understatement."

"So, you know the place?"

"Not personally. But an associate was there last week. If he's to be believed, you must ask for Dany. She was all he talked about for the two days after he returned to Bordeaux."

"She is a waitress there?" Peter Ellis played the naïf. The man shot his fellow salesman a look of humorous disbelief. Then, both men roared with laughter.

"She will certainly serve you, M. Ellis, but the menu is very limited."

This comment sent the two salesmen into a fresh paroxysm that lasted almost half a minute. Finally, the man who had been speaking to Peter Ellis took out a handkerchief, removed his glasses and wiped his eyes.

"I apologize for laughing so much, M. Ellis. It is just that this so-called 'club', from what my associate tells me, is, in truth, an upscale house of prostitution and gambling. Of course, they don't advertise themselves as such, and the girls are not common streetwalkers. But, if a man shows enough interest," he rubbed his thumb and fingers together, "he will be given very special service in one of the back rooms."

"Forgive me for being so dense, monsieur, and thank-you for the information. You have piqued my interest. I think I shall have to see what 'Le Gentle-man' has to offer."

"Well, M. Ellis, bring plenty of money. My associate came home without a <u>sou</u>. He had a pretty time explaining that to his wife!"

Peter Ellis left as the salesman recounted the particulars of his associate's dilemma for his fellow diner, with almost every sentence bringing a new burst of laughter.

***

It was after ten when Peter Ellis arrived at the 'Le Gentle-man' club. After he paid the admission price, high even by Biarritz standards, and suffered the scrutiny of the two, young, Mediterranean louts at the door, he decided to make a quick, cursory inspection of the premises before cashing in his precious drink vouchers. He wasn't expecting any trouble tonight, and he certainly wasn't going to look for any, but it was always wise, he had long ago discovered, to know the layout of your adversary's territory.

The club was divided into three large, over-decorated 'theme' rooms: "Hollywood", to the right; "Edouard VII", to the left; and, "La Belle Epoque", taking up the entire back of the main building. The rooms were decorated in a predictable manner. "Hollywood" featured framed movie posters and blown-up photographs of Marilyn Monroe, Brigitte Bardot and other former celluloid sex goddesses, with and without matching initials. "Edouard VII" had several large, grainy depictions of Biarritz's most infamous, royal philanderer surrounded by photographs and drawings of the kind of scantily clad, buxom women to whom he was allegedly partial. "La Belle Epoque" was a celebration of that wonderfully frivolous and self-indulgent time in Paris made famous by Toulouse-Lautrec and his artistic brethren. The furnishings and décor throughout fell somewhere between that of an upscale brothel and a set designer's idea of an English club in the Sherlock Holmes era, a mind-boggling mélange of heavy oak, brass, leather, synthetic velour and fake Oriental carpets. Peter Ellis settled on the Belle Epoque room not so much for the theme as for the fact that it had an exit door to the right of the bar and two unmarked doors to the left, one of which, he decided, must be to an office.

He ordered a Macallan on the rocks with a side of Evian. The barmaid, short and big-breasted, wore a low-cut white sweater, no bra and a black vinyl mini-skirt that barely revealed the crotch of her pantyhose when she stretched, on tip toes, to reach the Scotch bottle. Also revealed, he presumed by design, was her lack of under-wear. When she had finished pouring what was, by any standards, a generous double, she shot him a not-too-subtle look to see if he was paying attention. Peter Ellis gave her a warm smile of acknowledge-ment, of what he was not at all sure. Certainly a sense of juvenile, voyeuristic guilt, he thought. As the barmaid returned with his drink, he wondered if he looked as sheepish and transparent as he felt. The hand squeezing his left forearm took him completely by surprise. He turned abruptly, his heart jumping as if from an electric shock.

"Excuse me, sir, I didn't mean to startle you. I just wanted to ask if you would permit me to join you?"

It took an instant for Peter Ellis to find his voice.

"Of course, if you are expecting someone, I do not wish to disturb you."

"No, not at all. Please." He indicated the adjoining, heavily pad-ded barstool. "Would you care for a drink?"

"What are you having, monsieur…?"

"Pierre."

"Pierre, I am Dany." She offered a small, very white hand.

"Delighted to meet you, Mlle. Dany. And to answer your question, I am having a Scotch on the rocks."

The girl gave a faint stutter. "That is too strong for me, thank-you."

"Something else, then?"

"Would you mind if I ordered a little Champagne?"

"Of course not." He turned to the barmaid, who had been keenly following their exchange. "Mademoiselle, a <u>coupe</u> of Champagne for Mlle. Dany, please."

"With pleasure, monsieur." She flashed him a knowing smile, complete with lipstick-stained teeth.

Peter Ellis turned to face the girl. "So, Mlle. Dany, do you often come to "Le Gentle-man'?"

"Almost every night."

"That is a high recommendation for the club. It seems I was sent to the right place. Evidently, one can have a good time here."

"You might say that it is my job to see that you do." She smiled and gave his wrist a slight squeeze.

"You work here, Mlle. Dany?"

"More or less, though we don't call it work. It is my job to see that our clients have as good a time as possible."

"That doesn't sound like a bad job."

"It has its moments, like any other. But I suppose you are right. For the most part, it is very agreeable. The boss says I have the perfect personality for it. What do you think?"

"I think your boss is very perceptive."

The conversation was interrupted by the barmaid delivering the girl's glass of champagne.

"Will that be all, monsieur?"

"Yes, for the moment. Thank-you."

"With pleasure." She winked at the girl. "Just call when you need anything else."

Peter Ellis lightly touched his glass to that of the girl named Dany. "Chin-chin!"

"Merci!" She took a small sip. "I love champagne."

"So, Mlle. Dany, where were we? You were telling me about your job, I think?"

"There is really not much to tell. I talk to the clients, try to make them feel at home. Especially if they are by themselves."

"I see. That is why you are talking to me. It's too bad."

"What do you mean?"

"For a moment, I thought I was maybe a little different. But I see now that I am just another single man who needs cheering up."

"Oh, don't say that!" She gave him a mock-pouty look then placed her right hand on the inside of his left thigh. "I think you are different. I said that to Marie-Thérèse, my friend over there, the minute you sat down." She pointed to a tall, small-breasted girl at the far end of the bar. She bore a striking resemblance to a very young Genevieve Bujold. Her look of innocence was in marked contrast to the demeanor of her male companion, a short, fleshy, olive-skinned boy with close-cropped, curly black hair. "You can ask her if you like?"

"That is not necessary, Mlle. Dany. You have made your point." He put his left hand lightly on the hand that was now gently massaging his upper thigh. "Anyway, I would not want to disturb your friend. She seems to be very much occupied at the moment with that young man."

"That's Carlos. He works here, or at least is supposed to. Marie-Thérèse can't stand him. But he won't leave her alone. He thinks he's some kind of hunk. Just look at him. He's so disgusting!" She swallowed a large gulp of champagne.

"If he upsets her, why don't you complain to the boss?"

"We have already spoken to her twice."

"Her?"

"Mme. Janine. Who did you think was my boss?" A slight, apprehensive edge had come into her voice. She removed her hand from his leg.

"I thought M. Gambia owned this club. His friends call him Jojo. I must have been misinformed."

"You know M. Gambia?"

"No, but I was hoping to make his acquaintance. I believe we have some friends in common in Paris."

"You live in Paris?" Her tone immediately brightened.

"Yes. I just stopped in Biarritz for a little relaxation before going to Spain. I hope to be doing some important business there." He looked to see if she picked up on his insinuation. "You see, I am an importer. I am expecting a shipment in Bilbao in a couple of days. I have found that everything works more smoothly if I am at the port when the boat arrives. But you don't want to hear about my boring business." He touched her hand lightly. "Let's have another drink and you can tell me where I should go while I am here. You see, that's why I was asking about Jojo – I figured he would know the best places to go. What do you think?"

"I would be delighted to help you, especially if you force me to have another <u>coupe</u> of champagne. Perhaps <u>I</u> can show you some of the best spots personally."

"Excellent. This calls for a little celebration!" He motioned for the barmaid. "Mademoiselle, may I see your list of champagnes, please?"

He perused the list quickly and ordered an overpriced bottle of Veuve Cliquot. If he was going to pretend to be big time, he thought, he had best act the part. He felt certain it would pay at least a small information dividend.

"Veuve Cliquot! It is absolutely my favorite! How did you guess?" Dany's small, round face was beaming.

"I didn't tell you?" He made a show of looking intently into her dark brown eyes. "I have the gift of mental telepathy. So watch out what you think, mademoiselle. I can read minds like most people read books."

She laughed, the skin wrinkling around her small nose and at the edges of her eyes. Much to his surprise, Peter Ellis realized he was beginning to feel a kind of tenderness toward the young 'hostess'. In her expression, he detected a kind of mischievous openness that he guessed had been developed to mask her youthful vulnerability and insecurity. She was certainly not beautiful in any normal sense of the word. She did not even have the pouty, adolescent good looks of her friend at the end of the bar. But she did have a kind of impish sexuality that she wore like a constant dare. He was just reminding himself that he was at the club for business, not pleasure, when she began rubbing the inside of his thigh again.

"So, M. Pierre, if you can read minds, tell me what I am thinking now." She grinned widely at him.

"There are certain thoughts I am not at liberty to read aloud. And what you are thinking is one of them. That does not mean that I disapprove of it however. Anyway, it would be impossible to do anything here in the bar."

"Oh, I don't know about that! We have several private rooms where our special customers can relax. Of course, Mme. Janine or M. Gambia must give their approval. If you like, I can ask them when they arrive. They should be here soon."

"You are very kind, Mlle. Dany. I am certainly flattered. But you forget, we have a bottle of champagne to drink. Also, it is one of my special rules to talk for at least an hour before the first kiss."

"I have never heard that rule before, but I think it is very charming. What do you want to talk about?"

"Why don't we begin with where you grew up and what brought you to Biarritz and 'Le Gentle-man'?"

It was as he had thought: She came from a small town in the Béarn, the child of a strict, hard-drinking father and a religious, long-suffering mother. As soon as she was old enough, she left home to work in a small restaurant between Bayonne and Biarritz. One of the food salesmen, a M. Duchon, introduced her to M. Gambia, who offered her a job as a cocktail waitress in one of his other clubs. She had only been working at 'Le Gentle-man' a month and, so far, liked it much better than her previous job, especially the money. Also, as she announced, with pointed reference to him, she met a better class of people at 'Le Gentle-man'. Of course, there was always the occasional jerk, but they showed up everywhere, didn't they?

When it was his turn to talk, Peter Ellis stuck to the truth regarding his personal life, refraining from elaboration. He was saved from having to fabricate his business career in Paris by the arrival of two stocky, middle-aged men and a busty, well-dressed woman.

"Et voilà, Mme. Janine and M. Gambia are arrived."

The group had taken barely three steps into the bar when the woman brusquely grabbed the shorter of the two men by the arm, spoke no more than ten words to him, and pointed in the direction of Dany's friend and the boy named Carlos.

"It looks like Carlos is about to get it. Maybe they will boot him out the door this time!"

"Your Mme. Janine <u>does</u> look serious, that's for sure."

The boy, Carlos, was so involved in his conversation with the girl that he was taken totally by surprise. Gambia gripped him by the shoulder and forcefully spun him around. The boy started to raise his fist then, with a look of shocked recognition, realized who it was. Gambia said a few words to the girl, who nodded and began walking down the bar toward Dany and Peter Ellis. Gambia then clamped his hand tightly to the boy's upper arm and led him unceremoniously through the sparse bar crowd to the door.

Peter Ellis had turned to watch Gambia deal with the boy and he did not notice Janine Destin and her companion take the seats next to Dany. It was only when she removed her hand from his leg to greet them that he realized their presence.

"M. Pierre, permit me to introduce you to the owner of 'Le Gentle-man', Mme. Janine Destin."

"Delighted to meet you, Mme. Destin. My name is Pierre. Pierre Edwards. Your club is very charming, as are your girls." He indicated Dany.

"Thank-you very much, M. Edwards."

"Please! Call me Pierre. I feel old enough as it is."

"I know what you mean, Pierre. Getting old is a bitch, if you'll excuse the expression. It is even worse for us women. That I can assure you!"

"I don't see you have reason to worry about that, Mme. Destin."

"You lie well, Pierre. Keep it up. And, if I am to call you Pierre, then you must call me Janine. Okay?"

"With pleasure."

"Since Janine has obviously forgotten <u>my</u> name, monsieur, permit me to introduce myself. My name is Jacques, but my friends call me Jacky. And this beautiful creature is Marie-Thérèse."

Peter Ellis shook both their hands in turn. So, he thought, this is the famous Inspector Jacques LeClerc, who determined that the death of Kevin Duffy was nothing more than an accident. He doubted this swaggering good humor would be in evidence when the inspector learned <u>his</u> true identity.

"You are an associate of Janine, Jacky?" He meant the question in a business sense; however, LeClerc, smirking drunkenly at him, decided to make a joke of it.

"No. I have been trying, but she keeps turning me down. Is that not so Janine?"

"Pierre, believe nothing that Jacky says at night. His acquaintance with the truth vanishes altogether at sunset."

"You are too cruel to me, Janine. You know well enough that I <u>always</u> tell the truth."

"You and every lawyer I know."

"Now <u>that</u> is a low blow, Janine. You will pay for that one."

While Janine and LeClerc were caught up in their adolescent bantering, Peter Ellis studied the girl, Marie-Thérèse. It was evident that she was painfully shy. Just as it was evident that her striking appearance would most likely cause her more pain than pleasure. He managed to catch her eye for a moment; but, she immediately averted her gaze, looking as though she were guilty of some unnamed indiscretion.

Peter Ellis saw Gambia re-enter the room, briefly survey his clientele and make his way toward them. Dany enthusiastically introduced them. Gambia insisted that Peter Ellis use his nickname.

"With pleasure, Jojo. Delighted to make your acquaintance. I have heard a lot about you from a friend in Paris, who says he knows you well."

Earlier, Maurice had given him the names of two known associates of Joseph Gambia in Paris. Peter Ellis hoped his information was correct.

"Pedro Delgado assured me that you could get me into whatever trouble I desired here on the Cote Basque."

"You know Pedro 'LeFou'?"

"We do a little business together. He can be very amusing."

"Amusing? Did you hear that, Janine? Amusing? That is really excellent, my friend. I doubt Pedro has <u>ever</u> been called that before. Insane, yes. Outrageous, certainly. But amusing? Never in his life!"

"Now that you mention it, he was a bit wild the last time I saw him."

"How many <u>nanas</u> were with him?"

"He was with three women, I believe. All very charming."

"I'm sure. So, have you come to Biarritz for business or pleasure?"

"I am in Biarritz purely for pleasure, and I feel certain I have chosen the right club to begin my pursuit." He gave Dany's hand a quick squeeze. "However, as I was telling your delightful hostess here, I am on my way to Spain to meet a shipment. I have a small importing company and must be down there on Monday to meet the ship and make sure everything clears customs without difficulty. I have found that even if you employ an agent, it is best to be there in person in case a problem arises. I'm sure you have found the same to be true in your business."

"Have I ever! I could tell you stories."

"Excuse me, M. Pierre, for interrupting, but before Jojo begins telling stories, I need to have a few words with him in private."

"Now Janine?" Exasperation was evident in his voice.

"Yes, if you don't mind? I think our friend here is in good hands with Dany." She indicated the girl, who gave her a knowing smile.

"I shall do my best, Mme. Destin. Will it be okay to show M. Pierre one of our private rooms?"

"Of course, Dany."

"You are all very kind," Peter Ellis glanced at his watch, "but I really must be going soon. I am meeting some old friends from Paris tomorrow for lunch. They live in a little village close to Pau. I know too well how I shall feel tomorrow if I drink another bottle of Champagne."

"Whatever you think is best, M. Pierre. I'll leave it to you and Dany to work out. I certainly hope you will come back to visit us before you leave for Spain."

"I'm sure I'll see you again." He stood and shook her small hand. "And you, messieurs." He gripped their hands in turn.

"Jacky, are you staying?"

"If Mlle. Marie-Thérèse would agree to join me for a drink, and perhaps a game of backgammon, I'll certainly stay."

"As you like, M. Jacky. But you know I am not a very good player."

"Then let me give you a lesson!"

Peter Ellis was left sitting alone with Dany. He emptied the bottle into their glasses.

"To truth and friendship."

"And to surprises." She tapped his glass with hers.

"Surprises?"

"You'll see. Come with me."

"Dany, I must tell you, frankly, that I did not intend on having a late night this evening. I only brought a few thousand francs with me."

"You have been very kind, Pierre. Not like most of the others. I like you. Now come on, tonight's my treat."

She took him by the hand and led him to the door next to the one Janine Destin and Joseph Gambia had entered. She reached in her small purse, produced a key and unlocked the deadbolt. Again, taking him by the hand, she led him down a short hallway to a simple, small room. One side was taken up by a huge bed surrounded by three mirrored walls. The opposite side was divided into a small bathroom and a separate seating area with a plush, faux-leather sofa and glass coffee table. In the corner was an entertainment center with a television, VCR and rows of hand-labeled video cassettes. Dany took Peter Ellis's glass of wine and placed it with hers on the coffee table. Then she turned to face him.

"So, what do you think?"

He thought she was asking him about the room. He was trying to formulate an appropriate reply when she reached up and gently pulled his face down to hers. Without thinking, he put his arms around her and returned her kisses, gently at first then roughly, suddenly filled with passion. He moved his right hand down her back, cupped her youthfully hard buttocks and pressed them against his groin. She began rubbing herself against him and making low, purring noises. Suddenly, she pushed herself away from his grasp. The abruptness of the movement startled him.

"Is there something wrong, Dany?"

"Yes. You have too many clothes on."

She reached down and began to unfasten his belt.

"You don't have to do that, Dany."

"I know. But I want to. Like I told you a minute ago, Pierre, I like you."

He did not know what to say or what to do. So he stood there like a mute and allowed her to unzip his pants and pull down his briefs. She took his erect penis in her small hand and began gently to massage it. Without stopping, she knelt in front of him. She raised her eyes to meet his.

"You don't have anything, do you Pierre?"

"No. I was recently examined."

She began licking the tip of his penis. Soon she was running her tongue down its length. Finally, she guided it into her mouth and started working it in and out of her tightly closed lips. Peter Ellis held her head lightly with both hands and followed her back-and-forth motion. When he came, he felt a gentle shudder. He released her head and she raised her eyes once more to meet his, this time the look more playful. She ran her tongue over her lips.

"It was alright, I think?"

"It was more than alright and you know it. It was marvelous."

"The next time I want you inside me. You make me so hot. I almost came myself."

"I'm sorry I was so quick. It has been some time for me."

"Do you have a girlfriend in Paris?"

"Not now. She went back to America several weeks ago."

"Is she coming back soon?"

"No. It's over."

"Maybe I can visit you in Paris sometime?"

"Yes, that would be nice. We must exchange numbers before I leave Biarritz. I'll know more about my schedule in a few days."

"You are really serious, Pierre?" This time, she looked at him with the imploring look of the child she was.

"Of course. What do you take me for?"

"I'm already getting excited!" She bent her head and lightly kissed his spent member. "I promise you we will have a good time!"

CHAPTER FOURTEEN

Peter Ellis overslept and when he did wake it was with a hangover derived in more or less equal parts from champagne and guilt. And the guilt, in turn, was two pronged: although he had just met the Dutch woman, Anya, he somehow felt he had betrayed her trust; and, he had deceived the girl, Dany, for his own purposes then had acquiesced in, even promoted, her advances, ending by agreeing to see her in Paris. It occurred to him that he was acting with a sleaziness befitting the people he was after. Duchon would have been proud of his behavior.

He arrived at the beach of Chambre d'Amour a little after nine, more than an hour later than he had promised Marc Dufau. He found his friend's car and saw that a note had been left under the windshield wiper. It informed him that he was missing some of the best surf in weeks and asked him what kind of trouble he had found last night. If you only knew, Peter Ellis thought.

His friend had not exaggerated about the waves. On the drive over, he had debated whether, given the state of his head, he would get in the water at all. But when he saw the almost perfect conditions—light offshore wind and pristine six-foot faces—he knew he had no choice. He must go out, if only for half an hour. And not just because he would never hear the end of it from Marc if he didn't. It was precisely for days like this that one surfed.

He decided to walk the length of the boardwalk to get his blood flowing and build up a little body heat. The wide cement walkway was crowded with surfers, their friends and several white and blue-haired retirees walking their dogs. A handful of photographers with cameras mounted on tripods and equipped with long, wide-angle lenses were busy taking shots of the riders in the water. Peter Ellis turned his attention to the surf in time to see someone on a board, prominently featuring the logo of a well-known wetsuit manufacturer, take off at the peak of a solid six-footer, lean into an incredibly acute bottom turn, power back up the face, snap off a re-entry through the lip, shoot ahead of the rushing whitewater and tuck into the curl midway up the collapsing blue wall, kicking out at the last possible instant before it closed out. The entire ride had been seamless. He had not seen anyone take apart a wave like that since the last time he had watched Tom Curren at Lacanau. He did not know who the rider was but guessed he was a visiting professional who was in the region for the tournament at Guètary on the coming weekend.

While the unknown surfer paddled back out, Peter Ellis scanned the line-up until he found Marc and his distinctively colored board. Within minutes, his friend dropped in on a head-high left, carved an elongated, horizontal 'S' across the wave face, cut back to set up a short, slashing arc that launched him, almost upside down, over the top of the wave. As he landed, back-first, in the water, the wind caught his board, causing it to flutter wildly before the tightening pull of the leash landed it three feet from Marc's out-stretched, head-protecting arm.

While Peter Ellis was struggling into his wetsuit, he saw the nameless surfer manage another perfect, late takeoff, execute an elegant, deep rail turn, do an expertly-timed stall that positioned him in the barrel, disappear briefly inside the wave and end the ride with a floater off the lip, all three fins visible as he rode the cascading sheet of water down to the bottom. Another seemingly effortless performance. Well, he thought, it wouldn't be for lack of inspiration if he didn't surf well today.

The coldness of the water made him forget about the pain in his head, both mental and physical. The first surge of whitewater rushing over his body and penetrating the neck band of his suit momentarily paralyzed him. He saw a break in the sets and he paddled fast and hard and was just able to claw his way over the steepening wall of the first wave of the next set. When he was safely outside the breakline, he waved to Marc, who immediately paddled over to join him.

"Who is that guy in the blue-trimmed wetsuit? I've just seen him get two perfect rides."

Marc mentioned a name he had never heard. "Some people here think he's the next Tom Curren."

"I can see why. His style even reminds me of Curren's. Is he here for the tournament?"

"Yes. And for shooting part of a new surf film here and in Mundaca. He and the crew stopped by my restaurant last night with a mutual friend. They have recently arrived from Scotland where they apparently had some amazing waves."

"I've heard it can be very good there. But, God, the water must be frigid!"

"I hear you need a snail tool to find your penis when you get out of the water. Which reminds me, what kind of trouble did you get into last night?"

"It's a long story. I made a little fact-finding visit to 'Le Gentleman'. It was very interesting. And fruitful."

"I'll bet it was fruitful. You must tell me all about it later. Look!" He pointed toward the horizon. "Here we go!"

Peter Ellis's first wave was a shoulder-high left. He made a precarious entry and a wide bottom turn that put him too far in front of the wave. When he tried to cut back, he buried the rail of the board and was thrown, sprawling, into the water. After two more error-plagued waves, he finally managed a decent ride: After a solid take-off, he sliced to the bottom then midway back to the top where he was partially covered up by the collapsing wave. He raced ahead of the curl then cut back and cranked a hard bottom turn, cutting a gash of whitewater out of the glassy surface. He finished off the ride with what he felt was, at least for him, a moderately graceful re-entry.

It ended up being his best wave of the day. He was agreeably tired when he finally unstrapped the leash from his right ankle and carried his surfboard out of the shore-break. He changed into dry shorts, tee shirt and a large, grey sweatshirt with 'North Carolina' emblazoned in dark blue lettering across the chest. Maurice was waiting for him at La Chope, one of the small bars facing the beach. He was speaking with a middle-aged, blond woman, who had begun laughing at some remark he had just made.

"So, Maurice, I see you are in good form today."

"Enfin, you have finally finished with your surfing. Madame Marie, permit me to introduce you to an old American friend, Peter Ellis."

"Delighted to meet you, Madame Marie. It looks as though Maurice has been entertaining you well on this beautiful fall morning."

"Yes, indeed! He has been sharing a very funny story about an old widow we both have the dubious privilege of knowing, who acts as though she is a constant source of amusement for us. Is that not so, Maurice?"

"Yes, it is very true. We have had many entertaining moments at her expense." The inspector turned to Peter Ellis. "And how were the beautiful waves of Chambre d'Amour today, my friend?"

"Cold and unforgiving but a source of great pleasure and only a small amount of pain. I can tell you, however, that I am ready for a large, hot bowl of café au lait. And a croissant, if you please, Madame Marie."

"With pleasure, sir! If you and M. Maurice will choose a table, I shall bring your coffee immediately. Another tea for you Inspector?"

"Yes please, my dear."

They found a small table by the window. Peter Ellis immediately began recounting his evening at 'Le Gentle-man'. When he told of his private tour of the back room, he decided to limit the sex to heavy petting. Maybe when the affair was over, he would come clean with Maurice. For the moment, he found his weakness a bit too embarrassing.

"It will be interesting when they discover my true identity. I doubt little Dany will be so generous with her affections. Nor do I think she will want to visit me in Paris, since she may need to find new employment if we are successful in closing down M. Gambia's operations."

"From the way you describe her, I do not think she will have difficulties finding a new situation."

"Yes, I'm afraid you're right. But enough of Mlle. Dany. I have been worrying about another young lady recently, Maurice."

"Who might that be Pierre? Your new Dutch friend, Mlle. Anya?"

"No, Maurice. I am speaking of Chantal Clairac. Do you think she is in any danger?"

"It is strange that you should ask me that question at this time, my friend. It is something I have just been asking myself this morning. I do not <u>believe</u> she is in any danger at the moment. But, depending on what happens with our little friend, Duchon, on Monday, we may have to come up with a way to ensure her safety until this business is resolved one way or the other. Do you have any suggestions?"

"I could ask my friend Olga, if she would mind having a guest at the farm for a few days. I know she has an extra room."

"That is an excellent idea!"

"I have also been thinking that if Chantal were to stay there, Olga may be able to put her more at ease where we are concerned. Do a little 'female bonding'."

"I think you have a point. From what I remember of your friend Olga, she is an extremely perceptive woman, who has a gift for making strangers feel at ease."

"That is certainly true. So, how do you propose we convince Mlle. Clairac to move to the country for a few days? We can't just kidnap her."

"Let us hope it won't come to that; however, if that's what it takes to guarantee her well-being, I would say it is an option we will have to consider. I shall perhaps broach the subject this afternoon when I talk with her."

"You are meeting her this afternoon?"

"Yes. I decided this morning that it would not be a bad thing to pay a visit to Dodin's this afternoon to take some tea and to apologize for misleading the girl. Eat what I believe you call in English some 'humble pie'. I shall also attempt to ask her a few more questions. Specifically, I would like to find out more about her so-called 'lost weekend'. I have been thinking that it almost certainly has a bearing on her relationship with Duchon. I am also curious to know if he has spoken to her since his meeting with us."

"I can already answer that one for you: Of course he has."

"Yes, that is what I think too. But what did he say and how did he say it? Did he threaten her, for example?"

"Well, I wish you luck, Maurice. If anything important comes up, leave a message at the hotel. Otherwise, I shall check in with you tonight. I hope to be agreeably occupied until then."

"Ah yes, the Dutch artist. Let me give you a little fatherly advice, my friend. Take things slowly. Try to wait for her to make the first move, no matter how desirable you find her. I believe you are maybe a little vulnerable at the moment?"

"You may be right, Maurice. Ah, here comes our order! God, I am hungry." He began unwrapping a packet of sugar cubes. He glanced at his old friend, who was looking at him with a curious, almost melancholy expression. "I really do appreciate your advice, Maurice. And I shall do my best to heed it."

"I'm sure you will, Pierre. Bon appétit!"

Peter Ellis arrived at Olga's farm a few minutes before noon. As he rounded the corner of the house, he saw Anya sitting behind a portable easel in the middle of the small yard. She waved and gestured for him to join her. Just catching sight of her had sent a shiver through his heart. He had not realized, in his preoccupation with last night's lapse of discipline and this morning's session with Maurice, how excited he was to be seeing her.

She stood to greet him. She was wearing a short, faded-denim skirt and a red-and-white checked cotton work shirt with large breast pockets. Her skin was light pink from the sun. Peter Ellis tried to think of the last time he had felt such desire for a woman, and not merely desire in a sexual sense. He realized that it was when he had first met Burke.

He studied Anya's nearly completed painting. It was a simple, yet warmly evocative rendering of Olga's farmhouse.

"You should quit your job at the bank immediately. You are wasting your talent there."

"You are very kind to say so, though I believe you exaggerate for the sake of flattery. Still, thank-you."

"Actually, I am serious, Anya. Will you allow me to buy it?"

"Not for any amount of money!"

He was about to ask what he had done to upset her when she looked up and gave him a beautiful, wide smile that crinkled the skin at the edge of her eyes.

"But there is a very good reason why I won't, Peter. It is a gift for Olga."

"She will love it."

"I think I can finish it in the time it takes you to drink a beer. Would you mind terribly waiting a little?"

"Of course not. May I bring you something to drink as well?"

"A cold beer would be wonderful."

"I'll be right back."

True to her word, she finished the painting no more than two minutes after he had finished his beer. She packed up her easel and paints and Peter Ellis stored them in the trunk of the car. By one o'clock, they were crossing the bridge over the Gave d'Oloron at Peyrehorade. He had decided to take the longer, river road to Sauveterre-de-Béarn to show her some of the typical Béarnais countryside. The day was clear and unseasonably warm, with only the occasional cottony clump of cumulus drifting lazily across the sharp blue sky. They drove with the windows down, the rushing wind giving a heightened sense of exhilaration to their movement. When they reached the turnoff to Sauveterre, Peter Ellis slowed the car and pointed to a rambling, decrepit building on the left.

"That, Anya, used to be my favorite auberge in the whole region. In the early seventies, I went there often. Their specialty was fresh salmon from the Gave d'Oloron grilled over a fire made from grape-vine cuttings. It was served with the best sauce Beàrnaise I have ever tasted, before or since. Also, the old couple who owned the place had invested in some very good classified growth Bordeaux in the fifties and sixties, which they sold at reasonable prices. More often than not, I would rent a room for the night after eating there, the pros-pect of driving being at best distasteful after such an experience."

"What happened to the old couple?"

"I am embarrassed to say that I don't know. I was away from France for about ten years beginning in late seventy-three and when I returned the place was abandoned. It made me very sad. I'll ask about them today at the hotel where we are going to eat."

They had reached the river and, to their right, the ruins of the old fortified town rose dramatically from the nearly vertical cliff face at the edge of the rushing green water.

"Oh Peter, what an exquisite place! I could paint here for weeks."

"Anya, wait until you see the town itself and the view from up there."

"Thank-you so much for bringing me here. I'm so excited."

"I'm glad. For me, Sauveterre is a very special place. I was a little nervous about bringing you here. Everyone has different tastes, as you know."

"Well, so far, I think we share many of the same ones."

She had lightly touched his hand with hers when she made the remark. Although slight, the gesture, most probably unconscious, made Peter Ellis immeasurably happy. It had, indeed, turned into a beautiful day.

He drove up the steep, curving road through one of the for-merly fortified stone gates of the town (it had been chartered in 1080 by Centulle IV of Béarn as a 'place of refuge'), then slowly made his way down the narrow main street. The small, family-owned shops that lined the street were closed for the traditional midday lunch break and the sidewalk was deserted, save for the occasional homeward-bound diner, clutching a baguette. At the end of the short thoroughfare, Peter Ellis found a parking space in the public lot facing the early Romanesque church of Saint André. He locked the car and led Anya to the low, rock wall at the edge of the cliff. To their right, the jagged remains of la tour Montréal, the rectangular stone tower of the former fortress, rose forty or more feet above them. Into the thick walls were cut intermittent rows of four-by-fifteen inch slits through which Middle Age defenders of the town let fly their arrows. The openings now were nearly completely filled with cooing, nesting pigeons. Below them, the shallow, sparkling green river flowed over a rocky riverbed and forked around an elongated, wooded island toward a fortified drawbridge stretching halfway across the river. At its end, a thin, rectangular, grey stone tower, that once held the chains supporting the long-since rotted wooden half of the bridge, stood sentinel over the rushing waters.

"What a beautiful little bridge! Or perhaps I should say half a bridge."

"It is called the Pont de la Légende. I'll tell you the story of the legend over lunch, which we had best see about. In these small towns, they keep fairly strict hours. I hope you are hungry."

"I am famished. I only had coffee and a croissant for breakfast."

"Good. Afterwards, you can paint to your heart's content while I re-acquaint myself with that charming island down there."

They walked down the main street until they came to a some-what dilapidated, three story manor house called the Hostellerie du Chateau. They entered through a wide hallway at the end of which was a small oak bar. A short, middle-aged woman in an old-fashioned black and white server's uniform led them into an ample, high-ceilinged dining room and seated them at a table next to a large window. The view it offered was of a neglected rectangle of lawn framed by a wide pebble border on which was scattered a handful of red café tables and chairs.

The almost square dining room was decorated in an equally haphazard fashion, any attention to detail having long since been abandoned. Which is not to say that it lacked charm, albeit of a rural quality. In the middle of one wall was a large fireplace into which a gas heater had been inserted, the tall, brass andirons having been left to stand guard over it. Above the mantle was a small, faded heraldic painting surrounded by pock-marked plaster. On the far wall was an asymmetrically arranged series of paintings of bullfighters. In the far corner stood an old clock with a huge pendulum that made a loud, constant clucking sound. On the back wall was a bas-relief of a cherub around which were several old china plates, again hung with no attention to symmetry. The room had an ancient oak floor and dark oak wainscoting, with a foot-high triangular detail in the middle of each panel. Above the wide doorway through which they had passed was mounted, much like a set of trophy horns, a ragged old cutting of grape vine. Next to it hung a painting of the Pont de la Légende with the chateau, after which the hotel was named, towering over it under a black, stormy sky.

Peter Ellis noticed Anya studying the room. "The dining room at the Ritz it certainly is not; but there is something about it that appeals to me."

"To me as well. I see they have a picture of your legendary bridge. When am I to hear the famous story?"

"As soon as we have ordered and I have had a taste of Jurançon wine for inspiration."

The same woman who had seated them took their order and returned within minutes with the wine. Peter Ellis had chosen a dry Jurançon called Amistous, named for the delicate purple flowers featured on the label. It was a pale straw in color and had a pungent, apple-pear taste. After an appreciative sip, he began the story of the Pont de la Légende.

"Alright Anya, here is the story as I understand it: Around 1165, a certain princess named Sancie, the daughter of the king of Navarre, married Gaston V, the viscount of Béarn. When her husband, the viscount, died in 1170, Sancie was with child. When she finally gave birth, it was to a deformed baby who died almost immediately. Rumors soon began circulating that the mother was responsible for the child's death by inducing a premature birth. Sancie's brother had, by this time, succeeded their father as king of Navarre. The scandal was such that he decided that the only way to settle the matter to everyone's satisfaction, with the understandable possible exception of the vicomtesse herself, was to subject the accused to the 'test of the waters'. It seems that similar appeals to the 'judgment of God' were much in favor at that time in the Pyrenee region. This particular form of trial consisted in binding the person in question by the ankles and wrists and throwing them off the bridge into the river. If they somehow managed to escape drowning, then they were judged innocent.

"As you can well imagine, Anya, subjecting the vicomptesse to a trial by water proved to be a wildly popular event. Peasants from the surrounding countryside thronged to Sauveterre and joined the local townsfolk and gentry, lining the banks of the Gave. After a brief prayer that justice be served, the victim was launched into the rushing water as the hushed crowd looked on in suspense. To this day, no one has a definitive explanation for what followed, though several theories have been expounded over the centuries. That it happened, however, there is no doubt. Instead of disappearing under the water, the princess stayed on the surface, where the current carried her unharmed to the riverbank, some 'three arrow flights from the bridge', a measure of distance I take to have been popular at the time. As you might imagine, the crowd went crazy, having been witness to a seeming miracle, and Sancie's would-be executioners declared her innocent in the death of her infant. And that, Anya, is the 'legend of the bridge', as I understand it."

"What an extraordinary story! I dare say if we subscribed to that type of trial system, we would not have to worry about building prisons."

"I'll tell you, I would have no qualms using it on a couple of the local gangsters I am presently dealing with. Or, at least, having the option of using it. It would make getting at the truth a much easier undertaking."

"Have there been any developments in the case?"

Peter Ellis gave her a judiciously edited version of his evening at 'Le Gentleman'. He told of his suspicions about Gambia and his three young enforcers and the police cover-up. He explained the ultimatum he and Maurice had given Duchon and spoke of his concern for Chantal Clairac.

"Do you really think she is in danger, Peter?"

"Not for the moment. But if we can manage to scare Duchon enough to help us implicate Gambia, or if we can figure out some other way to tie him to the boy's death, then I think it would be wise to find someplace for her to stay until things are settled. In fact, I had even thought of asking Olga if she would let me rent her extra room at the farmhouse."

"I am certain she would be happy to help you. But why do you think Chantal is in danger, Peter? Does she know something that could make trouble for this Gambia man or for her former lover, Duchon?"

"Anya, I think I may have to hire you as an assistant. What you ask is precisely what I have been asking myself. There is a question of a 'lost weekend' that she experienced about six months ago that bothers me. Maurice is going to attempt to speak with her this afternoon, try to gain her trust and, hopefully, enlist her aid. But I have a distinct feeling that Chantal Clairac is hiding something, for whatever reason, that would be very helpful to us."

"Do you think Maurice will be able to convince the girl to help you? It doesn't sound very promising."

"Oh, I don't know. You have not seen my old friend in action. He has a way of coaxing information from unwilling subjects. No doubt, it comes primarily from his career in the Brigade Financière where it was his job to learn people's most intimate financial secrets. But he also has a native gift for convincing even the most suspicious of persons to trust him. I have often thought he literally charms them into submission, much like an Indian snake handler."

"You have certainly aroused my curiosity to experience the charms of your old inspector friend. When will I be able to meet him?"

"Maybe this weekend. Perhaps we could dine together."

"I shall have to think about that, Peter. I'm not sure if I shall be able to eat anything for a week after this meal."

They were on the second course of a four course meal, an enormous omelette of jambon de Bayonne with fresh parsley. The locally-cured ham was much saltier than the commercial variety and the omelette included small, crispy chunks of meat as well as large, succulent slices. Their first course had been a steaming tureen of potage paysan, a variation on the traditional Béarnais soup, garbure, with carrots, leeks, white beans, vermicelli and ham in place of confit de canard.

"I can't believe these people eat like this every day! I'm surprised they all don't have heart attacks by the time they are forty."

"It is certainly food made to sustain hard, physical labor. Though it is a lot healthier than you may think. I had a wonderful old friend from Artix, a town not too far from here, who ate like this daily. When he died two years ago at eighty-eight, he was as spry as an old rooster. Of course, he worked outside almost every day of his adult life."

"I'll take your word for the health benefits. All I know is that we have two more courses coming and I am already about to burst. What was that funny-sounding entrée you ordered?"

"A gigot de mouton with green beans and roasted potatoes."

He had no sooner described the main course than the waitress arrived with a large, chipped porcelain platter laden with grilled lamb and vegetables.

"Good God, Peter. It is enough for an entire family!"

"Yes, the chef is generous with his servings. Nouvelle cuisine it is not."

"What are we going to do? It is so much food."

"Eat what we can and bring the rest to Olga's dog, Rubens. I'm sure his appetite will make up for ours."

Peter Ellis had ordered a 1985 Chateau de la Motte Madiran to drink with the gigot and the cheese plate to follow. It proved to be an inspired choice. The deep garnet wine had a strong, fruity bouquet, a taste with hints of current and blackberry and a pleasant, dry finish.

"The wine is delightful, Peter. Is it local?"

"More or less. It comes from the region around Auch, about an hour and a half from here."

"I must get some to bring back to Amsterdam. Will you help me choose a few bottles?"

"I would be honored. Cheers!" He raised his glass. "To the wine-maker, whoever he is, for the pleasure he has given us."

They finished the bottle with the last bites of a soft, mild goat cheese. After coffee and a glass of Armagnac, they walked across the hotel's ragged yard to the edge of the cliff. For a moment, they stared silently down at the Pont de la Légende and the cold, rushing waters of the Gave d'Oloron. The early afternoon sun bathed the landscape in a soft, warm light.

"Peter, thank-you for a wonderful meal and a wonderful day." She took his hand and lightly kissed it.

"It is not over yet."

"I know. I just felt like saying it. For the first time in I don't know how long, I feel totally happy."

"Yes, I know what you mean."

"Days like this are extremely rare. One must drink them in like that wonderful wine just now, let them possess you."

"I hope this will be the first of many for us."

"Yes, it is possible. But let's not think about the future now. The present is so delicious. Now, if I can only capture a tiny bit of it on canvas this afternoon."

"I am sure that you will do much better than that, Anya."

CHAPTER FIFTEEN

All morning, Chief Inspector Jacques LeClerc had suffered the effects of the previous evening's over-indulgences while having to deal with several bureaucratic departmental problems. He was forced to eat a hurried meal at the non-descript bistro around the corner from his office. The steak was tough, the fries were greasy and the carafe of <u>vin ordinaire</u> was worse than ordinary and settled roughly on his queasy stomach. Even the glass of cognac that he thought might help settle his stomach proved to be little more than colored firewater. Such were the sources of his ill humor when he returned to his office a little after two o'clock and decided to call Maurice Claverie-LaPorte. He had intended on delivering his sermon of fire and brimstone to the former inspector in person. But after studying his face in the bathroom mirror at headquarters, the third time he had done so since arriving at work, he decided that his facial puffiness and bloodshot eyes would betray his night of dissipation and undermine the force of his message. So he picked up the telephone and dialed the former inspector's home number, vaguely hoping that his call might exorcise some of the morning's pain and frustration.

Maurice had been mentally preparing himself for the tiresome ordeal of a personal visit from LeClerc. The telephone call came as a pleasant surprise, given the options. The inspector's harangue was predictably loud, crude and histrionic, full of thinly veiled threats that Maurice knew were ninety percent bluster, with virtually no legal grounding. He listened patiently for almost fifteen minutes, smiling to himself and occasionally answering "Yes", "No", "I understand, Chief Inspector" and, finally, "I shall try not to let it happen again."

"No, not 'try' M. Claverie-LaPorte. You will make certain it does not happen again. And if you want my advice, I suggest you and the American boy's uncle stay away from Mlle. Clairac. She has had a hard enough time without your interference and meddling. The case is closed and the sooner everyone accepts that fact, the better. Don't you agree?"

"I would truly like to, Chief Inspector, as would the boy's uncle. What we are both interested in, as I'm sure you are, is the truth. Unfortunately, certain inconsistencies in your conclusion of accidental death are bothering both of us."

"Have you not heard a word I have been saying?!" LeClerc's voice was like an explosion and caused Maurice to move the receiver away from his ear. "The case is closed! The boy's death was an accident, caused, it seems to me, by his own stupidity and reckless behavior. Much like your and this uncle's behavior in trying to find something that does not exist. You are already guilty of impersonating an officer. I shall, against my better judgment, forget about that little liberty, provided you keep your nose out of affairs that do not concern you. If you decide to continue poking around where you shouldn't, I shall make more trouble for you than a whore with the clap. Understood?"

Before Maurice could answer, the telephone line went dead. He calmly replaced the receiver in the cradle. After several minutes of contemplation, he took out his pocket notebook, perused it for a moment, picked up the telephone receiver again and dialed the number of Chantal Clairac's mother. After a short, satisfactory conversation, he got up from his desk, stretched lazily like an old tomcat, walked out to his small balcony and settled himself into a padded chaise-longue for a short siesta.

At four o'clock sharp, a well-rested Maurice Claverie-LaPorte entered the Dodin patisserie shop and walked to the counter where Chantal Clairac was serving two ancient, blue-haired women. They

were debating, in spirited tones, whether, in addition to their lemon
and cherry tarts, they should split a pet de nonne. While the girl
patiently awaited their decision, she glanced furtively at Maurice,
who immediately acknowledged her look with a pleasant smile and
a touch to the brim of his tweed cap. She quickly averted her eyes.
Another waitress appeared and asked Maurice if she might be of assistance. He thanked her and said that he would wait for Mlle. Clairac
to finish, as he had a little surprise for her and held up a small bag
with the logo of a well-known Parisian fashion house.

"It is a peace offering for my rudeness to Mlle. Clairac two days
ago."

He said this just loud enough for her to hear. He saw her cheeks
flush. She fumbled slightly with the plump pastry that the two crones
had finally agreed on. He knew he had trapped her and felt a pang of
remorse for making her feel so evidently ill at ease. Still, it was necessary that he talk to her. She finally finished with the two women, but
only after an additional debate between them regarding whose turn
it was to pay for the pastries and whether some special consideration
should be given the addition of a third item.

"Please forgive me, Mlle. Chantal. I did not mean to cause you
any discomfort. But it was necessary that I speak with you. You feel
alright?"

"Yes, monsieur." Her voice was barely audible.

"I shall be frank, mademoiselle. When I last spoke with you, I misled you as to my official position. But you are already aware of that
fact, I believe?"

"Yes, monsieur."

"Was it M. Duchon who told you?"

"Yes, monsieur."

"And he probably also told you not to speak with me again. Is that
not so?"

"Yes, monsieur."

"Well, your friend was perhaps correct in one thing: it was wrong
for me to make you think I was speaking in an official capacity. I assure you, however, that my intentions were honorable. Still, I would

like you to accept this small gift as a token of my apology. I am sincerely sorry if I caused you any pain and I am also sorry for misleading you."

"The gift, it is not necessary, monsieur."

"Necessary or no, I beg you to accept it for my own selfish reasons. It will go a long way in easing an old man's conscience."

"Thank-you very much."

"You are very welcome, mademoiselle." He paused, forcing her to look directly at him. "I wish I could say that presenting you with a little gift was my only reason for this visit. But, alas, it is not. You see, Mlle. Chantal, I would like to speak with you this evening after work. It is very important."

"But I can't. Jean-Claude is sure to find out and…" Her voice trailed off.

"And he will be very upset with you. Will he physically harm you again?"

"Please, monsieur. Do not ask me these things. They are stronger than I am."

"Once again, I am sorry Mlle. Chantal. I do not mean to upset you. I shall say only one thing more: I am going to take my afternoon tea here. If you would prefer, you may ask another girl to serve me. But before I leave, I must ask you to call your mother. That is all."

"My mother?"

"Yes, mademoiselle, your mother. If, after what she says, you do not want to speak with me again, I promise you, on my word of honor, never to trouble you again. Is that fair?"

She nodded her head in tentative assent.

"Excellent. Now, which of these sinful pastries do you recommend today?"

***

After a short telephone conversation with her mother, Chantal Clairac agreed to meet Maurice Claverie-LaPorte at the Café Royalty after work. At ten minutes to seven, the former inspector entered the dark, subdued confines of the old Basque-style café and chose a corner table in the spacious rectangular club room to the left of the bar. As he waited for the waiter to arrive, he made a cursory inspection of the clientele seated in small groups around him. He was pleased to note that he recognized no one. He ordered a glass of dry sherry from a thin, elderly waiter attired in the old, classic fashion, his long, white apron reaching almost to his ankles.

"And one more thing, monsieur."

"Yes sir?"

"I am expecting a pretty young lady sometime after seven. She is rather tall and has long, auburn hair."

"If I see her, I shall direct her to your table. Is that all, monsieur?"

Maurice detected the slightest trace of disapproval in the old waiter's voice. Or it could have been just jaded resignation. Whatever it was, he felt compelled to add: "She is a friend of my niece."

"I understand, sir. I shall look out for her."

His lie was so transparent and the waiter's recognition of it for what it was so obvious, Maurice felt his face begin to flush. But the old waiter was nothing if not discreet and was already taking the order of an adjoining table.

Chantal arrived at seven fifteen. Maurice was looking at the entrance to the bar when she appeared, escorted by the old waiter. As she walked toward his table, Maurice stood to greet her. He immediately noticed that virtually every man and not a few of the women had turned their gaze on the striking, long-legged girl approaching his table. She wore pressed blue jeans and a black V-neck sweater, a simple combination that did no injustice to her figure. She carried a beige London Fog raincoat draped over her left arm. He offered her the chair to his immediate left, so that he might speak to her discreetly. That one never knew whose ears might be listening at the next table was one of his abiding axioms.

"Thank-you very much for coming, Mlle. Chantal. I shall not keep you long. Would you care for a drink?"

"Thank-you monsieur. I have ordered a Coca-Cola from the waiter."

"Very good. Then I shall tell you why I have asked you here. Please forgive me, Mlle. Chantal, if I speak bluntly. In view of the circumstances, I feel it is necessary to be straightforward. There is no time to waste. You see, I don't believe the death of your American friend was purely an accident. I think young M. Duffy died while trying to escape from three thugs sent by Joseph Gambia. Furthermore, I think your friend Jean-Claude Duchon asked M. Gambia to send the three to intimidate M. Duffy into leaving Biarritz. I shall tell you frankly, mademoiselle, that I do not care for M. Duchon; in fact, I find him and his type—for he is distinctly of a type all too prevalent in our country—extremely distasteful. But for all that, I do not believe he meant for your friend to die. For that matter, I do not even think that Joseph Gambia intended for him to die. The fact remains, however, that your friend is dead; and he is dead as a result of actions put in motion by the jealous M. Duchon and his accommodating friend, M. Gambia. I apologize for being so blunt, mademoiselle, I realize that it is painful for you to hear your friend's death discussed in such an impersonal way. Please don't think I am insensitive to your feelings. It is just that I intend to bring M. Gambia and any others directly involved in M. Duffy's death to justice. And to do this, I need your help."

"But how can I help you? I know nothing of what happened that morning."

"I am sure that is so, mademoiselle. But if you will permit me to ask you a few questions—and I must warn you that some are of an extremely personal nature—I feel certain that you can provide me with some important information that even you don't realize is pertinent to your friend's death. Will you allow me this liberty, Mlle. Chantal? I promise to hold anything you say in the strictest confidence."

"Yes, monsieur."

Maurice barely heard her whispered reply. He painfully noted the resigned, almost mournful expression on her face. He felt as though he was about to violate a child. Mercifully, the old waiter arrived with her Coca-cola.

"Another drink for you sir?"

"Yes, please. And a small bottle of Vittel as well."

"Very good, monsieur."

"With your permission, Mlle. Chantal, there is one other person with whom I would like to share your information. He is an old American friend from Paris named Peter Ellis. He is a respected journalist who has come down to aid me in this matter. I can guarantee you that he will not repeat anything you choose to tell me. I would like for you to meet him; however, that is for you to decide. Is this acceptable to you?"

"Yes, monsieur."

"Thank-you very much, mademoiselle. Now, let me begin by asking when you last saw M. Duchon?"

"He was waiting for me when I came home yesterday."

"Was he upset with you?"

"Not at first. He wanted things to be like before. He doesn't understand. It is impossible for things to be like before. Not after everything that has happened."

"Did he threaten you?"

"He said I was not to talk to you. He said if I wanted to talk to the police, I should call Inspector LeClerc's office."

"You know Inspector LeClerc?"

"I saw him sometimes when Jean-Claude and I went to the clubs of M. Gambia and Mme. Janine. I have never spoken to him."

"Never? Not even during his investigation of your friend's death?"

"I spoke with one of his detectives. I forget his name. He kept asking me if Kevin had been upset about anything."

"What did you tell him, Chantal?"

"That I didn't think so. It is the truth, monsieur! We were happy together."

"What about M. Duchon's threats?"

"Kevin told me not to worry about Jean-Claude. He said he could take care of himself."

"Did the detective ask you anything else?"

"He wanted to know if Kevin was planning to meet anyone that morning."

"And was he?"

"I don't think so. He often went to the Perspective Park in the morning to look at the waves. He usually went by himself."

"Did you ever go with him?"

"Only two or three times. He loved it there. He wanted to show me how beautiful it was early in the morning. He couldn't believe I had never been."

"Mlle. Chantal, I must apologize for asking you this. I know it is a painful question for you, but it is something I must know: Did your friend, M. Duffy, ever stand on the wall of the large overlook, you know, in order to have a better view?"

"No, monsieur, I never saw him do that. There is no need. The view is clear from that spot."

"Exactly! That is what I noticed myself."

"Do you think someone pushed Kevin from the wall of the overlook, monsieur?"

"I fear I do not know the answer to that, Mlle. Chantal. I do know that he was not alone that morning. There were at least three others on the overlook with him. These others, I feel sure, were sent by M. Gambia."

"Did they kill Kevin? Oh my God! It is because of me that he is dead. I knew it!"

"Please, Mlle. Chantal, calm yourself. One thing I do know: you are certainly not to blame for your friend's death. Like I said earlier, I think I know who is to blame, at least indirectly, for his death and I fully expect him to be punished. But please, mademoiselle, don't think for a moment that you are in any way guilty of anything in this sad business. That is, unless you are hiding something from me."

"I swear, monsieur, I am hiding nothing! Nothing!"

"It is as I thought, mademoiselle. Now, may I ask you just a few more questions?"

"Yes, monsieur." She took a bar napkin and dabbed her eyes.

"Good. Now, how well do you know Joseph Gambia? You said earlier that you saw him sometimes when you went out with M. Duchon.

Did he ever ask you to work for him in one of his clubs, or did M. Duchon ever suggest it?"

"I know M. Gambia only from the parties I went to with Jean-Claude and his friends. I met him the first time I went out with Jean-Claude. Mme. Janine had arranged a small soirée in an apartment she keeps for entertaining her clients. It is in a building behind the Casino Municipal. It is very chic. She said Jean-Claude might help me find a position in a better establishment. At the time, I was at a small shop around the corner from Mme. Janine's residence. The owner was a pig, always touching me and suggesting things behind his wife's back. But the wife was just as bad in her own way. Mme. Janine came in almost every day to buy our pastries and, often, to take tea. She was very nice to me, she always asked how I was doing. Two or three times, she came with Jean-Claude. At first, I thought he was her husband. I asked her one day and she couldn't stop laughing. She apologized afterwards because she saw I felt bad for saying what I had said. She was nice like that, always caring about my feelings. Then one day she asked if I wanted to come to a soirée. She said she was sure I would like it and she had invited someone special for me to meet, someone who might be able to help me, because she knew I was unhappy where I was. She never said it was Jean-Claude, the man I thought was her husband. I was so embarrassed when I saw him, you can imagine."

"So it was Mme. Destin who introduced you to M. Duchon and M. Gambia?"

"Yes. And she was right about Jean-Claude. He found me a place at Dodin's almost at once. Of course, it was at Mme. Janine's suggestion."

"Was M. Gambia at the party?"

"Yes, but he barely spoke to me. He was very rude to Mme. Janine in front of her guests. I found out it is his way. I have never liked him. But I could never say anything bad about him in front of Jean-Claude. He was always talking about Jojo—that's what he calls M. Gambia—how Jojo did this or Jojo did that for him. I just think M. Gambia is egotistical. Mme. Janine was smart to leave him. She is much nicer and much smarter. She's the one who really knows about business. Jojo just plays the part of the big shot."

"Did M. Gambia ever ask you to work for him at one of his clubs?"

"He made the suggestion the next time he saw me. Mme. Janine told me she didn't think it was a good idea. And she also reminded Jojo that they did not have any positions available at that time."

"So that was when you began seeing M. Duchon, after Mme. Janine's soireé?"

"That was when he started calling me. We would have drinks after work. He was very nice. Mme. Janine often joined us."

"If I may be indiscreet, Mlle. Chantal, when did you begin having more than drinks with M. Duchon? You must trust me, mademoiselle. I have a good reason for wanting to know this fact."

The girl looked questioningly at the former inspector. It was evident she was weighting whether or not to answer. Maurice took a sip of his drink and waited. Finally, she spoke.

"It was about a month later. There was another party at an apartment of M. Gambia. Mme. Janine was in Paris. But I didn't know that when I went. I guess Jean-Claude knew I might not go if he told me she was out of town. By then, he knew I didn't like being around M. Gambia, especially when he was drinking."

"Was Inspector LeClerc there by any chance?"

"I think he came later."

"You mean after you left?"

"No."

Maurice waited several minutes for the girl to continue. But something, he couldn't decide what, had dramatically caused her mood to change. She sat silently, her head bowed, her hands nervously folding and unfolding her cocktail napkin. He studied her face in profile. Her high, prominent cheeks had colored noticeably. But even in her agitated, downcast state, he couldn't help but think what a stunning young woman she was. And with this thought came the companion realization that this gift of physical beauty would be a curse for her well into middle age. Finally, he placed his large hands lightly over hers and gently held them still for a moment. When she raised her eyes briefly to meet his, he noticed that tears were forming around the edges.

"Mlle. Chantal, did I say something to upset you? If so, I apologize."

"No, monsieur. I was just thinking about that night of the party. I have never spoken of it with anyone. It makes me so ashamed."

"I am sure it is not so bad as that."

"I still do not understand what happened. I was not myself. It was horrible."

"If you try to tell me, perhaps I can help you. What is it that you do not understand? Please, try to tell me. Had you been drinking?"

"M. Gambia had made a special frozen drink with strawberries. It was like a dessert. It was not strong like a cocktail. But he must have put something strong in it. I only remember having three or four. I was dancing with Jean-Claude when I started feeling funny. I told him I was feeling strange. He said not to worry, that he would take care of me. By this time, there were several other girls in the apartment. They were all around M. Gambia, laughing and dancing with each other. Then one girl took her shirt off and started to dance like she was performing in a club. M. Gambia and his friends began clapping and whistling and then the other girls began undressing. Jean-Claude had stopped dancing to watch what was going on. All of a sudden, one of the girls came over to me and asked me why I wasn't dancing. She took my hand and led me to where the others were putting on a show for the men. The girls by now were only wearing their string panties. The one who had come over to get me said I had a nice body and should not be afraid to show it. Everyone had started looking at me. I was the only girl still wearing my clothes. All of the girls were dancing around me and the men were shouting for me to undress. I have never done anything like that before, I assure you, monsieur. I didn't know what to do. Everyone was dancing around me, even Jean-Claude. I know it was stupid, monsieur, but with all they had given me to drink, I was not myself. It was like a bad dream. You must not believe I am really like that."

"I am sure you are not, Mlle. Chantal. Under certain circumstances, we are all of us capable of doing things that are out of character. And under the influence of alcohol or drugs, watch out! It is very easy to become someone else."

He paused to sip from his drink. The girl wiped her eyes with the cocktail napkin she had been clutching. He gave her several minutes to regain her composure.

"I know this is extremely painful for you, mademoiselle, but I must ask you to continue. I presume that something else happened that evening, something even more difficult for you to recount. Am I correct?"

"Yes, monsieur, it was terrible. I never thought I could speak of it with anyone. I am still not sure I can."

"Please try, mademoiselle. Often it helps to talk to a sympathetic stranger about things you can not tell those that are close to you. And I am not sure why, but I have a hunch what happened that evening has a distinct bearing on the mystery surrounding your friend's death. Take your time, mademoiselle, but please try to tell me, as best you can remember, what else happened that evening. How long did the dancing last?"

"I am not sure. I can barely remember anything until I went to the bedroom with Jean-Claude."

"Excuse me, mademoiselle, I do not understand. Was this bedroom in the apartment where M. Gambia was having the party?"

"Yes. There were three or four bedrooms. I don't know exactly what happened. I think I fell down. I remember Jean-Claude taking me into this room. There was a very big bed and mirrors everywhere. It was like the funhouse at a fair. I remember I was very confused. I saw myself everywhere. And everywhere I was naked. Jean-Claude told me to lie down, that he would get my clothes. I must have fallen asleep. The next thing I remember, he was on top of me. He had taken his clothes off. He was trying to make love to me. I told him to stop. I tried to push him off me. He wanted to know what was wrong. He said he thought I liked him. I don't remember what I said except for him to please stop. Then he became very angry. He called me names. He said it was my fault for getting him so excited. He pushed me away and started dressing. He told me to sleep well and left. I don't know how long I was there before he came."

"M. Duchon came back?"

"I thought it was Jean-Claude at first. It was very dark. But then he came closer and I saw it was a much bigger man. Then I saw the mask and screamed. I'll never forget the horrible sound of his voice telling me to shut up or else. I have never heard such a voice! I started begging him to please not hurt me."

"You did not recognize him or recognize his voice? You had never seen him before? Please, mademoiselle, try to think."

"There is not a day since then that I have not thought about him, I assure you. There was definitely something familiar about him, I am sure of that; but, as hard as I try, I can't recall what he looked like. I remember only that black mask and his voice. It was like a growl, monsieur, like the growl of some beast. And that was how he acted, like some wild animal. I was so terrified, so scared, I didn't know what to do. He started rubbing himself, holding it close to my face, telling me to look at it, saying he knew I wanted it, saying all the young girls wanted it, they just pretended they didn't, wasn't that right? Then he said 'Tell me you want it' and called me a name. He said it again. And again. I'll never forget the sound of his voice repeating those words. He spread my legs and started touching me. He was very rough, he was hurting me. He said he wanted me to beg him for it. I was so afraid. Then he forced himself in me and then, all of a sudden, it was over. I had closed my eyes as tight as I could. I don't know what happened next, but when I opened my eyes, he was gone. I lay still for a long time, then I got up to go to the toilet. Where he had forced himself, I had a terrible pain. When I turned on the light in the bathroom, I saw blood on my legs. Oh monsieur, it was so terrible! I am so ashamed."

This time, her whole body shook with her sobbing. Maurice took a handkerchief from an inner pocket and offered it to her.

"You have absolutely nothing to be ashamed of, Mlle. Chantal. You are an extremely brave young woman. I apologize with all my heart for making you relive that horrible incident. But your story has given me some important new ideas about this whole terrible affair. On my word of honor, mademoiselle, I shall see that Justice has her way with the cowardly man who did this to you.

CHAPTER SIXTEEN

Peter Ellis helped Anya set up her easel and painting kit on the gravel apron next to the short wall at the edge of the escarpment. Below them, the Gave d'Oloron, jade green in the slanting rays of the mid-afternoon sun, rushed swiftly over the shallow rock riverbed, past a narrow, heavily-wooded island, toward the Pont de la Légende then around a sandy bend and out of sight. It was still very warm and only the bright orange-and-yellow canopy of fall foliage spreading out below him reminded Peter Ellis of the actual season.

While Anya arranged her painting things, Peter Ellis surveyed the panoramic scene below them. He watched a small flock of larks chase each other around the tour Montréal, diving, swooping, circling and climbing with a quickness and ease that made him suddenly long to join them. Then, as if she had willed it, he looked over at Anya, who was smiling broadly at him, and decided that his earthbound fate might not be that bad after all.

Having agreed to meet her in the vicinity of the church in an hour or so, he set off on the steep rock stairway leading down to the riverbank. The stairs led to an ancient stone walkway that slanted toward the Pont de la Légende. As he walked, he passed growths of cactus, Spanish bayonet, palmetto and banana palms, green evidence of the tropical micro-climate of the south-facing cliff. He walked under the ruins of the old chateau, a series of rugged, dilapidated, lichen-covered rock walls perched precariously on the edge of the bluff. As he approached the old drawbridge, he entered a vaulted tunnel, open to the river side, that ran under a typical galleried Béarnais house with a burnt orange tiled roof. The house stood on the corner of the entrance to the legendary old bridge where the river turned upstream in a rush of noisy rapids. The house had been for sale for at least three years and Peter Ellis had, during that time, often entertained the fantasy of owning it. He had even broached the subject with Burke, who had dismissed it as unrealistic but wonderfully romantic. (Having said this, she then proceeded to make an exhaustive photographic study of the house that she later assembled into a small, hand-bound book, which she presented him on his last birthday.) He smiled ruefully at the memory. He should have expected Sauveterre to trigger thoughts of Burke but, up until that moment, his mind had been wholly occupied by the world of possibilities that Anya had opened for him.

As had become his habit on visits to the medieval town, Peter Ellis decided to climb the steep, spiral stone stairway that led to the cramped, upper level of the drawbridge tower. The ascent was in near total darkness, the only light coming from two foot long, vertical embrasures in the thick, stone wall of the small room that had formerly housed the lifting mechanism of the bridge. The darkness, coupled with a malodorous dampness permeating the claustrophobic space, gave an eerie feeling of foreboding. He half expected to see the ghost of the princess, Sancie, hands and feet still bound, seeking vengeance for her false accusal. What he did see this time was a slightly embarrassed young couple whom he had obviously interrupted in mid-embrace. They quickly brushed past him with identical, cursory 'Excusez-mois'. No sooner were they out of sight than Peter Ellis heard a muffled, high-pitched giggle echoing through the narrow stairwell.

From the Pont de la Légende he walked a short distance to the pedestrian bridge that gave modern-day access to the island. He followed the well-worn path around the perimeter toward the eastern end of the deserted, natural preserve. Along the riverbank, haphazard piles of flotsam, lodged against rocks and tree roots, served as evidence of previous flooding. He came to a large oak which had fallen across the path, the stubby remains of its crown splayed out above the cold, shallow water. As he scrambled over the horizontal trunk, he noticed three mountain goats, a male and two females, foraging in the dense undergrowth. They had heard him approaching and stood motionless, staring in his direction, curious as to the nature of the intruder. He walked toward them slowly. The two females, quickly satisfied that this particular two-legged visitor posed no threat to their well-being, recommenced chewing their respective clumps of brambles. The male, however, perhaps sensing the opportunity for some like-gender bonding, walked over to the edge of the path. Peter Ellis stopped next to him and gingerly reached out a hand to the animal, hoping he would not mistake it for an entrée. The goat gently nudged it with the top of his nose and lowered his head as if to say, 'This is where I want to be scratched'. Peter Ellis instinctively obeyed this universal animal gesture and received a kind of guttural groan of satisfaction in thanks.

After several minutes of head-scratching, the goat decided that it was time to return to either his dinner or his harem, Peter Ellis wasn't sure which, since they both occupied the same patch of ground. He wished his new friend 'bon appétit' and continued along the path to the end of the island. It was shaped like the prow of a large ship. Looking down at the rushing water as it divided into two distinct currents, he had the momentary illusion of forward motion. He stood for several minutes trying to detect the exact point of divergence, his mind hypnotized by the green, translucent river. Some sudden movement below the surface, the shadowy darting of a barely perceived fish, broke his reverie. Immediately, for no apparent reason, he thought of Anya. He looked up at the steep, partially buttressed escarpment rising above the flood plain. Just beyond the low, cemented-rock wall, he could barely make out the back of her blond head and the brown A-frame of her easel. The distant glimpse of the woman triggered an earlier vision of a supine, nearly naked body lounging in the afternoon sun. For an instant, he thought of himself, naked, lying next to her. Almost in the same instant, he realized how foolish he was being. He had known Anya barely twenty-four hours. He had merely invited her for lunch and a visit to a small, medieval town. He had detected a certain natural affinity during their conversation in the restaurant, at least he thought he had. She did seem to look at him with more than professional, painterly interest—at least he thought she did. Still, it was ridiculous to get one's hopes up based on such slim evidence. Better to have no expectations. Remember what Maurice had said about vulnerability.

Resolved to this sensible course of action—or inaction—Peter Ellis retraced his steps back to town. When he came to where the oak had fallen across the path, the three goats were nowhere to be seen. After crossing the river, he walked up the steep, stone-paved road through the massive town gate that had once been part of Sauveterre's perimeter fortifications. He tried to retrace the former fortress walls, which led him to a lengthy exploration of the town's narrow, back streets. He stopped briefly at a low-ceilinged, rustic bar for a quick beer and to update his journal. He thought briefly of Gambia and Duchon but quickly concluded that he didn't want to sully such a beautiful day with the filth they represented. There would be ample time to deal with them the following week. When he finally found Anya in the small park behind the church, it was nearly four-thirty.

Standing behind her, he studied the drawing she was working on. It was a detailed rendering of the large, barrel-like apse of St. Andre, flanked by two smaller circular rooms, all surmounted by a massive square stone bell tower with four, intersecting, triangular, tile roofs. A small crucifix rose from the shared apex.

"It's very nice. I have always loved the solid simplicity of this church."

"Oh Peter, it is beautiful! The whole town is beautiful. Do you think we might come back one day this week? I realize you are going to be busy; I guess I could borrow Olga's car and come by myself."

"Don't be ridiculous! I introduced you to Sauveterre and I'll not have you visiting it without me, at least this week. It is our first adventure together. And I hope it won't be our last."

"I suspect it won't be." Her eyes smiled at his. "Now, if you can just give me about fifteen minutes to finish this."

"Are you sure that is all the time you will need? I am certainly not in a hurry to go anywhere."

"Perhaps I could use just a little more time." She looked questioningly at him. "Peter, would a half hour be too much to ask?"

"Not at all. It will give me enough time to visit a little wine shop I discovered on my walk. It looks to have an excellent selection of local wines. If you like, I'll pick out a small selection for you as well, a few bottles you can take back to Holland, a souvenir of Sauveterre."

"That would be wonderful, Peter. Perhaps you could choose six or eight bottles for me."

"Do you have a preference between red or white?"

"Not really. I'll leave the decision to you. After what you chose for us to drink at lunch, I don't anticipate having any complaints. If you don't mind, would you also get two or three extra bottles that I can give Olga for her hospitality? You know her taste. The price is not important."

"I'll see if the store has any '85 or '86 Jurançon doux. It is her favorite local wine and those are both excellent years."

"Perfect. I'll try to be finished when you return."

As was his habit, Peter Ellis ended up buying twice as much wine as he had planned and spending almost twice as much time. The patron of the ancient little shop was both passionate and knowledgeable about his wines. He was a classic example of a rural, Béarnais shopkeeper, complete with long blue work apron and large black beret. When he discovered that his American client shared his enthusiasm, if not his home grown intelligence, he insisted on sampling two or three excellent 'petits coups'. When Peter Ellis finally returned with the car to pick up Anya, a warm wine glow suffused his body. He was barely out of the car when he began his apologies. She stopped him in mid-sentence.

"Peter, please, there is absolutely no need to apologize. As long as I have my drawing pencils and a tablet of paper, I can amuse myself for hours. Anyway, you are only fifteen minutes late."

"You are generous in your estimations. I believe the figure is closer to thirty minutes."

"That's possible, but I must tell you that I don't get too serious about punctuality when I am on holiday. Of course, if you had been this late for an appointment with me at the bank, I would have had to scold you. And seriously question your ability to pay back a loan in a timely manner." She smiled mischievously at him.

"I shall keep that in mind if I ever need to see you for a loan. Still, I appreciate your understanding. I'm afraid it happens regularly when I find a good wine shop. I always get carried away, both with time and purchases."

"But you found what you wanted?"

"That and more. The owner was a typical local character and extremely knowledgeable. When he found out that I knew a little of the region and of its wines, he insisted I taste some of the wine made by the local farmers. He said it was from his private stock, but was quick to add that he would gladly sell me a few bottles if I would kindly keep the sale between ourselves."

"Why did he insist on your discretion? Is it illegal?"

"Very. You see, local farmers, by law, are allowed to make a certain amount of wine every year for their personal consumption. It is not unusual for them to make a good deal more than the legal limit as a way to supplement their income, as well as to show off their wine-making skills. As you can imagine, it is rare to see a printed label on one of these bottles. You are lucky if they have taped a scrap of paper with the year on the bottle. But the wine, as a rule, is excellent and without chemicals."

"How fascinating! I can't wait to try it. If you like, I can make some hand-painted labels for your bottles. They would force you to think about today every time you take one out to drink."

"That would be very nice, though certainly not necessary."

"Meaning what, precisely?"

"Meaning, number one, that I feel sure that my memory of this day with you will need no such reminders."

"I see. And number two?"

"That as soon as the bootleg wine was stashed safely in my car, the old shopkeeper took from his pocket a small packet of labels that he had had printed for just such sales. He even gave me a few extras as souvenirs."

"The old devil thinks of everything. Well, so much for my new career as a label designer."

"Maybe not."

"What do you mean? You just said the shopkeeper gave you labels for the bottles."

"Precisely. He gave me the labels but they are in my pocket, not on the bottles." He reached in his breast pocket and handed her a sample of the black-on-white labels. "As you can see, they are pretty rudimentary."

"I've got an idea. What if I hand colored them? Would you mind?"

"Are you kidding? I think it's a great idea. But enough of this talking about wine. What do you say we have a drink before driving back?"

"I would love that. In fact, I was going to suggest it myself."

"Good. I know a wonderful little auberge on the other side of the town square. We can leave the car here and walk."

After packing Anya's easel and paint box in the snug, shallow trunk, they started across the gravel walkway toward the red awning of the small bar. In front of the Church of St. Andre, they stopped to admire the bas-relief stone tympanum above the double-arched doorway. The scene, bathed in the warm, golden glow of late-afternoon sunlight, depicted Christ, seated in a pose of benediction, surrounded by the four animals symbolizing the evangelists. Above them, on either side of the robed, central figure, sat human embodiments of the sun and moon, favorite symbols of primitive, Christian artists. At the extreme right and left of the keyhole-shaped arch, two angels holding censors completed the striking apocalyptic composition.

"It is truly a beautiful piece of work, don't you think, Anya?"

"Absolutely breathtaking. I always wonder what these medieval Christian artists were like. They must have realized what a special talent they possessed, to create something so moving."

"And all for the love and glorification of God. I've always thought it quite amazing that, for the most part, we don't even know their names. You know, I wonder how many artists, of all mediums, we would have today if there was a law stipulating that anyone creating art must remain anonymous?"

"I can tell you, Peter. We would have the same number of true artists and a lot less narcissists with paint brushes, chisels, cameras, pens, pencils- whatever – in their hands. Several years ago, I read an interview with a well-known English writer—I forget his name now, I'm embarrassed to say—in which the author, in response to the question of publication, stated that if he were told that nothing he wrote from that moment on would ever be published, he would not change his writing habits at all. That, in effect, he wrote for himself, not others."

"He might have added that writing, or any other creative practice, is a sickness with which one is afflicted. I think it is something that chooses you rather than the other way around. God, listen to me! "

"Well, God <u>did</u> have something to do with it." She indicated, with a slight upward turn of her head, the bas-relief above the doors of the church. "At least a beautiful representation of Him did."

"So He did. Do you think He's trying to tell us something?"

"I don't know if He is, but I think the anonymous creator of this tympanum is."

"And what do you think that is, Anya?"

"That you indulge me a quick tour of the church. I meant to visit it earlier but became carried away with my work."

"An indulgence is hardly required. It would be a pleasure." He held open the heavy oak door for her. "After you, mademoiselle."

The inside of St. Andre's was dark and somber. It possessed that characteristic odor shared by every old French church Peter Ellis had ever visited, a haunting mixture of incense, must, beeswax and dried widows' tears. They walked side by side down a narrow side aisle, their footfalls echoing loudly off the ancient stone floor and walls. When they reached the small altar, they were holding hands. To their right was a tarnished metal stand of votive candles. Peter Ellis deposited two ten franc pieces into the slotted box and handed a long wooden match to Anya and indicated for her to light a candle. He then lit one himself. They stood motionless before the flickering candles for almost a minute. Walking back by way of the opposite aisle, they stopped several times to admire the stained glass artwork illuminated by the slanting afternoon sun. During the ten or so minutes they spent inside the church, neither of them spoke. Nor did they let go of each other's hands.

In marked contrast with the church, the auberge was teeming with activity when they entered. Or more precisely, with one particular activity, the local card game called belote. Peter Ellis ordered a small carafe of white Béarnais vin ordinaire from a round-faced, rosy-cheeked young woman in a black skirt and white embroidered peasant blouse. He handed a glass of wine to Anya, who had been observing, with intense interest, the local men in their afternoon ritual. Huddled in groups of four around wine-stained deal tables, the card players furtively peered at their cards, their eyes hidden under the wide, lowered brims of black berets. They smoked incessantly and cajoled each other after every loud slap of a card on the table.

"Well, I'd say we have made a smooth transition from the sacred to the profane. Though they both have this in common." He clicked his glass against hers. "Here's hoping our wishes come true. You did make a wish before lighting the candle, didn't you?"

"Of course. But don't even think of asking me what it was."

"I wouldn't dream of it. But there is something I would like to ask you, though I don't want you to take it the wrong way. It's just that I've enjoyed this afternoon more than any I can remember in a long time. I know this is sounding stupid. I realize I barely know you, but..."

"We have to start somewhere. I'd say we've made more than a good beginning today." She took his hand in hers and began massaging his fingers one by one. "I, too, have a confession to make, Peter.

It has been a long time for me as well. I had almost forgotten what the feeling was like. To be so comfortable and so—I don't really know how to put it any other way—so excited at the same time. Does that make any sense?"

"All the sense in the world, Anya."

"I feel like such a schoolgirl. I know I must be blushing like one. I thought you wanted to ask me a question. Isn't that how all this got started?"

"I do. How would you like to join me for dinner tonight in Biarritz? I promise to be on good behavior."

"In that case, forget it. Though I might reconsider it if you promise to introduce me to your friend, the inspector."

"Tonight? I'm not sure that will be possible. I seem to recall Maurice saying he was meeting someone for dinner."

"I can wait until tomorrow to meet him then, provided you don't mind my spending the night. If there is a problem with that, I certainly understand. I realize I'm being quite brazen, inviting myself like this."

"I'll forgive you this time. Just don't let it happen with anyone else."

"I won't make any promises, but I'll try."

"I guess that will have to do."

"I will need to stop by the farm to pick up a few things and let Olga know that I won't be returning home this evening."

"You don't think she'll mind that I'm stealing you for the night?"

"I'm sure of it. She said something before leaving this morning that led me to believe she anticipated my absence this evening. When I asked her what she meant, she just gave me that funny smile of hers. You surely know the one: like she is sharing a joke with herself."

"Or like she has seen what you're going to do before you even think about doing it, and finds it all very amusing. Oh yes, I know the look only too well. Sometimes I think she can read my mind."

"Well, it looks like she was right this time."

"She usually is, Anya, she usually is." He squeezed her hand gently. "I guess we'd better be going, while there is still a little light left. I thought we might go back by way of Salies-de-Béarn. It's a bit longer but it will give you the chance to scout some potential places to paint. What do you think?"

"What do I think?" She paused theatrically, then flashed him a wide, mock-seductive smile. "I am yours, sir. Take me where you will!"

CHAPTER SEVENTEEN

The phone call from Janine Destin had surprised Duchon. He had seen very little of her in the last couple of months, especially since her most recent falling out with Gambia over an affair he had had with one of their girls. He had felt a certain unspoken pressure to take sides and had tried to remain neutral. But Gambia, especially since Chantal had taken up with the young American surfer, had been much more forthcoming with his sympathy and little favors, especially the little secret favors. For a short time, these favors had even made it possible for him to forget about Chantal. Janine, on the other hand, had merely advised him to leave Chantal alone and let her have her fling. She was still a young girl, wasn't she? She would soon come to her senses. That was easy for Janine to say. She had LeClerc following her around like a puppy. He and Gambia had often joked about it, though never in front of either of them.

The setting for these troubling reflections was the bar of the Café des Colonnes where Jean-Claude Duchon was nursing a Ricard and waiting, nervously, for Janine, who was already fifteen minutes late. Gambia had gone to Spain for the weekend to attend to some unspecified business, most likely drugs Duchon guessed. Maybe she wanted to use her partner's absence to check up on him. She was certainly aware that they had been spending a lot of time together. Even before she had introduced him to Gambia, when she and he had first become friends and spoke almost daily, he remembered how she used to pump him for information. Duchon doubted there was a single member of Biarritz's feline community who surpassed her in curiosity.

Whatever the reason, he thought, as he took another drink of the pungent, cloudy cocktail, the call couldn't have come at a better time. His wife had invited her sister from Pau to lunch, and the sister had brought a friend who was even more prone to gossip and inane chatter than she was, which was no mean accomplishment. He had held his tongue during lunch, which was not difficult, given the Babel-like atmosphere at the table. In those rare moments when one of the women remembered he was there and sought confirmation of an opinion, he had responded with a diplomatic "Indeed, you have a point, madame!" if the question came from one of his guests; or, an emphatic "There can be no doubt!" if it came from his wife. He had managed to take his leave without incident, while the three gourmands were passionately debating, between heaping forkfuls, the respective merits of their three, individually-chosen desserts. He smiled to himself as he pictured the scene: three fleshy faces attempting to argue and eat at the same time. The animated voiced of Janine Destin, like the unexpected report of a pistol, abruptly shattered this picture of prandial excess.

"My God, is that you, Jean-Claude! I can't believe it! Where have you been keeping yourself? I thought you had taken a trip or something. How long has it been? Christian, s'il vous plait," she waved to the barman, who was barely four feet away, "a Jack Daniels and Coke and I suppose Jean-Claude wants another of these disgusting pastis drinks. We must celebrate! There is nothing like running into an old friend." The pistol had become a machine gun.

Duchon looked bewildered. "But I thought we were supposed to meet…" She cut him off with another rapid burst of words.

"What are you trying to tell me, Jean-Claude? Don't feed me any of your nonsense, you old devil. You forget, I know how you are. Come, let's get away from these guys. They are worse than old maids with their talk of sports. Look, there's a table over in the corner all by itself. I want you to tell me everything you've been up to. And don't shake your head and pretend you've been doing nothing. Christian, will you please have a waiter deliver our drinks over there? And Christian, would you mind making mine a double? Running into Jean-Claude like this has made me feel a little reckless. And why not?"

Duchon followed Janine Destin to the other end of the large room, his mental state one of total consternation. He wondered if she had begun her drinking early and had somehow forgotten her invitation, though that was not like her at all. He had never known her to let her celebrated fondness for whiskey interfere with her work.

When they reached the corner table, Duchon pulled it back to allow Janine Destin to seat herself. She arranged herself on the banquette in a short ritual of feline movements, like a pampered cat settling into its favored upholstered chair. She was wearing black leather slacks, a low-cut black cashmere sweater cinched at the waist with a wide, gold-buckled Hermes belt and black suede spiked heels with a touch of gold trim. While she was checking her make-up in a small Chanel compact mirror, Duchon seized the rare moment of silence.

"Excuse me, Janine, but I thought you asked me to meet you here after lunch. When you called me earlier at home. Did I misunderstand you?"

"Of course not, silly. All that, back there, was just an act for old big ears, behind the bar."

"You mean Christian?"

"The biggest gossip in Biarritz. Anything you say in front of him, you may as well publish in the <u>Sud-Ouest</u>. In fact, you would do better to publish it in the paper; at least that way you could be sure half of it was reported correctly."

"What's wrong with our meeting together? Everyone knows…" With a raised hand, she stopped him in mid-sentence to allow the waiter to deliver their drinks without the possibility of eavesdropping.

"Jean-Claude, will you give me your word that you will keep everything I am about to tell you absolutely confidential? I assure you, it will be in your own best interests."

When she spoke, he made a conscious effort of keeping his eyes on hers, though occasionally he found himself staring at the deep, trembling chasm between her massive breasts. He had just caught himself in one of these lapses, but not before Janine had noticed.

"Jean-Claude, are you listening to me?"

"Of course, Janine. Absolutely confidential."

"And when I say confidential, that means Jojo as well. No, let me put it more bluntly: that means especially Jojo."

"Has he done something wrong, something to upset you?"

"You, of all people, should know the answer to that. Unless my information is inaccurate, I understand that you are still having problems because of that unnecessary business with Chantal's American friend. I believe you have been threatened by a relative of the boy?"

"His uncle. A real bastard. But he's about to be given a big lesson."

"So I have heard. But you'll forgive me if I seem to lack confidence in Jojo's new plan—after the brilliant way Carlos and his buddies handled the American kid. You and Jojo are just lucky that Jacky took over the investigation."

"Janine, I didn't want the kid dead. I just wanted him to get the hell out of town!"

"What, are you looking for forgiveness from me, Jean-Claude? If you had taken my advice and let the affair run its course—and a short one it would have been if you want my opinion—you wouldn't have anything to feel guilty about. And I wouldn't have some old former inspector from the Brigade Financière trying to use Jojo's macho stupidity to fuck with my business."

"You mean Claverie-LaPorte? Jojo said he was harmless. Anyway, hasn't he been put out to pasture?"

"Jojo is not always the greatest judge of people. I would have thought you would have noticed that by now, Jean-Claude. I know a fair amount about former Inspector Maurice Claverie-LaPorte. He's not a man to be taken lightly. He has given all of us more than a few headaches over the years. I don't suppose Jojo told you that the old inspector almost busted him about a year ago. Thank God I had a

<u>little</u> influence with one of his superiors, if you catch my meaning."
She startled Duchon by suddenly puffing out her chest and passing the splayed, crimson-tipped fingers of one hand slowly across it,
illustrating exactly the kind of influence she meant. She cast him a
coquettish look, then abruptly let out a loud snort of laughter. "You
can close your mouth now, Jean-Claude. I didn't mean to shock you.
Are you ready for another drink? I think you need one."

"Sure, Janine."

"Good. Because I certainly need another one."

She hailed their waiter and ordered two more drinks. "And tell
Christian to make this one a real double. I <u>can</u> tell the difference."

"Yes, madam. Thank-you madam."

"Now, where was I? Oh yes, our old friend Claverie-LaPorte. Let
me just say his early retirement came not a moment too soon for
some of us. He had set a clever little trap which Jojo fairly leapt into,
even though I had specifically warned him about it. I told him it was
a deal too good to be true. But his eminence, the Cardinal Richelieu
of crime, Monsieur Macho, he says "Don't worry, I know what I'm doing." The next thing he knows, the old inspector has him by the balls
and he's squeezing. I was tempted to take my losses and let Claverie-
LaPorte have the imbecile. But I knew the old fart wouldn't stop
there and I had one or two friends to think about who are in very sensitive positions, who have been very helpful in arranging certain legal
matters. I couldn't risk anything happening to them. And, I know
Jojo too well: I didn't spend five years putting up with his bullshit
for nothing. He talks big but underneath it all he's just a punk from
a little village in Corsica, who's only looking out for one thing: his
own dumb ass. He'd turn in his mother if it came down to the choice
of her or him doing time. Which, finally, is why I called you, Jean-
Claude. I'm worried. And, I guess I feel a little responsible for being
the one who introduced you to the brilliant M. Joseph Gambia."

"But what are you worried about, Janine? Jojo said he was going
to take care of the American uncle on Monday. I'm supposed to call
him and set up a meeting at his place. Jojo said he would deal with
the rest."

"It's the rest that I'm worried about, Jean-Claude. If we have another screw-up like the one a couple of weeks ago with the American kid, it could mean real trouble for Jojo."

"What do you mean, Janine? What kind of trouble? What can this American do without the diary? He can't go to the police on hearsay. And if he tries, LeClerc could certainly take care of that."

"Yes, he could. Provided he had a mind to."

"What is <u>that</u> supposed to mean, Janine, 'Provided he had a mind to'?" It was as if she had touched him with an electric prong, the way his heart jumped. The waiter arrived at that precise moment to deliver their drinks. His sudden, unseen arrival almost caused Duchon to knock over his glass.

"Excuse me, sir. I didn't mean to startle…"

Janine Destin cut the waiter off in mid-apology. "Well, let's see if Christian put any whiskey in this one." She tasted the drink. "Will wonders never cease, a real drink! Tell Christian he's improving with age."

"With pleasure, madam. Will that be all?"

"For the moment. But don't forget that we're here. Now, Jean-Claude, what was it you were just saying?"

Duchon waited until the waiter was out of earshot. "Please, Janine, what are you trying to do to me? I thought everything was arranged. That after Monday we could forget about this whole damned affair. Jojo said everything would be okay. Now you're telling me there's a problem with LeClerc. And that Jojo might be in trouble. Which means I might be in trouble. I can't believe it. I feel sick. I swear, Janine, I can't take much more of this. Not to mention Chantal! After all I've done for her!"

"Take it <u>easy</u>, Jean-Claude. If you keep on, you're going to give yourself a heart attack! Take a drink and try to calm yourself. There. Now listen carefully to what I am about to tell you. You are an old friend and I want to help you provided you want to help yourself. You <u>do</u> want to help yourself, Jean-Claude?"

"Of course, Janine. You know I do."

"Even if it means taking my side, if necessary, against Jojo?"

"Do you think that is going to be necessary, Janine? I mean, it could be dangerous for you."

"No, you mean it could be dangerous for you, if Jojo finds out. That's what you mean, is it not, Jean-Claude?"

"You know how Jojo is when he loses his temper. He does things without thinking. He's like a crazy man."

"Bravo, Jean-Claude! Bravo! I knew you would agree with us. I told Jacky not to worry. I told him you would appreciate what we were doing."

"I'm afraid I am missing something, Janine. Sorry."

"Not at all, Jean-Claude. On the contrary. You put your finger on why Jacky and I have run out of patience with Jojo. It is precisely as you said just now: He does things without thinking! This plan of dealing with the American uncle, or whoever he is, is a perfect example. It's not only stupid, it's very dangerous. Especially for you."

"How can it be dangerous for me, Janine? All I'm doing is making an appointment to meet him at his hotel. Jojo and the boys are doing the rest."

"Exactly. And what if the American does not scare easily? That is provided they don't screw up and kill him like they did the other one."

"That was an accident, Janine. Even LeClerc said so."

"For the papers he said so, Jean-Claude. Don't kid yourself. But that's history. Let's think about the present. What if this other American, the supposed uncle, decides to file a complaint after Jojo's boys pay their visit? Who do you think he's going to name? Think about it, Jean-Claude. Who's the only one he can name? Who set up the appointment?"

"Oh shit! I see what you mean. I am an imbecile, I didn't even think about that possibility. Jojo told me not to worry. What is he trying to do to me, Janine? I thought he was my friend. I'll be ruined. I'll lose my job. I'll lose Chantal. I'll lose everything!"

"I see, Jean-Claude, that you begin to appreciate the nature of our problem with Jojo."

"But what about Inspector LeClerc? Inspector LeClerc could deal with any complaint the American might try to file. Couldn't he, Janine? Or maybe I won't make the appointment. Then anything that happens happens. It has nothing to do with me. That's what I'll do, Janine. I just won't make the appointment! And if the American's not there when Jojo's boys arrive, I'll say he must not have wanted to see me. What could Jojo say to that?"

"Slow down, Jean-Claude, and listen to me. Are you listening to me?" He nodded his head. "First of all, let me make one thing perfectly clear: You <u>are</u> going to make the appointment with the American. Do you understand?"

He looked at her dumbfounded. Now he really didn't understand anything. He wondered if the whiskey was finally getting to her. As if reading his thoughts, she quickly continued with her explanation.

"No, Jean-Claude, I haven't lost my mind, if that is what the goofy expression on your face means. Nor am I trying to get you arrested. In fact, just the opposite. Remember what I said earlier about Jacky interceding if he had the desire to? Well let me assure you that in this case the desire is definitely there. So you need not worry about any complaints from the police. That is, if everything works according to plan. And I can see no reason why it shouldn't, unless someone gets cold feet."

Here she paused impressively and looked pointedly at him.

"You, you don't have to worry about me, Janine. I swear!"

"I didn't think so, Jean-Claude. As I was saying, if everything works according to plan, you will not only be rid of this meddlesome American and the old inspector, Claverie-LaPorte, but you will also stand a good chance of regaining Chantal's affection. You see I do have <u>all</u> of your best interests at heart. And I think you will agree that if anyone can help you with Chantal, it is certainly old 'Aunt Janine'."

"There's no question about that. In fact, I've been wanting to ask you to talk to her for me but I wasn't sure how you'd take it."

"Come, come Jean-Claude. We are old friends. Much older friends than you and Jojo I might add. You should have said something. What are friends for? Anyway, it's not necessary now. Within a week I bet you will be having your way again with that poor innocent creature. So you better rest up, you old dog, if you plan on keeping her happy. You know, Jean-Claude, we girls do like to be kept happy."

"I assure you, I have never had that problem, Janine, provided I had a partner who inspired me. You are not playing with me, are you? You really think Chantal will come back?"

"I guarantee it."

"Janine, you can't know how happy that would make me. I would do anything to get her back. My life has been unbearable since she left. Tell me exactly what it is you want me to do."

"That's more like it, Jean-Claude. A positive attitude. I knew I could count on you. In fact, I was so certain of it I even brought you a little present that you may find useful in the future, something every man should have. Call it a small token of appreciation for the help you are giving Jacky and me." She deftly produced a Hermes shopping bag from under the table and handed it to him. The weight of it surprised him. "I would prefer that you open my little package later if you don't mind, Jean-Claude. Things like this always embarrass me in public."

"I understand perfectly what you mean. I am that way myself. I do hope you realize, though, that this was completely unnecessary."

Janine Destin just smiled at him and signaled for the waiter.

CHAPTER EIGHTEEN

At ten minutes to seven, the precise moment that Maurice Claverie-LaPorte was entering the Café Royalty to wait for Chantal Clairac, Chief Inspector Jacques LeClerc was riding the elevator up to Janine Destin's penthouse apartment. Cradled confidently in the crook of his left arm was a gift-wrapped bottle of Jack Daniels Black Label whiskey. Janine had suggested they meet at her place to, as she put it, 'avoid any distractions'. LeClerc wasn't exactly sure what she meant by the phrase, but he felt certain, by the way she said it, by the slight inflection of her voice, that his luck with her was about to change. In fact, things were looking up on all fronts. Within the week, with any luck at all, he foresaw a tidy resolution to all of his problems involving Joseph Gambia and his bumbling Corsican crew, a resolution even that old pest, Claverie-LaPorte, would be likely to applaud. The door to Janine's apartment was slightly ajar. He opened it enough to crane his neck around the edge.

"Janine? Are you there?"

"Come in, Jacky, make yourself at home. I'll be with you in a minute. What are you doing arriving early, anyway? That's not like you."

"Oh, I didn't realize, Janine. I'm sorry."

"You almost found me in the shower!"

"Then I shall come earlier next time, Janine. Maybe I'll get lucky."

"You are a scoundrel, Jacky. What would Mme. LeClerc say if she heard you talk like that?"

"She wouldn't care, Janine. All she cares about is shopping and making sure she's the first in her group with the latest style of shoe, however idiotic it is. You should have seen the pair she brought home yesterday. Absolutely ridiculous. And six hundred francs to boot!"

"Maybe you should get a divorce. I'll make sure you don't get lonely."

He had walked out to the balcony and was admiring the view of the lighthouse and the Pointe St. Martin. He turned at the sound of her voice close behind him.

"I would if it wasn't for the repercussions it would have for my career…" He stopped in mid-sentence. Janine stood, barefoot, five or six feet away. She was wearing a knee-length, cream-colored silk robe, tied loosely at the waist. Her hair, still wet, was combed straight back from her forehead. She spread her arms wide, palms up, in a gesture meant to illustrate her predicament. LeClerc could clearly see the outline of her large nipples through the thin, silky material.

"You see, I haven't even had time to dress. What are you doing with your coat and tie still on? I thought I told you to make yourself at home. Perhaps I forgot in my excitement." She stepped up and kissed him quickly on the mouth before he could say anything. "I'll be right back. I think a little celebration is in order."

She returned several minutes later with an ice bucket, a sweating bottle of Mumms and two crystal champagne flutes.

"Will you do the honors, Jacky?"

"With pleasure. What's the occasion?"

"To launch our new partnership. They use champagne to launch ships, don't they? I thought about breaking the bottle over your hard head but decided that would just be a waste of good wine and probably wouldn't teach you anything anyway."

"You are most likely right about that. If all the cracks on the skull I received in rugby didn't teach me anything, I doubt a little tap with a bottle will do any good. But still, that wasn't a very nice thing to say to your new partner. And who knows what else?"

"Listen to you! Already looking to take advantage of my female weakness."

"Janine, I can think of many words to describe you, but 'weak' is certainly not one of them. 'Sexy,' yes. 'Provocative,' absolutely, especially this evening. But 'weak'," he paused to let the pop of the champagne cork provide the exclamation point, "never! Whoops." The champagne had bubbled over and a thick stream of foam ran down the neck. "What did you do, Janine, shake up the bottle in the kitchen?"

"Of course not, Jacky. You must have gotten the bottle excited with all that talk, trying to put ideas into my head." Her raspy voice exploded in raucous laughter. She raised her glass. "Here's wishing that imbecile Jojo a bon voyage. And may the trip be a long one.

"So, Jacky, have you worked out all the details—or should I say 'travel arrangements'?" She burst into a fresh peal of laughter at her own cleverness. "It's a shame we can't send him into space like the Russians used to do with their monkeys. He'd fit right in. Just picture it, Jacky: the expression on that big dumb mug of his, peering out from one of the space suits with all the tubes, waiting for us to push the button. God, that would be good!"

LeClerc had been grinning smugly at Janine's performance. He took her extreme good humor as another positive sign of things to come.

"I'm not sure I've ever seen you in such good spirits, Janine."

"Well Jacky, unless I am very much mistaken about the future, you had better get used to it. Hell, we haven't even begun to have fun." She reached over and pulled his head down to hers. She fastened her mouth on his for several seconds. The movement caused the belt of her robe to loosen, revealing an enormous, surprisingly firm breast. Before LeClerc could follow-up on her overture, she had settled back into the opposite corner of the couch and was deliberately re-arranging her robe. "But I'm getting carried away—first things first. What exactly is the plan, Jacky?"

"Janine, you are going to be the death of me, you know?"

"There are worse ways to go, my dear."

"I certainly won't argue with that. But I would hate to die from anticipation."

"In that case, you'd already be dead." Again she let out a snort of laughter. "I'm sorry, Jacky, I don't know what's come over me. Please, if you'll refill my glass, I promise to sit here quietly and listen to what you've planned for dear Jojo."

"You promise?"

"I promise. I swear."

"Okay, here's what I see happening…"

The trap he had set for Gambia was wonderfully simple, as he proudly pointed out to Janine Destin. And the real beauty was that their partner could not possibly recognize it for what it was, since it was triggered by actions of his own devising. What Inspector LeClerc did not point out to his smiling companion, lounging suggestively at the other end of the couch, was how his plan would almost certainly resolve another, strictly personal problem that had bedeviled him for months. Consistent with the thorniest problems, it was, even he had to admit, entirely of his own making.

"And so, more or less, that's the plan, Janine. By this time Monday, Jojo should be well on his way to self-destruction. What do you think?"

"Bravo, Jacky, bravo! I think it is brilliant. Of course, I would have expected no less from you."

She extended her hand to him. "If you'll help me up, I'll see if I can find another bottle of champagne."

He pulled her close and kissed her hard on the mouth. His right hand moved under the silky material of her short wrap, quickly and expertly finding a nipple. It instantly hardened to his touch.

"Oh Jacky, not now! Let's wait until this whole thing is over. It will be so much better then."

"But it feels so good, Janine. Doesn't it?" He continued to massage her nipple. He began kissing the back of her neck.

"It feels great, Jacky. It feels just like I always thought it would. But please, let's wait. I promise you, it will be even better."

She pulled back from him and, as she did so, her robe fell open, revealing a moist pink gash between large, light-brown lips. While LeClerc had been outlining his plan for Gambia, Janine had been secretly touching herself. When LeClerc saw the glistening, clean-shaven place between her legs, he literally fell to his knees. His crotch riding her dangling left foot like a small saddle, he began running his tongue between the slightly parted, wet lips.

"Jacky, what are you doing? Oh Jacky! Easy, easy, oh yes, now you've found it. Easy, easy."

She was holding his head by the ears and was trying to guide him, but it was too late. He was rubbing himself furiously against her foot and ankle. Within two minutes he had come. He groaned then went limp, resting his large head between her sweating thighs. It was only after the telltale wetness had soaked through his underwear and thin trousers onto her foot that Janine Destin spoke.

"Jacky, please, you are crushing my leg."

He raised his head and awkwardly rolled to one side. "I'm sorry, Janine." He looked up and noticed for the first time a small tattoo directly above her clitoris. The image was chilling: a small blood-stained dagger with a handle in the shape of a rose.

.

CHAPTER NINETEEN

P eter Ellis and Anya arrived in Biarritz shortly after sunset. He
parked on the rue Million next to his apartment building.
As soon as he had brought the car to a stop, he felt the wind,
heard it above the sound of the idling engine. He reached for Anya's
hand.

"Come, let me show you something. But be careful when you
open the door. The wind can be dangerous here."

"I noticed. Is it always like this?"

"Just about. In fact, in my experience, this part of the rue Million
is arguably the windiest spot in Biarritz, with the possible exception
of the walkway out to the Rocher de la Vierge. If you like, we can go
there before dinner and you can judge for yourself."

"We'll see, Peter. I may just take your word for it. But didn't you
just promise to show me something here?"

"And so I shall."

Leaning slightly into the wind, they crossed the rue de La
Perspective and stopped by the short cement-and-stone fence bordering the cliffside park. Spread out before them was the southeastern
elbow of the Bay of Biscay and the mountainous expanse of the
Spanish Basque coast. In the sky, an afterglow of dull orange melted
into an ever-darkening ink wash of green and purple.

"I see what you mean about the most spectacular view in Biarritz.
It is truly breath-taking."

"Yes it is, Anya. Unfortunately, it has recently proven to be breathtaking in a quite literal sense: Just below here is where the Duffy boy fell to his death."

"I'm so sorry, Peter. I should have known."

"How could you have?"

"From what you said at Olga's yesterday. You said it happened right in front of your apartment."

"Well, even if I did, there was no way for you to know it happened right here. Anyway, it is I who should apologize for mentioning it in the first place. Now is no time to talk about death. Tonight we celebrate life."

He put his arm around her shoulders and pulled her close. He kissed her lightly on the temple. They stood silently for several minutes, watching as darkness gradually enveloped the wind-whipped ocean.

"Come, Anya. Let's have a drink in the hotel before we go up to change. I'll introduce you to my second family."

Arlette was behind the reception desk at the back of the dining room. She motioned for them to walk back. Peter Ellis introduced Anya to her and the two women exchanged greetings.

"You have arrived at the perfect moment, Pierre. I was just now preparing to leave you a message."

"Oh yes?"

"A man just telephoned for you, a strange man I think. He would not leave his name; he said you would know who it was."

"What did he want?"

"He said he had decided to accept your offer. He said he would be here Monday morning at eleven o'clock."

"Excellent! Did he say anything else?"

"He said to be sure to tell you that he would only speak with you alone. That if anyone else was here, he would leave immediately. Then he asked for the number of your apartment."

"And did you give it to him?"

"Of course not, Pierre! You know me better than that, I hope. I said for him to call back tomorrow and that I never gave out room numbers without the permission of the guest. I fear I was not very polite with him. I found his tone of voice extremely rude."

"I have no doubt but that it was. It is the kind of man he is. In fact, 'rude' is probably too charitable a word for him. But I am surprised, Arlette, that you did not recognize his voice. The man is someone you know. That may be why he didn't want to leave his name."

"You're kidding. Who is he?"

"Your favorite food salesman, Jean-Claude Duchon."

"I don't believe it! Are you sure?"

"Unless I am very much mistaken."

"Well, it has been some time since I have spoken with him. Still, I am surprised I didn't recognize his voice. It is somewhat distinctive. So, I may give him your apartment number when he calls back?"

"By all means. And you may tell him that I look forward to our meeting."

"Anything else, Pierre?"

"No, except to ask if you will join Anya and me for a drink?"

"You are very kind, Pierre, but I don't really have time. I have a large party arriving early to celebrate a birthday."

"Come, Arlette, you have time for a small glass. You work too much."

"Very well. But it will have to be a small one."

"Excellent! Anya, what will you have?"

After a pleasant interlude of small talk and drinks, Peter showed Anya up to his apartment. While she was showering, he telephoned Maurice and told him about the message from Duchon.

"So, my friend, it looks like our fish has risen to the bait."

"That appears to be the case. However, there is one thing that bothers me, Maurice."

"Which is?"

"His message was extremely vague. It gave no indication what he intends to do. It merely says to meet him here, alone, at eleven on Monday. He makes a point to insist that I be alone."

"Does that worry you? Do you think he is setting some kind of trap?"

"Are you kidding, Maurice? Worried about Duchon? And if he were planning something, why advertise it? It would be stupid."

"That is true. So what is bothering you, Pierre?"

"I don't know. I just have a funny feeling about it."

"Well, don't let it spoil your weekend with your new Dutch friend."

"Don't worry. There is no chance of that."

"Good. I am glad to hear it. And where are you taking her for that important first dinner?"

"I thought we might go to Albert's. Why don't you join us? She is eager to meet you."

"Eager to meet me? What lies have you been telling her?"

"Nothing but the truth, Maurice. Why don't you come? It would give me pleasure as well."

"Thank-you, Pierre. You are very kind but I already have dinner plans this evening. Perhaps we can meet for coffee in the morning. Not too early, you understand? Say about ten o'clock? At La Chope?"

"Perfect. We'll see you there at ten."

"Tell your friend, Anya, I look forward to meeting her."

"I'll tell her as soon as she gets out of the shower. A demain, Maurice. Sleep well."

He placed the handset in the cradle.

"And just what will you tell her as soon as she gets out of the shower?" Anya was leaning against the bathroom doorjamb combing out her damp blond hair, a bath towel wrapped around her.

"That Maurice regrets that he can not join us for dinner this evening, but that he looks forward to meeting you tomorrow morning for coffee. I took the liberty of accepting on your behalf. I hope you don't mind."

"Of course I don't mind, provided it's not too early. I refuse to get up early when I am on holiday, unless it's absolutely necessary."

"We agreed to meet at ten in Chambre d'Amour. There's a wonderful little café there called La Chope. I think you'll like it."

"If you say so, Peter, I feel sure I will, after what you've shown me this afternoon. I don't imagine you have a hair dryer. I left mine at Olga's."

"I'm afraid I have very little need of that particular appliance. I can call down to the desk and ask if they can locate one for you."

"That's not necessary, Peter. My hair should be almost dry by the time we go out. We aren't leaving immediately, are we?"

"No. I thought maybe in about half an hour. Longer if you wish."

"Good" She stopped combing her hair and walked over to where he was standing. She reached up and put her arms around his neck, looking directly into his eyes and smiled. It was one of the loveliest, most purely provocative smiles he had ever seen. "That should give us just enough time to get ready."

She pulled his fact down to hers. She ran her tongue gently over his lips and kissed him, softly at first, then passionately, pressing her lips tightly against his. She stepped back and began to unbutton his shirt. He made to unbuckle his belt but she stopped him with her hand.

"Please, Peter, let me do it all. It has been so long since I have felt like this."

After she undressed him she unfastened the towel and let it drop to her feet. Her body was still warm and slightly damp from the shower. She ran her fingers lightly over him, her touch feathery. He wet the tips of his forefinger and thumb and gently squeezed her erect nipples. When they embraced it was with such force and abandon that Peter Ellis felt a shiver run through her body into his, like a small electric charge. They stood holding each other until they were both wet with a pungent blend of perspiration and passion. She interlaced her fingers in his and led him to the bedroom.

In bed, touching her, Peter Ellis had the impression of silk dipped in aromatic oil. He worked himself into her slowly, penetrating a fraction deeper with each successive movement. When he was totally inside her, he felt inner muscles fasten around him. He pressed his hips hard against hers, holding her tight and motionless, trying to make the moment last. The tension was almost unbearable.

ACCIDENTAL DEATH IN BIARRITZ

Then he felt her grip suddenly tighten and release, felt her soft, shuddering liquid surrender. It rendered any further attempt at discipline futile.

When his heart finally stopped racing, he carefully propped himself up on his forearms and studied Anya's face. Her eyes were closed and her glistening skin was flushed with the pink afterglow of sexual contentment. After several seconds, she opened her eyes and looked up at him, the look so direct that he wondered briefly if anything might be wrong. Then she did something he was totally unprepared for: she smiled. It was a smile he instantly knew he would never, could never forget. It was a smile both open and enigmatic, serious and playful, radiant and knowing. It was a smile that articulated everything wonderful and ineffable about the experience they had just shared.

They arrived at Albert's restaurant a little after eight-thirty. Peter Ellis asked for and received an isolated table in the back corner. He wasn't expecting to see Gambia or any of his associates but, like Maurice, he was a firm believer in discretion in public places. He never ceased to be amazed at how often, even in Paris, he overheard conversations about people he knew. Once, he had even heard the female occupant of an adjoining table deliver a self-described first-hand account of a philandering episode in which he had a starring role. That night, as he was leaving the restaurant, he thanked the concerned party for the publicity. Tonight, in addition to choosing an isolated table, he took the added precaution of briefing Anya on the fictional persona he had created for Gambia's benefit.

"And who am I to play in this charade, my love? I am too old to be a call girl, though that sounds like an appropriate mate for this handsome scoundrel, Monsieur Edwards." She grinned mischievously at him.

"Oh, I don't know. Perhaps Monsieur Edwards prefers mature companions."

"So your Monsieur Edwards has brains in addition to good looks."

"The two have been known to co-exist in some members of my sex, though I'll grant you it seems to be a rarity. Ah, what have we here?"

The maitre d' had reappeared with a half bottle of Veuve Cliquot that Peter Ellis had secretly ordered on their arrival. "Please don't tell me that you dislike champagne, Anya."

"Au contraire, monsieur. It is one of my great weaknesses. I have been known to drink an entire bottle by myself. All my friends in Amsterdam kid me about it. They have seen me do some pretty wild things after I've had a bit too much."

"Such as?"

"I'm afraid you will have to ask them. Or perhaps I shall tell you when I've had more to drink. Right now it would embarrass me too much to tell you."

"That bad, huh?"

"Not really bad. Just very childish."

"Then I totally approve."

After filling their glasses and waiting for their approval of the sparkling wine, the maitre d' explained the specials of the day and asked if they had any questions about the menu. In his explanation and answers, he was honest and informative and did not affect the air of condescension and superior tone of many in his profession. He returned five minutes later to take their order. After confirming what he had scribbled on his pad, he smiled warmly, gave a slight bow and wished them an enjoyable meal. When he was gone, Peter Ellis reached across the table and lightly squeezed Anya's left hand.

"Anya, I realize this is probably none of my business, but how is it that you are not attached? I am certain it is not for lack of suitors."

"How do you know that I am not?"

"I'm sorry, Anya, I just assumed it from some things you said in Sauveterre. And then after what happened earlier, I guess I jumped to the conclusion that you were not with anyone. I apologize."

"No, Peter, it is I who needs to apologize. That last remark was uncalled for. It was not a nice thing to say, particularly to someone who has been so wonderful to me."

"The pleasure has been equally mine. And I am not only speaking of the lovely thing we just shared at the apartment. There are no words to do that justice."

"Yes, I know what you mean. I must confess, though, that I have been thinking about making love with you all afternoon. I felt sure we would be good together, but I had no idea it would be so perfect. I actually find myself a little frightened."

"Why is that?"

"I have a small confession to make, Peter."

"Don't tell me you are engaged."

She laughed and reached for his hand. "No, my love, nothing like that. In fact, quite the opposite. You see, after you left Olga's the other day, when we had made our date for Sauveterre, I did some investigating of my own."

"And you still agreed to see me?"

"It was a close call. After what Olga said about you, I thought you were too good to be true. Which is not to say she thinks you are perfect. But I'll tell you something Peter, which I think you already know: if you have a bigger fan than Olga, then you are truly a lucky man. She cares for you very much."

"Yes, I know. And I can assure you the feeling is mutual. I sometimes feel guilty that I have not done enough for her since Roger's death."

"Well that's certainly not the impression she gave me. In fact, it was she who was concerned that she had let you down."

"So, she told you about Burke."

"She said she had never heard you sound so depressed."

"It is true, Anya. I can't remember ever being so down. I was very much in love with her."

"You don't think there is any chance that you will be together again. I know it is impertinent for me to ask you such things. I guess I am feeling a bit vulnerable all of a sudden. If you don't want to talk about it, though, I certainly understand."

"No, it's alright Anya. I think it might be a good thing to talk about it. Of course, I may be asking you a few personal things as well."

"Which I shall answer as truthfully as I can, beginning with your first question just now about being unattached: Up until this past December, I was living with someone, a self-proclaimed poet named Joost. I spent almost five years with him."

"Why do you say 'self-proclaimed'?"

"I realize it sounds very cold but it's true. At first I was taken in by the image of the struggling, tortured writer whose inner pain no one can understand. I have since learned that, with him, many people are so taken in at first, especially young women. I think that now, he actually is tortured, but it is by his own behavior, his lying both to himself and to others."

"How did you meet him?"

"A friend of mine brought him to the opening of my first show in a real gallery. She thought we would be perfect together, both artists, both sensitive, I'm sure you've heard the same thing yourself."

"I guess we all have, Anya, and the results are usually dismal."

"Well, he said all the right things about my pictures. He was just critical enough to imply I was good but still had a long way to go before I could call myself a real artist. Knowing what I know now, it was a textbook example of his style of manipulation. He asked if I might be interested in illustrating a book of erotic poems he was working on. Don't laugh, Peter, I know that proposal, if nothing else, should have made me suspicious."

She paused for a sip of champagne. For several moments she seemed lost in a place very far away. She took another quick drink and continued.

"After what I've said, you must be wondering why I fell for him. I must say, in my own defense, that I did have my initial doubts. But Joost is nothing if not charming. And, at least initially, he was very amusing. He made me laugh a lot which, at the time, given the situation at the bank, counted for more than you might guess. Nor will I pretend that I was not affected by his looks. He is still considered a handsome man, even though his life for the last couple of years has been spent primarily in bars. When I met him, he had just returned from six months in Greece. In contrast to the pasty-white faces around me, his body was almost god-like. Within two weeks he was living with me. At first, everything was great, or seemed great. Constant sex has that effect I have found."

"Yes, it certainly does. I think that whoever said masturbation will make you blind only got it half right. So, what happened, Anya?"

Before she could answer, the waiter arrived with the raw oysters Peter Ellis had ordered as an appetizer. They were carefully arranged on a conical silver rack above a mound of crushed ice and bright yellow lemon wedges. The waiter then produced a tall green Muscadet bottle for their inspection. After a nod of approval for the sample taste he had poured, he filled their glasses with the pale, straw-colored wine. After receiving their assurance that everything was satisfactory, he wished them a smiling 'bon appétit' and disappeared.

"These look fantastic, Peter!"

"They are beautiful, aren't they? They come from the island of Oleron across from La Rochelle. They're called 'verts' because of the green tint around the edges. They tend to be very salty. What do you think?"

"Oh Peter, they're delicious."

"They are my favorites. Perhaps one day, before you go back, after I have completed this business with Gambia, I can show you where they come from. I have a good friend who has a restaurant in St. Pierre d'Oleron. It's a charming little town. We'll surprise him with a visit."

"I'd love that."

While they sipped the crisp, fragrant dry wine and relished each succulent, salty morsel, Peter Ellis spoke a little of Oleron and the village of St. Pierre. He added a short history of his friendship with Etienne. He decided not to press her to finish her account of the relationship with Joost. However, as soon as they had finished and she had declared the oysters to be the best she could ever remember eating, she abruptly continued.

"If you don't mind, Peter, I shall finish my depressing little tale of the smart girl who wasn't so smart."

"If you are sure you want to, Anya."

"I am sure, Peter. I want you to know the whole story. I want you to know just how foolish the woman to whom you have paid so many compliments today can be."

"Aren't you being a little hard on yourself?"

"Listen, then you be the judge."

"I am sure I shall be a more merciful one than the storyteller."

"We'll see. Now, as I mentioned earlier, within a couple of weeks, Joost had moved in with me. Since his return from Greece, he had been staying with friends. One night, after we had had a great deal of champagne, (he had quickly discovered my one big alcoholic weakness), he wondered aloud whether it wouldn't make sense to pool our resources and live together. I found out much later that his friends had, the day before, given him a week to find another place to live. It seems they were tired of his helping himself to their beer and food.

"At first, the fact that he contributed almost nothing to our living expenses did not really bother me. I have never been overly concerned about money, and I had just been promoted. Also, I had begun to sell a painting here and there. Initially, Joost was very happy for me when I sold something. But before long, he began to take my modest success as a personal attack. He would say things like that I should feel lucky to be working in a medium that was so commercial, that poets did not practice their art for monetary gain. Of course, it did not occur to him that he might do something else to make money and still write poetry."

She stopped to take a long, slow sip of wine. Peter Ellis could see that her recollection had suddenly opened the floodgates to a turbulent flow of pent-up frustrations.

"I am sorry, Peter. I did not realize how very angry I still am, both at him and at myself."

"You can store up a great deal in five years, Anya. Are you familiar with Robert Graves?"

"Isn't he a writer, a writer of travel books?"

"Yes, among other things. He is also a celebrated poet. He was once asked why, given the commercial success of his travel books, he continued to write poetry since it had never made him any money. His reply was that, while there might be no money in poetry, there was certainly no poetry in money. In other words, if you choose to write poetry, you should be under no illusions about making a living doing it. Your friend sounds like he may have been writing for all the wrong reasons. The only reason you should do it is for yourself. I don't think your friend understood this fact. I'm sorry Anya, I know I'm rambling. But you have touched on a topic close to my heart. After hearing about your friend, I wasn't going to tell you this for fear of scaring you away. Since you are sure to find out before long, I might as well tell you now that I, too, occasionally attempt to write verse. It is not something I publicize. In fact, I don't even write under my own name."

"Yes, I know. You use an old family name. I also understand that you are very good."

"So Olga told you everything?"

"She wanted very much for me to like you. She was actually very funny, almost like a mother. I finally had to tell her that she had nothing to worry about."

"You did? When?"

"Last night. I don't know why. I surprised myself when I said it. I just had this feeling." She laughed and flashed him an impish smile. "I decided to risk it."

"Well, I'm certainly glad you did."

"So am I. Now, let me finish my story, that is if you still want to hear it."

"If you're sure it's not going to upset you. This day has been too perfect to spoil with an unpleasant ending."

"It's alright, Peter. I feel much better now. I'll try to make it short. Where was I?"

"You began selling some paintings and Joost couldn't handle your success."

"Ah yes. Well, at the time, that seemed to be the beginning of our trouble. I now realize that there had been many more small problems that I had chosen to ignore. As I said earlier, he could be very charming. He seemed to have a sixth sense when something was beginning to upset me. Inevitably, he would show up at home with a present or take me out for a surprise dinner. It was strange. He always seemed to have money when he needed it then. I am still not sure where it came from, though I have my suspicions.

"You may wonder how I could have stayed with him for so long and I confess I don't have a good answer even now. I guess Joost, for all of his faults, represented a kind of security. And, as I said, he could be very amusing. Until the very end, he could almost always make me laugh.

"For at least the last year we were together, I knew that whatever we had was gone, that I could never be happy with him. But, as you know, change takes effort. Between the bank and my painting, I just didn't have the energy, for I knew he wouldn't go without a fight. It is possible that I would still be with him if he had not begun seeing other women and lying about it. I found out at a bank party before Christmas last year.

"As so often happens, it occurred totally by chance. Another woman at the bank, a young secretary from a different department was talking to an adjacent group about this great-looking poet she had recently met. Normally, I wouldn't have paid attention, since Amsterdam is full of young men who call themselves poets. But, when she mentioned the little bar where she had first seen him, my heart stopped. It was one of Joost's favorite haunts, a dingy little basement bar at the entrance to the red light district. The owner is a former prostitute with artistic pretentions, who prides herself on her down-at-the-heels, bohemian clientele. The bar is also one of the preferred places for the district's working girls to take their breaks and trade war stories. I went there with Joost several times during our first months together. I tried to like it for his sake, tried to appreciate what he called 'the inferno of lost souls' that made up the habitués. But finally, I had to admit that I found the place simply distasteful. If

189

he wanted to go there on his own, I had no objections. Anyway, when I was able to get this young secretary alone, I mentioned, in an off-hand way, that I had overheard a bit of her conversation and said that I used to frequent the bar in question. I innocently asked if she had run into an old friend of mine, an amusing character named Joost. I added that he, too, was a poet.

"Well, Peter, you should have seen the expression on the young girl's face. After giving a little yelp, like an excited puppy, she began telling me all about their affair. It seems he referred to me as an older woman who couldn't understand his passion for poetry, but who paid the bills in return for the occasional 'mercy fuck'. The little fool laughed when she repeated the expression, saying they were Joost's exact words and wasn't he so cute and naughty. I forced myself to listen for several more excruciating minutes, then pretended I had just seen a colleague arrive with whom I needed to speak. I made her promise to give Joost my regards and wished her good luck."

"God, Anya, what did you do?"

"I left the party almost immediately, blaming a sudden headache, not an entirely untrue excuse. As soon as I reached my apartment, I called an all-night locksmith. By the time he had changed all the locks, I had packed-up all of Joost's clothes and personal items. I left them all in a pile on the landing with a note suggesting he call the young secretary—I forget her name now—and see if she thought his poetry deserving enough for free room and board. I realize the note was somewhat childish and I don't blame you for finding it amusing. In retrospect, I find it funny myself. But you must realize that, at the time, I was blind with anger, much of it directed at myself for being so damned stupid. I still cannot believe it took me so long to kick him out!"

"Anya, I understand exactly how you felt. I doubt there are many of us who, by the age of twenty-five, have not had a similar experi-ence. And I was not smiling because I thought your behavior adoles-cent; I was smiling at the thought of your friend arriving home, no doubt a bit drunk, and finding his things on the landing. I think I have discovered a woman after my own heart. Cheers!" He touched his glass to hers and drank. "So what happened? It must have been a wonderful scene."

She smiled sheepishly and started shaking her head. "Not so wonderful really. I think 'pathetic' would be a more appropriate word to describe it."

"I'm sorry, Anya. I don't mean to make light of your story. It's just that, after hearing your description of Joost, I can't help but imagine his shock, maybe I should say disbelief, at finding his things in a pile and the locks changed."

"Yes, I must say that it did take some time for it to sink in, for him to understand it was not a joke. When he finally realized I was serious about not letting him back in, he went berserk. He started screaming obscenities at me, calling me a 'capitalistic bitch' and other worse things, saying my art was just so much shit, that it had no soul because I had no soul. When he started trying to break down the door, I called the police. Before they escorted him away, I told him that if he ever bothered me again I would file harassment charges. Thank God that has not been necessary."

"And you haven't heard from him since?"

"Not a word. I dare say he took his hard-luck story to that little secretary and convinced her to take him in. I actually thought about calling her department to find out if that is what happened. I guess I was thinking about warning her. But then I realized she would think that anything I said was just sour grapes."

"Well Anya, you can be sure that any story Joost told her was carefully embellished in his favor. And we both know that, however unfortunate, some lessons can only be learned through experience. Speaking of which, I believe you are about to experience one of the great delicacies of the region."

The large, milky-orange salmon steaks that the waiter placed in front of them were grilled to perfection, the outside slightly crispy, the inside flesh flaky, tender and moist. The warm Beàrnaise sauce had a velvety texture and just the right amount of tarragon. The accompanying vegetables were a classic match: finely-cut green beans and boiled baby potatoes, exquisite with the rich sauce. Peter

Ellis had decided to splurge on wine and had ordered a 1978 Cos d'Estournel to accompany the salmon. He had asked the waiter to decant it right away so that it might have time to open up. He now raised his glass and, holding it toward the candlelight, studied the deep ruby clarity of the wine.

"The color, it's extraordinary don't you think, Anya?"

"I don't think I've ever seen anything quite like it."

"What should we toast?"

"Well, after the day we have had, perhaps we should drink to the glories of France."

"To the glories of France, then!" They touched glasses. "So, what do you think of the wine?"

"I believe it might just be the most wonderful wine I have ever tasted. It's even better than any champagne I have ever had. And it's absolutely perfect with the salmon. Once again, you have introduced me to something new and exquisite. Just like Sauveterre."

"Strangely enough, Anya, it was in Sauveterre where I myself first had this wine with salmon. It was at La Grange de Guinarthe, the auberge I mentioned earlier. It was in the early seventies. The owner was a great <u>amateur</u> of wine and had assembled quite an extraordinary cellar. Today, the collection would be worth a small fortune. One night, on his recommendation, I chose a 1964 Cos d'Estournel to accompany his version of this same dish. I have never forgotten that meal."

"Nor shall I forget this one. If you spoil all your women like this, I'm surprised you don't have a harem."

"I only spoil the ones that deserve it."

"Well I'm not so sure I deserve it, but I appreciate it more than you can know. You have made me feel very special."

"Which is exactly what you are. I was beginning to wonder if I could ever feel like this with anyone again. So perfectly content and excited at the same time. So alive and so wanting to be alive. I realize I'm not explaining all this very well, but I have a feeling you know what I mean."

"Yes, Peter, I know exactly what you mean. I feel exactly the same way." She reached across the table and squeezed his hand. "It's so wonderful, it's frightening."

"How do you mean?"

"Please, don't be angry with me for saying this. It's probably something I shouldn't say, especially tonight."

"What is it? Have I said or done something I shouldn't have?"

"No, not at all. It's nothing like that. It's just that I feel myself becoming so close to you so fast. I guess I'm feeling a little vulnerable. Olga told me how close you were to your friend Burke and how devastated you were when she left. I can't imagine why she left you. But I can imagine her realizing what she had and deciding to come back. And if that happened, I really couldn't blame you for getting back together with her. As much as I want to be with you, I don't want to put myself in that position. Can you understand that, Peter?"

"Yes, I understand perfectly. I would be lying if I said it is something I have not thought about myself. I'm not really sure <u>what</u> I would do if she were to walk into the restaurant right now, except perhaps crawl under the table."

"A suitable male response."

"Exactly."

"At least I'm with a man who knows his own sex, so to speak."

"I try, Anya. 'Know thyself' and all that. But seriously, I don't think that's a dilemma I shall be facing. Burke made it very clear when she left that I should not wait for her. I did not want to believe her, of course. Call it pride or arrogance, but I really thought she would change her mind after a month or so. Even though I guess I knew, somewhere deep down, that she wouldn't. Or couldn't. If you knew her, you would understand. You, especially, would understand."

"Would it be entirely inappropriate and rude to ask you to tell me about her, about what happened? If you don't want to talk about it, I'll certainly understand."

"No, I don't mind at all. In fact, I would like to tell you the whole story. I'll be as objective as I can, which might not be all that objective, given how I feel. But I'll try."

By the time Peter Ellis finished telling Anya about his and Burke's time together, the salmon had been eaten, the wine drunk, the plates cleared and espresso and dessert ordered.

"After all you've told me, Peter, I really don't understand why she left. If her only complaint was the dangerous nature of your work and if you really did offer to change the type of reporting that you did, then I fail to see why she left. Unless there was another reason you don't want to talk about."

"There was another reason, but I don't mind talking about it. Maybe your female perspective and sensibility can help <u>me</u> understand it."

"Don't count on <u>that</u>, my dear. But I'll certainly listen and tell you what I think."

"Understand, Anya, that it's just my opinion. It is not something Burke said, though I think she wanted to. I think she was afraid it would hurt my feelings. And it probably would have. But it would have been better than this forced silence. It's not being able to talk with her, to hear from her, to communicate in some way with her that really hurts. It was the only request she made when she left: not to attempt to contact her until she contacted me. She said it would be easier for her that way. She said she understood it would be painful for both of us, but that staying in touch, long-distance, would only prolong the pain. I must say that I disagreed with her then and I disagree with her now."

"Understandably, Peter. I think I would have as well. What did she say in response to your disagreement?"

"She said it was something she wasn't able to explain. And even if she could, it was probably something I couldn't understand anyway. To use her words, I 'just wouldn't get it'."

"That seems a little unfair."

"I certainly thought so at the time, even though I knew it was just her way of saying she was not ready to settle down with me. Which was something I already knew but kept trying to deny."

"So that was the real reason she left. She was not ready to settle down with you."

"That's what I think, though she repeatedly denied it. She said it was a question of proving herself professionally. It was something she had to do by herself. And it was something she had to do in New York City. Like the Sinatra song: "If I can make it there, I can make it anywhere". In fact, she even sang part of the song to try to make me smile. I told her I never had agreed with those lyrics, no matter how many times Old Blue Eyes crooned to the contrary. So, in the end, I wished her luck, told her I loved her and would miss her very much and expressed the hope that she would change her mind, at least about communicating. As you can see, she has not."

"Well, Mr. Ellis, from this particular female perspective, it sounds like you loved this Burke woman very much."

"I can not deny it."

"And continue to love her very much."

"Again, guilty as charged, though not in the same way. Something has changed and…" Anya had started to say something. Peter Ellis raised his hand, palm out, and signaled for her to wait. "I think I know what you are about to say, Anya. Please let me finish. Then, if I am wrong, you can have your say. Okay?"

"Since I have no choice in the matter, I shall agree. But I won't promise to keep your punishment limited to words. Something physical may be called for."

"Fair enough." He paused for several seconds. "Let me explain what I meant when I said something had changed. It has nothing to do with meeting you, though it certainly has a bearing on how I reacted to you. When I said something had changed, I meant that I have come to the painfully slow realization that Burke did not love me in the same way that I loved her. I know she cared about me a great deal. But caring about someone, however strongly, and loving someone are two distinctly different feelings. With love, you have no choice in the matter. It is all-consuming. It will not take 'no' for an answer. You can choose to care about somebody or you can choose not to. Love leaves no possibility of choice. It chooses you. Am I making any kind of sense, Anya?"

"The most wonderful kind in the world. And the most frightening."

"Yes, that's the rub. Love does not guarantee reciprocation. In fact, I would have to say that the odds are stacked pretty heavily against it. Which can lead to behavior of the most hideously irrational kind. The classic example, to my mind, is the murder of the loved one by the one spurned followed by his or her suicide."

Anya had caught Peter Ellis's eye and caused him to pause and look around. The waiter was standing just behind him holding a laden tray.

"Excuse me, monsieur, your dessert and espresso. Will there be anything else?"

"No, merci. Just the check."

"Very good, monsieur. It has been a pleasure serving monsieur and mademoiselle. Bonne soirée!" He bowed slightly and left as quietly as he had come.

"I'm sorry to have gotten on such a tangent, Anya. I guess what I have been trying to say is that I have known for some time now that things were over between me and Burke. I did not want to admit it. I kept waiting for the phone to ring, even though I knew, deep down in that ruthless place where we truly know things, that it wouldn't ring. Or that if it did, it would be to say that she had found somebody else."

"You don't think she ever really loved you?"

"I believe she tried to love me. I think she tried very hard. You must understand there was a tremendous amount of affection between us and not a small amount of sexual compatibility. The two, in combination, can serve as a pretty convincing counterfeit of love. There was a short period of time when I feel certain Burke had actually convinced herself that she was in love with me. At least I know she convinced me. But it wasn't long before I began to detect a certain restlessness in her behavior. Her mind often seemed to be elsewhere. She wasn't smiling or laughing as much as before. Time has a way of uncovering deeply hidden truths. With Burke, it was just a matter of time before she recognized that what she felt toward me was not love."

"At that point, then, she should have just told you of her feelings. In a nice way, of course."

"In retrospect, I think she did try to tell me on more than one occasion. That she didn't succeed is my fault. I think that in both word and action, I made it virtually impossible for her to tell me. It's a cliché, but it's certainly true: Love makes you blind. In my case, it made me not just blind but deaf and dumb as well."

"I think you're being a little hard on yourself, Peter. As you said earlier, we have no control over love. At least you experienced the emotion with Burke. I don't even have that to look back on with Joost."

"Yes, I do have that. And it's a memory I'll always treasure."

"Please don't be mad at me for saying what I am about to say. I know it's very selfish. Since I can't pretend not to be glad your friend, Burke, failed to realize what she had, I would like to make a suggestion: Why don't we both try to forget about the bad tastes left by the past and concentrate on the delicious ones of the present, beginning with this absolutely wonderful dessert. What did you say it was called?"

"Gateau basque. And you are quite right. It is quite wonderful. Almost as wonderful as the woman sitting across the table from me."

"Now that is unique praise indeed. It is certainly the first time I have been compared to a small cake."

"But a very wonderful small cake."

"Yes, that is true. Still, I may have to discuss with you later the implications of being a small cake. Be prepared!"

"In that case, I must suggest we pay a visit to the Player's Bar and see my friend Philippe, the barman. I feel the sudden need of some fortification, some 'French courage' if you will. Philippe has recently discovered a new pear eau-de-vie. It comes from the region around St. Jean Pied-de-Port. He says it is extremely good, which means it's extraordinary."

"Let us go then and see if we can find you some of this special courage."

On their way to the bar, they stopped often to look and comment upon the window displays. They went by way of the Place Eugenie and the rue Mazagran because Peter Ellis wanted to show Anya his two favorite Biarritz art galleries, that of local artist Laulié and the small, venerable gallery of print dealer, Lena Reneteau. Anya especially admired the Laulié paintings. Peter Ellis promised to take her by the artist's studio the following week.

At the Place Clemenceau, the sidewalks became crowded with townspeople taking their after-dinner strolls, seeking out their favorite cafes and clubs where they might celebrate the end of the work week. At the Café Royalty, the narrow sidewalk became almost impassable. Peter Ellis took Anya by the hand and negotiated a path through the small groups who had stopped to talk with friends seated at the outdoor tables. In the confusion of the crowd, he did not notice Jean-Claude Duchon squeezed between two large women at a small second row table. The food salesman, however, bored by the predictable babble of his constantly yapping wife and her equally loquacious companion, had been paying close attention to the passing crowd and noticed the American and his shapely companion right away. On an impulse, he decided to follow the hand-holding couple. Citing an important client he had just seen passing and with whom he needed to speak, he excused himself from the table and hurried down the street, his wife's warning to be quick about his business ringing in his ears.

As he followed them, Duchon was taken by the closeness between the American and his attractive blond friend. He immediately concluded, by the way they walked and touched each other, that they were both friends and lovers. A man did not act that way with a mere acquaintance. Nor did a man act that way with his wife, at least no man of Duchon's acquaintance did. The woman could be a high class prostitute, he thought, but he immediately dismissed the notion. They were too obviously friends, and one rarely became friends with a prostitute in his opinion. Anyway, she did not look like any hooker he had ever seen, even in magazines. When they stopped in front of a book store to study the window display and the man named Peter Ellis lightly kissed the girl on a wispy blond temple, Duchon was certain of his conclusion.

He followed them to the rue Gardères, where they turned down the narrow, sloping street toward the beach. He cursed to himself because here the sidewalk was much less crowded and he was more likely to be spotted. The last thing he wanted now was another confrontation with this damnable American who was threatening him with the Duffy boy's diary. Suddenly he relaxed and smiled to himself. How could he have been so stupid. Their destination was obvious. They were going to the Player's Bar. It was where he had earlier met with this American bastard and the meddling old retired inspector, Claverie-LaPorte.

He waited until he saw them enter the bar, then followed the steep sidewalk down to where he could discreetly observe them through the large bank of windows bordering the street. He was curious to see if they were meeting anyone, especially anyone he recognized. He was not sure what he would do if he saw Chantal with them. He told himself to be calm. He would be rid of the American by Monday, one way or another. Gambia had assured him of that. And Janine had assured him that if he followed her instructions, she would use her best efforts to convince Chantal to resume their relationship. He knew from experience that Janine usually got what she wanted, that she was a woman to be both respected and feared. Based on the surprising present she had given him earlier at Les Colonnes and the promise of financial help if things worked out the way she wanted, he felt fairly certain that she must trust him. Tomorrow he would give her the first proof that her trust was justified by reporting his present observations. He wasn't sure what she would make of them, but he thought she would find them interesting. He certainly did. In fact, what he was seeing was quite extraordinary.

It seemed that the man named Peter Ellis had come to the Player's Bar specifically to see the barman, whose name he recalled was Philippe. They were carrying on like old friends, their obviously animated conversation frequently punctuated by laughter and tell-tale hand gestures. They appeared to be talking about the clear liquor they were drinking from small snifters, some kind of eau-de-vie Duchon guessed. The barman was pointing out to the American something of interest at the bottom of the label. The American was nodding his head in evident approval. All three of them seemed to be enjoying themselves to a degree Duchon found distasteful, if not downright disgusting. Especially since he suddenly had become aware of how long he had been gone. He stole a final, furtive look at the man and his beautiful blond companion. The barman had evidently said something amusing because they both had begun laughing. In that instant he thought of Chantal and the way she used to laugh. He wondered where she was tonight and what she was doing. Under his breath, he uttered an extended profanity. Things were going to be different after Monday. One way or another, he resolved, things were going to be different. Muttering a parting curse in the direction of the laughing group at the bar, he turned, spat emphatically on the sidewalk, and slowly began walking back to the Café Royalty and his squawking wife.

CHAPTER TWENTY

Peter Ellis was awakened early by the married sounds of gusting wind and rattling shutters. He lay on his side, his back to Anya, whose warm body was curled to fit snugly against his. He could feel soft breathing on his neck and the steady, faint beating of her heart against his back. Her incredibly soft skin, almost like silk, was slightly moist from their combined body heat trapped under the two layers of blankets. He lay still for several minutes listening to the wind and the distant rumble of the surf, basking in the perfection of the moment, trying to capture it complete on the capricious sensory film of memory, knowing that the very effort doomed him to failure. Anya's left arm was flung carelessly over his, her fingers loosely touching the back of his hand. He moved her hand gently, freeing it so that he might remove the top layer of covers. The slight movement caused her to moan softly and to rearrange herself more tightly against him.

"What is all that noise, Peter?"

"Just the wind against the shutters."

"It sounds terribly strong, the wind. Is it early? Do we have to get up?"

"It is early and we don't have to get up. At least any time soon."

"Good. It feels too good to move."

"I know."

He turned to face her, slipping his left arm under her head. With his right, he pulled her body close against his and buried his face in her hair. He breathed deeply, registering the full range of intermingled scents. He kissed the downy hair on her temple and released the pressure of his right arm. Anya made a little burrowing movement, settling herself comfortably against him.

"Um-m-m-m. Just right. Is it okay for you?"

"It's perfect."

Within minutes, Anya made three or four little twitching movements and drifted back into sleep. For a time, Peter Ellis made an attempt to join her but finally gave up, realizing that his consciousness of the moment, his total sensory awareness of it, made sleep impossible. So he listened to the gusting, whistling wind, listened to the shutters rattling against the window frames, listened to the distant booming surf and wondered if he was not, in fact, dreaming.

When Anya woke again, it was nearly nine. After some leisurely, almost unnecessary foreplay, they made love and then showered together. They dressed quickly and were on the road to Chambre d'Amour by nine forty-five.

The sky was a foreboding iron grey and a barely perceptible mist dampened the air. The wind was gusting but not as strongly as Peter Ellis had feared. The chill he felt came not so much from the temperature as from the swirling moist air. He had briefly thought of bringing his surfboard with him then decided against it. When he reached the parking lot overlooking the break at Chambre d'Amour, he knew he had made the right decision. The ocean was a cauldron, the waves extremely large and ragged, breaking haphazardly, the water choppy and boiling with large clumps of foam. Still, the parking lot was packed with cars equipped with surf racks and the wide boardwalk was teeming with surf-related activity. They found a parking space just north of the main surf break and began walking among the huddled groups of shivering surfers and their bundled companions toward the block of small cafes that included La Chope. In front of the long green-black jetty that extended out next to the main surf break, Peter

Ellis stopped to watch two surfers who were precariously picking their way across the slippery wet rocks.

"What is it, Peter?"

"Those two out there on the rocks." He pointed to the end of the jetty. Just as he did so, one of the two wetsuit-clad young men slipped as he started to cross from the angled face of one boulder to the relatively flat face of another. With his free hand, he managed to break his fall and keep from sliding between the two large rocks. It was an extremely close call.

"My God, Peter, what are those two doing out there? They could get killed."

"Yes, they could. Especially on a day like this."

"What exactly are they trying to do? Why don't they use the beach to enter the water?"

"Basically they are trying to cheat Mother Ocean. They are trying to get out past the breakline without having to paddle through it which, on a day like today, can be extremely difficult. For some, and I include myself in my present physical condition, paddling out on a day like today is a daunting proposition. I take it as nature's way of telling me I have no business being out there. Those two obviously do not share my belief. Hopefully, they are locals and have experience getting out that way on nasty days like this."

"Still, Peter, it looks very dangerous, the way the waves are breaking against the rocks."

"It is very dangerous. You have to time your entry perfectly. Otherwise you will be washed back against the jetty. You will see in a minute or two. They are just about where they need to be."

Within three minutes, the two surfers had managed to launch themselves successfully from the jetty, the first one cleanly, the second not so cleanly. Peter Ellis shook his head and breathed an audible sigh of relief. He took Anya by the hand and continued down the wide cement promenade. After several steps she glanced over at him and gently squeezed his hand.

"The second one was lucky, wasn't he?"

"Yes, I believe he was, Anya. I believe he was very lucky. Let us hope his luck holds out. Speaking of luck, there is my friend, Maurice, about to claim that parking space right in front of the café."

The old inspector was in the process of trying to lock his car door when Peter Ellis and Anya arrived, unseen.

"So even old policemen must lock their cars in Biarritz these days. What is the town coming to?"

"Especially old policemen. I think these young hooligans of the ocean take perverse pleasure in targeting the old and decrepit. I sometimes wonder why the ocean is so merciful with them. There, finally! I think there must be a sadist at Renault who designs these damn locks." He turned to face Peter Ellis and was startled to see Anya standing next to him.

"Please excuse my language, mademoiselle. I thought Pierre was alone." He extended a hand. "I am delighted to meet you."

"The pleasure is mine. I have heard so much about you."

"Well, I hope you did not believe everything my friend here said about me. He is a writer, after all, and tends to embellish things."

"I have told Anya nothing but the truth, Maurice. In your case, there is no need to embellish. The figure is larger than life."

Maurice gave him a playful slap on the shoulder. "You see, Mlle. Anya, what kind of friend I have. Now he is making fun of my eating habits. Is it my fault that I live in a country with the best food in the world?"

"M. Maurice, I think you look very distinguished. I suggest we leave this old surfer to his beloved waves and see what delights this charming little café has to offer."

"An excellent idea, Mlle. Anya."

After they had settled into a corner table and placed their orders, Maurice asked Anya for a detailed account of their previous day's activities. Maurice listened with interest as she recounted how she had fallen in love with Sauveterre.

"Yes, Sauveterre is a charming and historic old town. But you must make our friend here take you to Navarrenx. It is just up the river from Sauveterre and equally as charming. And the restaurants are far superior."

"I'm not so certain they are far superior, Maurice. Perhaps equally as good."

"Pierre, please! Be objective. You know the restaurants of Navarrenx are, on a whole, better than those of Sauveterre. You said as much the last time we were there. Do you not remember?"

"It is possible. Then again, I may have been trying to appease the pride of a native son." He smiled broadly at Anya.

"You are from Navarrenx, M. Maurice?"

"My family has been there for over five hundred years. It is one of the most celebrated names in the region, in spite of my personal lack of distinction."

"Again, I must disagree with you, Maurice. Just from what I know of your career, I feel safe in saying that you have done more for the good of France than even your famous cousin, the World War I flying ace. His fighting career only lasted four years, yours has lasted a lifetime."

"But think of the dangers he faced, Pierre. It is a miracle he survived the entire war. Very few of his fellow pilots did."

"Of course, you have a point. But I must say that the dangers your cousin faced were certainly no worse than the ones you have faced over the years. And continue to face, I might add. Gambia and LeClerc are not pussycats."

"No, they certainly are not. In fact, I have learned that they are even more despicable than I had previously thought."

Maurice proceeded to recount for them Chantal's story of the fateful party at Gambia's apartment. He speculated how Jean-Claude Duchon, under the guise of friendship, had used the girl's ensuing predicament to his own advantage. He told them of his conversation with LeClerc and of his suspicions regarding LeClerc's relationship with Gambia and Janine Destin. Finally, he asked Peter Ellis about Duchon's message.

"So you think he will show up?"

"I think someone will show up. Either he or LeClerc."

"What about Gambia?"

"No, I don't think he would be that stupid. And even if he wanted to, LeClerc wouldn't let him. Not after what happened to the Duffy boy."

"Are you going to tell him your real identity?"

"That depends on what he tells me, Maurice. At this point, I would prefer not to."

"Do you want me to have my friend Rectoran send a couple of his men to watch your place Monday morning, just in case Duchon tries something funny?"

"I don't think that will be necessary, Maurice."

"Peter, are you sure? These sound like very dangerous people."

"Some of them are, Anya. Duchon isn't one of them, though."

"Still, they could send someone with him."

"If they decide to use force, it will come later, Anya. And, they won't give me advance notice, I assure you. Also, I brought a little protection of my own, just in case. I'll be alright. Don't worry."

"What do you think, M. Maurice?"

"Our friend here is very hard-headed, mademoiselle, but he usually knows what he is doing."

"Thank-you for such an enthusiastic vote of confidence, Maurice."

"I speak only the truth, as you well know."

"M. Maurice, may I ask you a question? It may be none of my business, and you may say so if it is."

"My dear, you may ask me as many questions as you want and I will do my best to answer them all. What is it you would like to know?"

"Who do you think raped the girl, Chantal?"

"Mademoiselle, your question is at the heart of this mystery. And I wish I knew the answer to it. I believe Chantal knows who it is; however, the trauma of the attack has caused her to develop a case of selective amnesia. I believe…" Maurice's speculations were interrupted by a young man, clad in a wetsuit unzipped to the waist, who rushed through the doorway and shouted to the waiter to call an ambulance. He reported, in a loud, excited voice, that there had been an accident, that a surfer had been washed into the rocks of the jetty.

"Oh Peter, I wonder if it was one of the boys we saw earlier. The ones you said were lucky."

Maurice was already on his feet. Peter Ellis had never seen his large friend move so quickly. "Pierre, we must go and see if there is anything we can do. I have my training, you know, and I always carry an emergency medical kit in my car. You never know what you will come across on the roads these days."

A large group of onlookers had gathered on the sidewalk close to the jetty. Peter and Anya followed Maurice as he forced his way through the crowed. A young man in a wetsuit was attending to the boy with what looked like, to Peter Ellis, professional competency. An attractive woman in a one-piece Speedo bathing suit was assisting him. Maurice approached, identified himself, and asked if he could be of assistance. The young man looked up quickly shaking his head, then noticed the first aid kit in Maurice's hand.

"If I may have the use of your medical kit I would be very grateful, monsieur. I am a doctor but, as you can see, I did not come prepared for such an emergency. Also, if you could try and have the crowd move back, it would aid me very much."

By the time the ambulance arrived ten minutes later, Maurice, with the help of Peter Ellis, had managed to move all but one of the group of onlookers from the immediate vicinity of the supine, bloody body. The young man who remained was sitting on the sidewalk a few feet from the injured surfer, clutching his knees to his chest. His hands were stained red and his pale lime wetsuit was covered with dark purple splotches. Next to him was a surfboard with a ragged gash in the nose. After the doctor had supervised the transfer of the injured surfer to the ambulance, he returned to where the distraught young man was sitting. His female assistant was already kneeling next to him, talking in a low voice, her arm around his trembling shoulders. She said something to the doctor. He nodded his head and bent to help the injured surfer's friend to his feet. After a short exchange with his assistant, he lead the shaking young man to the ambulance. The assistant packed up the first aid kit then walked over to where Maurice was huddled with Peter Ellis and Anya.

"My husband asked me to thank you for your help. He is going to accompany the two boys to the hospital. The friend of the injured one seems to be in shock. He thinks it is all his fault. It was he who suggested they jump off the jetty. It is a foolish thing to do, especially if you do not know this beach well. It seems they are both from up around Bordeaux. They came down to watch the contest in Guètary. They decided to try a few waves before going down there. It was their first time surfing here. Can you imagine? On a day like this!" She indicated the wind-whipped surf and shook her head. "They are lucky to be alive."

While the woman was speaking, Anya had moved close to Peter Ellis and put her arm around his waist. "Could your husband tell how badly hurt the other boy is?"

"The external injuries do not appear to be too serious; however, he is concerned that the boy may have hit his head on the rocks. He is going to ask for immediate tests to make sure there is no internal bleeding. Now, if you'll excuse me, I told the friend I would take his surfboard to the shop over there for safekeeping. Once again, thank-you for your help."

Maurice did not say a word on the way back to the café. Even after they had re-claimed their table, he remained silent, a strange, intent expression on his face. Peter Ellis noticed how closely Anya was studying Maurice's frozen features.

"What is the matter, Maurice? Are you feeling ill?"

He reflected for several moments, slowly coming back from the troubled place his thoughts had taken him. "Yes, I suppose I am feeling a bit ill. But not in the sense you mean, Pierre. I am not exactly sure what it is. Suddenly I am feeling very troubled. I have this premonition. We must learn something, I believe, from what we have just seen. We must not do anything foolish. We need to be very careful from now on."

***

Peter Ellis and Anya arrived in the coastal Basque village of Guètary just after noon. The sky was heavy with low, dark clouds and the air was damp and misting. They parked close to a Basque-style café in the center of town and walked over the railroad bridge and down the steep, curving, narrow road to the small fishing port and short strand of rocky beach. The wind had abated and turned almost offshore. Long before they reached the oceanfront, they could hear the thunderous surf. On the drive from Chambre d'Amour, Anya had barely spoken, and then only in response to some observation or commentary by Peter Ellis. Since leaving the car, she had said nothing.

"Anya, is something wrong? If you do not care to stay and watch some of the contest, we can leave. The weather is terrible. I can just leave a message for Marc, say we'll meet him later in town."

"No, Peter, I don't mind staying. And the weather is fine. In Amsterdam, you learn to live with this kind of weather."

"Have I done something to upset you, then?"

"Now you are being silly, my love." They were holding hands. She raised his hand to her lips and lightly kissed it. "You have been wonderful. I guess that's the problem. Ever since we left Maurice, I've had this feeling that something very bad is going to happen. I can't explain it."

"You mean you believe this thing about a premonition."

"Yes, I guess that has something to do with it. And then there was that boy who was washed onto the rocks. All I could think about, looking at him, was that it could have been you."

"Now you are being silly. First of all, Maurice tends to exaggerate things. I think he has become even more dramatic in his old age. He certainly worries more about things now that he has so much time on his hands. Secondly, I can assure you that you will never see me surfing even remotely close to any rocks in the kind of conditions you saw at Chambre d'Amour this morning. I, for one, don't subscribe to that macho, no fear school of surfing. I surf for the enjoyment and exhilaration. A little fear is normal, even necessary if you want to experience the rush of taking off on a big wave. But I am far too old to take unnecessary risks when I'm surfing. Or doing anything else, for that matter. The only person at risk in this business with Gambia, as far as I can tell, is the girl, Chantal. She is my only real concern."

"You really think she is in danger, Peter?"

"Yes, I think she might be. It depends on what she knows. It also depends on what Duchon decides to do. I have very little confidence in his judgment. I don't think he realizes how serious this thing is. He thinks it's just about the death of the Duffy boy."

"What do you think he'll do?"

"I don't know. The only thing I am certain of is that he will do whatever he can to get Chantal back. And I'm sure Gambia knows that as well. What I must do on Monday is convince Duchon that Gambia can no longer help him."

"How do you intend to do that, Peter?"

"I really don't know right now. But don't worry, Anya, I won't do anything foolish. I've just met someone who I would like to get better acquainted with. I think that she and I could become very good friends."

"Just friends?"

"Well, she is kind of sexy…"

"Now you are making fun of me."

"Au contraire, mademoiselle."

They had reached the bottom of the steep hill and were walking along the road parallel to the rocky beach. At the end of the road were several raised viewing platforms and a handful of tents emblazoned with the names of the contest's sponsors. Cars and vans with surf racks lined the two-lane road, their license plates representing virtually every European surfing country, from Portugal to Scotland. Next to several of the vehicles were shivering surfers, wrapped in blankets, sweaters and hooded sweatshirts, surrounded by friends and fans. Peter Ellis recognized a local surfing acquaintance walking briskly toward them, a surfboard under one arm and a large towel covering his dripping head, Arab-style. After a brief exchange of surfing small-talk, Peter Ellis learned that his friend, Marc Dufau, had just left to paddle out for the next heat. He and Anya continued along the road until it abruptly ended in a wide, concrete ramp that led down to the rock-strewn beach. They found an elevated vantage point from which to watch Marc's heat.

The surf was breaking several hundred yards out and the surfers were difficult to see in the misty, seaspray-washed distance. Peter Ellis judged the wavefaces to be in the ten-to-twelve foot range. They were thick, ragged, unpredictable and unforgiving. In surfspeak, they epitomized the term 'gnarly'.

"My God, Peter, I can't believe people surf in these conditions. And so far out."

"Better them than me. Of course, I doubt I would even make it out to the break on a day like today."

"Wouldn't it be easy to be killed by waves like these?"

"Very easy, if you are not both in shape and know exactly what you are doing. The guys that surf these tournaments are all in great shape and probably know the ocean better than they know themselves."

"What about accidents? Surely they must happen, even to the best surfers."

"Unfortunately they do, Anya."

Their conversation was interrupted by three loud, strident blasts of an air horn. Peter Ellis turned and saw that the flag signaling the start of the heat had been raised. He turned back and quickly scanned the line-up where the five contestants were paddling for position.

"Can you see Marc?"

"Not yet. I'm not sure what board he is using. I think it's the new one he was telling me about yesterday. I can't remember what color he said it was. As soon as he catches a wave, though, I'll recognize him. Like all good surfers, he has his own distinctive style."

The first rider to catch a wave misjudged his takeoff point and had to pull out to avoid a collapsing section. The second rider made the same mistake as the first, then compounded it by trying to power through the section. A chorus of empathetic groans from the crowd accompanied his hard wipeout. As soon as the third rider had stroked into the wave and made his bottom turn, Peter Ellis knew it was Marc and told Anya. His friend had learned from the mistakes of the previous two contestants and had been able to stay ahead of the dangerous section, though not by much. He worked the wave conservatively, insuring himself a long ride and the good score that went with it. When he kicked out of the wave, there were scattered shouts of approval from the crowd.

"The people here seem to like Marc's performance."

"As well they should. He rode the wave well but, more importantly, he rode it intelligently. He didn't try to do too much. In conditions like these, it is especially important to have a good first wave score. It does not have to be great, just good. It has a great settling effect and gives you a huge boost of confidence. Not to mention the message it sends to the other guys in the water. Let's see how they react."

When the horn ending the heat sounded, Peter Ellis calculated his friend to be the likely winner. He led Anya down to the beach and waited for Marc to come in. A young woman who had been standing close by, holding a thermos and a large towel, ran to meet him as soon as he stepped out of the water. They exchanged a quick embrace. She handed him the towel then poured him a steaming cup of something from the thermos. Peter Ellis noticed the unspoken intimacy that existed between them and smiled to himself. Just then Marc saw him and waved.

"So Peter, you decided to come and see how bad Guètary would work me today. And I see you brought a friend to witness my punishment. You must be Anya." He extended a hand. "I am delighted to meet you."

"The pleasure is mine, Marc. Peter has told me so much about you."

"I hope you didn't believe everything he said. He has been known to exaggerate."

"Not true, Marc. You are going to give your friend here the wrong impression." He indicated the woman who had brought the towel and thermos.

"Please forgive me. The cold water must have frozen my brain. Permit me to introduce you to my friend, Christine."

"Marc has also spoken of you often, Peter, but you need not worry. I know him too well to believe everything he says."

"Well Marc, I see you have a very perceptive friend."

"Sometimes I think she's maybe too smart for her own good. Isn't that so, Cherie?" He gave her a light kiss on the cheek. "But she certainly takes good care of me. She's even brought a thermos of my favorite soup to inspire my performance."

"It seems to have worked. According to my calculations, you won the heat. Though not by much. The guy in the red vest made an incredible comeback after a disastrous first wave."

"He was the one I was most worried about. He's from the island of Oleron and is one of the best surfers in France."

"Well, unless the judges show undue favoritism, you got the best of him this time." Just then, there was a burst of applause from the crowd. They all turned and looked up in the direction of the judges' platform. One of the officials was posting the results from the recently-completed heat. At the top of the board was Marc's name and number.

"Congratulations, old friend. When is your next heat?"

"Probably in about an hour and a half. But don't even think about keeping Mlle. Anya out in this weather. I doubt I'll get past the next heat anyway. There are some very famous surfers entered in the contest this year. I was just lucky out there a while ago."

"Christine, since when has Marc become so humble?"

"I believe in about the last five seconds. Of course, he has it all wrong. Luck had nothing to do with his success."

"What _was_ the reason for my success in your opinion, my dear?"

"The soup, of course." She slapped him playfully on his backside. "Now, let's get your friends out of this wet, cold wind. You'll have plenty of time to talk about surfing this evening at dinner. You might even find time to tell Peter what you have discovered about the loveable M. Duchon."

"You have found out something we can use against Duchon, Marc?"

"Yes, I think so. I can take no credit for the information, however; Christine did all the work. I think you will be impressed with what she uncovered."

"I am certain I shall be if you say so. What time shall we meet?"

"How about nine o'clock at my restaurant? It is not too late for you, Anya?"

"No, not at all. I prefer eating late when I am not working."

"Excellent. Until nine this evening, then."

***

During the climb up the steep, narrow coastal access road, Peter Ellis suggested they stop at the Basque-style corner café in the center of the village for lunch. Afterwards, they could drive to St. Jean-de-Luz and, weather permitting, take a walk in the hilly park overlooking the town's large, horseshoe-shaped bay. Their lunch was excellent- big bowls of Ttoro, the hearty Basque fish soup, simple house salads with a garlic and onion vinaigrette, a plate of assorted local cheeses and a chilled bottle of Irouleguy rosé. By the time they had finished, the sky had partially cleared, though the wind was still gusting strongly out of the southeast.

In St. Jean-de-Luz, Peter Ellis found a parking place next to the bayside asphalt promenade on the Boulevard Thiers. In spite of the cold, windy weather, the boardwalk was teeming with walkers of all ages and description, from young mothers pushing elaborate baby carriages carrying red-cheeked infants to tightly bundled retirees shuffling along with the help of a cane or a supporting arm. Peter Ellis and Anya climbed the short set of steps leading up to the wide walkway and joined the diverse crowd of afternoon strollers taking in the brisk seaside air. They walked in the direction of Sainte Barbe, the undulating grass-covered promontory overlooking the northern entrance to the bay. As they walked, Peter Ellis told Anya the story of the marriage between Louis XIV and the Infante Marie-Thérèse of Austria, celebrated in the 14th century church of Saint-Jean-Baptiste in the center of St. Jean-de-Luz. He promised to show her the door-way that was blocked up following the ceremony so that no one of lesser blood would ever darken the portals that the newlyweds had graced with their royal presence. When they reached the end of the Promenade des Rochers, Peter Ellis paused at the base of the path that snaked up the face of the headland to show Anya the place next to the massive breakwater where he had surfed many years before with some friends from Florida. It had been a memorable day because, according to the locals, no one had previously surfed the spot.

"That does not surprise me, Peter. It looks extremely dangerous. With all these rocks, it's a wonder one of you didn't break your neck."

"We probably <u>were</u> fortunate no one was hurt. The conditions that day were really frightening. As I recall, at least two boards were broken on the rocks. Back then, before board leashes, mistakes were much more costly, both in lost time and lost money."

"I think I'm beginning to understand why you chose your particular profession. It seems you have been attracted to danger since your youth. I'm surprised you have not tried mountain-climbing."

"Actually I have, back around the same time I surfed right here."

"Oh God, I should have guessed!"

"It wasn't like you think, Anya. I was with an old friend who had always wanted to climb the Matterhorn. He had been going to Zermatt with his family since he was a child. He had become fascinated with the challenge. He wanted someone to climb it with him."

"And of course you volunteered. It's a good thing he hadn't spent his youth in Tibet. He would have had you climbing Everest."

"No, it wasn't like that at all, my dear. I assure you I have never had a death wish. We were with guides who had climbed the mountain at least two hundred times. It really wasn't that dangerous. I'm not saying that there were not times, especially during our training on the sheer rock face of the Rifflehorn, when I was absolutely terrified."

"I'd say it served you right, though it doesn't seem to have taught you much." With a forefinger she jabbed him mock-seriously in the chest. "Does it now?"

"To the contrary, my love. In my old age, I have grown much wiser. As you can see," he indicated the gentle slope of the Sainte Barbe headland, "I now limit my climbing to less threatening heights."

"When you are not chasing the mafia around the southwest of France, which I would say is at least as dangerous as climbing the Matterhorn. A mistake doing either one can easily get you killed."

"Only if you are not careful and don't take every precaution available to you. It is like tying yourself off on the mountain in case you slip. Don't worry Anya, I won't do anything foolish." He put his arm around her shoulders and squeezed her close to him. He kissed her lightly. "Especially now."

As they climbed the headland, the panorama of green ocean, red-tile roofs, dark blue bay and distant, cloud-covered mountains spread out before them. Peter Ellis pointed out, across the mile-wide bay mouth, the old fort of Socoa and the neighboring village of Cibourne, home to most of the local fleet's commercial fishermen and birthplace of the composer, Maurice Ravel. He indicated the line of mountains that arbitrarily divided the Basque country into French and Spanish sectors. He located the specific mountain on the distant Spanish coastline that towered over the port of San Sebastian. Anya bemoaned her lack of at least a sketchbook and charcoal pencils and voiced her desire to return in the near future for an afternoon of drawing and painting.

They chose a different, meandering path down to the Boulevard Thiers and followed it to the rue Gambetta, the town's de facto main street. (Several years earlier, the municipality had converted the narrow, medieval street into a pedestrian mall, with self-evident positive results.) Peter Ellis and Anya immediately found themselves part of a large crowd of afternoon shoppers regaling their senses with the unique offerings of the various small establishments lining the bustling street. Especially prevalent were shops catering to France's ubiquitous twin passions for fashion and food. From Marquis de Sade-inspired footwear to clownish ensembles designed to be fashionable for no more than a single season, Madame and Monsieur might stroll down the rue Gambetta and find whatever was necessary

to make an up-to-the-Parisian-minute sartorial statement. But even
more impressive, at least to Peter Ellis's eyes and nose, were the
scores of shops dedicated to the decoration and provisioning of the
French dining table. From delicate, white Basque linen bordered
with characteristic red and blue geometric designs to gold-rimmed
table settings from Limoges, everything to make the table an elegant-
ly attired model for an artist's still life was available on the street. As
for the food to put on this finely set Gallic table, the choices offered
by the small purveyors in this vibrant town center could be said, without any exaggeration, to cover the gastronomic alphabet from anise
to zucchini. With every few steps, Peter Ellis found himself salivating
from some new visual or olfactory stimulus: freshly-baked baguettes,
pungent ripening fromage de brebis, baskets of large langoustines
and pale-green crevettes, strings of garlic and red peppers hanging
above mounds of neatly arranged fresh vegetables and fruit.

When they reached the Place Louis XIV next to the fishing port
at the end of the street, they stopped for a drink at one of the cafes
surrounding the square. Although the walk had sharpened his appetite, Peter Ellis decided to put off eating a snack until they reached
the Bar Basque on the Boulevard Thiers, not far from where he had
parked the car. It was his favorite café in St. Jean-de-Luz and had
tapas rivaled only by those of the Santa Maria above the Port Vieux
in Biarritz. While Anya lingered over a glass of semi-dry Jurançon,
Peter Ellis gulped two glasses of Kronenbourg 1664 and told her
a little about the town and its counterpart, Ciboure, on the south
side of the river Nivelle: how its fishing fleet, the largest tuna fleet
in France, had been an established enterprise for many centuries,
accounting for the fact that the town's population was twenty-five per
cent larger in the 18th century than at present; how the town had
only developed into a fashionable beach resort after the middle of
the last century; how it's suburbs boasted two of the best golf clubs in
Europe, thanks in great part to legendary tennis star, sportsman and
local inhabitant, Rene Lacoste; how, because of its large, protected
bay, it was celebrated for its good wind-surfing.

After they had finished their drinks, they took a leisurely walk around the harbor. At the sight of the small fleet of brightly painted Basque fishing boats, Anya immediately decided that she would have to return there as well with her easel and paint box. They admired the Maison Lohobiague where Louis XIV had resided during his famous marital visit and the elegant Maison de l'Infante, where Marie-Thérèse had stayed in the company of her queen mother, Anne of Austria, awaiting her marriage to the Sun King. When they reached the lighthouse marking the mouth of the Nivelle, they turned onto the beachfront promenade. They followed it as far as the large municipal casino, with Anya giving a running commentary on what pleased and displeased her, architecturally, in each of the large residences overlooking the curving beach. At the casino, they turned right and soon found themselves in front of the long wide terrace of the venerable Bar Basque.

They entered the high-ceilinged main room with its massive wooden beams and herringbone-patterned parquet floor and walked over to the long, impressive oak bar. Carved into the thick face of the bar were painted low-relief murals depicting typical Basque village life, the most notable among them an awkward portrayal of bereted peasants hoisting a wine glass against a background of large bunches of grapes. Hanging from one of the thick beams above the bar were curved links of chorizo and large Bayonne hams. Spread at intervals along the bar were glass-covered plates of freshly-made tapas. After examining the selection, Peter Ellis and Anya seated themselves at a secluded corner table where, almost instantly, a well-groomed, classi-cally-attired young waiter appeared and took their order.

"What a wonderful bar, Peter!"

"It is, isn't it? I think it is one of the most comfortable places for drinking I have ever known. And wait until you taste the tapas."

"You know, my dear, I am beginning to wonder if you will ever take me to a place I don't like."

"Oh I'm sure I shall, and probably in the not-too-distant future. So far, it has been easy. I've just taken you to all my local favorites. I think you will agree that it's hard to go wrong with places like

Sauveterre. And if you <u>hadn't</u> liked Sauveterre, it would have been a clear indication to me that our future together was going to be short-lived. Of course I don't expect you to swoon over everything and every place I happen to like."

"You don't? Are you sure? I think that's exactly what you expect."

"Am I that transparent?"

"Perhaps in some things. And don't forget, I <u>am</u> a banker and good bankers have a nose for dishonesty."

"I stand warned. It's a good thing Duchon is not a good banker. I would be in big trouble if he could see through me like you do."

"Please, Peter, let's not talk of him or the others any more until this evening when we meet your friend, Marc. I don't want to be difficult, but the whole business does upset me. When the time comes, I can deal with it. If there is one thing I know, it is that I am strong. Maybe even too strong for my own good sometimes. I've begun to think a little vulnerability, or maybe a little weakness, is not such a bad thing. I think for true love to be possible, it may even be a necessary thing. I guess if I'm feeling it now, it might have something to do with how I am feeling about you. I know you have a job to do and I admire you for doing it, I really do. I just don't want to think about it right now. I hope you understand, Peter." She reached over and took his hand and gently brought it to her lips. She held it there for several seconds, willing him to look at her. When he did, what he saw in her eyes was so passionate and honest, so powerful and so vulnerable, that he suddenly felt he might start to cry, tears being the only release for his sudden swelling of emotion. Anya seemed to sense what he was feeling. She lightly kissed his hand and laid it back on the table, letting her soft grip linger. Peter Ellis felt the built-up pressure gradually release. With a soft brush of fingertips, Anya removed her hand. The waiter had suddenly appeared with their order.

"Peter, will you excuse me for a moment? I'll be right back, but please don't wait for me to begin."

"I'll give you five minutes."

"Really, Peter, I don't want you to wait for me."

"But that's exactly what I am going to do. The anticipation will just make everything taste that much better."

"You really are hard-headed, aren't you?"

"I can be. As can someone else, I believe. Now, weren't you going someplace?" He waved her away with a backhand shooing motion. He took a sip from the sweat-beaded glass of Heineken. It tasted wonderfully crisp and fresh. He admired the selection of tapas on the large, colorful plate: round slices of chorizo with boiled egg; thin cuts of jambon de Bayonne with sweet butter; large, pink shrimp with aioli; small mounds of fresh crabmeat with spicy homemade mayonnaise. When he heard the deep-voiced, Marseille-accented greeting, his first thought was that the speaker must be addressing someone at the next table. He even smiled to himself: the accent always reminded him of the Pagnol film classic, Marius. It was only when the greeting was repeated, at much closer range, that he looked up, with evident shock, saw Gambia standing at his elbow and realized that the words were directed at him. Or, more precisely, at the persona he had assumed, Peter Edwards.

"Please excuse me, M. Edwards. I did not mean to startle you. I saw you come in with that beautiful woman and wanted to take the opportunity of her absence to congratulate you. Your friend is quite magnificent. And- I could not help but notice- she seems to think highly of you, you old dog." He raised his eyebrows knowingly and slapped him lightly on the shoulder. "My little Dany will be very disappointed. I really believe she has a thing for you. But she is young and knows how to please a man. She'll get over it."

"M. Gambia, what a surprise! How are you doing?"

"Please, call me Jojo. 'Monsieur' is so formal and it makes me feel old."

"Pardon me, Jojo. I agree totally. But only if you do the same."

"Entendu." He slapped him on the shoulder again and fixed him with a look of mock-consternation. "I don't even know who Monsieur Edwards is! Do you?"

"Absolutely no idea. Some rich American playboy, no doubt." Gambia joined him in a conspiratorial laugh. "So, Jojo, what brings you to St. Jean-de-Luz. I thought you said, when we spoke the other night at your delightful little club, that you were spending the weekend in Spain."

"You have a very good memory, Pierre. I like that in a man. I did go for a day and a half, but a little problem has come up that I must take care of. Even though I have partners, it seems I must do everything. I'm sure, in your business, you know how it is. If you want something done right, you must do it yourself."

"I certainly do, Jojo. Well, good luck. I hope the problem is not too serious."

"It's nothing. Just some little prick sticking his nose in my business."

"It sounds like a good way to get a broken nose!"

"What an excellent idea, Pierre. That's how we shall begin with him."

"I am glad I could be of service."

"But wait, my friend. I believe you have given me an even better idea. I shall not just break the bastard's nose, I'll cut off a little piece as well. That should send a clear message to anyone who sees him: Stick your nose into Joseph Gambia's business and you risk losing a piece of it! What do you think?"

"I think you have a point there. Or will have when you are finished with him, if you get my meaning."

Gambia burst into raucous laughter. "I like it! I like it very much. I begin to think we are men of very similar tastes."

"It is quite possible."

"I am sure of it." He nodded his head in the direction of Anya, who was returning to the table. He stood quickly and moved to pull out her chair. "Permit me, please, mademoiselle."

"Thank-you, sir."

At her arrival, Peter Ellis had stood as well. As Anya was taking her seat, she looked up at him inquiringly. She seemed to sense something was wrong.

"Anya, I would like you to meet my friend Joseph Gambia. He has a charming little nightclub in Biarritz."

"I am very pleased to meet you, M. Gambia." She flashed him a wide smile.

"I assure you, mademoiselle, the pleasure is all mine. But please, call me Jojo. All of my friends do."

"In that case, I take your request as a compliment. Thank-you."

"You are Dutch, are you not, Mlle. Anya?"

"You are very perceptive, Jojo. Yes I am. I come from Amsterdam."

"A wonderful city. I have passed many amusing times there. And what brings you to the Pays Basque at this time of year?"

Peter Ellis had been expecting the question and quickly interceded.

"Anya is my primary distributor in Holland, Jojo. She has kindly agreed to come down and assist me in Spain with our new shipment. She decided to surprise me by coming a few days early."

"What a nice surprise for you. I am jealous. Lately, the only surprises I have received are the kind one can live without."

"Actually, Jojo, I think she came early to see that I did not get into any trouble, if you know what I mean?"

"That is totally untrue, Peter. You are going to give your friend the wrong impression of me. Jojo, I came early to see for myself if all the wonderful things he has told me about this part of France are true."

"And what is your impression so far?"

"I think your region is even more beautiful than he described. I look forward to spending much more time here in the future."

"Well, I hope you can find the time to visit me in Biarritz. It would please me greatly to take you both to dinner one night after you have completed your business in Spain."

"You are very kind, Jojo. I'll see what we can do. I have already asked Anya to consider staying a few extra days."

"Excellent. You can always reach me at night at the club." He reached into his jacket pocket, took out a gold-embossed business card, and handed it to Peter Ellis. "I shall look forward to hearing from you. Good luck with your affairs in Spain."

"Thank-you very much."

Peter Ellis waited until Gambia was well out of earshot before speaking.

"I am so sorry, Anya. I can't believe he just showed up like that. The last thing I want is for you to get involved in this business."

"It's okay, darling. You had no way of knowing. I actually enjoyed playing the part once I recovered from the initial shock. What do you think? Did I pass the audition?"

"With flying colors. In fact, I think you may have missed your calling."

"Well, just as long as I didn't give anything away."

"If anyone gave anything away, it was yours truly. I almost fell out of my seat when I looked up and saw him."

"I can imagine. It certainly seems that your twin, Peter Edwards, made a good impression on him the other night at the club. I hope you didn't have to do anything too bad to establish your authenticity."

"Bad enough. It's not something I'm very proud of. When this whole affair is over, I'll tell you all about it if you want to discover how low I can go in the line of duty."

"If and when you want to talk about it, I shall be happy to listen. Otherwise, my dear, don't worry about it. I shall still adore you."

"You really are an extraordinary woman, you know that?"

"Of course I do. And I shall be even more wonderful if you can manage to have our garcon bring me another glass of wine. I seem to have developed a slight case of nerves."

CHAPTER TWENTY-ONE

Peter Ellis and Anya had arrived in Biarritz just after sunset. Anya suggested they take a short siesta before getting ready for their dinner with Marc and his friend, Christine. As soon as they were in bed, she began caressing him, first with her fingers, then with her lips and tongue. She lingered over him for several minutes, not allowing him to interfere with her lovingly deliberate movements. When he was almost on the verge of climax, she straddled him and, kneeling, gently lowered herself onto him. For at least two minutes she sat motionless, staring intently, almost fiercely, into his eyes, the only movement an achingly sweet clasping of small, interior muscles. Then, she raised herself slowly to almost his full length, held herself there for one shivering moment, then collapsed onto him in an all-enveloping embrace. They held each other with a trembling tightness for several minutes afterwards. And it was only much later, as they lay side by side, spooned, that their heartbeats returned to normal.

They overslept and did not get to the restaurant until nine-twenty. Marc and Christine were waiting for them in the small bar.

"Enfin, Pierre, you have arrived."

"I'm sorry to be so late, Marc. We decided to take a little siesta and I didn't think to set an alarm."

"Your timing is perfect, my friend. I have only now finished working. I didn't expect to be so busy, given the time of the year. I allowed one of my waiters the night off to visit his family in Pau. So I had to help the others out a little."

"How did you do in the second heat?"

"As I expected."

"He was robbed, Pierre. We all thought so. I think the sponsors are paying off the judges."

"Come now, Christine. You know that's not true."

"Pierre, I tell you, Marc should have taken the second spot. He surfed much better than the one who advanced in his place. He was much more graceful, much more natural. The other one, he showed no finesse."

"What my dear Christine means, Pierre, is that I did not do some of the things the judges look for. For a while, I think I forgot that I was surfing in a tournament. It was very close. The other guy did have some longer rides. But I assure you, I had more fun."

"Still, cheri, I think you were better than he was. Much more natural and in harmony with the waves."

"It sounds like Christine knows something about surfing, Marc. It also sounds like I would have chosen you to advance had I been a judge."

"Well, you're both very kind, but it's over now. And I, at least, am not going to worry about it. In fact, I feel almost relieved. Tomorrow I can go out somewhere and just surf for myself. Perhaps you will join me, Pierre?"

"I'd love to, Marc, but Anya and I have plans to eat with Olga and Maurice in Navarrenx."

"We'll do it later in the week, then. Now, I hope you are hungry. I have taken the liberty of preparing a selection of some of our signature dishes. Since it is Anya's first time here, I've decided to show off a little. Nor have I forgotten you, Pierre. For the main course, I have prepared one of your very favorite things."

"Let me guess. Gigot d'agneau à l'ail."

"With green beans and scalloped potatoes. And I have raided my wine cellar for two bottles of what should be excellent St. Emilion."

"I warned Anya on the way over here to be ready for a feast."

"Well, I see you so rarely these days, I must take advantage of my few opportunities. So, let's get started. If you'll excuse me for a few minutes, Christine will see that you get something to drink."

Marc disappeared into the kitchen. Christine led them to a secluded corner table at the back of the restaurant. A waitress immediately appeared with a chilled bottle of dry Jurançon. She had barely finished filling their glasses when Marc and a waiter arrived with three exquisitely garnished plates.

"I have decided on two separate entrée courses. The first, as you can see, is a selection of delicacies from both river and ocean: smoked trout from St. Jean-Pied-de-Port; slightly seared tuna au poivre from St. Jean-de-Luz; and, finally, some local langoustines with aioli. The second course will feature three celebrated spécialités from the three regions that comprise this little corner of France: truffled paté de foie gras from the Beàrn; cepe mushrooms from Les Landes sautéed in duck fat; and grilled quail from the area around Sare in the French Basque country. So Anya, do you see anything you like?"

"Oh Marc, this is too much. I feel like I'm in some kind of gastronomic dream. And the presentation is so beautiful. Each plate is like a painting. It seems a shame something so visually pleasing must, by its very nature, be so temporary."

"Like life itself, Anya. But thank-you for what you say about my small creations. Coming from a true artist, I take your comments as a great compliment. I must say, though, that unlike your paintings—which Pierre tells me are exquisite—my little culinary works only achieve their aesthetic potential by being eaten. So, for the sake of art, let us begin. Bon appétit!"

Their conversation during dinner was both lively and wide-ranging. It was only after the dessert plates had been cleared and the digestives poured that the talk turned to serious matters. Christine needed no prompting.

"So Pierre, let me tell you what I have learned about this absolutely despicable man, Jean-Claude Duchon. I must warn you that it is a very upsetting, very sad story; however, it is also, at least in my opinion, extremely incriminating. Hopefully, it will help you stop him and his associates from ruining the lives of any more young women."

"This does not sound very pleasant. Are you sure you want to hear this, Anya?"

"Anything that concerns you Peter now concerns me. I think I may not like what I hear, but I need to hear it. So Christine, please begin."

"Well, when Marc told me about why you had come to Biarritz and mentioned Duchon's connection to the affair, I immediately thought about what had happened three years ago to a young girl named Madeline Delay. For you to appreciate fully her story, it will be necessary for me to provide you with some background information, so please bear with me. I shall try to be as brief as possible.

"When Madeline first came to town, she worked in the restaurant of one of our old friends, Jean-René Renaud. It's a small place not far from Les Halles and caters primarily to traveling salesmen and local merchants. In fact, it was one of the regular customers, a salesman from Tarbes, who recommended Madeline for the job. He had met her working in a roadside café in Artix. She came from a small farming community nearby and, having completed her basic school requirements and being of working age, was determined to make her way to the big city. Taking a job in the café on the route Nationale was her first step in that direction.

"Madeline was a very clever young girl, perhaps too clever for her own good. From a very young age, it seems, she became almost addicted to popular magazines, like <u>Paris</u> <u>Match</u> and <u>Marie</u> <u>Claire</u>. As a result of all this reading, and in her case believing, she affected a soi-disant cosmopolitan air. She became fashion conscious to the extreme. To make the picture of Madeline at this time complete, though, I must add finally that she was one of the most stunning young women I have ever seen. By that I do not mean she was beautiful in a Catherine Deneuve sort of way. With Madeline, it was her extraordinary, almost feline body. She moved with a combination of animal grace and muted sensuality. She also possessed enormous, ice blue eyes.

"As you can imagine, Madeline did not have trouble finding dates. In fact, the running joke around the restaurant during those first few months was whether there were any male customers who wouldn't ask her out. This is not to say she accepted many of these invitations. I soon discovered from Jean-René that the only proposals she accepted were for dinner, and then only if dinner was to be in one of the fancy restaurants in town. She had the additional peculiar habit of stipulating that her dates both pick her up and drop her off not at her apartment but at a small café around the corner from it. When one young admirer complained about this arrangement in front of the barman at the café, she apparently told him that it was the only way she could think of to protect her reputation in Biarritz and that if he didn't like it then perhaps he would find it preferable to eat alone. All of this concern for reputation changed, however, about a month after she met Duchon.

"In the three or so weeks between their initial meeting and their first date, Duchon had become an almost daily visitor to the restaurant. He inevitably came in late for lunch and stayed long after most of the other diners had left, talking with Madeline at every opportunity. One afternoon, after Duchon had stayed an inordinately long time talking with the girl, Jean-René took her aside and asked whether the food salesman was bothering her by hanging around for so long. To his great surprise, she replied that, to the contrary, she found his conversation both informative and stimulating. It was not long after this that they had their first dinner date. Everyone at the restaurant was amazed that she had accepted his invitation. The explanation was soon advanced that she must be feeling sorry for him. Still, even if that was her reason, it was generally held to be an ill-advised and potentially dangerous thing to do, given the fact that he was married. Not to mention that he was known to associate with some very questionable characters. You can imagine the degree of disbelief and universal disapproval that greeted her announcement, a week or so after this first date with Duchon, that she had decided to take a part time job in a nightclub owned by one of his friends, in her words a 'charming and very sophisticated gentleman from Marseille named Joseph Gambia'. My friend Jean-René was at first stunned but then became very angry. It is a very good thing Duchon did not show his face in the restaurant that afternoon, for I fear he would have left with it somewhat disfigured. But then, he probably knew what the reaction would be to Madeline's announcement and stayed away on purpose. She, on the other hand, was evidently oblivious to the consequences she might suffer as a direct result of her proudly-delivered news. It did not take long, however, for her to find out. As soon as the day's lunch service was completed, Jean-René took her into his office and, after establishing that she did indeed want to work in Gambia's club, gave her a simple choice: his restaurant <u>or</u> Gambia's club. He said he would give her time to think about it. The next day she came in and gave her notice. To her credit, she offered to work until Jean-René could find someone to replace her.

"In spite of her petty vanities, Madeline was, at heart, a fun-loving, quick-witted, very decent young woman and was universally well-liked. Everyone at the restaurant was sad to see her leave. Many of the people who had come to know her, myself included, tried to convince her to reconsider her decision. Jean-René, especially, pleaded with her to think about the potential dangers of working in a place like Gambia's club. He even offered to help her find a position in a more exclusive restaurant if all she really wanted was to work with a more upscale clientele. She thanked him for his offer but said that her mind was made up. She wanted to work in the club. To this day, I don't know how Duchon managed to get to her, but get to her he did.

"At first, it was like a dream for Madeline. Her fantasy world had suddenly become real. Men were throwing money and compliments at her. For about a month, she came into the restaurant almost every day, showing off her new clothes and telling anyone who would listen about the latest important person she had just met at the club. Then, all of a sudden, she dropped out of sight. Initially, no one at the restaurant thought anything of it. It was generally assumed that she was spending time with her new 'more important' friends from the club. A week passed and her best friend at the restaurant, after failing to reach her by phone, decided to check with the barman at the café around the corner from her apartment, which she had previously used as a rendezvous for her dinner dates.

"The barman's name is Jean-Louis. As fate would have it, he grew up in a village not far from the farm of Madeline's parents. Although he only knew them slightly, the fact that he and the girl were from the same region immediately created a special, almost parental bond between them. In view of this special relationship, you can imagine her friend's surprise when her inquires about Madeline only elicited a shrug from the old barman. Apparently, he had talked to her only once after she had begun seeing Duchon and said he had no desire to see or talk to her as long as she was with the food salesman, who he called a 'dirty little weasel'. When the old barman learned, however, that Madeline had not been seen for a week, he immediately softened and promised to see what he could find out.

"Her friend's next thought was to check at the club. Jean-René kindly volunteered to perform this distasteful task. None of the employees seemed to know anything. They all repeated the same story. She had just stopped coming to work a week ago. That's all they could tell him. He came away with the distinct impression, though, that at least two of the girls he had questioned seemed to be hiding something. He had asked each of them if they could think of any reason why Madeline would stop coming to work. In each case, the girl hesitated before saying no and suggesting he talk with their boss, Joseph Gambia. It was only after Jean-René threatened to call the police about the girl's disappearance that he was granted an interview. Gambia said he had last seen the girl a week ago at a party with her friend Jean-Claude Duchon. Although he could not say for certain why Madeline had stopped coming to work, it had not really surprised him. It was his opinion that she was a bit too naïve to work in his kind of club. On this point, Jean-René could not disagree.

"The next step was to contact Duchon, but it proved to be unnecessary. The old barman, Jean-Louis, found Madeline the following morning. He convinced the concierge of her building to let him into her apartment. And there she was, curled up on her bed. She had been there the entire time. She was in such a frightening state, the old concierge was certain she was going to die. She had hardly eaten for a week. Initially, she didn't recognize Jean-Louis. When she did, she burst into tears and began shaking uncontrollably. The barman sent for a doctor who immediately put her in the hospital. It was there discovered that she had been repeatedly raped in every possible way. As soon as it was deemed safe, she was questioned by the authorities about what had happened. From the very beginning, she said she was unable to talk about it. Duchon, of course, was questioned and pleaded total innocence. He said they had had a falling out the previous week at a party and he had not seen her since that evening. In the end, the authorities, frustrated by her apparent lack of cooperation, lost interest and the whole incident was quickly forgotten.

"As soon as Madeline was over the worst of her trauma, she moved to Pau where she was hired by a friend of Jean-René's who has a small but relatively famous <u>nouvelle</u> <u>cuisine</u> restaurant. She seems to have made a complete recovery and I try to speak with her about once a month, though never about what happened here. That is until yesterday. After Marc told me why you had come and how Duchon had apparently done the same thing to this girl, Chantal Clairac, that he had done to Madeline, I decided to risk talking to her about what had happened three years ago. Well, not only did she agree at once to tell me exactly what had happened that traumatic night, she also insisted on telling me everything she knew about the workings of Gambia's nightclub and exactly how Duchon was involved in the operation. She even had some very interesting things to say about Gambia's partner Janine as well as the esteemed Chief Inspector, Jacques LeClerc. I knew from her time at Jean-René's restaurant that Madeline was an extremely observant young girl; however, I learned yesterday that I have very much underestimated her powers of observation. As have Gambia, Duchon and the rest. Her youth and naïveté appears to have put them totally off their guard. It seems they did and said some very indiscreet things in front of her. She remembers them all and says she is willing to put everything into a sworn affidavit if it will help put an end to what Duchon and the others have been doing to girls like her and Chantal."

"Christine, this is too good to be true. With this information, there is no way Duchon can refuse to cooperate. I don't know how I can adequately thank you."

"Knowing it may help put these disgusting bastards out of business is, in itself, thanks enough. Now, if you don't mind, let me take a short break. I took some notes during my long conversation with Madeline and I'd like to consult them for a few minutes. We can have another drink and then I'll recount, to the best of my ability, everything she told me about Gambia's operation."

CHAPTER TWENTY-TWO

—————

The call from Janine Destin came as a complete and very agreeable surprise to Duchon. His wife had answered the telephone. After an initial yelp of feigned incredulity and a short barrage of perfectly inane questions inquiring after the health of the caller, her dog, her neighbor and the owner of her neighborhood patisserie, she passed the phone to her husband. But only after assuring the caller that she was doing as well as could be expected, given her bad back and constant headaches, which were caused, she was sure, by continually worrying about poor Jean-Claude. He was always so tired when he came home at night. Did Janine really think so? Oh, it would be the answer to her prayers. She was really too kind.

Unlike the babbling of his wife, Duchon's remarks were brief and monosyllabic and served to frustrate her insatiable curiosity. She pounced within seconds of his replacing the receiver in its cradle. Given the degree of her frustration, her diplomatic approach was admirable and entirely uncharacteristic. To Jean-Claude Duchon, it provided further incontrovertible proof, not that he needed any, of Janine Destin's ability to manipulate even the hardest cases, among whom he numbered his gorgon of a wife.

"Well, I must say, Jean-Claude, it is most reassuring to me to know that you have friends like Mme. Destin. I don't say that I understand it. She is such a thoughtful and chic woman. I have learned, however, never to look a gift horse in the mouth. Mme. Destin said she might

be having some good news for you. She said it involved a very pleasant change in your situation. She said you should be the one to tell
me."

"And I certainly will, as soon as I discover what it is myself."

"You don't have to take that tone of voice with me, Jean-Claude!"

"I did not realize that I was employing an offensive tone of voice.
Please excuse me."

"Well, you were." She paused briefly to let her words have their intended dramatic effect. "Now, you mean to say you have no idea what
Mme. Destin was referring to when she talked about a change in your
situation?"

"I have a suspicion. I should know more after I speak with her.
She asked if I might meet her in town at four this afternoon. I presume you have no objections since you have your sister coming over
for tea at the exact same time."

"Of course I have no objections if it involves a change for the
good around here. We are certainly overdue for that. But I don't see
why she couldn't have invited me as well. I could have called my sister
and put off our tea. She would have understood. Mme. Destin and I
are friends, after all, even if we don't see each other often. And I am
your wife."

"Indeed you are, Cherie. And it is precisely because of that fact
that she didn't invite you. You know how she is when it comes to mix-
ing business and pleasure. I believe she tried to explain it to you the
last time we were together. Don't you remember?"

"Of course I remember. Do you take me for a cretin? I just don't
think I agree with her on that particular issue. I feel I have a right to
know if it is something that is going to affect my situation as well. I
don't want to have to wait and read it in the newspapers."

"And I certainly would not <u>want</u> you to read it in the newspapers,
I can assure you. Trust me a little. I will let you know everything as
soon as I know it's going to work out. You'll see."

"Well, I guess I have no choice in the matter. At least remember
to give Mme. Destin my regards. Perhaps I should give you a <u>tarte aux</u>

pommes for her. She certainly will find none better in Biarritz, even in the high-priced patisseries like Miremont."

"That would be very nice. I'm sure she would appreciate one of your famous tartes aux pommes."

***

Jean-Claude Duchon arrived at the café a few minutes after four. In addition to the celebrated tarte aux pommes, he carried, in the fancy shopping bag his wife had insisted using, several carefully-wrapped, sugary specialties of the Duchon kitchen. The café was around the corner from Janine Destin's apartment building and she used it as a kind of informal office. It held many bittersweet memories for Jean-Claude Duchon. It was here that he had first met Chantal Clairac with Janine and it was here that he had spent many hours and not a few francs courting her. Janine was waiting for him in her customary corner booth, sipping from a fluted glass. On the round, marble-topped table in front of her were two additional glasses and an antique silver ice bucket in which was chilling a bottle of Mumm's Cordon Rouge.

"Please excuse me, Janine. I have been trying to leave the house for the last half hour. My wife kept thinking of some other pastry you might want to try. I finally had to put my foot down."

"Something you should have done many years ago, if you want my opinion, Jean-Claude. And put it on her mouth. It would serve two good purposes at least. It would shut her up and it would keep her from stuffing it with these disgusting pastries. Even her tarte aux pommes is excessive. I don't see how you can eat it."

"It's not easy, Janine. I assure you."

"Well, enough talk about La Reine Duchon. Let's talk about someone you may find just a bit more amusing. Let's talk about a certain charming young lady with a singing name. Do you know who I mean?"

"Of course, Janine. But please don't tease me. You know how I feel about Chantal. It's driving me crazy not being able to see her."

"Jean-Claude, you should know me better than that! I am not making fun at your expense. To the contrary. You see the two other glasses?"

"Yes."

"Who do you think the third one is for?"

"Chantal?"

"Bravo, mon vieux. She should be here in a few minutes."

"Janine, why didn't you tell me she was coming? Look at me! And these clothes! I look like I'm going to church. What will she think?"

"She'll probably think it would be a good idea for you to go, given what happened to her young American friend."

"I had nothing to do with that, Janine! You know that. It was Jojo and that imbecile, Carlos. I didn't want the kid dead. I just wanted him to leave town."

"Save your pleading for a more sympathetic ear, Jean-Claude. I am not interested in your little self-deceptions."

"But I had nothing to do with it!"

"You had everything to do with it. Don't kid yourself. Who asked Jojo for help? As I recall, it was you, monsieur. Or am I mistaken?"

"I didn't ask him to kill the kid."

"And he didn't mean to have it done. Even he is not that stupid. But when you give a child a pack of matches, fingers usually get burned. Is that not so?"

"Yes. Of course."

"When you asked Jojo for help, you supplied the matches. If you had not asked him to aid you, that boy would still be alive. Is that not also true?"

"I guess so."

"I know so. And so do you. So stop kidding yourself and, please, stop trying to kid me for God's sake. I didn't ask you here today to listen to a pack of pathetic lies."

"Why did you ask me here, Janine? To accuse me of murder? To make me feel worse than I already do?"

"Please, Jean-Claude! Stop whining! I asked you here to help you get back together with Chantal. But I want to be certain you know how things stand. I shall help you and, God knows, you are going to need it after all that's happened. But I expect help in return and absolute loyalty. I don't want you getting confused about who your true friends are. Do we understand each other?"

"Of course, Janine."

"Is there anyone else who can help you with Chantal the way I can?"

"You know there isn't."

"Yes. As a matter of fact I do know that. I am extremely pleased to see that you recognize it as well. So then, with that in mind, is everything arranged for Monday morning?"

"I think so. I talked with Jojo like you asked me to."

"And what was his response?"

"He said he'd take care of everything. He told me to keep my appointment with the American bastard but to make sure I arrive thirty minutes late. He said it was very important and that I should have two reliable witnesses who can say they were with me for at least the first fifteen of those thirty minutes. When I asked him why, he said I would understand afterwards. He said it was for my own protection. Are you sure I'll be all right, Janine?"

"Absolutely certain, Jean-Claude. It is almost too perfect. Let us drink a toast." She raised her glass, looked at Duchon's puzzled face and suddenly let out a howl of raspy laughter. "But I have forgotten to pour you any champagne! Please forgive me. I guess I was thinking of keeping it all for myself. How typical. There. Now we're ready. Here's to getting what we both want!" She chimed her glass against his. "And it looks like some of us will be getting it sooner rather than later. Don't look now and try to stay calm. When she gets to the table, act surprised but don't overdo it. And, above all, let me do the talking at first."

Janine Destin waved Chantal over to the booth.

"Over here, my dear. Look who I ran into on the way to the café. I hope you don't mind that I asked him to join us. I thought it might be like old times."

"No, of course not, Mme. Janine. How are you, Jean-Claude?"

"Very well, thank-you. And you?"

"Very well."

"Chantal, will you take a glass of champagne with us? Please?"

"You are very kind. Thank-you."

"There. Now, let me propose a little toast. I know things have been very difficult for you these last few weeks, Chantal. But things have been difficult for others as well." She nodded slightly toward Jean-Claude. "You are both my dear friends and I want nothing but happiness for both of you. There have been certain misunderstandings, on both of your parts. But it is nothing that can't be worked out, especially with the help of a trusted and sympathetic friend. So, with that in mind, and as a demonstration of forgiveness and friendship, I propose we drink to new beginnings. Agreed? Chantal?"

"Yes, Mme. Janine."

"Jean-Claude?"

"With all my heart. You are a true friend, Janine."

"Excellent. I feel better already. Don't you, Chantal?"

"I am trying, Mme. Janine. But it is very difficult. I don't know what to think anymore."

"Well perhaps I can help you, my dear. I think I know what is bothering you. May I speak very frankly?"

The girl slightly bowed her head.

"Good. The problem is very simple. You think Jean-Claude had something to do with the unfortunate death of your American friend. Based on his behavior, I believe you have good reason to suppose this. He has acted very foolishly in this matter."

Duchon began to protest. She raised her hand, palm out, and cut him off in mid-sentence.

"Please, Jean-Claude, let me continue. The truth must be told. When Chantal began seeing her American friend, you became very jealous. It is true, is it not? As I recall, I even told you not to worry. Young girls <u>will</u> have their little flings; but, that is all they are. Little flings. I had faith in Chantal but you did not. Is this not so?"

"I tried to have faith Janine, but it was very hard. She did not realize how much she was hurting me."

"That may be the case, but still, is what I said not true? You lost faith in Chantal."

"I suppose I did."

"I <u>know</u> you did. And that loss of faith led you to take matters into your own hands. You went to see the boy and tried, in a very clumsy and embarrassing way, to convince him to stop seeing Chantal. But your efforts failed miserably. I am not exaggerating am I, Jean-Claude? Is this not precisely what happened?"

"I was in love with Chantal, Janine. I was not thinking clearly."

"No, you certainly were not. That I will accept. And, I believe Chantal will as well. Won't you, my dear?"

"Yes, Mme. Janine."

"So what did you do next, Jean-Claude? I shall tell you. You went to see my partner, Jojo, who lately seems to have completely lost his mind. You mentioned your predicament to him. And he, for reasons I cannot understand even now, offered to help you. I know this for a fact because that imbecile, my partner, told me."

She stopped to take a sip of champagne. She reached over and took Chantal by the hand.

"After your friend suffered his tragic accident, my dear, I confronted Jojo. I had my suspicions about his involvement. I forced him to tell me everything. This is what he told me. It is the truth. It is necessary that you know it. I know it will be painful, but try to be brave. Will you do that for me, Chantal?"

The nod of her head was barely perceptible.

"There. That's a brave girl. Now then, let me tell you exactly what happened: Jojo told Jean-Claude that he would send three of his boys to scare your friend into leaving town. Jean-Claude insisted there should be no violence. Jojo promised there would be none. But when the men Jojo sent confronted your friend, he panicked and tried to escape by jumping over the wall of the overlook. It seems he slipped on some loose gravel, lost his balance and fell awkwardly. When he landed, his head hit part of the rock retaining wall. The blow killed him immediately. According to Inspector LeClerc, it was an extremely unfortunate, freak accident. No one, especially Jean-Claude, wanted anything like this to happen to your friend. You do realize this, don't you Chantal?"

"Yes, I think so, Mme. Janine."

"You also realize the risk I am taking in telling you about Jojo's involvement in the accident? He would kill me if he knew I was talking to you both like this. I mean that seriously, Chantal. I consider it a risk worth taking, however, if it will help to repair the damage between you and Jean-Claude. You see, he really did have nothing to do with the death of your friend. His only crime is being blinded by his love for you. You see that now, don't you?"

"I am not sure what to believe any more, Mme. Janine. Everyone tells me different things. I am so confused."

"Well, you should not listen to everyone, Chantal. You should only listen to your friends. And you will not find two better friends than Jean-Claude and me. Either of us would do anything for you. Is that not correct, Jean-Claude?"

"Absolutely, Janine. Anything in the world. And I do mean anything."

"You see, Chantal? And I feel exactly the same way. You must promise me two things, my dear. Will you do that for me?"

"If I am able, Mme. Janine. I will try."

"Good. I am sure you will not find it difficult. First, I want you to promise to tell me if anyone, besides Inspector LeClerc or his men, of course, tries to talk to you about your friend's accident. I am being very selfish in asking this, but it is absolutely imperative that I should know for my own safety. I am presently in very great danger, you see."

"I don't understand, Mme. Janine. How can the death of my friend put you in danger?"

"I tell you this in very strict confidence. Both of you. It is a final proof of how much I trust you. Jojo has made many enemies here. This would not concern me if we were not partners in the club and three other enterprises. I have tried to buy him out, but he refuses to even listen to me. His enemies are very jealous of the success he has had and the way he has used it. They have been trying to make trouble for him in business for some time now. Many of these people are in very high places. If they can connect Jojo with the death of your friend in any way, it would make things very difficult for me. I could lose almost everything I have worked so hard for. Thank God Inspector LeClerc is a close friend. He is working- very secretly I should say- to bring the persons directly involved in your friend's accident to justice. It is a very delicate operation. Any outside interference, even by those who are well intentioned, could ruin the whole thing. If the operation is successful, not only will those most responsible for your friend's death be punished, but I should be able to force Jojo to sell his share of the businesses. When the police question Carlos and the others, they will certainly have to implicate Jojo. It will be their word against his. His will carry more weight so he will not face arrest. But I think he will be made to see the advantages of relocating to some other part of the country. He has many friends in Paris and could set himself up quite nicely there, especially if I and some of my government acquaintances put in a good word for him. So you see, Chantal, the importance of not interfering with Inspector LeClerc's investigation in any way?"

"Yes, Mme. Janine. I didn't realize the police were still concerned about what happened to Kevin. I'm sorry if I have caused any trouble."

"Don't worry, my dear. Inspector LeClerc thinks everything will be alright. Everything should be over in the next two or three days. If anyone approaches you before that time, please call me immediately and I shall see that you are not bothered. That goes for you as well, Jean-Claude."

She caught his eye and gave him a furtive, knowing wink.

"I understand completely, Janine. And I must say that I take it as a very great compliment that you feel you can trust me with this very sensitive information. I am sure Chantal feels the same as I do."

"You are very kind, Jean-Claude. I should have probably spoken to you both earlier. I feel a little responsible for my dear Chantal's misunderstanding of your innocent role in this terribly unfortunate tragedy.

"This brings me to my second request, Chantal."

She again reached across the table and took the girl's hand. "My dear, I realize this may be hard for you to think about now. I don't ask you to think about it right away. However, when you have had sufficient time to recover from the shock of your friend's terrible accident, will you promise to give Jean-Claude another chance? I know that he loves you and will take good care of you. I know he would have left his wife earlier, had he been financially secure. And I know something else—something Jean-Claude himself is only now about to learn—that will finally give him the means to leave that selfish, unappreciative woman and become a free man."

"What are you talking about, Janine?"

"It is very simple, mon vieux. When I buy out Jojo's shares, I shall need a man to assist me. A man I can trust, a man I can trust completely. A man that valuable would deserve a share of the business. A share both big enough to enable him to live well and big enough to inspire him to increase the value of the business for both his and his partner's sake. Can you guess who I have in mind for this position, Jean-Claude?"

"You can't be serious, Janine. This is like a dream come true."

"But I am serious, Jean-Claude. And I can tell by the look on your face that you are wide awake and not dreaming."

"How can I possibly thank you?"

"First, by working harder than you have ever worked in your life. Second, by doing everything in your power to make this wonderful girl here take you back. Now, let us put an end to this serious talk and have another bottle of champagne. Waiter!"

CHAPTER TWENTY-THREE

Peter Ellis had fallen asleep to the sound of gusting wind and rattling shutters. When he awoke shortly after eight the following morning, he immediately felt something was wrong. He lay perfectly, warily still and listened. All he could hear was Anya's low, regular breathing next to him. It was as though something that was a part of the room was missing, had been removed while they slept. He looked around the apartment. Sunlight leaking through the louvered wooden slats bathed everything in a soft, muted grey. Suddenly he realized what it was or, more precisely, what it wasn't: For the first time in three days, he could not hear the wind. Trying not to wake Anya, he carefully slipped out of bed. He walked over to one of the ocean-facing windows, gently unlatched them and pushed open the shutters. Sunlight streamed into the room.

"What are you doing, Peter? Is it time to get up?" Anya's voice was groggy with sleep.

"No darling. We can stay in bed all morning if you want. We're not meeting Olga and Maurice until after one."

"What's the weather like?"

"Absolutely beautiful. Almost too good to be true for this time of year."

"Why don't you come back to bed for a little while?"

"Do you want me to leave the shutters open?"

"If you don't mind. It's so wonderful to wake up to sunlight. Especially with your lover next to you."

Peter Ellis lay on his back with Anya's left leg curled over his thighs and her flaxen head nestled on his chest against his neck. He soon felt her left hand begin a slow, deliberate exploration beneath the covers. At first her touch was feathery and all-inclusive, moving ghost-like between stomach and thigh. Then, little by little, almost imperceptibly, she narrowed her area of interest, began measuring with her fingertips the length and heat she had created. Their love-making was deliciously slow and delicate up until the final, shuddering moment of wild thrust and release. When it was over, they collapsed into each other's salty embrace and, within minutes, fell asleep.

They both slept soundly and did not wake until almost ten. By the time they had showered and dressed, it was past ten-thirty and Peter Ellis realized that the hotel's kitchen was already prepping for the midday meal. He suggested they walk over to Au Haio, a venerable old neighborhood café on the rue Gambetta, for a quick, light breakfast. The day was magnificent, a bright visitation of Indian summer, the sky almost cloudless and the temperature already in the sixties. They walked hand-in-hand and Peter Ellis could not remember when he had felt so perfectly content.

"Oh Peter, I feel so lucky to be alive on such a beautiful day in such a beautiful place. I feel as if God is smiling down on us."

"If He is, I'll bet He's blushing."

"Don't be so sure. Whoever or whatever God is, I doubt that any behavior based on true love would surprise or embarrass Him. Or Her."

"I guess you are right. I must admit, though, I have never thought of God in quite that way."

"Perhaps it's time for you to start."

"You know, Anya, I believe it is."

Though they were both very hungry, they limited themselves to croissants, a bottle of Badoit sparkling water and bowls of steaming café au lait in anticipation of the large meal Maurice had promised them. After their small breakfast, they spent almost an hour strolling in the cliffside park and along the wide sidewalk overlooking the beach of Côte des Basques. A little before noon, they left Biarritz for the hour and twenty- minute drive to the old fortified Bèarnais town of Navarrenx. They found Maurice and Olga waiting for them in the dining room of the Hotel du Commerce.

"So, my young friends, I am very glad to see you have finally found your way to the humble town of my birth."

"We are not late, are we Maurice?" Peter Ellis glanced down at his old Rolex. "You did say one-fifteen, didn't you?"

"Indeed I did. And you have arrived with three minutes to spare. I only meant that, after all your complimentary remarks about Sauveterre, I am very pleased for you to visit this second, and for me very special, jewel of the Gave d'Oloron. How do you find it, Mlle. Anya?"

"Absolutely charming. It is different from Sauveterre but equally as beautiful, from the little I have been able to see."

"Peter, your friend is a born diplomat, though I believe she speaks the truth regarding Navarrenx. In any event, you will be able to judge for yourselves after lunch, for I intend to give you a unique guided tour of the town. But now, let us sample some of the delicacies of this little region. I hope you are hungry. I have ordered a small feast."

The old inspector did not exaggerate concerning either the quality or the quantity of the food. As an added, unexpected treat, he delivered, with each of the five courses, a short lecture on its preparation and provenance. Even Peter Ellis was astonished by the depth of his friend's culinary knowledge. While the dessert plates were being cleared, he suggested that, as it was an unusually beautiful day for that time of year, they repair to the hotel's small garden for a glass of something to aid in the digestion of the meal they had just eaten. He knew for a fact that the hotel bar possessed an excellent choice of Armangacs. Virtually in unison, the two women groaned at the prospect of consuming a bite or a drop of anything more. Olga proposed that she and Anya take a much-needed constitutional and leave the two gentlemen to the enjoyment of their brandy. They would rendez-vous within the hour for the promised guided tour.

Peter Ellis insisted that Maurice choose the Armangac. While they waited for the barman to deliver it, he began recounting the story Christine had told the previous evening concerning Duchon and the waitress, Madeline. Maurice expressed first disbelief then displeasure with himself that he had heard nothing of the affair until that moment. He agreed that it certainly seemed to cement their case against Duchon and provided invaluable insurance for the trap they had devised for him and Gambia, should they prove cagier than anticipated. When Peter Ellis told of his chance meeting in St. Jean-de-Luz with Joseph Gambia, the old inspector was even more incredulous. His shock quickly turned to concern when Peter Ellis recounted the conversation they had had.

"Do you not think that it must be you he is speaking of when he refers to someone—how did he put it—poking his head into his affairs?"

"I believe he spoke of someone 'sticking his nose' into his affairs, which I find much more appropriate in a country once ruled by DeGaulle. And yes, I do think it was me he was referring to, albeit not the Peter Edwards version of me that he has befriended. I must say that I hope to be present when he learns Peter Ellis and Peter Edwards are the same man. It should be quite amusing."

"More amusing, I wager, than if he decides to send some of his thugs to your apartment instead of Duchon. You recall his warning of making sure to be alone."

"Indeed I do, Maurice. But I can't believe Gambia would be so stupid as to send any of his people to my apartment. What I am expecting is that he will have Duchon try to lead me into a trap, much as we ourselves are trying to make Duchon lead him into one. Which works in our favor provided we can make Duchon cooperate."

"That is possible, Pierre. Still, I think it would not be a bad idea to take some added precautions. Why not have my friend Inspector Rectoran hidden somewhere close by at the time of the meeting."

"Provided Inspector Rectoran lets no one else know what he is doing, I have no objection, Maurice. I do not have a great deal of faith in the discretion of the local police department."

"Nor do I. But they are not all corrupt. I have known Rectoran for many years now. He is as straight as they get. He is also a good man to have around if the going gets rough. He used to be in a special anti-terrorist unit of the army. I can assure you that he is even more fed up with LeClerc and his cronies than we are. He has been keeping a private watch on them for some time, which is how I have learned much of what I know about their involvement with the local underworld."

"Why has he not been able to do anything about them? He must have some proof of their involvement by now."

"Rectoran is a very careful man, Pierre. I think it comes from his time in the anti-terrorist unit. Also, he knows how well connected LeClerc is, which is something even I did not appreciate until it was too late. I believe if we are successful in what we are trying to do, he will have what he needs to go to the proper authorities. At least, that is what he has indicated to me."

"I didn't realize you and he have been working so closely together."

"I can't tell you everything, my friend. It would not be discreet."

"Touché, you old devil. I am glad to see that certain of your skills have not diminished with age. The blade of the sword remains as sharp as ever."

"As one would expect from someone coming from the same region as D'Artagnan and Cyrano."

"A fine point, if you do make it yourself."

"Indeed I do. Now then, we are in agreement about having Rectoran stay close-by tomorrow when you meet with Duchon in case Gambia decides to do something foolish?"

"Absolutely."

"Do you think we have time for another Armagnac before the ladies return?"

"I am certain of it."

"Très bien! There is something new on the list that the barman said we should try."

"In that case, I think it would be in very poor taste not to act on his recommendation."

The second snifter of Bas Armagnac was even better than the first, possessing a delicacy and smoothness rarely encountered in even the absurdly priced designer cognacs. Olga and Anya arrived as they were savoring the final memorable sips.

As promised, Maurice gave them a comprehensive guided tour of the old town, his running commentary informed with tidbits of information that only a native son might possess. The tour ended with a visit to a small tavern owned by one of his childhood friends. He was a thin, hawk-nosed, merry-eyed man who insisted they all join him in a bottle of Jurançon from his private reserve. By the time Peter Ellis and Anya left his little bar, it was nearly four-thirty.

At Anya's request, they stopped at Sauveterre on the way back to LaBorde. Saying she had overlooked a few important details in her painting of the Church of St. Andre, she suggested that Peter Ellis wait in the small café across the square while she made the sketches necessary to rectify the oversight. The afternoon light was already beginning to fade and she would have to work fast if she were to finish before nightfall. Peter Ellis took advantage of the time to scribble some final notes for his meeting with Duchon, incorporating some suggestions Maurice had made earlier over their glasses of Armagnac.

They spent a quiet evening at LaBorde, Anya working behind her easel in a corner of the farm's large atelier, he and Olga catching up on news and recalling stories from the summer when he had been a part of the Van Cys family, a glorious summer of self-discovery, friendship and young love. At nine-thirty, Olga announced that she could keep her eyes open not one minute longer. She wished them both goodnight and promised to make sure they were awakened by six-thirty.

CHAPTER TWENTY-FOUR

P eter Ellis left the farm early, reaching Biarritz shortly after eight. He parked his car on the narrow service road that ran behind his apartment and the adjoining hotel. He walked to the corner of the rue Million and crossed the coast road, La Perspective. He stood next to the short shell and cement fence bordering the cliffside park and spent several minutes gazing out at the ocean and the jagged, rocky southern edge of the Pointe Atalaye and the Cachous rocks beyond. There were large waves breaking against the point and the surrounding rocks as well as those buttressing the winding seawall. Normally, he would have taken the path down to the overlook for a closer inspection of the surf. Today, however, there would be no time for the riding of waves. Looking out over the ocean, he detected a high, almost straight line of clouds approaching from the northwest. He turned his back to the building wind and crossed the road to Les Flots Bleus.

The dining room was filled with the usual lively collection of traveling salesmen and saleswomen. They were seated on either side of a long central table discussing their day's destinations and clients between mouthfuls of croissant and gulps of coffee. He shook hands with a couple of regulars whom he had come to know over the years then took a table by the front window-wall and ordered café au lait and a sandwich of jambon de Paris. Before going up to his apartment to shower and prepare for Duchon's arrival, he checked at the reception desk to make sure he had received no messages.

When he entered his apartment, he immediately became aware of a distinct chill in the air. A quick inspection of the room revealed the reason for the coldness: he had forgotten to close one of the bedroom windows he had opened the previous morning when Anya was there. After securing the window and turning up the thermostat, he took a long, hot shower. He was shaving when the men came.

Three loud knocks on the apartment door shattered the morning silence. He called out that he would be there in a minute then quickly but carefully stroked the remaining lather from his face. He put down his razor and glanced at his watch which he had placed on the narrow countertop next to the sink. It was a few minutes past nine-thirty. His meeting with Duchon was set for eleven. As he approached the door, his insistent visitor knocked again, only louder this time.

"I hear you! Who is it?" He searched his pocket for the door key then realized he had left it on the bedroom dressing table.

"It is yours, the white car parked at the corner of the alley?"

"The white Porsche?"

"Yes, with Paris plates."

"Yes, that is my car. Is there something wrong?"

"There has been a slight accident. I did not expect a car to be parked so close to the corner. Luckily, the damage is minor, just a small dent. There is no need to call the police. I am willing to pay a reasonable sum to repair your old car, even though it was parked in a bad place. Provided the police are not involved."

"My car was where I always park it!"

"I suggest, then, that you choose a more suitable place."

"Wait a minute, I'll be right down. We can decide how we are going to handle the repair bill when I see the car."

"As you wish, monsieur. I shall be waiting for you."

As Peter Ellis walked back to the bathroom to rinse his face, he silently cursed the man behind the door. And not just because of his arrogant attitude. The body of his beloved old 911 had been meticulously restored and repainted the previous spring, a mere six months ago. Hopefully, the damage was indeed slight and it would be possible for him and the rude stranger to settle on a price for the repairs. The last thing he wanted this morning was a visit from the local police. He went into the bedroom, pulled on a Lacoste knit shirt, retrieved his key from the dresser and walked back into the small vestibule. He fitted the large key into the worn lock and carefully worked the ancient mechanism. The heavy bolt disengaged with a loud, metallic clank. In that instant, the door seemed to explode in on him. A short, stocky man burst into the room, pushed him hard against the table and quickly stepped aside. Two other, taller men rushed in behind him. Peter Ellis lunged at them. They wrestled him awkwardly back against the table, one on either side of him. He was still fighting to get free when the first man stepped forward and pressed the barrel of a small pistol against his stomach.

"Enough!"

Peter Ellis immediately stopped struggling and, for the first time, focused on the short, wide, olive-skinned man holding the gun. It was the same man Dany, the 'hostess' from Le Gentleman, had identified as Carlos that first, adultrous night in the club. Unlike that night, today he was dressed as though he had just escaped from the set of The Untouchables: dark, pin-striped, double-breasted suit, wide white tie and light grey fedora. Were it not for the gun, Peter Ellis would have had to laugh at his theatrical get-up.

"That's better. Stay calm and no one will get hurt." He motioned with the short barrel to the row of dining chairs lined up against the interior wall and addressed his two accomplices. "I think our friend would be more comfortable if he sat there while we take care of our business. Why don't you help him into one of those chairs?"

The two men, each one holding an arm, guided Peter Ellis roughly into one of the chairs. They remained standing on either side of him.

"Now then, M. Ellis, why don't you put both of your hands on top of your head? That way, I will know where they are." Peter Ellis did as he was instructed. "Good. You take orders well. That is very important. You know why, M. Ellis?"

Peter Ellis sat motionless and stared blankly at the man called Carlos. He said nothing.

"You don't? Well, then, let me tell you. It is very simple. It will keep me from shooting you." He paused and grinned at Peter Ellis, showing several bad teeth. "You know what I think? I think we should make a deal. You do nothing stupid and I won't shoot you. Agreed?"

Peter Ellis slightly nodded his head.

"No, let me hear you say it. Say 'I agree'."

"I agree."

"Much better. That's settled then." He backed away from Peter Ellis and motioned to his two companions, pointing the gun in the direction of the bedroom door. "You two have a look around in there. You never know what you might find in a man's bedroom. And see if he has a radio or something. I feel like we may need some music later on. Music makes work much easier. Don't you think so, M. Ellis?"

Peter Ellis stared straight ahead and said nothing.

"You don't have much to say, do you? That's too bad. I like talking to men who have something to say. When my friends here finish their search, we must see what we can do about this talking problem you seem to have."

Carlos waved his two accomplices away then seated himself on the edge of the massive Basque oak table across from Peter Ellis. He began to whistle a popular pop song. Peter Ellis, hands on his head, began to look around the room and assess his predicament.

He was fairly certain that the thing Carlos had sent his accomplices to find was Kevin Duffy's diary. Of course, there was no risk of their finding it. What they would find would be his notes for the Kevin Duffy article. Since it was doubtful any of them read English, they might mistake his notes for the diary, seeing the repeated names of Chantal, Gambia and Duchon. In addition to looking for the diary, he figured Carlos and his two nameless friends had been sent (no doubt by Gambia) to intimidate him into leaving Biarritz. He suddenly thought of Maurice's description of the knife wound on Kevin Duffy's neck. Peter Ellis had had a lifelong phobia of knives and of being attacked with them. They always made him think of the shower scene in the movie, <u>Psycho</u>. He began to look around the room for possible ways to escape. The situation was not promising: The front door, to his left, was locked with the key safely in Carlos' pocket. Two old French doors, to his immediate right, opened onto a small, second-floor balcony and, he speculated, were probably not locked. The balcony was at least twenty feet above the enclosed gravel courtyard and so posed no security risk. He thought he could make it through the doorway and over the waist-high, wrought iron railing were it not for the pistol Carlos held in his right hand. He decided that, for the moment, he had no choice except to wait and see what developed. He could not believe that Gambia would be so stupid as to have him seriously injured. He had to realize such a course of action would only further complicate any cover-up by his friends in the police.

For the first time since he had been surprised by Carlos and his two accomplices, Peter Ellis began to feel better about his plight. But then, suddenly, he recalled his chance encounter with Gambia in St. Jean-de-Luz. He saw Gambia's grinning, wolfish face and heard Gambia's conspiratorial voice congratulating him on his suggestion of how to deal with an adversary who poked his nose into one's business. He pictured Carlos slicing off the tip of his nose with his switchblade, no doubt the same knife he had used on Kevin Duffy's arm and throat.

"So, just how fast will that old Porsche of yours go?" The question from Carlos interrupted Peter Ellis's disheartening speculations.

"I'm really not sure. Close to 200 kilometers, I imagine."

"Is that all? I wouldn't have a car like that if it didn't do at least 240. It would be embarrassing to have a Porsche that didn't do at least 240 or 250."

"I'm sure it would be embarrassing for someone like you."

"What is that supposed to mean, 'someone like me'? Are you trying to make fun of me?"

"Not at all."

"I think you are. I think you are trying to be cute, trying to make fun of me. That's not very smart, monsieur. I do not like people trying to be cute with me. Understand?"

"You made the statement. I was just agreeing with you."

"Maybe I don't think that's true. Maybe I don't like how you are speaking to me."

"That's too bad."

Carlos slapped him hard across the face. Peter Ellis moved his hands and made to defend himself against additional blows. Carlos quickly stepped back, leveled the short, black barrel at his chest and began screaming at him.

"You move anymore and I'll shoot you. Put your hands back on your head! Now!"

The sound of his raised voice brought his two accomplices rushing into the room, both talking at the same time.

"What's going on? Is everything okay, Carlos? Take it easy! Be calm, Carlos!"

"Shut up, both of you." He waved the gun in their direction. "I have everything under control. I was just teaching M. Ellis a lesson in respect. Now he knows my name, thanks to you bright boys. Maybe I should give him both your names as well. And your addresses. That way he'll know where to send the police."

"I already knew your name, Carlos."

"What?"

"I said I already knew your name. In fact, I know where you work and who you work for."

"What are you talking about? How could you know any of that? I think you are lying. You just heard them say my name."

"You think so? What if I told you that you have been chasing a certain young lady named Marie-Thérèse? And, having very little success, I might add. I don't recall your two friends here saying anything about her, do you, Carlos? How could I have known about her?"

"He has a point, Carlos. We didn't say anything about little Marie."

"Shut up, Marco."

"What if I also told you, Carlos, that your bosses, Jojo and Janine, are not very happy with what you've been doing. And I'm not just talking about your work at the club."

"That's a lie. How can you know what they think?"

"Maybe I'm not who you think I am."

"What do you mean?"

"I mean that maybe I'm someone else. That maybe you've made a big mistake."

"I haven't made any mistakes. Jojo told me exactly where to go."

"Perhaps <u>he</u> has made a mistake, then. Maybe he's trying to set you up. I can think of at least one good reason why he might want to. Can't you, Carlos? Think about it."

"What I think is you better shut up. Right now!"

"Carlos?"

"You shut up too, Marco."

"But Carlos, listen to me. I've seen this guy before. And I just remembered where."

"What are you talking about?"

"He was at the club the other night. Talking with Dany. You remember, the night Jojo, Janine and Inspector LeClerc showed up while you were talking with Marie-Thérèse, and Jojo got so mad with you. Remember?"

"Enough, Marco. Of course I remember that night. How could I forget? So, our friend here was with that slut, Dany? That explains why he's acting like he knows so much. I've warned that bitch about her big mouth. This time she's gone too far. I don't think Jojo's going to be too pleased when he hears that she's been talking about our business to strangers, do you Marco?"

"But Carlos, that's just it. Jojo was talking with this guy too. Whoever he is. He was talking with him like they were old friends. Laughing. Making jokes. He even let Dany take him in the back."

"What? Are you sure?"

"Of course I'm sure. Ask Pipo. He was there with me."

"Is that right, Pipo?"

The one called Pipo was standing across the room on the other side of the table. He had brought Peter Ellis's portable cassette player from the bedroom and put it on the table. He had also brought Peter Ellis's travel case of cassettes. While the others were talking, he had been examining the collection. He had removed one cassette and was reading the song titles. At the mention of his name, he looked up from the cassette.

"What did you say, Carlos?"

Carlos waved the gun at him. "Put that shit down and pay attention. This is important."

He tossed the cassette box carelessly on the table. The lid popped open and the cassette slid across the table, stopping less than six inches from the edge. Peter Ellis looked down and saw it was an early recording by Dire Straits.

"I have been paying attention."

"So? Answer my question."

"It's like Marco just said. This guy was in the club the other night talking with Dany. When Jojo and the others came in, they started carrying on like old friends. I didn't recognize him when we first got here, but now I'm sure he's the same guy."

"Son of a bitch! There's something wrong here. I don't like it when shit like this happens."

"That's what I've been trying to tell you, Carlos. You and your buddies are being set up by Jojo."

"You," he leveled the pistol at Peter Ellis's face, "you shut up. When I want you to talk, I'll tell you. Or make you." He turned suddenly and handed the pistol to the one called Marco, who was standing behind him next to the front door. "Here. Take this and put it in your pocket. I don't want you shooting me by mistake. Pipo, you go back to the bedroom and see if you can find anything with this guy's name on it. And be quick. I'll take care of things in here. This guy seems to know so much, I think it's time he started sharing what he knows with us."

He turned to face Peter Ellis. As he did so, he reached into his coat pocket and removed a narrow black and silver knife handle. The end protruded two inches past the grip of his thumb and forefinger. With an almost imperceptible movement, he flicked open the long, thin shiny blade.

"Is that the knife you used on the American boy down in the park?"

"What are you talking about? What American boy?"

"Don't play dumb, Carlos. I know how you cut Kevin Duffy on the neck, how you forced him off the lookout at knifepoint, how you, in other words, killed him."

"Killed him? That's crazy. The stupid American bastard took off and jumped. We weren't there to hurt him, only to scare him."

"You did a very good job of it. You scared him to death. I think that's called murder."

Carlos took two quick steps forward and laid the cold blade of the knife on the underside of Peter Ellis's jaw.

"Carlos! Be careful! Remember what the boss said." The one named Marco had stepped over and put his hand on Carlos's arm. Carlos stepped back but kept the tip of the switchblade pointed at Peter Ellis's face.

"Listen to me! Listen very carefully! I did not kill that American guy. My knife slipped. That's all. Then the crazy bastard decided to jump. Just like that. I did nothing to make him jump. Ask Marco or Pipo. They were there."

"Yes, I know they were there. I have talked with witnesses who saw them there. That makes them accessories to murder, even though they really didn't have anything to do with it. The way I see it, it was all your fault, Carlos. Why should they suffer for your mistake? What do you think, Marco? You have the gun now. Are you going to let Carlos kill me too? How do you think your boss, Jojo, would like another 'accidental' murder to worry about? I don't think he'd be very happy."

"You! Shut up!" Carlos waved the knife in Peter Ellis's face. "I've had enough of your mouth. You are beginning to make me mad."

"Take it easy, Carlos. Look. Here's Pipo."

"It's about time. What have you found? Did you find the diary?"

"I don't know. I found these papers but I can't read them. They're in English."

"Let me see them."

"They're in English, Carlos."

"So? I studied English in school. Let me see them. We don't have all day, remember?"

Peter Ellis immediately saw that the papers Pipo had found were indeed his notes on the Duffy case. He was not sure how well Carlos read English. It hardly mattered. He was certain to recognize all the names. He watched as Carlos quickly perused the top page. Carlos looked up with a smug, humorless smile.

"M. Ellis - if that is really your name - I think you have been telling my boss lies. My boss has a thing about people who tell him lies. I don't know what games you've been playing, but I know how to make you tell me."

He pointed the long, thin blade at Peter Ellis and sighted down its length dramatically, like a matador sighting down his sword before the kill. Then he slowly moved it to his left in the direction of the cassette machine Pipo had placed on the table.

"Pipo, put on some music. I don't want our little interview with M. Ellis to disturb any of his neighbors."

"I can't figure the damn machine out, Carlos. It's some kind of new model."

"My God, Pipo, I don't believe this. And you wonder why Jojo put me in charge."

"You try it then, if you're so smart. I'm telling you it doesn't work like the ones we have."

"Okay, okay! Enough. I believe you. I'll take care of the music. Go back and see what else you can find in M. Ellis's bedroom. And hurry up." He turned and pointed the switchblade at Peter Ellis. "Would you be a good little boy and put that cassette on for us?" He indicated the Dire Straits recording which lay on the edge of the table. "And please, don't try anything stupid. I am not in the mood for any more games. Marco, keep an eye on our friend here while I see what these papers are all about."

With a quick flick of his wrist, Carlos retracted the blade and dropped the knife into his pocket. He then began shuffling through the Duffy article notes. Peter Ellis slowly rose from his chair and

walked deliberately to the far end of the massive oak table. He picked
up the Dire Straits cassette that Pipo had thrown down and reached
across the table for the small recording machine. He clicked open
the playback compartment and inserted the cassette. Then he looked
over to where Carlos stood with Marco next to the locked front door.
Carlos had turned to face his friend so that his back was to Peter Ellis.
He was discussing something with Marco in a low voice. Peter Ellis
slowly moved his hands away from the cassett machine to the edge
of the table. He tightly gripped the underside bracing, lifted the end
chest-high in one quick movement and pushed the table as hard as
he could toward the two men, pinning them against the opposite
wall. The action was accompanied by a chorus of obscenities. He pivoted and found the working handle of the French doors. He tried to
turn it but nothing gave. It was like a bad dream suddenly become reality: the doors were locked. Though the dream lasted only a couple
of seconds, the realization had the effect of freezing time. He tried
the handle again and, all at once, felt something give. Accompanied
by the grating sound of rusty metal forced into movement, the long,
locking mechanism of the double doors disengaged. He pulled
sharply on the old oval handle. The left door slammed against an
adjoining chair exploding the bottom glass panel. He clambered over
the balcony's waist-high railing of ornamental ironwork and dropped
down the twenty or so feet to the gravel courtyard. A burning jab
of pain shot through his right ankle followed by a cracking sensation as the right side of his body hit the ground. He jumped up and
started running toward the alleyway behind the hotel. Just outside
the entrance to the courtyard, he nearly ran into the back of Joseph
Gambia, who was standing next to the wall smoking a cigarette. He
stopped abruptly, just as Gambia flicked the butt on the pavement
and turned to face him. He had begun to say something but all Peter
Ellis could make out was a prefatory expletive and the name 'Carlos'
before the gangster stopped in mid-sentence. On Gambia's face what
had been an expression of angry impatience had changed to one of
outright astonishment.

"You were expecting someone else, Jojo?"

"What are you doing here, M. Edwards?"

"I could ask you the same question, Jojo, but I already know the answer. You see, I have just been talking with some friends of yours up in my apartment. It was very interesting for awhile. But they became extremely rude. I decided to leave early."

"What are you talking about?"

"The three punks you sent up to see me. Carlos and his buddies, Marco and Pipo. The same three punks you sent to scare Kevin Duffy into leaving Biarritz. Or did you mean for them to kill him?"

"What? Are you crazy?"

"No, I am not crazy. What did you send them up to do to me, Jojo? Kill me too? Or just cut off a piece of my nose? Carlos, he's very proud of that big switchblade. Too bad he's so stupid and has such a bad temper. But then, it's hard to find good help these days."

"Who are you?"

Peter Ellis suddenly heard the rattling slam of his apartment building's heavy iron and glass front door.

"My name is not Edwards, it is Ellis, Peter Ellis. I am a journalist. You must now please excuse me. I must make a telephone call to the police." He took off at a trot toward the hotel's service entrance. One of the hotel's cooks had just come out to smoke a cigarette. He waved to the cook then glanced briefly back over his shoulder. Gambia had intercepted Carlos and his pals. The four of them had begun walking briskly in the direction of the rue Gambetta.

Peter Ellis found Arlette, the hotel manager, at the reception desk working on the day's receipts. She looked up instinctively at the sudden sound of his approach.

"Arlette, may I please use your telephone?"

"Of course, Pierre." She smiled as she handed him the telephone. The smile immediately vanished when she noticed how his hand was shaking when he took the receiver from her. Then she saw the expression on his face. "Pierre! What has happened? You are shaking. Is something wrong?"

"I have had a little unpleasant surprise. But don't worry. It is all over now. It was something I should have expected. I have been very stupid and reckless. I must call Maurice immediately and explain what has happened. You may listen so that you will know as well."

"You are sure, Pierre? It is perhaps none of my business."

"I am absolutely certain, Arlette. It is something I think you should know. It is not something I want to keep secret."

Maurice picked up the telephone on the first ring. He had obviously been keeping a kind of phone-side vigil. Peter Ellis quickly gave him a short summary of what had happened. He left out most of the details of Carlos's knife-play, not wanting to alarm Arlette. When he had finished he heard Maurice grunt with disgust.

"It is unbelievable, no? Gambia, he thinks he is above the law."

"Or working with it. LeClerc must have known what he was planning to do."

"I am not so certain of that, my friend."

"Come on, Maurice. They are partners, aren't they?"

"Yes. Of course. But I can't see LeClerc doing something so stupid. So brazen. Although I detest the man, I must give the devil his due. For all of his faults, Inspector LeClerc is an extremely careful and clever man. He did not get to where he is solely on his rugby reputation, though that did not hurt him either."

"So what do you think then?"

"Mon ami, I think, upon reflection, that we both may be right. It does stand to reason, as you have pointed out, that Gambia would alert LeClerc to an undertaking so risky for all of them."

"What do you mean, 'all of them'? Who else might be involved?"

"Janine Destin. The third partner. And the smartest, I might add. If LeClerc was aware of Gambia's plan, he would certainly have told her. Unlike Gambia, Janine Destin is not one to take undue risks. If she had advance knowledge of the plan to intimidate you in such a heavy-handed and dangerous way and allowed it to proceed, it leads me to believe there is more going on here than we realize."

"I think I see what you are getting at, Maurice. There is trouble in paradise."

"Exactly, mon vieux. But it seems you have foiled their plan with your fortuitous escape."

"Not necessarily, Maurice."

"I don't understand."

"At this moment, only Gambia and the three punks know about my escape. As far as the others are concerned, I am still in my apartment, condition unknown. What time is it right now? About ten o'clock?"

"It is five after."

"Duchon is not scheduled to arrive until eleven."

"You intend to return to the apartment and wait for him? After what just happened? What if they return?"

"Even Gambia is not that stupid, Maurice. But don't worry. This time I shall take precautions before opening the door to strangers. Perhaps you can contact your friend, Rectoran, and have him come over right away and take up his position. Just in case."

"I shall call him immediately. It will take him about ten minutes to get there from the station. I suggested he wait there and keep an eye on LeClerc until just before eleven. I'm sure he will be ready."

"Good. I'll wait here fifteen minutes and have a drink. I think I need one."

"Pierre, what do you think is going to happen?"

"I really have no idea, Maurice. But I feel certain that <u>something</u> is going to happen. We will just have to wait and see."

"Well, be careful, mon ami."

"Don't worry. I think I have learned my lesson."

"I shall wait here by the phone. Call me when you have news. Good luck!"

"Thanks. I shall talk to you soon." He handed the receiver back to Arlette. "I know it is early, Arlette, but I think I need a beer."

CHAPTER TWENTY-FIVE

A t ten-twenty, Peter Ellis returned to his apartment next to the hotel. The door gaped open and, inside the vestibule, the large Basque table lay on its side surrounded by overturned chairs. Cassettes and their empty plastic boxes littered the floor next to the entrance. His portable cassette player rested at an angle against the right wall close to where, less than an hour ago, he had sat at knifepoint and been interrogated. At the far end of the room, the old French doors groaned as they swung in the breeze, the left door banging loudly against the radiator with every intermittent small gust of wind.

Peter Ellis entered the room and closed the door. He found that, in their haste to leave, Carlos and his friends had left the key in the lock. He turned the key to engage the bolt then walked over and closed the French doors. He set about righting the furniture and picking up and re-boxing the scattered cassettes. When he had finished, he went into the bathroom. He found his watch on the ledge by the sink. He strapped it on and noted the time. Duchon was scheduled to arrive in twenty-five minutes. While he completed his morning's interrupted toilette, washing his hands and face and brushing his teeth, he speculated on possible scenarios. Whether Duchon showed up or not, one thing was certain: the morning's events had raised the ante for those responsible for Kevin Duffy's so called "accidental death".

The absolute disarray of his bedroom put a momentary halt to his speculations. If not thorough, Marco and Pipo had been tornado-like going through his room. Drawers had been emptied and discarded, his bed had been stripped and partly dismantled and his closet had been laid bare. Everything lay scattered across the floor. He stepped carefully over to his desk. Next to it, as if by some miracle, his trash basket stood upright. He reached down and retrieved the heavy Colt automatic from under the plastic lining. He checked the clip, flicked off the safety and placed the pistol on the edge of the desk. He began straightening up the mess made by his mid-morning visitors, beginning with his papers which seemed to be scattered everywhere. He had nearly finished getting them all back in order when he heard two loud knocks on his door. He looked at his watch. It was exactly ten minutes past eleven. He retrieved his pistol from the desk and walked into the vestibule. As he reached the door, the knocking was repeated. Everyone was insistent this morning it seemed.

"I'm coming! Who is it?"

"The police! Open the door immediately!"

"Who?"

"Chief Inspector LeClerc! Open the door now or I shall break it down."

Peter Ellis smiled to himself. It would take an ax or a sledgehammer to break down the old oak door. Holding the gun by his side, he unlocked the door and stood aside. LeClerc took three quick steps inside and glanced quickly around the room. He looked a bit perplexed.

"May I help you, Inspector?"

"You are M. Peter Ellis?"

"Yes."

"You are here alone?"

"For the moment."

"You are expecting someone?"

"It is possible. I was not, however, expecting you, Inspector. May I ask why you have come?"

"I have received a complaint."

"About me?"

"Yes, about you, M. Ellis."

"May I ask from whom?"

"I prefer not to say at this time."

"Then may I ask what it concerns?"

LeClerc strode suddenly across the room, seeming to ignore the question. He stood for a moment in front of the French doors, gazing outside. He turned just as Peter Ellis was pocketing his pistol, which he had held out of sight during his brief exchange with the inspector.

"What is that you are putting in your pocket?"

"My pistol. I have a permit for it."

"Your pistol? What are you doing with a pistol?"

"My work is sometimes dangerous. It is necessary to protect myself. I could have used it earlier this morning."

"Your work? What is your work? I thought you were in Biarritz because of what happened to that young American man, M. Duffy. I understood you were a friend of the family."

"It is true. I am here because of what happened to the young man, Kevin Duffy. But I lied about being a friend of the family. I am a journalist."

"A journalist? You are American, yes?"

"Yes."

"I am very surprised that a story about the accidental death of a reckless young American surfer would merit sending a journalist all the way to France. Unless your paper is one of those that likes to make trouble,that fabricates the facts to fit the story. I must warn you, M. Ellis, if that is the kind of paper you work for, watch out! I shall not support lies being told about me or my force."

"Thank-you for the warning, Inspector. I agree with you about those kind of papers. What we call tabloids in the United States. You need not worry."

"I hope not."

"You see, I was not sent here from the United States. I live in Paris. I work for the European News Bureau. I write free-lance features for papers and magazines both here and in the United States. Perhaps you have read some of them. I recently did a three part series that was published throughout France."

"With respect, M. Ellis, I have never heard of you."

Peter Ellis had been building to this moment. He paused and looked meekly at LeClerc, affecting embarrassment at his pitifully evident lack of renown. The acting job elicited the desired response. As if on cue, the inspector became smugly apologetic.

"I'm very sorry, M. Ellis. It is not personal."

"There is no reason to be sorry, Inspector. It is entirely understandable. In fact, I would be worried if you <u>had</u> heard of me. It would mean a lapse of security at the Bureau."

"What are you talking about, M. Ellis? Why would you be worried if I had heard of you?"

"Because I write under a pseudonym, Inspector. For reasons of self-protection. Unfortunately, every now and then, someone discovers that Jean LeBlanc is actually Peter Ellis." He looked directly into the inspector's widening eyes and gave him his best disarming smile.

"You are Jean LeBlanc? You are the one who did the series about that racket in the mustard industry in Dijon?"

"So you <u>have</u> read one of my pieces?"

"Merde! I do not believe it!"

"Is something wrong, Inspector? Perhaps you did not like the piece on Dijon? Perhaps it was too hot for you?"

LeClerc ignored the question and feeble pun. His expression had turned to stone. His voice was all business.

"M. Ellis, please hand over your gun. Then tell me exactly what you are really doing here."

"But I have a permit for my pistol."

"If you have a valid permit for it, I shall return your pistol when you leave Biarritz. Now, if you please, give me your gun. And be careful."

Peter Ellis retrieved the pistol from his pocket and handed it, butt first, to LeClerc.

"Now, please tell me why you have come to Biarritz."

"I have told you, Inspector. I have come to investigate the death of Kevin Duffy. You see, unlike you, I do not think the death was entirely accidental. In fact, I <u>know</u> it was not entirely accidental."

"May I ask how you know that?"

"It is very simple, Inspector. The person who caused the young man's death told me exactly what happened that morning. He even showed me the knife he used to cut him. If I had chosen to stay around, I believe he would have done more than show me the knife."

"What in the world are you talking about, M. Ellis? What person?"

"His name is Carlos. He works for Joseph Gambia. He and his friends, Marco and Pipo, paid me a visit almost an hour ago. You understand, it was not a social call."

"Merde! I should have known! What an imbecile!"

"It sounds like you know of Carlos and his friends."

"It is my business to know of such people, M. Ellis."

"Yes, I suppose it is, Inspector."

"What did they want with you?"

"They wanted to see if I had Kevin Duffy's diary here. They also came, I believe, to scare me into leaving Biarritz. The same way they tried to scare Kevin Duffy that morning down in the park. Unfortunately, he was not as lucky as I was when he jumped to escape from them. I now know exactly how he felt that morning. You really should take that knife away from Carlos the next time you see him. You might also consider arresting him before he kills someone else."

"Do not tell me how to do my job, M. Ellis. Why do you think I am here now?"

"You came here to arrest Carlos? I thought you said you had received a complaint about me, no doubt from Jean-Claude Duchon. Evidently, he told you about our meeting today."

"I knew of your meeting this morning, it's true. But it was not M. Duchon who told me. In fact, he has no idea that I do know about it. I learned of your meeting with Duchon from an acquaintance who, from time to time, supplies me with discreet information. She owns an establishment frequented by many of our small-time hoodlums. Carlos has become one of her best clients. She heard about the meeting from him. He likes to try to impress her with his tough guy act. He told her about your meeting with Duchon and how he was going to surprise you. Since she knows of my interest in Carlos, she immediately telephoned me."

"So you knew Carlos and the others were coming here today. It was nice of you to warn me."

"I was not absolutely certain they would come. Also, I did not know how you would react if you knew. It was important for me to catch them in the act. If I had known who you really were, perhaps it would have been different. I did not think for a moment that you would be in any danger. I planned to be close by."

"It's just as well you did not tell me, Inspector. Had I waited for you to come and rescue me, I would be missing part of my nose and who knows what else."

"They tricked me. I did not expect them to come so early."

"You should have confirmed the time with your friend, Joseph Gambia. He certainly knew exactly when Carlos and his pals were coming."

"Why do you say M. Gambia knew when Carlos was coming?"

"Because I nearly ran into him in the alley after I managed to escape by jumping from that balcony. He was standing there waiting for Carlos to finish with me."

"M. Ellis, I must ask why you refer to Joseph Gambia as my friend."

"It is true, is it not?"

"I know him, yes. Like I know many people in his line of work. He is an acquaintance. That's all."

"Excuse me, Inspector, but when I saw you with him the other night at Le Gentleman, you two appeared to be more than acquaintances."

"When were you at Le Gentleman? Wait, now I remember. That is why you look so familiar. You were there the other night when I gave Janine a ride to the club. We ran into M. Gambia in the parking lot. As I recall, you were at the bar with the new girl, Dany."

"You have a good memory, Inspector. It was a very interesting evening. Mlle. Dany is a lively young girl. But I am sure you already know all about her special charms."

"Be careful what you say, M. Ellis. It is very dangerous to talk of things of which you know nothing. I think you are forgetting who I am."

"Please forgive me, Inspector. I assumed that you were familiar with all aspects of the club. As part of your job, of course."

"That is enough, monsieur. I am beginning to lose my patience. Will you please tell me what you were looking for that night at Le Gentleman?"

"What I was looking for, I found, Inspector. Your 'acquaintance', M. Gambia, was very helpful. Of course, he was under the impression that I was someone else. This morning, he realized his mistake. I believe it came as quite a shock to him."

"M. Ellis, you have not answered my question! Will you please tell me precisely why you went to the club that night?"

"Am I being interrogated, Inspector LeClerc?"

"I am seeking your cooperation in an investigation, M. Ellis. You can choose to answer my questions here or you can accompany me to my office and answer my questions there. It is a serious offence to threaten an officer with a pistol, even if one does hold a permit for it. If we go to my office, I will be forced to charge you with threatening an officer with a concealed weapon. You understand?"

"Perfectly, Inspector."

"Very good. Proceed then."

"With pleasure. I went to Le Gentleman that night primarily to make the acquaintance of Joseph Gambia. I am familiar with some of his associates in Paris and with some of their habits. I decided to present myself as Peter Edwards, a friend of Pedro Delgado, one of these associates. Perhaps you know whom I am speaking of. He is also called 'Pedro Le Fou'."

"I have heard of him, that's all."

"He is a very colorful character. That's to say he has certainly earned his nickname. M. Gambia was very impressed that I knew him. But then, some people are easily impressed, don't you think?"

"Why did you want to meet M. Gambia?"

"From information that had come to my attention, I was certain that he was directly involved in the death of Kevin Duffy. I wanted to find out the details before writing my exposé."

"Is that all?"

"I also wanted to discover how he managed to have the real cause of death covered-up by your department."

"M. Ellis, listen to me! There has been no cover-up by my department. If you write that there has been, I shall have you in court, or worse. Do you understand?"

"Then I must ask you, Inspector, to explain your statement in the newspaper, Sud-Ouest. As I recall, you told the paper that Kevin Duffy's death was accidental and that the case was closed. I have read nothing recently from you to contradict that statement."

"M. Ellis, because of your reputation, I am going to confide in you. What I am going to tell you is in strict confidence and off the record. Do I have your promise not to reveal anything I am going to tell you until after I have completed my investigation and arrested those who are guilty?"

"Yes, provided what you tell me does not involve the cover-up of a crime."

"I assure you, M. Ellis, it involves nothing of the kind. If anything, I am putting myself at risk by having confidence in you. You see, it is a very delicate matter in the department. So, do I have your promise?"

"Yes."

"Very good. Let me then explain the situation. At first, I did believe that the young man's death was an accident. There was no evidence to prove it otherwise. No one saw anything. The cuts on the body could have been caused by the fall. The rocks there are very sharp. In effect, I had nothing to go on, nothing to indicate that the young man's death was anything other than an accident. I had no choice but to close the case and make my findings public. The day after the announcement appeared in <u>Sud-Ouest</u>, I received a call from the informant I mentioned earlier. She said Carlos had been in drinking and bragging about a job he had just done. He was laughing about how he had taught a surfer how to fly.

"At that point, I re-opened my investigation, but in a discreet way. I mentioned it to no one, not even my colleagues in the department. I did not want any information leaking out. I had gathered almost enough evidence to make an arrest when your associate, the retired Brigade-Financière inspector, M. Claverie-LaPorte, began making clumsy inquiries and interfering with my investigation. Then you arrived and began scaring people and making wild accusations. This is why I became so angry with M. Claverie-LaPorte. Yesterday, when I heard you were to meet with M. Duchon and that Carlos was going to take his place, I felt this might be the break I needed. It occurred to me that something might happen."

"Well, something certainly happened, Inspector. May I ask what you plan to do about it? Apart from threatening to remove part of my face with his knife, Carlos as much as confessed to causing Kevin Duffy's death."

"There is no need to worry any more about Carlos. I shall issue a warrant for his and his accomplices' arrest as soon as I return to my office."

"What about M. Gambia?"

"Ah, now that is a different affair. For the moment, I do not have enough evidence against him for an arrest."

"How much more evidence do you need, Inspector? He was waiting in the alley down there for Carlos and his pals to finish their job, one he obviously sent them to do. Just as he was seen waiting on a bench out front on the morning of Kevin Duffy's death. Does it not strike you as highly coincidental that he should be in the neighborhood on both occasions? In fact, almost miraculous."

"Not at all, M. Ellis. It is perfectly natural."

"What? Am I missing something here? You do not find it strange that he should be in this precise neighborhood on both occasions?"

"Not at all."

"Then my I please ask why?"

"Certainly. It is very simple. M. Gambia happens to live in the large apartment building next door, Le Nadaillac. At least in France, it is not against the law to frequent one's own neighborhood."

"Still, Inspector LeClerc, there is plenty of other evidence."

"It is all circumstantial. It is possible Carlos acted on his own and M. Gambia discovered what he was doing. In any event, I shall get to the bottom of it as soon as I have Carlos and the others in custody."

"What about Duchon?"

"I intend to question him as well. If you have no objection, M. Ellis, I would like to wait and see if he shows up after all. Perhaps he is running late."

"I have no objection, Inspector. But in that case, don't you think it would be a good idea to call one of your men and have him pick up Carlos before he has time to leave town?"

M. Ellis, please do not tell me how to do my job. I know where to find Carlos. He is not going anywhere."

"I hope you are right."

"I know I am right, M. Ellis. You will see. Now, if you will please..."

Three loud knocks interrupted the inspector in mid-sentence. The unmistakable high-pitched voice of Jean-Claude Duchon called out from behind the door.

"M. Ellis? M. Pierre Ellis? It is Jean-Claude Duchon. Are you there, M. Ellis?"

Peter Ellis opened the door just as he was turning to leave. Duchon seemed surprised to see him.

"You were expecting someone else, M. Duchon?"

"No. Not at all. It is just that since I am late, I thought perhaps you had left."

"Yes, you are late. Thirty minutes late, to be precise."

"I had an appointment in Bayonne with a new client. It lasted longer than I anticipated."

"How convenient for you. And unfortunate for me."

"What do you mean? I don't understand."

Inspector LeClerc stepped suddenly from behind the door. "What M. Ellis means, M. Duchon, is that he has had some unexpected visitors this morning who apparently knew of your plans to visit him. They threatened him, he says, with a knife. Had you been on time, it is possible you might have come to his aid."

"That is not exactly what I meant, Inspector."

"Oh yes. M. Ellis also believes, M. Duchon, that you may have had something to do with their visit. There were three men. The leader was named Carlos."

"Carlos? I know no one named Carlos! This is preposterous! I have come here in good faith and now I am being accused of a crime I know nothing of. It is too much! This man here is trying to ruin me, Inspector."

"Calm yourself, M. Duchon. I do not believe that M. Ellis is trying to ruin you. He has just survived a frightening ordeal. He is very upset. It is understandable. He has certain suspicions. Again understandable."

"But I was with a client in Bayonne!"

"As you have already said, M. Duchon. Still, I think it would be a good idea if you came down to my office for a few questions. I will not keep you long. Perhaps you can arrange to meet with M. Ellis later."

"I have no time later today. I am busy all afternoon. And I won't know my schedule for tomorrow until late this afternoon when I return to my office."

"I shall call you then, M. Duchon. At what time exactly will you be in your office?"

"After four. If my boss or anyone else answers, you must mention nothing. You must say you are a client. Understood?"

"I understand your dilemma perfectly, M. Duchon. I suggest we try to meet around noon tomorrow. See if you can arrange to be free then."

"I shall try but I can make no promises."

"Try very hard, M. Duchon. I am quickly running out of patience with you."

"You see, Inspector LeClerc? He is threatening me again!"

"Enough! Both of you. Come, M. Duchon, let's go to my office. M. Ellis, I shall contact you as soon as I have made an arrest. Until then, please do not interfere with my investigations. That also goes for your friend, M. Claverie-LaPorte. Do you understand?"

"Perfectly, Inspector LeClerc. Au revoir."

***

As soon as LeClerc left with Duchon, Peter Ellis called Maurice and arranged to meet him after lunch at La Chope. At one forty-five, he left for Chambre d'Amour under a dark sky heavy with charcoal layers of low, threatening clouds. He parked north of the beachfront complex of shops, restaurants and cafes and walked over to the edge of the rock-buttressed seawall. The wind was gusting out of the northwest, raking the sets of large, ragged waves with diagonal lines of foamy chop. For several minutes, he stood and watched the small band of black neoprene-clad figures struggling in the strong cross-currents of the cold, treacherous beachbreak. He was very glad not to be among them. He checked his watch and walked across the street to La Chope. He greeted the barman, ordered a Kronenbourg 1664 and joined Maurice at a corner table overlooking the terrace.

"Eh bien, mon ami, how goes it?"

"Much better now."

"I can imagine."

"For a time, I must say that this punk, Carlos, had me very frightened. I really believe that he is mentally sick. I was certain he was going to make a mistake and do more than he was sent to do."

"You were very lucky to escape."

"It's true."

"So tell me about it."

Peter Ellis was on his second beer when he finished recounting the events and conversations of the morning.

"I found it very interesting that LeClerc took Duchon before I could question him. I also had the distinct impression that Duchon was as surprised as I to see the inspector at my apartment. I think there is something going on that we are unaware of, Maurice. What do you think?"

"Well, from what you have told me, it certainly sounds as if the good inspector is covering his backside. I think he realizes finally that there is a limit to how far he can go in protecting Gambia. Particularly now that he knows who you really are. He has his political friends to think about, the ones responsible for putting him where he is. A scandal could be disastrous for him. And them."

"Who precisely are you talking about, Maurice?"

"I wish I could give you their names, Pierre. I have done much digging and I have my suspicions but no concrete evidence. I had an interesting conversation this morning with Inspector Rectoran. He, too, has been trying to find out who LeClerc's political supporters are. We have narrowed the list somewhat but we are still far from being able to positively identify them. Two things about them are certain: these men hold government positions of great power and they are not helping him out of kindness."

"So what is our next step?"

"How did you leave things with Duchon?"

"I said I would call him this afternoon to arrange a meeting tomorrow. I suggested he try to get free around noon. I think the time has come to begin tightening the screws."

"Yes, I think you are right; however, there is one thing that bothers me about putting him in a desperate situation."

"What's that?"

"The girl, Chantal Clairac. We must make sure there is no way she might be caught in the crossfire. I could not live with myself if anything happened to her because of what we are doing."

"Yes, I've been thinking about that possibility as well. What do you propose by way of protecting her?"

"Do you think your friend, Mme. Olga, would mind if Chantal stayed at her farm for a few days?"

"Not at all. I have already spoken with her about that possibility."

"Good. I shall talk with Chantal's mother at once and ask for her permission and help. I think she will listen to me. Then I shall speak

with her boss. She is an old friend and a very sensible woman. I have
no doubt she will allow Chantal a few days of vacation."

"Is there anyone you don't know in Biarritz, Maurice?"

Biarritz has become a very large town. There are many people
here now that I don't know, but they are all, for the most part, people
of no importance."

"I am happy to see your humility is still intact."

"I speak only the truth."

"Without doubt."

"Mon ami, let us continue our conversation later. I do not mean
to be rude, but I have much to do this afternoon. Will you be able to
meet me and Mlle. Chantal at Dodin this evening when she gets off
work?"

"Of course. What time?"

"I believe she finishes at seven. Is there anywhere I can leave you
a message in the next hour?"

"I'll be at my apartment packing up. I am thinking it might be
wise if I, too, stayed at Olga's for a few days, until we have resolved
this thing with Gambia. I don't want to be too easy to find. I've had
enough surprises for one week."

"A very wise decision, mon ami. At this point, there is no telling
what Gambia or, for that matter, the good Inspector LeClerc might
try. They seem to be getting desperate. You go pack your things
and I will let you know when to meet us as soon as I have arranged
everything."

When Peter Ellis returned to his apartment, he called Olga and
told her of Maurice's request. She agreed immediately to have Chantal
come and stay with her. Next he packed up his writing things as well
as an overnight bag. He fabricated a story for Arlette about spending
a couple of days with his new friend, Anya, showing her around the
Pays Basque and the Beàrn. He said he was not sure where he would
be staying but that he would check in every morning and evening for
his messages. Maurice called while he was talking with Arlette and said
that he would be waiting with Chantal Clairac at precisely 7:15 in front
of the Dodin patisserie shop. He asked Peter Ellis not to be late.

CHAPTER TWENTY-SIX

Jean-Claude Duchon followed the impressive, broad-shouldered back of Inspector Jacques LeClerc down the stairs and through the gravel courtyard of the old apartment building. Duchon knew that LeClerc was a close friend, and maybe more, of both Janine Destin and Joseph Gambia. He had seen them together often at the club and at parties. This was the first time, however, he had been alone with the imposing inspector or made more than brief small talk with him. He remembered Janine's assurance that 'Jacky' was a close friend and would look out for him. Still, he was more than a little concerned by the present turn of events. The inspector had asked him, and not very nicely at that, to come to his office for questioning. He had no idea what kind of questions the inspector wanted to ask him, but the prospect of sitting across an official table from the large man in a small, brightly lit police interrogation room was not at all appealing to the nervous food salesman. When they reached the street, Duchon could contain himself no longer.

"If you please, Inspector LeClerc, can you tell me how long you think I shall be detained at the station?"

To his utter surprise and bewilderment, the inspector began laughing out loud.

"You will forgive me my little joke, Jean-Claude. You need not worry yourself. We are not going to my office. That scene back there in the apartment was all for show. Just follow me to my car. I shall not be keeping you for more than a few minutes."

They reached his car and the inspector waved him into the passenger seat.

"Jean-Claude, I realize we only have a passing acquaintance but I feel like I know you from all the things Janine has told me about you. She speaks very highly of you, you know. You should be very proud to have such a friend."

"Thank-you, Inspector LeClerc. Janine has truly been a loyal friend to me. I am very lucky."

"There is no need to be formal with me, Jean-Claude. I dare say we will be seeing a great deal of each other in the future. So please, call me Jacky." The inspector gave Duchon a friendly pat on the shoulder.

"That's very kind."

"It's nothing. Now, Jean-Claude, I must ask that you keep what I have to say to you confidential. You may, of course, mention anything to Janine, since she is already <u>au courant</u>. Understood?"

"Yes, of course."

"I make this clear because I realize you are also Jojo's friend, as I am. I know all about how he tried to help you get Mlle. Clairac back from that unlucky young American man. Unfortunately, he sent that imbecile, Carlos, to do the job. The same imbecile he sent this morning to M. Ellis's apartment, with nearly equally disastrous results. I don't think it is necessary to go into the problems Jojo's lack of judgment has created. For you, for me and for Janine."

"No, it has been a catastrophe."

"Exactly. And it must stop before it goes any further. Do you not agree, Jean-Claude?"

"Are you kidding? I will be ruined if anything else happens."

"We all will be if we don't do something. If not by Jojo and Carlos, then by this meddling journalist we have just left."

"The American up there, M. Ellis, is a journalist? I thought he was a friend of the dead kid's family."

"As did I until this morning when I discovered that he is a journalist, and a very well-known one at that. You have heard of Jean LeBlanc?"

"Shit! That guy is Jean LeBlanc? What is he looking for here?"

"He says he is here because he thinks the death of Kevin Duffy was not an accident."

"It is not true! Shit!"

"But I think he is here for more than that. I think he is after our mutual friend, Jojo. He is using the accident involving the American surfer as a way of getting to him. That is why he wants to talk to you, to scare you. He wants to establish the connection between Jojo and the accident. He is obviously working at the request of old Claverie-LaPorte, the retired Brigade Financière inspector who lives here in town. The fat old fart has been after Jojo for years. I don't know how he found out about the connection between you and Jojo and the kid's death. That's a problem I will deal with later. But the fact is that he did find out and was smart enough to recognize Jojo's vulnerability. My guess is that as soon as he saw this new opportunity of trapping Jojo, he called this journalist, Peter Ellis, alias Jean LeBlanc, and asked for his assistance. I think they must have worked together before."

"What are we going to do? I am supposed to meet this damned American journalist tomorrow. You heard what he said. What if he writes about my affair with Chantal and what happened to the kid. I will be finished!"

"Don't panic, Jean-Claude. That is not going to happen. I will see to that. And remember what Janine promised you yesterday. She told me all about it. She has big plans for you. I think your future looks very bright. Provided we work out our present problems. To do that, I shall need your help."

"Anything. I'll do anything. Just tell me, Inspector. Oh, excuse me! I mean Jacky."

"First, I want you to meet this M. Ellis tomorrow as he requested. Try to find out what he is really looking for. Be agreeable but not too agreeable. I don't want him to become suspicious. Act like you are only willing to do what he wants because he is forcing you. Tell him about Jojo's offer to help you convince the Duffy kid to leave town."

"You want me to tell him _that_? He'll say the kid's death was my fault."

"You are not listening, Jean-Claude. I said to tell him _Jojo_ offered to help _you_. He insisted. It was _his_ idea. Of course, you wanted the kid out of the picture. You can admit that. It would be understandable. You wanted Chantal to come back to you. You can even say that Jojo promised you that there would be no violence. It's your word against his."

"But what's going to happen when he talks to Jojo?"

"He will not get that opportunity. With your help, I will see to that."

"With _my_ help? I don't understand."

"It is the second thing I want you to do for me, Jean-Claude. You must meet with Jojo as soon as possible and find out if he plans to see this journalist, Ellis, again."

"I am supposed to meet Jojo for a drink at Les Colonnes tonight at eight."

"Perfect. Tell him about your meeting with the journalist tomorrow and see what he says. See what he knows about him, if anything. Make sure you arrange to meet M. Ellis in a very public place in case Jojo decides to join you or plans a surprise visit. If he even hints at that possibility, let Janine know immediately. In any case, call her this evening and let her know where the meeting with the journalist is to take place. I shall take care of everything else."

"You are certain it is wise to meet with this bastard, Ellis, tomorrow?"

"Trust me, Jean-Claude. By this time tomorrow evening, we all should have cause to celebrate. You, me _and_ Janine. I must be going now. I need to pick up that imbecile, Carlos. It has been a pleasure speaking with you, Jean-Claude, despite the unpleasant circumstances." LeClerc offered him a large, heavy hand to shake. "I anticipate we shall be seeing much more of each other in the future."

Jean-Claude Duchon walked back to his car slowly, his mind filled with worrisome thoughts and disheartening images. Despite LeClerc's upbeat, optimistic outlook, he could think of nothing pleasant to look forward to in the next twenty-four hours, try as he might. The prospect of being grilled again by the meddling American, Ellis, made him cringe. It was no wonder the bastard had gotten under his skin during their first conversation at Player's Bar. He was a damned journalist—and a famous one at that! He hated journalists, had always hated journalists. They reminded him of his wife, always prying into other people's lives and fabricating stories. Why couldn't they just mind their own business and live their own lives like he did. It was, no doubt, because they were like his wife and had no life of their own worth living. So they spent their time taking pleasure in ruining the lives of others.

This perverse line of speculation was followed by one that was equally depressing. As much as he did not look forward to his meeting tomorrow with the damned journalist, Jean-Claude Duchon positively dreaded his meeting at eight that evening with Gambia. Even in the best of times, Jojo had a tendency to bully him. And these were far from the best of times. After the disaster this morning at the journalist's apartment, there was no telling what kind of mood he would be in. At least they were meeting at Les Colonnes where Jojo was well known and not likely to make a scene. But what if Jojo somehow discovered that he had begun working in league with Janine and LeClerc against him? What would he do? He was, after all, a somewhat irrational and often violent man. It was all too much to think about!

These and a dark succession of similar disturbing thoughts turned what would have normally been a relatively pleasant afternoon of calling on clients into what Duchon could only liken to an extended visit to the dentist, with its seemingly interminable torture of slow-drilling and raw-nerved pain. The stress evidently showed. Several of his clients asked whether he was feeling ill. He told them all the same thing: He had woken up that morning with a bad toothache, so bad that he feared the tooth would have to be pulled. They all expressed dismay at such a drastic prospect and offered their sympathies. When he finally arrived at his office just before four, it was with the sense of having survived a minor but lengthy ordeal.

The journalist called at precisely four-fifteen. Their conversation was brief, business-like and altogether anticlimactic: Did Duchon know a cafe in Chambre d'Amour called La Chope? Yes he did. Could Duchon meet him there at 11:30 tomorrow morning? Yes he could, but only for half an hour. He had forgotten it was a holiday. He was obliged to take his wife and some friends to lunch. The journalist assured him that would not be a problem: the meeting would not take more than thirty minutes. Duchon would be sure to come alone? Yes he would. Very good. A demain. Click.

Duchon hung up the telephone with an immense sense of relief. At least they were not meeting at a place in the center of town where he was likely to run into someone he knew or, worse still, where the owner was a client. He took out his private address book and looked up Janine Destin's unlisted number. She picked up on the third ring. The sound of her friendly, cheerful voice was the most reassuring thing he had heard all day. He gave her the time and place of his meeting with the journalist.

"So how are you holding up, Jean-Claude?"

"I will not lie, Janine. It has been a rough day for me."

"I can well imagine. Jacky said you behaved very sensibly, that you showed great strength and composure under difficult conditions."

"Inspector LeClerc was very kind."

"He is a good friend as you will, no doubt, come to see."

"Has he found Carlos yet?"

"Unfortunately not. He has located the other two imbeciles, Marco and Pipo. Though they are not to blame for what happened, he has locked them up for safe keeping. He wants to teach them a lesson."

"Where do you think Carlos is?"

"When Jacky questioned the other two, they said that he had gone off with Jojo. That was all they knew. Jacky thinks you should bring up Carlos's name when you meet with Jojo this evening. Say something critical of him and see what Jojo's reaction is. Maybe it will give us an idea of where he's hiding."

"Do you think that's a good idea, Janine?"

"Trust me, Jean-Claude. Act like you are upset that Carlos's mistakes have caused you so many problems, including problems now with the police. Even Jojo should understand that. I am going to say the same thing to him when I see him later at the club. That is why I can't meet you for a drink like I had intended. I had hoped to give you some good news."

"You have talked with Chantal today?"

"I went by Dodin this morning. She was very busy but I did manage to have a few words with her. I suggested the three of us have drinks together tomorrow evening when she gets off work."

"What did she say? Did she agree?"

"She was hesitant but gave me the impression she would like to see you. I think she needs a little confirmation of how you still feel."

"What should I do?"

"I think if you were to bring her some flowers tonight when she gets home from work it would not hurt your chances with her. Maybe also buy a nice vase that will remind her of you when the flowers fade. Don't be pushy when you give them to her. Don't try to talk her into coming. Simply ask her to consider it. Let the flowers do the talking. I will stop by Dodin tomorrow morning and see what I can do. It will be your reward for having to meet with that nosy journalist."

"You are too nice, Janine. How can I thank you?"

"You can begin by doing everything Jacky asks you to do."

"No problem, Janine. It will be a pleasure."

"And one more thing."

"What's that?"

"Make sure you pick out some nice flowers. And lots of them. A woman likes to feel special."

"I am going to the florist right now."

Jean-Claude Duchon was not exactly telling the truth with this last remark. Before he could go anywhere, he had to endure the fire of the dragon, which was how he looked upon any encounter with his wife. She had left a message with the office receptionist that he call her as soon as he came in. It was urgent. Such messages were not unusual and usually concerned something she had forgotten to buy for dinner. Since he was going to be late for dinner, he sat pensively at his desk for several minutes fabricating a plausible excuse. These fictive efforts proved to be unnecessary. Before he could utter one false word, Mme. Duchon called and informed her husband that he would have to eat alone that evening. She was très desolée but an old classmate had unexpectedly arrived in town and had invited her to an early dinner at the Cafe de l'Océan. She didn't think she would be too very late but one never knew who one might encounter at the Cafe de l'Océan. Duchon tried to sound disappointed though not too disappointed. She might suddenly decide to invite him to join them. As he hung up the telephone, he realized he had not even thought to ask his wife the name of her old classmate.

At the florist, Duchon spent a small fortune on a large spray of exotic flowers personally chosen by the owner who described the selection as fit for a queen. He spent a larger fortune on a gold-rimmed green glass vase. Then, finding himself with almost two hours to kill before Chantal returned home from work, he decided to go for a long overdue, well-deserved drink at Le Sportif. Brimming with new-found confidence, he entered the little cafe and proudly showed off his purchases to Achille. The barman immediately pronounced them magnificent. Chantal was certain to be stupefied when he presented them to her. What girl in her right mind wouldn't be? Beaming with self-satisfaction, Duchon ordered a Ricard.

"And make it a large one, Achille."

"With pleasure, M. Duchon."

"I have had a long, hard day."

"And who knows," the barman winked suggestively, "but that you won't have a long, hard night."

"You are terrible, Achille!" Duchon grinned lewdly at the barman. "I'll be right back. I must go check on Monsieur." As he strutted toward the door marked 'Hommes' in the far corner of the cafe, Jean-Claude Duchon resembled a scrawny over-confident rooster whose security comes from the knowledge that he has the henhouse all to himself.

***

At the precise moment that Jean-Claude Duchon was enjoying this good-natured banter with the barman, Achille, Joseph Gambia was sitting in his office at Le Gentleman Club across his cluttered desk from his partner, Janine Destin, and Inspector Jacques LeClerc engaged in a conversation far less amusing.

"So let me get this straight, Janine. You are insisting that I sell out to you?"

"I am giving you that option. It is a generous offer under the circumstances."

"How was I to know the guy in the apartment was the journalist who writes under the name of Jean LeBlanc?"

"No matter who you thought he was, you should not have sent Carlos and the other two to attack him. You would have done better to send the Three Stooges. At least when they screw up they don't use switchblades or kill people. What were you thinking, Jojo, after what happened to the kid in the park? Where it close to Easter, I would be forced to conclude you had given up thinking for Lent."

"That's enough, Janine. Save your feeble jokes for your little gigolos. I imagine that for the money you give them, they're expected to laugh at your jokes as well as fill your tired old hole."

"At least they can fill it. You certainly never did."

"Oh really? It seems your memory is going as well."

"Stop! Both of you! We are here to discuss business, not your past sex life."

"Sorry, Jacky. I lost my head."

"It's not the only think you've lost, though it might be the biggest thing."

Inspector LeClerc pushed his chair away from the desk as if to leave. "If you are going to continue, Jojo, then I'm going to leave. And if I leave, you're on your own to deal with the mess Carlos has made. And, in case you have forgotten, you're the one this journalist, Ellis, is after."

"How do you know that for sure, Jacky?"

"Let's just say a little bird told me, a little high-flying bird with very keen eyesight. I have never known this little bird to make a mistake in such things."

"So what if I don't want to accept Janine's so-called 'generous' offer?"

"That's entirely up to you, Jojo. But whether you accept it or not does not alter the fact that you must leave Biarritz for at least six months."

"And why is that, Jacky?"

"Because otherwise I will be forced to arrest you."

"Arrest me? Are you crazy? Arrest me for what? I have done nothing. I thought we were friends, Jacky, as well as associates."

"We are, Jojo, but you have left me no choice. As you know, this guy Ellis saw you this morning outside his apartment buliding waiting for Carlos and his pals. He knows you sent them. If you stay around and I don't arrest you, he'll be after my ass as well as yours."

"What about Carlos? He's the one that's screwed up everything. You just said so yourself."

"And who is Carlos going to say put him up to it?"

"He won't be able to say anything if you don't find him alive."

"But I am going to find him alive, Jojo. You are going to make sure that I do."

"Why should I do that? So he can testify against me? That would be smart."

"As if you knew anything about being smart."

"Shut up, Janine. Don't think I don't know what you're up to. If I didn't know better, I would say you're paying Carlos to frame me."

"I would not pay Carlos to frame a piece of toilet paper, which would be about the same thing."

"I'm surprised. If you used it first to wipe your fat ass it would be a self-portrait."

"Listen! Both of you! We need to make some decisions. And make them right now. I can't keep this guy, Ellis, quiet forever."

"Why not? I certainly could. Haven't you ever heard of fatal accidents? They happen all the time. It would solve everything."

"I don't believe what I am hearing, Jacky. Do you?"

"Jojo, don't even think about doing anything to that journalist. In case you have forgotten, there has already been one fatal 'accident', which I've had to risk my ass covering up. It's not like I'm the only inspector around here. I have several colleagues who would like nothing better than to see me take a fall. That self-righteous bastard, Rectoran, would be especially pleased."

"What if the accident were to happen outside of your district? Maybe even in Spain."

"No, Jojo! And that's final. As long as M. Ellis is in the area, nothing 'accidental' is going to happen to him. That is, unless you want to be charged with murder. Now <u>that</u> would take care of all our problems. Maybe I could arrange for you and Carlos to be cellmates since you seem to be so fond of him."

"You've been talking a little bit too much about putting me in jail, Jacky. I'm beginning to wonder if that's not what you're really planning to do as soon as I sign my part of the business over to Janine. I'm sure she has promised to make it worth your while, one way or the other. I would, from personal experience, advise you to take the money and leave the other alone. The rose might be nice to look at but the smell is not all that pleasant. Not to mention the thorns."

LeClerc slapped the right arm of his chair a loud, sudden blow and stood up abruptly.

"Jojo, you are starting to piss me off. I didn't come here to listen to your bullshit or to your insults. I came here to help you to save your ass. If you don't want my help, fine. And good luck. Otherwise, let's decide what we are going to do. Janine has offered to buy you out. With that money, you could set yourself up somewhere else. You could go to the Caribbean for a few years. I hear there's money to be made in St. Martin and St. Barth these days. And in the kind of business you seem to prefer now. It wouldn't be like Napoleon in Elba. Think about it."

"What about Carlos?"

"I have to have Carlos. It's the only way I can make it work."

"If he talks, I'll be fucked. This guy, Ellis, will have a field day. I won't be able to work anywhere. Even in St. Barth."

"Let me worry about that. Janine and I don't want him to talk any-more than you do. I am sure I can convince him to do a deal."

"And what if he decides he doesn't want to?"

"He'll do a deal, one way or another. Don't worry. Leave it to me. I'll take care of your little macho friend. He'll be begging me for a deal when I finish with him."

"Give me one good reason I should believe you."

"You have no choice, Jojo. Now, tell me where you've hidden Carlos. As I've said, we don't have a lot of time. Ellis is meeting with Duchon tomorrow. There's no telling what that cretin is going to tell him. When he arrived at the guy's apartment this morning, he was like a scared rabbit. That's why I told Ellis that Duchon had to come with me for questioning. I was afraid of what the little weasel might say."

"You don't have to worry about Jean-Claude, Jacky. I have him under control. I'm meeting him later this evening at Les Colonnes. I'll tell him what to say tomorrow to the journalist."

"I suggest you tell him to say as little as possible. You might also tell him to get in touch with me the next time a stranger contacts him about one of my cases. I don't even want to think about what could have happened if I had not been in the office when Ellis reported the attack."

"Wait a minute, Jacky. From what you're saying, I don't un-derstand why Jean-Claude should even meet with this guy, Ellis, tomorrow."

"He should meet with him because I <u>want</u> him to meet with the guy."

"But why?"

"To buy me some time to deal with Carlos. That's why you need to tell me right now where that punk is hiding. I need to pick him up as soon as possible. Once I have him in custody and under my thumb and you have mysteriously left town, our journalist friend can do nothing but speculate about what really happened to Kevin Duffy. He will not be able to confirm anything. So where's Carlos, Jojo?"

"Not so fast, Jacky. Don't you think we are forgetting something?"

"Forgetting what?"

"Money. 'Janine's generous offer,' as you so diplomatically put it."

"This is too much! I need a drink." Janine Destin stood up and started walking toward the door to the bar.

Joseph Gambia stood up as well. "That's the most intelligent thing you've said today, Janine. Why don't we all have a drink and calm down. We are all friends here after all. The more I think about it, the more I like the idea of spending some time in the islands. Your offer is not exactly the figure I would come up with myself, as you can imagine. But it serves as a starting point. There are many ways to skin a cat and I feel certain we can find one to suit our purposes. Provided we do and provided you give me the appropriate written assurances, then I shall arrange for Carlos to be at a place where he can be easily apprehended. Does that sound fair, Janine?"

"I guess so, as long as you are reasonable about the money and give me enough time to come up with it."

"What about you, Jacky? Does my little proposal sound okay to you?"

"If it's okay with Janine, it's okay with me. You two are the official partners. Just tell me when I will be able to get my hands on that imbecile, Carlos."

"Tomorrow afternoon, provided I get an adequate down-payment and the papers have been drawn up and signed."

"Shit! Tomorrow's a holiday, Jojo. All the banks will be closed. And all the law offices."

"So it is, Jacky. So it is. Well, let's have a drink and see if we can figure something out. I'm a reasonable man. I realize how serious the problem is now. I'm sure we can work out a solution."

CHAPTER TWENTY-SEVEN

When Peter Ellis pulled up in front of Dodin's to pick up Chantal Clairac, he found Maurice pacing nervously, back and forth, on the sidewalk. His old friend immediately hurried over, opened the passenger-side door and leaned his head inside the car.

"Good evening, Maurice. Is everything alright?"

"As good as can be expected under the circumstances. The girl is in a very fragile state. Please be gentle with her. And be careful yourself. Make sure no one follows you from her apartment. I can't imagine anyone waiting for you there, but one can never be certain. Here she comes now. Telephone me tomorrow after your meeting with Duchon. I'll be waiting at home for your call."

"Very good, Maurice. I'll talk to you then."

Maurice stepped back and held the car door open for the girl.

"Chantal, this is my good friend and associate, Pierre Ellis. He will take you by your apartment to get your things and then take you to the farm I mentioned. It is a charming place and Olga, the owner, is looking forward to meeting you. I doubt you will have to stay for more than a couple of days."

"Thank-you, M. Maurice."

"Be brave, my dear, and call me if you need anything. Pierre, I'll talk to you tomorrow. Bonne route!"

"Au revoir, Maurice. A bientôt."

Peter Ellis started the car and slowly pulled away from the curb. They rode in virtual silence to Chantal Clairac's apartment, their only conversation having to do with what streets to take. While Peter Ellis waited in the car for Chantal to get her things, he discreetly scanned the surrounding streets and adjacent small park for anyone who might be waiting for her. Except for the occasional neighbor returning home with an evening baguette, the streets were deserted. He noticed a small cafe called Le Sportif midway down a connecting sidestreet bordering the park. If anyone was waiting for her there, he would easily spot the person before he could get close to them. Still, he decided he might as well take a few unnecessary turns on his way out of town just to be safe.

Chantal had told him she wouldn't be very long. True to her word, she emerged from her building in less than fifteen minutes carrying a suitcase in one hand and a black leather coat in the other. The change in her appearance was striking, tight-fitting blue jeans and a black cashmere turtleneck replacing her prim, frilly server's uniform. Normally he would have let his gaze linger for several appreciative moments on her stunning body, on the elegant, long dancer's legs and the high, rounded breasts. Instead, he found himself studying her sad, solemn face, especially her large, downcast eyes. In the lamplight, he couldn't make out their color, but thought he detected a glint of moisture in them. As he took her suitcase and coat, he stupidly asked if she were doing alright. She nodded once and quickly averted her face.

Peter Ellis did not speak to Chantal Clairac again until they were on the other side of Bayonne and he was certain no one was following them. Whenever it had been necessary to stop at an intersection, he had furtively glanced over to check on her. Each time he did so, her attitude was always the same: she sat rigidly straight, motionless as a statue, her eyes staring blindly at the road ahead.

"May I call you Chantal?"

The question seemed to startle her. Her body shivered and she let out a slight, barely audible exclamation.

"I'm sorry, mademoiselle. I didn't mean to startle you."

"It is not your fault, monsieur. In my mind I was somewhere else. Then I heard my name. Did you ask me something?"

"I asked if I may call you Chantal."

"Yes, of course."

"If you do not care to talk, I will understand. I know that all of this is very difficult for you. I thought it might make it easier if I explained what Maurice and I are trying to do. Would you like me to do that?"

"If you want to, monsieur."

"Do you want me to, Chantal? And please, call me Pierre."

"I guess so. I don't understand anything anymore."

"Do you know why you're coming with me to Olga's farm?"

"Your friend, M. Maurice, said it was for my safety. He talked to my patronne and to my mother. He convinced them that I should go."

"So you did not want to leave Biarritz?"

"I didn't understand why it was necessary. Who would want to hurt me? And why?"

"You know M. Duchon's friend, Joseph Gambia, I believe?"

"He is a salaud! A dirty, disgusting, bad man. I detest him. I tried to tell Jean-Claude but he would not listen to me."

Peter Ellis was surprised by the girl's sudden show of emotion.

"I agree with you, Chantal. He is now also a very desperate man. Maurice and I are afraid he might try to harm you."

"But why? I have done nothing to him."

"Let me explain. Did Maurice tell you what happened to me this morning?"

"No. He just said something had happened that made him worry about my safety."

"Then let me tell you. Under the circumstances, you deserve to know. It is all related to the death of your American friend, Kevin Duffy."

Peter Ellis proceeded to give the girl a sanitized version of the morning's events. For her own protection, he left out most of the details of his conversation with Inspector LeClerc.

"So you see, Chantal, when M. Gambia found out about my meeting this morning with M. Duchon, he decided to send Carlos and his buddies to scare me, to try to keep me from talking to him. Just like he sent them to scare your friend, Kevin, into leaving town. The next time, it is possible that you might be the target. Maurice and I decided we could not risk that possibility."

"But why would M. Gambia want to hurt me? What have I done?"

"You have done nothing, Chantal. It would be his way to keep M. Duchon from telling me anything. You see, I am meeting with him tomorrow morning. As of today, M. Gambia knows who I really am and what I am doing here."

"I thought you were a friend of M. Maurice, that you were helping him find out what really happened to Kevin."

"That is correct. I am also a journalist. I work for the European News Bureau in Paris. I came to Biarritz to help Maurice put Joseph Gambia out of business, to expose him for the criminal he really is. We both suspected he had something to do with your friend's death. We thought that if we could prove it, it would give us a way of revealing his other activities. This morning, Carlos admitted that it was M. Gambia, his boss, who sent him and his buddies to try to scare your friend, Kevin."

"Yes, I know. But poor Kevin tried to escape and he slipped on some gravel and fell. He hit his head on the rocks."

"How do you know all this, Chantal? Did M. Duchon or Inspector LeClerc tell you?"

"No. A friend told me. She told me not to speak with anyone about the accident. Except Inspector LeClerc."

Peter Ellis said nothing for several seconds, his mind racing to comprehend all the new implications the girl's use of the female pronoun had unwittingly revealed. When he finally did speak, he tried to conceal the enthusiasm in his voice.

"Your friend gave you very good advice. But that does not surprise me. Janine Destin is very intelligent. One would expect good advice from her."

"You know, Mme. Janine?"

"No. Unfortunately I have not had the pleasure of meeting the distinguished lady. I know her only by reputation. I understand she is a woman of considerable charm and intelligence. I'm sure you feel lucky to have such a good friend."

"Mme. Janine has always been very kind to me, though she is not that way with everyone. She can have a very bad temper. I have seen what she can be like when she is upset with someone. I don't know what I would do if she were ever that way with me."

"How did you meet her, Chantal? Did M. Duchon introduce you?"

"No, not at all. It was she who introduced me to him. She used to come to the little cafe where I worked before I started at Dodin. Her apartment building is around the corner. She often met clients at the cafe. She used to joke about it being her office. One day Jean-Claude came there to meet her and she introduced us. She said she thought I might find him amusing."

"I see. Was she upset when you started going out with Kevin Duffy?"

"Not at all. Like me, she was not happy with how Jean-Claude was behaving at the time. He was spending a lot of time with M. Gambia and was beginning to act like him. Very arrogant and rough when he did not get his way. Mme. Janine said he needed to be taught a lesson. She told me to have fun with Kevin but to be careful. She did not want to see me hurt."

"When was the last time you talked with Mme. Destin?"

"Yesterday afternoon. She asked me to meet her at my old cafe. She didn't tell me Jean-Claude would be there. She pretended she had just run into him on the street. I guess she knew I might not come if I knew he was going to be there. But he was very nice, like he used to be. I think Mme. Janine must have said something to him."

"It sounds like she wants you to give M. Duchon another chance. Is that what she wanted to talk to you about?"

"Yes. That and other things."

"And are you going to give him one?"

"I don't know. There is so much to think about. Mme. Janine said it will be different when he begins working for her. He will have money to get a divorce."

"I'm sure he will. I presume he will start after Mme. Destin has bought out her partner, M. Gambia."

"Yes. How did you know that?"

"It was just a guess. M. Gambia has been doing a lot of stupid things lately. I imagine Mme. Destin is not very happy with his behavior. If I had a partner who did such things, I would certainly want to get rid of him. Wouldn't you?"

"I suppose so. But I should not be talking to you about all this. Mme. Janine would be furious if she knew. She made me promise."

"Don't worry, Chantal. I will not tell her."

"What if you are one of the people she talked about who are trying to hurt her? She told Jean-Claude and me yesterday that there are some people trying to ruin her business."

"I have already told you, Chantal. It is M. Gambia I want to put out of business—him and those who work for him, the ones who caused the death of your friend, Kevin. But I do not want to talk about anything that makes you uncomfortable. Forgive me."

"It is not you, monsieur. So much has happened, I don't know what to think anymore. That's all."

"I understand, Chantal. It is all very confusing. Let us talk about something else."

For the remainder of the drive, Peter Ellis concentrated on engaging the girl in disarming small talk. He told her about Olga and the farm and about meeting Anya. He spoke about Paris and his work, telling her about the article he had just finished on the gastronomic delicacies of autumn. This led to talk of the regional specialties of the southwest of France. By the time they reached the farm, he had discovered her preference for the mountain cheese of Laruns, her love of omelettes made with fresh cêpes from Les Landes and her friendship with a certain peasant farmer named Aurrisset who made wonderful Jurançon wine at his vineyard near Monein.

He also discovered that, once put at ease, Chantal Clairac was quick to laugh and possessed a charmingly unaffected sense of humor.

***

Joseph Gambia left his apartment on the corner of the rue Million and rue La Perspective at seven-forty to walk to Les Colonnes where he was meeting Jean-Claude Duchon at eight o'clock. As he slowly made his way down the rue Gambetta towards the center of Biarritz, he had the semi-dazed look of a man completely lost in thought. The reason for this appearance of total preoccupation was not difficult to explain: At around the time he had professed himself a reasonable man to Jacky and Janine, he had already begun to suspect that they had no intention of buying him out, that their plan was as he had initially thought, to implicate him, with the help of Carlos, in the death of the American surfer and the attack that morning on the guy who turned out to be a well-known journalist from Paris. By the time his meeting with them had concluded, he knew, beyond any doubt, that this was in fact what they planned to do. The agreement they had worked out had been far too easy. Janine had barely complained about the higher price he had demanded or about certain strict penalties he had insisted upon in the case of non-payment. And Jacky had suddenly become far too matter-of-fact about how he would deal with Carlos and the journalist.

Now, as he walked down the narrow, sloping sidewalk past Les Halles, Joseph Gambia assessed his predicament. Thanks to the incredible bumbling by Carlos and the others, Jacky and Janine held a distinct and formidable advantage. Still, he had no intention of playing the little end game they had planned for him. What he needed was to find a way to turn the tables on them. Ruthlessly and completely. That's what he needed and he needed to find it right away. Jacky had been correct about one thing: His problems had reached a critical stage and time was short.

The more he thought about the situation, the more he came back to the journalist, the man who had befriended him as Peter Edwards. It was strange. He could not put his finger on why he felt so certain. Maybe it was intuition. For some curious reason, Joseph Gambia was suddenly sure that the journalist was the person destined to provide a solution to his predicament. What <u>was</u> his real name? It was something similar to the alias he had used, the same initials. Then he remembered. Ellis. His name was Peter Ellis. He reflected on how bizarre it was: When he had met the guy as Peter Edwards, he had taken to him at once, had felt a certain kinship with him. Could he really have been so mistaken? Was his judgment really that bad? Had it all been an act, a ruse to trap him as LeClerc had insisted?

At first the thought depressed him, but then he saw it in a different light and smiled to himself. If it <u>had</u> all been a performance, it meant the guy was really good. And what he needed was someone really good to help him if he was going to have any reasonable chance of getting rid of Janine and Jacky without ruining himself in the process. It came down to leverage, he now realized. What lever could he use on Peter Ellis to force the journalist to help him? This critical question occupied his thoughts as he crossed the Place Clemenceau and then the Avenue Edouard VII. He was still searching for a suitable answer when he entered Les Colonnes at two minutes after eight.

He stopped in the entryway and looked around the crowded cafe for Duchon. His friend was apparently running late. He walked over to the bar and was immediately and enthusiastically greeted by Christian, the unctuous barman Janine always called "Big Ears".

"M. Gambia, how are you? I have missed seeing you."

"It's true, Christian. It has been some time since we have seen each other. It's my work. I've barely had time to walk the big dog, if you know what I mean." He gave the barman a knowing smirk.

"'Work'. It is a dirty word is it not, M. Gambia?"

"To be sure, Christian."

"But there it is! There's nothing one can do about it! What may I offer you, M. Gambia? A Ricard?"

"No, I think I will have a beer. I have been walking and have worked up a terrible thirst."

"A draught?"

"Please, Christian. Kronenbourg."

"Very good, M. Gambia."

"By the way Christian, have you seen my friend Jean-Claude Duchon? You know, the food salesman. He was to meet me here at eight to discuss a new product line for the club."

"M. Duchon arrived about fifteen minutes ago. He's over there." The barman pointed to a table in the far back corner of the cafe. "You will forgive me for saying so, M. Gambia, but he looks terrible. He has me worried. It makes me think there may have been a death in the family."

It was no wonder Gambia had not spotted Duchon when he had entered the cafe. He barely recognized his friend even now, the way he sat hunched over the small corner table, his face buried in his hands. He hoped Duchon's histrionic pose had nothing to do with what had happened that morning at the journalist's apartment. He was in no mood for either whining or accusations, particularly from Duchon. If he hadn't tried to help the little fart get rid of that American kid, he wouldn't be in the mess he was in now. The barman arrived with his glass of beer.

"Christian, what is Jean-Claude drinking?"

"M. Duchon is drinking Ricard. As usual."

"Of course. Please have the waiter bring one over and put it on my bill."

"With pleasure, M. Gambia."

"Thank-you, Christian. And please, have a drink on me as well. Whatever you want."

"You are too kind, M. Gambia. Thank-you!"

Gambia made his way to the table where Duchon was sitting, motionless, elbows on the table, hands cupping his face, a hackneyed study in depression. When Gambia pulled back the facing chair and sat down, Duchon slowly looked up, his face frozen in a rictus of despair.

"My God, Jean-Claude! What's wrong? You look terrible."

"Jojo, he's taken her away! I was waiting for her in the cafe across the street, talking to Achille. I had bought her flowers. And a vase!"

"Take it easy, Jean-Claude. Calm yourself. You are not making any sense. Who are you talking about?"

"Chantal! Who do you think? My little Chantal! Janine said I should buy her flowers. To show her how I felt. So I did. I was waiting to give them to her. But when she came, she was with him. Then they left. Together! That bastard! He took her away before I could say anything, before I could give her the flowers and the vase. The dirty bastard! I'd like to kill him."

"Easy, Jean-Claude, easy. Get a grip on yourself. Here, I have ordered another drink for you."

The waiter placed on the table a small bowl of ice, a miniature pitcher of water and a tall glass with three fingers of anisette. He asked if they cared for anything else. Gambia ordered another draught beer then turned back to his distraught friend.

"Now listen, Jean-Claude. Calm yourself. Take a drink. It will help. There. Do you feel better?"

Duchon nodded, almost imperceptibly.

"Are you sure? Take another drink. It will settle your nerves. It's good medicine, Ricard."

Duchon did as he was told.

"Good. That's much better. Now, Jean-Claude, take your time and tell me exactly what happened. You said Chantal arrived with someone. Who was it?"

"That American bastard, the one from the apartment this morning."

"You are sure it was him? What kind of car was he driving?"

"Of course I am sure, Jojo. I saw him this morning, didn't I? The bastard was driving an old white Porsche."

"Okay, it was him. That's what he drives. So what happened? Did he go into the apartment with her?"

"No. And it's lucky for him that he didn't. There is no telling what I would have done."

"Yes, I can imagine, Jean-Claude. So, Chantal went into her apartment by herself. How long did she stay inside?"

"Fifteen or twenty minutes. She came out with her small suitcase and another small bag. He put them in the trunk. Then they left. Just like that! Before I could say anything, before I could give her the flowers! What am I going to do with them? They cost me a small fortune."

"Okay, Jean-Claude, okay. That's enough. Tell me, did they appear to be leaving town?"

"Of course they were leaving town! What do you think? Chantal was wearing jeans, boots and her leather coat. Exactly what she used to wear when we went for our little trips in the country. It's obvious. The bastard is taking her on a trip in the country. Can you believe it? I was supposed to see her tomorrow afternoon. Janine was going to talk with her. That's why I bought those damned flowers and the fancy vase. Janine said..."

Gambia let out a raucous bark of laughter that stopped Duchon in mid-sentence. He reached across the table and clapped his friend on the shoulder.

"Bravo, Jean-Claude! Congratulations!" He succumbed to another loud guttural whoop. "It's too much. It's perfect. You're a genius, Jean-Claude."

"What are you laughing at, Jojo? This is not a time for jokes. I see nothing funny about all this. That American bastard has taken my Chantal away to God knows where. And who knows for how long? Wait until I see that son-of-a-bitch tomorrow. If he doesn't tell me where she is he better watch out. It's too much! He takes Chantal away in his fancy car and all you do is laugh. Why, Jojo? I thought you were my friend."

"Jean-Claude, please shut up for a minute and listen to me. I am your friend. That's why I am going to get Chantal back for you. I'm sorry about laughing. I know you are upset. I laughed because you just gave me, without knowing it, the solution to a very big problem. I've spent hours racking my brain and you come out with the perfect solution just like that. You have saved my life, Jean-Claude. Do you know that? You have really saved my life. Santé!"

He touched his glass to that of Duchon then took a long drink.

"What are you talking about, Jojo? Have you gone crazy? What about Chantal? Where has that guy taken her?"

"Don't worry about your girlfriend, Chantal. I'll have her back to you before those pretty flowers of yours have had time to fade. And don't worry about this guy, Ellis, giving you any more problems. I'm going to take care of him at the same time I return Chantal."

"What? What are you going to do? If it's something like this morning when you sent Carlos and the others to his apartment, I want none of it, Jojo. I've had enough of your Carlos to last me a lifetime. All he's done is make problems. My life is hell because of him."

"I could say the same thing about you, Jean-Claude. Think about it."

"Me? What have I done? I've done nothing!"

"Exactly. You ask others to do your dirty work. Then after they try to help you, you blame them for making your life hell. You're something, Jean-Claude. You're really something. No wonder Chantal left you for that American kid. She probably got tired of your whining."

"That's enough, Jojo! You must not talk about Chantal like that."

"And why not? Is your little mistress a sacred subject? Or I should say 'your former mistress'. Do you want Chantal back or not? Just tell me that, please."

"Of course I do. What do you think?"

"Very good. And what about the journalist, Ellis? Would you like me to make sure he doesn't bother you anymore?"

"You know I would, Jojo. But Inspector LeClerc told me this morning that if you tried to do anything else to the guy, he would put me in jail as well as you."

"Fuck LeClerc! That's what he's already trying to do to us. Open your eyes, Jean-Claude."

"What do you mean? He told me this morning he was going to take care of the American bastard just as soon as he found Carlos. He said he had to find Carlos before he could do anything."

"Jean-Claude, wake up! This fucking journalist just left town with your lover, Chantal. Do you call that taking care of him? Because if you do, I'll leave you to work things out with LeClerc by yourself. But be careful. The good inspector only cares about one person. Himself. As Janine will soon find out. So tell me, Jean-Claude, is that what you want? If it is, I'll leave right now."

"I just want Chantal back and this whole mess over with. I don't want any more trouble. I can't take any more trouble. I'm going crazy, Jojo."

"What about me, Jean-Claude? What do you think my life has been like recently? A rose garden?"

"No, of course not."

"You can bet your ass it has not. And I've had enough. I'm going to do something about it. With or without your help. It's for you to decide. If you help me deal with this journalist, Ellis, you get Chantal back. If not, who knows?"

"You're not talking about killing him are you, Jojo?"

"Jesus, Jean-Claude! I used to think you had some brains. I guess I was wrong. Kill the guy? LeClerc would love that. It would be perfect. No journalist to make trouble for him and Janine and me wanted for murder. He would look like a hero. Hell no, Jean-Claude. I want that journalist, M. Ellis, very much alive and working. He is the key to the whole thing. That's why I need your help."

"I don't understand."

"Didn't you say you are supposed to meet Ellis tomorrow?"

"Yes. At 11:30."

"Where?"

"Jojo, you're not thinking about coming to the meeting too? LeClerc said you..." Duchon let the sentence trail off.

"What's the matter, Jean-Claude? Has the cat suddenly got your tongue? What exactly <u>did</u> Inspector LeClerc say about me?"

"He made me swear not to tell you. It's nothing important. Really."

"God damn it, Jean-Claude, you are really starting to piss me off. You sound like you're working for LeClerc. Is that what you're doing now? Because if it is, our conversation is over. As well as our friendship."

Gambia pushed his chair back from the table as if to leave.

"Don't go, Jojo. I'll tell you what he said."

"Well, I'm listening."

"He just asked me to tell him if you were planning to meet with the journalist tomorrow. That's all. I swear!"

"You are certain that is all he said, Jean-Claude?"

"I swear to you, Jojo. On the grave of my mother."

"I hope for your sake what you say is true. If I find out you are lying to me, there will be a new grave next to the one of your mother. You understand?"

"Yes, Jojo."

"Good. Now let's stop acting like women and get down to business. You want another drink?"

"Sure, Jojo."

Gambia motioned for the waiter to come over. This time he ordered a Ricard for himself as well.

"Now, Jean-Claude, where are you meeting this journalist, M. Ellis?"

"At La Chope. It's a little cafe across from the beach in Chambre d'Amour. It's not one of my accounts so I don't know much about it. I've only passed by it on the street. I think it's a hangout for surfers."

"And you're meeting him at 11:30?"

"Yes. I have to have lunch with my wife at 12:30 because of the holiday. I told the guy I could only meet with him for about half an hour."

"Well, make sure you talk to him for the entire half an hour. It shouldn't be difficult for you. You can talk about Chantal."

"Why the entire half an hour, Jojo?"

"You'll see tomorrow. It's better if I don't tell you right now. For both of us. It probably won't be necessary but I want to be safe."

"What if he doesn't want to talk that long?"

"Then you better think of a way to make him. That is, if you want Chantal back before your flowers start to fade. I have faith in you, Jean-Claude. You'll think of something."

"Is that all, Jojo?"

"That's all for now unless something unforeseen comes up."

"My God, I hope nothing does. I've had too many surprises recently."

"We all have, Jean-Claude. But don't worry. This time I'm taking care of things myself. Now I need to know one more thing. What time do you usually go to work?"

"I have to be at the office by nine but I usually leave home by seven. That way I can read the newspaper in peace at the cafe without having to listen to my wife babble."

"Would you be able to leave home earlier than that, say on the day after tomorrow?"

"If it was necessary, I could. Sometimes I have clients who want to meet with me before they open for business."

"Good. Then everything is set, except to talk about what I plan to do after I move to St. Barthèlemy."

"St. Barthèlemy? What are you talking about Jojo?"

"It is what you are going to tell Janine we talked about when you call her later this evening. You're going to tell her how much I am looking forward to moving to St. Barthèlemy."

CHAPTER TWENTY-EIGHT

When Peter Ellis pulled into the circular driveway, he found Olga and Anya waiting by the open front door of the old farmhouse. Framed by the warm yellow light of the entry hall, they struck him as radiant welcoming angels. He introduced them to Chantal. Olga immediately took her by the arm and led her into the house. She called over her shoulder for him to bring in Chantal's things. Left alone, Peter Ellis took Anya into his arms. He held her close for several seconds.

"God am I glad to see you. What a day!"

"From what you said on the phone, it must have been terrifying for you. Are you really okay?"

"I was very lucky when I jumped. It was a long way down. I could easily have broken a leg."

"You must tell me all about it, even the very bad things. Will you do that later?"

"I don't know if that's a good idea, Anya. I don't want to scare you off just when we are getting started. It's not as though this happens to me all the time."

"Listen, Peter, you are already a part of my life, for better or for worse. I want to know everything about you, the good _and_ the bad. You must know I am already absolutely in love with you. Nothing you say now can change that. How you act toward me is the only thing that can change my love for you. What you do in your work is separate. I know that it is not going to be easy, at times, to deal with the risks you take in your work. But I also know that I can't help how I feel about you. Do you understand?"

"I'm trying to. I don't know what I've done to deserve you but I hope I can keep doing it. It is almost too good to be true."

"What do you mean, 'almost'?" Still in his embrace, she pushed back from his chest and looked up at him with mock disapproval. He leaned down and kissed her.

"I stand corrected. It is altogether too good to be true."

"That's better but don't overdo it. Now sir, when are you going to tell me about what happened this morning?"

"I'll tell you after dinner when we are alone. I gave Chantal a heavily edited version of events while we were driving out here. There are certain things I don't think she needs to hear."

"How do you think she is doing?"

"Remarkably well, under the circumstances. She is very confused. People are pulling at her from all directions. I still don't think she has had a chance to come to terms emotionally with the death of her friend, Kevin Duffy. So many other things have been happening."

"She certainly is a very attractive girl. I must say I was not prepared for someone that sophisticated looking. She could easily pass for one of those long-legged models walking down the Champs-Elysées."

"I know what you mean but don't let appearances fool you. Beneath that chic cashmere exterior lies the innocence and sensibility of a country girl. That is not meant as a criticism nor as a commentary on her intelligence. In fact, from the little I have observed, she comes across as a fairly perceptive, quick-witted girl. I think you are going to like her. She was genuinely excited and a little incredulous when she heard you were an artist."

"Why on earth did you tell her I was an artist?"

"Because she asked me what you did. And because it is true."

"You're going to embarrass me."

Olga suddenly reappeared in the doorway. Peter Ellis still held Anya in a light embrace.

"I would ask what you two are doing if the answer were not so evident. I have already given Chantal a tour of the house and you, Peter, are still out here acting like a teenager."

"Where is Chantal now, Olga?"

"In her room freshening up."

"Is there a telephone in her room?"

"No. Why?"

"I don't want her making any private calls tonight. It's for her own safety. I don't want anyone, even her mother, knowing exactly where she is. If she wants to call anyone, I want someone to monitor the call."

"Why are you so worried, Peter? She did not give me the impression that she was upset or wanted to leave while I was showing her around."

"It's not that, Olga. It's something she told me in the car. The girl is extremely impressionable. She does not know when people are preying on her while pretending to be friends."

"Yes, I noticed that innocence. She reacted almost like a child when I showed her the studio and Anya's paintings. It was very touching."

"What did you think of her, Olga, apart from that?"

"I'll tell you when we get inside out of this wind. I can't believe you have kept Anya out here so long."

"You two go on in. I'll get Chantal's things out of the trunk."

"Did you remember the wine and the tarragon mustard?"

"Yes, madam. Can you tell me now what the surprise is for dinner?"

"No. You must come in and see for yourself. I don't think you will be disappointed though you will kick yourself for not figuring it out after all the hints I have given you."

When Peter Ellis walked into the dining room and saw the large tarnished brass pot and smelled the cooking oil, he felt like he had walked back in time. Beef fondue was something they often had on special occasions at the farm in the old days. Olga was right. After all the hints she had given him, he should have guessed.

When they sat down to dinner a short time later, it quickly became obvious that Chantal was unfamiliar with the communal boiling-oil cooking ritual of fondue. Olga and Anya seemed simultaneously to detect her self-consciousness and immediately set out to disarm it with a tactful combination of friendly instruction and self-deprecating humor. Peter Ellis sat back and marveled at how the girl responded to their attention. Within fifteen minutes she seemed totally at ease. By the end of the meal she was clearly enjoying herself and was the first to laugh when she or anyone else inadvertently left a cube of beef floating unskewered in the oil.

After dinner, at Anya's suggestion, they repaired to the studio for their coffee and digestives. Anya explained to Chantal that she had been working on a portrait of Olga for most of the day and was very close to finishing it. Olga had already agreed to sit for the hour or so Anya needed to complete her work on the face and body. She would do the background later.

"Of course, Peter, if you and Chantal would rather watch television in the living room, you will not hurt my feelings. I realize my request is selfish. It is just that I am so close to finishing that I don't want to risk losing the spontaneity of the impression."

"Well, Chantal, what do you think? Would you like to see the artist at work?"

"Oh yes. Very much. I have never seen a real artist at work except for M. Laulié once at the Port Vieux."

"Don't let Peter fool you, Chantal. I just paint pictures. I would not call myself a 'real artist'."

"Well I would, my dear, and so would anyone who knows the least bit about painting. Is that not correct, Olga?"

"For once, Peter, I must totally agree with you. I have been trying to convince her all afternoon to quit her job at the bank and concentrate on her art."

"You know I would like nothing more than to paint all the time, Olga, but the artist must eat."

"And have I not told you that you may stay here until you have established yourself? I promise not to let you go hungry."

"And who will pay my mortgage?"

"I am certain you would have no trouble renting your apartment in Amsterdam for more than enough money to cover your expenses there."

"You are very kind, Olga, and your offer is very tempting. Almost too tempting. I need time to think. Things have been happening so fast." She shot a quick glance at Peter Ellis. "There is so much to consider. Amsterdam suddenly seems so far away. Still, I have commitments there."

"What about the commitment to your talent? You are blessed with a very special gift, Anya. Roger recognized it from the beginning, when you were a student. I only wish he were here to see how your work has progressed. He would be very proud of you. He would also be giving you the same advice I am giving, though I am sure he would be using somewhat stronger language. But then, you already know that, after all the time you spent listening to his critiques."

"Yes I do, Olga. I also know he would be wondering why I am standing at my easel talking with my model instead of painting her."

"You see, Peter, what thanks I get for offering to help a starving artist?"

"They are all the same, Olga. No appreciation at all."

"Exactly. All she cares about is that I take off my clothes. She is no better than a man."

Olga had no sooner spoken these words than she became aware of how they might be taken by her impressionable young guest.

"Oh Chantal, my dear, I am so sorry. I was not thinking. That was a very crude thing to say."

"But it is true, Mme. Olga. That is how most men are, at least most men I have known. Don't worry, though, I know you were just joking."

"Thank-you, Chantal. You have taught me a valuable lesson: models should be seen and not heard. Is that not so, Anya?"

"Absolutely. Especially when it comes to giving advice to the artist."

"You see, Peter, your friend even has the ego of the artist. Next, she will be asking if I need help remembering my pose, this after I have held it for God knows how many hours today." She pointed an accusatory finger at Anya whose face wore a wide smile. "Is that not so?"

"I am guilty as charged. You know me too well, Olga."

"No, Anya, I knew Roger too well. I dare say you learned it from him. So I shall tell you the same thing I always told him when he asked if I needed help remembering my pose: No, do you?" With this, Olga pivoted like a high-fashion runway model and began walking with an exaggerated, hip-throwing stride toward the plastic beach recliner they had set up in the corner of the studio. As she walked she began to unbutton her blouse. When she reached the recliner, she threw the blouse aside and reached back to unclasp her bra. As she did so she looked back over her shoulder at Peter Ellis. "Monsieur, prepare yourself for the sunbathing Venus of St. Martin-de-Hinx!"

While Anya worked, Peter Ellis and Olga reminisced about old times and exchanged news of old friends. Chantal, at Anya's invitation, sat in a chair behind the easel and watched her paint. Every so often Anya would pause and explain to Chantal what she was about to do. The girl would listen intently, wrinkles of attempted comprehension furrowing her wide forehead. As soon as the explanation was complete, she would give a short nod of understanding and go back to following intently the work in progress. While stealing a look at Anya, Peter Ellis managed to observe one of these heart-touching, innocent interchanges. The scene was indescribably tender.

True to her word, Anya proclaimed her work finished within the hour. Olga got up from the recliner, retrieved her shirt and bra and announced that she was going to bed.

"All of this lying still and trying to look like a goddess has worn me out. I shall leave you young people to your own devices. Feel free to listen to music or watch television. I can hear nothing in my bedroom. Is there anything I may get for you before I retire, Chantal?"

"No thank-you, Mme. Olga. I, too, am very tired and am going to bed. You have been very kind. Thank-you for everything."

"It has been my pleasure, Chantal. Are you sure there is nothing else you need? Perhaps you would like to call your mother and let her know you are alright?"

"She goes to bed very early. I am sure she is already asleep. I will call her in the morning, if that is convenient with you?"

"Of course. Just let me know. Now if you'll come with me, I shall show you to your room."

After wishing Olga and Chantal goodnight, Peter Ellis walked over to the bar and poured himself and Anya small snifters of Armagnac. He went over to where she was standing. She was studying her just-completed work.

"So what do you think, Peter?"

"I think it is exceptional."

"You really do? You're not just saying that to make me feel good?"

"Not at all. I would never say something just to make you feel good. If it involved making me feel good as well then that's another matter. I think all this talk of going to bed has given me some ideas." He put his arm around her waist, squeezed her gently, then bent down and kissed her lightly on the temple. Her hair felt like silk and smelled faintly of lavender.

"I'll bet it has. I can't imagine what those ideas might involve." She gave him a playful jab in the ribs.

"But seriously, Anya, I am quite impressed. It is extremely good. Will you try to finish the background tomorrow?"

"Maybe tomorrow evening. It depends on the weather. If it is pretty in the morning, I am going to have Chantal model for me outside. That way we can both get some sun. I keep thinking about the gloomy, wet Dutch winter ahead of me."

"Have you already talked with Chantal about it?"

"Yes. We talked about it while I was working. At first she demurred but I could tell she really wanted to do it. She said she was afraid the picture might be seen by the wrong people. So I told her I would give it to her as soon as it was finished and she could keep it hidden in a closet if she wished. That seemed to gain her trust and she agreed."

"I think you have had her trust from the beginning. You should have seen the way she was looking at you while you were painting. She was like a child at her first magic show. Her face was filled with pure, innocent wonder. There was one moment, it was when you were explaining something to her and she was concentrating so hard on what you were saying and not seeming, at first, to understand."

"Peter, I know exactly when you mean."

"Then you said something and, suddenly, her face was beaming with comprehension. It was really a very touching scene."

"It is as I suspected, M. Ellis. At heart, you are nothing but a soft touch."

"Not usually. This is a special case."

"Yes, you're right. I should not be making jokes at this time, given Chantal's fragile condition. After what she's been through, I'm surprised she's doing as well as she is. Do you think that she is still in a state of shock?"

"To some extent. And that's what really scares me. How she will react when it all finally hits her. The death of her friend and the circumstances surrounding it. I'm afraid she is, ultimately, going to blame herself."

"I feel so sorry for her. I so much would like to help her."

"I think that you already are."

"Peter, will you tell me everything you know about her and what really happened to her friend?"

"Of course."

"And then will you tell me exactly what happened to you this morning?"

"My dear, I shall tell you everything I know on both subjects: however, I have one important stipulation."

"Which is?"

"That I tell you all this information from the safety and comfort of our bed upstairs."

So after he and Anya were curled up warmly against each other under a puffy old Swiss eiderdown comforter, Peter Ellis told her everything he knew about Chantal and the circumstances surrounding the death of Kevin Duffy. He left out nothing, feeling strangely confident that the beautiful and uncommonly intuitive woman curled up next to him might somehow hold the key to the rehabilitation of the emotionally scarred young girl asleep in the bedroom down the hall. Afterwards, he told her of his succession of morning encounters, first with Carlos and his playmates and then with Gambia, LeClerc and Duchon. In this telling, he left out only two or three small details.

"And now you know everything, Anya. The good, the bad and the ugly."

"There is so much I want to ask you, Peter, but I fear that the second glass of Armagnac is beginning to have its effect."

"There will be plenty of time to talk later. You can ask whatever questions you want tomorrow afternoon when I return from my meeting with Duchon."

"You promise?"

"Boy Scout's honor."

"Were you really a Boy Scout?"

"For about two months. I had trouble learning to tie the knots."

"I'll bet."

"It's true."

"Well, I'm too tired to argue. Do you have to leave early tomorrow?"

"Not really. I'm not meeting with Duchon until 11:30. So long as I leave by 10:45 I should be fine."

"Good. I think I may need to sleep late. I suddenly feel totally exhausted. You won't be mad if we save our love-making for the morning?"

"Of course not."

"Thank-you, my love." She leaned over and kissed him. "If you feel like reading, please do. It will not bother me."

"You are sure?"

"Positive."

Anya settled in close to him, resting her head on his chest. Peter Ellis reached over to the night table for his well-worn paperback copy of The Selected Poems of Wallace Stevens that he always carried with him on his travels. He opened to 'The Man with the Blue Guitar'. It was a poem he had never tired of and never ceased learning from. Anya squirmed a little, nestling her body closer to his.

"Are you comfortable?" He stroked the top of her head.

"Perfectly."

Anya was asleep within minutes, her regular breathing a soft counterpoint to his heartbeat. He read for twenty minutes then put down his book and switched off the table lamp. Taking care not to wake Anya, he gently turned so that his back fitted into the curve of her body. He fell asleep almost immediately.

Peter Ellis woke in the middle of a vaguely erotic dream. He felt as if he had slept for only a couple of hours, but then became aware of the first tentative chitterings and chirpings of early morning birds. Simultaneously, he became aware that it was not a dream he was having. Anya had her hand between his legs and was gently squeezing him with her long, soft fingers.

"Are you awake, Anya?"

"Mm-m-m-m-m."

He was lying on his back and she was settled in tight against his body, her head nestled in the crook between chin and shoulder blade. He raised his head and leaned down to kiss her sleep-softened lips. He slowly moved his right hand down her body and began to caress her. He gently probed and immediately felt a shuddering, electric surge. She moved in concert with the pressure of his fingertips and he could feel her tenseness build. This hidden dance lasted perhaps three minutes. Suddenly Anya removed his hand, rose up on her knees and, astraddle his hips, lowered herself onto him. This deep, liquid enveloping triggered an almost immediate bursting, shared release. Anya collapsed onto his chest, burying her face in the pillow next to his head. Peter Ellis held her heaving body tight against his, her salty love sweat mingling with his own, surrogate of another, profound intermingling.

They lay like this for several minutes, lost in the glorious exhaustion and cleansing emptiness of spent passion. All at once Peter Ellis became aware that Anya had begun crying. He turned and lifted her face up from the sweat-and-tear soaked pillow.

"Anya, what's wrong? Did I do something to upset you?"

"No, Peter, not at all. That's just it. It was all too perfect. I am crying because I am too happy. I feel more happiness than I am capable of holding."

"So you cry away the rest. It seems like a terrible waste of happiness."

"Now you are making fun of me."

"Hardly, my dear." Peter Ellis moved his head closer and kissed her, first on both eyelids and then on her tear-stained lips. He gathered her into his arms. "Let's stay like this for awhile."

CHAPTER TWENTY-NINE

It was a little after 8:30 when Peter Ellis and Anya came down to the farm's large kitchen in search of coffee. They found Olga and Chantal huddled together over the black cast-iron stove. Their attention was focused on the simmering contents of a gleaming copper pot. A sweet aroma permeated the room.

"What are you cooking, Olga? It smells wonderful."

The two women turned at the sound of his voice. Olga was holding a large wooden spoon.

"None of your business. It is a surprise, a secret recipe that Chantal has kindly agreed to share with me. It is for tonight's dinner."

"You may tell them if you like, Mme. Olga."

"No, Chantal, they must wait until this evening. It is their punishment for sleeping so late."

"Does our punishment also include no coffee?"

Olga scrutinized them both for several seconds, squinting her eyes in an exaggerated expression of concern. "No, that would be too cruel. You both look like you need several cups. Give me a few minutes. I shall make you a fresh pot. I may even let you have some of the fresh fruit and croissants that Chantal and I fetched this morning in the village."

"You are an angel, Olga."

"Don't exaggerate, Peter. Anyway, it is Chantal who is the angel. It was her idea to buy the fruit."

"Then I must thank you, Chantal. That was very kind of you."

"It is nothing, monsieur. You have all been very kind to me."

"Would you care to call your mother? We can do it while the coffee is brewing."

"It is not necessary, monsieur. I have already talked with her. Mme. Olga let me call her earlier."

"And is everything alright? She is not worried about you?"

"No, monsieur. I told her how nice everyone has been. She has also talked with your friend, M. Maurice. Everything is fine."

"Well, it sounds as though everyone has been quite busy this morning. Anya and I have some catching up to do."

"Indeed you do, Peter. By the way, when are you planning to leave for Biarritz?"

"Around 10:45, why? Do you want to come with me, Olga?"

"I was thinking that I might, if you don't mind stopping in Bayonne on the way back. I have a little shopping to do there. It won't take more than an hour. That way I can leave the car here with Anya in case she and Chantal decide to go exploring."

"An excellent idea, Olga."

"And you don't mind stopping in Bayonne?"

"On the contrary. I would enjoy it. It has been at least ten years since I've been to the center of town. I used to walk there often in the old days. I am curious to see how it has changed."

"Like everywhere, there have been changes: however, I still find the old quarter of the city quite charming. But you can judge for yourself soon enough. Now, if you'll excuse me, I must attend to this pot or else you will be having a burned surprise. Your coffee will be ready in a minute."

After a simple <u>petit-dejeuner</u> of fresh fruit salad, croissants and <u>cafe</u> <u>au</u> <u>lait</u>, Peter Ellis and Anya walked the short distance to St-Martin-de-Hinx. It was a clear and unseasonably warm day and Anya had never been to the tiny neighboring village.

"Can you believe this weather, Anya? It is a shame we cannot spend the day at the beach together."

"Yes, that would be lovely. But I am just happy to have such beautiful sunny weather for painting Chantal. I shall have her sit on one of the beach chairs and we can pretend our backyard is the beach. Perhaps I shall even paint in some sand."

"You will keep an eye on her for me, won't you, Anya? I don't foresee any problems—she seems genuinely happy to be here now—but one can never be absolutely sure."

"I shall guard her with my life, though I hardly think that will be necessary. Like you said, she does seem to enjoy being here now, and I am sure Olga has a lot to do with that. Did you notice how they were working together this morning in the kitchen?"

"Yes, I did. I also noticed how Chantal hung on your every word last night. Olga is not the only one responsible for making Chantal feel at home here."

"She is such a sweet and shy girl, Peter. I think it is a good thing that no one will be here while she poses."

"You mean you think it is a good think <u>I</u> am not going to be here when she poses."

"Yes, that too. But don't take it the wrong way. It is not just you."

"Not to worry, my dear. Anyway, I agree with you. And I certainly don't take it personally. I believe she would feel uncomfortable if any man were present. After what she's been through, it's natural."

"I'm glad you understand." She paused, as if trying to decide whether to add something else.

"What is it, Anya? Is there something else I should know?"

"It's strange. I don't know exactly why, but I really believe my painting her is going to be a good experience for Chantal. I think it is going to help her recover some lost self-esteem. Does that sound terribly egotistical?"

"Not at all. I can't imagine how it could be anything but a good experience for her. I hope it will be a good experience for you as well."

"I'm sure it will be. I just hope I can do her justice."

"I am certain you will." Peter Ellis paused to glance at his watch. "We had better get back. It's almost 10:15."

When they returned to the farm, they found Olga and Chantal lounging in beach chairs in the sunny side yard where Peter Ellis had first seen Anya. Unlike that memorable, life-changing day, this morning the two women sunbathing wore shorts and bikini tops. Telling Olga he would be ready to leave in five minutes, Peter Ellis went upstairs to shave and gather his things. He was rinsing his face when, in the mirror, he noticed Anya standing in the doorway of the bathroom. She had changed into her bikini. He turned and started to make a comment on the sexiness of her outfit when she walked over and silenced him with a quick kiss. She wrapped her arms around him and held him tightly for several seconds. Then, without saying a word, she disappeared downstairs.

Peter Ellis put on his shirt, grabbed his things and hurried down the stairs. He found Anya, Olga and Chantal outside standing by his car. Olga appeared to be telling the two younger women an amusing story. At the sound of his approach, she turned and smiled at him.

"So, Olga, what sort of scheme are you cooking up now?"

"Nothing that concerns you, monsieur."

"Are you ready to go? We should be getting on the road. I don't want to be late."

Olga held up a small beach bag. "I am packed and ready for the rigors of Chambre d'Amour."

Peter Ellis stored her bag in the trunk while she took Chantal by the hand and walked around to the passenger's door. Olga kissed the girl on both cheeks and opened the car door.

"Good luck, my dear. Be brave."

Olga started to get in the car but then stopped and leaned over and whispered something in the girl's ear. Chantal smiled broadly and nodded her head.

Peter Ellis kissed Anya goodbye and slipped in behind the wheel. He eased the car into gear and started down the driveway. He had barely traveled one hundred meters when Olga placed her hand on his arm.

"Peter, I'm so sorry. I just remembered something. Do we have time to go back? It will only take two minutes, but I think it is important. I don't want the girls to be frightened."

"Frightened of what?"

"Of old Pascal. He brings the cheese, milk and butter. Today is one of his delivery days. I think I should forewarn Anya."

"Is there something wrong with him?"

"Nothing that a hot shower and a good barber could not remedy. No, old Pascal is a sweetheart. We've been friends for years. But I've known his appearance to terrify the uninitiated. And that's before he opens his mouth. The locals refer to him as 'the Growler'."

"It sounds like Anya will appreciate the warning."

"I really am sorry for the delay."

"Don't worry, Olga. I think I can make up the time. And if I can't, tant pis. Under the circumstances, I think M. Duchon will wait for me."

**

In fact, Jean-Claude Duchon was waiting when Peter Ellis walked into La Chope's small bar at 11:40. He made a show of checking his watch.

"M. Duchon, forgive me for being late. Thank-you for waiting."

"I am a man of my word, monsieur. As I hope you are." He sipped from a glass of pastis.

"You need not worry yourself on that account, M. Duchon. When I say I am going to do something, I always find a way to do it. Would you care to sit down?" He indicated a table in the corner. "What I have to say you may not want others to hear." Peter Ellis ordered a Kronenbourg 1664 and followed the thin food salesman to the table. He took a seat with his back to the wall. "Very good, then. Where shall we begin, M. Duchon?"

"You may begin, monsieur, by telling me where you have taken Chantal. And why?"

"Unfortunately I can not tell you where I've take Mlle. Clairac at this time. I can assure you, however, that she is safe and is in good spirits. You may confirm this by calling her mother. In answer to your second question, I have taken her away for her own protection."

"Her own protection? Who would want to hurt Chantal?"

"Perhaps the people who paid me a visit yesterday morning, the charming young associates of M. Gambia. Or perhaps even you, M. Duchon."

"Me? That is ridiculous!"

"Correct me if I am wrong, M. Duchon. Have you not recently threatened Chantal? In fact, have you not recently even physically assaulted her?"

"I did not assault Chantal. That is an exaggeration. I merely slapped her, and not hard. She had made me very angry. After all I've done for her, she was still refusing to see me. I know it was wrong to slap her and I am sorry. I told her so afterwards. But I was not myself that day."

"Just as you were not yourself the day you abused Madeline Delay?"

"What does she have to do with this? I have not seen her in almost three years."

"And why do you think that is?"

"She decided to move away. I don't even know where she is. I believe she had a nervous breakdown."

"You have a gift for language, M. Duchon. I have never heard violent rape referred to as a 'nervous breakdown'."

"I had nothing to do with that. I swear to you on my mother's grave. Madeline was at a party and things apparently became crazy."

"'Apparently'? You are really too much, M. Duchon. Who, may I ask, brought her to the party, the party where she was drugged and raped? Will you please tell me that?"

"I did, of course. I admit it. But I had nothing to do with the other things. I was no longer there when those things happened. I had tried to take her back to her apartment but she refused to let me. So I left. You can ask anyone who was there or you can ask her."

"Madeline Delay refused to let you take her home because she was afraid you would try to molest her, as you had done once before.

Is that not true, M. Duchon? Was that another day when you were not yourself?"

Duchon sat in stony silence. Peter Ellis, keeping his eyes fixed on him, took a long, slow sip of beer.

"M. Duchon, you have professed to be a man of your word. Is Mlle. Delay lying or did you, in fact, try to rape her in her apartment the first time you two were there alone?"

"It was not like that. You make me sound like an animal. Madeline and I had been going out together for some time. She was beginning to return my affections, as well she should have what with all the money I was spending on her. I thought the time had arrived to take the next step. I thought she was ready."

"But she was evidently not ready so you tried to force her."

"We had been drinking. She invited me up to her apartment for a nightcap. She let me kiss her, and not just in a friendly way. She got me all excited. Then when I tried to touch her she slapped my hand away. She was trying to tease me. And I became angry."

"So it was her fault, then, that you pushed her down on the couch and jumped on top of her."

"Nothing happened. If she says otherwise, she is lying. But what does all this have to do with M. Gambia? I thought that was why you wanted to talk with me."

"Indeed it is, M. Duchon. I just want you to know what will happen if you decide not to cooperate with me and my associates. Mlle. Delay is a very smart girl and has a remarkable memory. She has agreed to give written testimony, if it proves necessary, about your part in procuring girls for M. Gambia as well as your part in her rape at the party. I think my readers would find the story quite interesting, if a little sordid."

"So that's it. You are trying to blackmail me. And that is why you have taken Chantal. To turn her against me as well."

"M. Duchon, I am interested primarily in one thing: to see those responsible for the death of Kevin Duffy brought to justice. I know the boy jumped because that goon Carlos was holding a knife to his throat and threatening to carve up his face. Carlos himself told me as much yesterday morning while he was threatening to do much the same thing to me. I also know it was Gambia who sent Carlos and his pals to intimidate the boy. In fact, I know M. Gambia was sitting on a bench overlooking the park at the exact moment the boy jumped to his death. Finally, I know that it was you who asked Gambia for help in getting rid of Kevin Duffy after your own attempts to scare him off had failed."

"What do you mean, 'my own attempts'? You have no proof that I tried to do anything to harm the boy."

"M. Duchon, please don't play games with me. I do have proof. The boy wrote about what you tried to do in his diary."

"Then you must know I certainly did not try to kill him or even do him any physical harm."

"M. Duchon, as much as I detest you and all that you stand for, I do not believe you are a killer. I can even believe that you did not take part in the rape of Mlle. Delay. Still, you contributed your fair share to the commission of both crimes and, no doubt, many others of which I am presently unaware. I am giving you an opportunity to make some small amends for the harm you have done by helping me and my associates to remove permanently from circulation the truly dangerous criminals."

"And you will keep my name out of the papers?"

"I do not know if that will be possible. It depends on the police. What I can do is not mention your affairs with Madeline Delay and Chantal."

"Has Madeline agreed to that as well?"

"Yes, provided M. Gambia goes to prison for what he and the others did to her. As far as Chantal is concerned, that is her decision. For some reason, I don't think she wants to make trouble for you."

"That is because she still cares about me. It is what I have been trying to tell you, monsieur. If that American boy had not come along, we would still be together. I still love her and intend to get her back, no matter what lies you have told her about me. You will see."

"M. Duchon, I have told Chantal no lies about you. In fact, I have not even told her most of the damaging truths I have learned about you. Yet. Whether I do tell her will depend on you. But let me give you fair warning: If any harm ever comes to Chantal because of you, I promise to ruin whatever life you have left. Do you understand?"

The food salesman sipped at his drink and said nothing. He rolled his left wrist slightly, revealing the face of his watch, then adjusted his shirt sleeve to cover it. He turned his half-clenched fist inward and made to study his fingernails.

"M. Duchon, do you understand what I am telling you?"

"Yes, I understand. But it is not your affair."

"You, M. Duchon, have made it my affair. Now, do you know where Gambia is?"

"No. But I know he wants to see you. He wants to talk to you."

"He wants to see me? Why?"

"I do not know. He said he has something important to tell you, something for your article."

"When did he tell you this?"

"Yesterday evening when I told him I was meeting you. He said he would call you here."

"And what does he think he can tell me that will make me change my mind about him, after all he has done?"

"I do not know. I swear to you. Maybe he wants to make a deal."

"I can not imagine anything he could tell me that would make me want to make a deal with him. So I think you and I should get down to our business. Are you prepared..."

Peter Ellis stopped in mid-sentence. The waiter had come over towards their table and was waiting a discreet five paces away. He waved the waiter over.

"Yes? What is it?"

"Excuse-me, gentlemen. There is a telephone call for M. Jean-Claude Duchon."

Duchon was quickly on his feet. "You see? I told you." He followed the waiter back to the bar, thanked him and picked up the headpiece. "Yes, hello?"

"Bonjour, Jean-Claude. I have someone who wants to say hello to you."

There was a momentary silence on the line, then a meek voice. "Jean-Claude? Is that you?"

"Chantal! Where are you? I went to see you last night. I was bringing you flowers. But you left before I could give them to you. I was so disappointed. I wanted to surprise you."

"Jean-Claude, why are these men here. Where are they taking us?"

"Jojo has come to rescue you, to bring you back home."

Suddenly Gambia was back on the line. "You see, Jean-Claude, I told you I would find Chantal for you. And I must say she looks more beautiful than ever."

"When can I see her?"

"Tomorrow. I shall personally deliver her to you, provided, of course, that you keep your mouth shut and do everything I tell you. Otherwise I cannot be responsible for what might happen to her. Her fate is in your hands."

"What do you want me to do, Jojo? I'll do anything. But please, do not harm Chantal."

"I shall call you tonight at home at eight-thirty. Now, let me speak to the journalist. I have a little surprise for him."

Peter Ellis had been studying Duchon intently while he talked on the telephone. In the course of his short conversation, his normally sour demeanor had undergone a series of quick transformations, from elation to agitation to dejection. This last expression is what Duchon wore as he turned and motioned with the headpiece. Peter Ellis quickly went over and took the telephone from Duchon's hand.

"Hello?"

The cheerful voice at the other end of the line was all too familiar. "M. Ellis! How are you doing? It's me, your old friend, Jojo."

"Yes, I recognize your voice."

"You do not sound happy to hear from me, M. Ellis. What a shame on such a beautiful sunny day. Perhaps, after our little talk, you should take a walk on the beach. I'm sure you will find many beautiful young girls there taking advantage of the sun and warm weather. Of course, they may not be as beautiful as the two young women I have just discovered sunbathing next to an old farmhouse.

Imagine my surprise, M. Ellis, when I recognized one of them as your friend from St.-Jean-de-Luz. I must say she looks even better without clothes."

Gambia paused to let the meaning of his words register. Peter Ellis suddenly felt sick. It could not be true. It could not. How could Gambia know where Olga's farm was or that he had taken Chantal there? He shot Duchon a quick, appraising look. No. It was not possible. He would have had no way of knowing. Or would he? Then he heard Anya's trembling voice.

"Peter? Is that you?"

"Anya? Oh Jesus! Are you alright?"

"Yes, I think so."

"Where are you?"

"We are still at the farm but are getting ready to leave. When we saw the van, we thought it was the deliveryman, Pascal." Then she was screaming. "No! Stop! Don't touch me!"

Gambia came back on the line. He was chuckling but there was no humor in his voice. "I must say, M. Ellis, your friend is quite a lively young woman. And strong. It is a good thing I have Carlos here to help me."

"Gambia, listen to me. If anything happens to my friend, anything at all, I will kill you. You understand? I will come after you and I will find you. And when I find you..."

"There is no need to threaten me, M. Ellis. I do not intend to harm your beautiful friend. I merely intend to hold her as insurance."

"Insurance? Insurance for what?"

"I want to talk with you tomorrow. Alone. It is very important. I have a deal for you. I think you will find it very attractive. Your friend is insurance that you will come alone and hear what I have to propose. Should anything happen to me during this meeting, should I not return to my little hideaway by a certain time, young Carlos here will be free to do whatever he wants with your friend. And I must say, he has not taken his eyes off her since we arrived. Of course, who can blame him. She is quite sexy."

"Gambia, I'm warning you. Keep that punk, Carlos, away from Anya. Do you hear me?"

"I give you my promise that nothing will happen to your friend, provided you cooperate with me."

"How can I be sure?"

"You have my word on it."

"And what if that is not enough?"

"Frankly, I don't see that you have any choice in the matter, M. Ellis. However, as an act of good faith, I shall bring Mlle. Chantal with me when we meet tomorrow. She can tell you what I say is true. Surely you will believe her. Do we have a deal?"

"Where and when do you want to meet?"

"Stay in your apartment in Biarritz tonight, but leave your car somewhere else, out of sight, perhaps in a garage in town. Do not let anyone know you are staying in town. Tell your landlord you are taking a short trip. Keep the shutters closed and the curtains drawn. M. Duchon will come for you early in the morning, before seven. He does not know this yet, so say nothing to him. The less he knows, the better. You understand?"

"Yes."

"Until tomorrow, then. And M. Ellis?"

"Yes?"

"Please do not get any clever ideas."

The line went dead. Peter Ellis replaced the headpiece and returned to the table, where Duchon sat waiting for him.

"You see, monsieur. I told you Jojo would call." In his voice there was more concern than triumph. "When does he want to meet with you?"

"Soon. He said he would let me know."

"Well then, that's settled! I must be going." He pushed his chair back from the table and started to stand up. Peter Ellis quickly grabbed his forearm and forced him back down into his seat.

"What are you doing? Are you crazy? Take your hands off me!" He struggled to stand up again.

"M. Duchon, please sit down and shut up. I'm not finished with you."

"I don't care. I must leave. I'm taking my wife to lunch for the holiday. I have a reservation at L'Océan. I must not be late."

"Have you told your wife yet that you plan to divorce her as soon as you begin working for Janine Destin? Or are you saving that for lunch?"

Duchon slumped back into his chair and covered his face with his hands. Peter Ellis waited several moments before continuing.

"M. Duchon, what I say is correct, is it not? I have it on very good authority."

"You tricked Chantal, you bastard. It was she who told you."

"I had a conversation last night with Mlle. Clairac, it is true; however, I did not trick her or force her. It was not necessary."

"I detest you!"

"And I you, M. Duchon. It is one thing we can agree on. Now, let us see if we can agree on a few other things. Listen to me very carefully. Are you listening, M. Duchon?"

"Go on. I am listening. But hurry up, I must not be late."

"Don't worry. This won't take long unless you make it. It is up to you. Understand?"

"Yes! I'm not an imbecile."

"You know that Gambia has kidnapped Chantal?"

"Yes. I just talked to her."

"Was it you who told him where to find her?"

"How could I have told him that? I did not know myself. How could I know?"

"Perhaps Janine Destin found out and told you."

"That is ridiculous. Janine does not even know she is missing from Biarritz. At least I have not told her."

"You are sure?"

"Of course I'm sure. I was waiting across the street at Le Sportif last night when you came with her to pick up her suitcase. I had bought her flowers. And a vase. They cost me a small fortune."

"So you told Gambia I had taken her but you didn't tell your future boss, Janine Destin. Why was that? I don't think she would be very pleased if she knew you were keeping things from her."

"I don't know. I was already supposed to meet Jojo. I was very upset. When I met with Jojo he told me he would get Chantal back, provided I did not mention anything to Janine. I knew she would be mad and would not understand. She is very upset with Jojo."

"In fact she is so upset, she is trying to get rid of him with the help of Inspector LeClerc. Is that not true?"

"I don't know. I think so."

"You don't know? Come, M. Duchon, you are not that stupid I hope. You have just said you are not an imbecile."

"Okay. Yes. She is afraid Jojo is going to ruin their business. She is going to buy him out."

"And she has asked you to spy on him?"

"I am not spying. She wants to make sure he doesn't do anything crazy before their deal is done."

"Like talk to me."

"Janine is concerned that Jojo might again try something stupid. Like yesterday morning. Inspector LeClerc is also concerned."

"Oh, I'm sure he is, as any good policeman would be. So, what are you going to tell them about our little meeting?"

"I'm not sure. I'll think of something."

"When are you meeting with Gambia?"

"I don't know. He's calling me tonight to let me know."

"Is he going to bring Chantal with him when he meets with you?"

"He said he was."

"What does he want you to do for him in return?"

"I don't know yet. He does not want me to mention anything to Janine."

"I do not envy the position you are in, M. Duchon. It is what we call in America a 'no-win situation'. I wish I could help you."

"You? Help me? Are you kidding? You are the cause of my problems. How could you possibly help me?"

"First, by not telling Janine Destin or Inspector LeClerc that Gambia has Chantal and that you told him where to find her."

"You bastard! I didn't tell him. I didn't know myself. I have already explained that to you."

"But they don't know that. Also, you did tell your pal, Jojo, that I had taken Chantal and yet failed to inform them. They will not like that."

"I was going to tell them."

"When, M. Duchon? When?"

"Today. I was going to tell them today if Jojo didn't call."

"Very convenient. And now? What are you going to tell them now? Remember, Jojo has Chantal. You know how crazy he can be. And violent. Who knows what he might do to Chantal if you show up tomorrow with Inspector LeClerc? Have you thought of that, M. Duchon?"

"Of course. That's why I can't tell them anything until I meet with Jojo. Until I have Chantal back."

"But you have to tell them something. They both know you were meeting with me today."

"I will think of something."

"No, M. Duchon, you will do as I say. You will not think. You will tell them only that you spoke with me about Gambia and his role in the death of Kevin Duffy. You will tell them nothing else. Absolutely nothing else. If they happen to ask about Chantal, you will say you know nothing. Do you understand?"

"Yes."

"I certainly hope so, M. Duchon, because if anything happens to Chantal, I shall hold you responsible. So don't do anything stupid."

"I am not an imbecile! You will see."

"I certainly hope that is true, M. Duchon. For you sake as well as mine. You may now go and meet your wife."

The food salesman quickly got up and made to leave.

"And M. Duchon."

"Yes. What is it now?"

"Bon appétit."

***

It had been all Peter Ellis could do to control himself after talking on the telephone to Joseph Gambia. Now, with Duchon gone, he looked down and noticed that his hands were trembling. He wondered whether the ferret-faced food salesman had seen how upset he really was. He did not think so. Nor did he think, having had time to reflect, that Duchon had actually had anything to do with Gambia's kidnapping of Chantal and Anya. He began to assess the situation. He sat there for a long time, sipping beer and thinking about what to do. When he left the cafe, it was nearly 1:30.

In bright sunshine, he walked north down the beach to the first rock jetty past the end of the boardwalk. There he found Olga sunbathing, reading a paperback, her back propped against one of the large black granite rocks. He took off his shirt, sat down next to her and, taking her hand in his, proceeded to recount what had transpired at the farm after they had left that morning. After an initial outburst of outrage, she grew pensive while Peter Ellis finished his story.

"You know, Peter, I think I saw a blue van when we were leaving this morning. It was backed into the driveway of the old abandoned farm down the road and I remember seeing two men in it."

"Did you notice the make or anything special about it?"

"It looked like one of those old police vans. I remember thinking at first that it <u>was</u> the police come to check on the farm. Then I noticed that there was a grey circle where the yellow police light normally is. How stupid of me not to say anything."

"Don't be silly, Olga. How could you know anything like this was going to happen? If anyone is stupid, it is me for leaving the girls alone. I just can't figure out how Gambia found out where I had taken Chantal. Do you think she may have made a call without our knowing it?"

"No. I am positive she did not."

"How can you be so sure?"

"Because I unplugged the kitchen phone and took it with me when I went to bed. Do you think Duchon could have told him?"

"I don't see how. He certainly didn't follow me out there last night."

"God, it makes me furious to have my house invaded like that. If I find out this Duchon man had anything to do with it, I will wring his neck."

"You will have to wait in line for the privilege."

"Have you thought about what you might be able to do to get the girls back?"

"Yes. I've made a plan. I'll tell you about it, such as it is, when we get to Maurice's apartment. I want to see what he thinks of it."

"Are we going there now?"

"I think that would be wise. There are calls to be made and things to be arranged."

"Well then, let's go."

Olga and Peter Ellis spent just over an hour with Maurice at his Anglet apartment. While they were there, Maurice called his friend, Inspector Rectoran, on a private line and set up a meeting for 8:30 that evening. Before leaving, Peter Ellis made a call as well, this on the official line, to the office of Inspector LeClerc and left an apologetic message saying that he had been summoned to Paris for two days to deal with a small problem at work and that he would get in touch as soon as he returned. From Anglet, they drove to Hotel Les Flots Bleus, where Peter Ellis had a short, discreet conference with Arlette. Then, leaving Olga to wait for him in the hotel's restaurant, he went up to his apartment and packed a bag. He went around to all the windows and, after first making sure the shutters were securely fastened, drew all the curtains. After locking the door, he set himself a small early-warning device using two matchsticks.

Over Olga's protests, Peter Ellis insisted on stopping, as planned, in Bayonne on their way home. As he explained it, there was nothing else to be done until evening and a little shopping would help take their minds off the day's troubling events. After Olga had completed her errands, they stopped at a cafe in the old district for drinks and a snack. Neither of them had eaten anything since breakfast that morning, a convivial time that now seemed removed by years rather than hours.

When they reached the farm, they found a lengthy note on the kitchen table attached to a carton of eggs. It was from Pascal, the deliveryman. In it, he explained that he had encountered a blue van leaving Olga's driveway when he had arrived to make his delivery. It was a van he did not recognize and the two men in it looked suspicious so he had written down the license number, which he here included. When he pulled up at the house, he found the front door wide open. Since Olga's car was in the driveway, he assumed she was home. When he discovered she was not, he immediately became alarmed, thinking that a burglary had been committed by the two men in the blue van. He had made a quick inspection of the premises. (He hoped Olga would not object, it seemed like the correct thing to do.) He could not find anything to be missing or out of place. Still, he decided to call the police and report the suspicious van— one never knew—only to discover the telephone line dead. He checked the connection outside and discovered that the line had been cut at the box. He was now on his way to Peyrehorade to alert the police and report the damage to the telephone line. He would stop by that evening after he had finished his deliveries to see if Olga had returned home. He was very concerned and hoped Olga was well and that nothing had been stolen. He signed the note, 'Your friend, Pascal, who delivers the cheese and eggs'.

"Peter, it is incredible, no? What did I tell you? The old devil, Pascal, is something!"

"He is certainly shrewd and observant. That license number may prove invaluable."

"Unbelievable!" Olga had walked over and picked up the receiver. "The telephone is working now. What a miracle. Pascal must have really raised a fuss to get it repaired so quickly."

"Let's try calling Maurice to be sure." He took a pad from his pocket and found the number. "I want to give him that license number. Maybe Inspector Rectoran can trace the van by this evening."

Maurice picked up on the first ring. His voice sounded more exasperated than normal. Peter Ellis identified himself and, after listening to and accepting a quick apology, asked his friend to get a pen and write down the license number of Gambia's blue van. He promised to explain how he came by it later that evening during their meeting with Rectoran.

During dinner, Peter Ellis tried to sound optimistic. It was not easy. He had not told Olga what Gambia had said about leaving Anya with Carlos. The picture of her alone with that smirking, pathological, slash-happy punk had haunted him since leaving Chambre d'Amour. Now, his stomach in knots, he forced himself to eat and, for the sake of his old friend, did his best to sound sanguine about their chances of rescuing Anya and Chantal unharmed.

The deliveryman, Pascal, arrived as they were clearing away the dinner plates. Olga embraced him warmly and thanked him profusely for all he had done and especially for being so observant in noting the number of the blue van's license plate. Peter Ellis shook the old peasant's calloused hand, offered him a glass of wine and explained with regret, that he was just on his way to Anglet for an 8:30 meeting. The old man nodded his head, grunted an expression of understanding and waved his hand as if to say 'so off you go'. Peter Ellis took the gesture as his cue to leave.

***

It had been a long, stressful day for Inspector Jacques LeClerc. It had begun with a call from Janine Destin who reported that Chantal had gone missing. Next had come a false alarm regarding the spotting and apprehension of Carlos. (His men really could be imbeciles sometimes—the punk they arrested did not even vaguely resemble Gambia's bumbling enforcer.) No sooner had he finished listening to the misapprehended youth's indignant accusations and threats of litigation than Janine had called again, this time to inform him that Duchon had reported in after his meeting with the journalist and seemed to be holding back information. LeClerc had exploded and immediately volunteered to pull in the food salesman and grill him. For some unvoiced reason, Janine had not liked that idea and, instead, had suggested he put an intercept on Duchon's home telephone line. Not an official one, she had added, as if he would even consider doing something so stupid. In order to get the phone tapped, he had been forced to call in a marker from one of his gambling friends who worked for the telephone company. The man owed him a sizeable amount of money and insisted that the entire amount be forgiven in return for the favor, citing the risk to his job and pension. Then, after an insufferable and overpriced late lunch with his wife at a chic new restaurant recently opened by a famous nouvelle cuisine chef, he had returned, hungry, to his office only to be greeted by a message from Peter Ellis. It informed him that the journalist had left for Paris for two days. He had slammed the message down on his desk with such force that he initially thought he had broken a bone in his hand. It was incredible! He, the fucking Chief Inspector of police, had expressly told the journalist not to leave town without his permission. Before it was all over, he was going to teach this Peter Ellis a lesson, one he was not likely to forget. It was while pondering the specific form his retribution would take that he had been interrupted by a third call from Janine. When he heard her voice, he had instinctively braced himself for more bad news. Instead, he had received an invitation to come up to her place after work for drinks and a little chat. She asked him to bring a bottle of good champagne 'just in case'.

Now, as he rode the elevator up to Janine's apartment, the day's depressing series of events were all but forgotten. In their place was a distinctly pornographic fantasy featuring large trembling breasts, inviting moist orifices and a strategically placed tattoo. He kept remembering her parting words, 'just in case', and the promise they implied. But Janine's coy, tantalizing words were not the only reason for Jacques LeClerc's buoyant, even expectant mood: Just before leaving his office, he had received the first fruits of the recalcitrant telephone man's wiretapping labors. And deliciously sweet they were. Sweet enough, he mused, to turn his penis-hardening fantasy into naked reality.

Janine met him at the door wearing a black and orange Balinese wrap-around skirt and a loosely-tied halter top, both featuring a crescent moon and star motif. She made him stand in the doorway while she modeled her new outfit, turning a slow, suggestive pirouette for him, her hands raised, ballerina-style, over her head. From the way the thin material clung to her body, it was evident she was wearing nothing underneath either skirt or top.

"So Jacky, how do you find my new outfit? It is not too risqué?"

"Not at all, Janine. It is very becoming. It makes you look like some native princess on a South Pacific island."

"With all the shit that has been going on recently, I would not mind being on an island right now, preferably lounging naked on the beach with a handsome young native."

"Why not with a not-so-young but still relatively attractive and athletic chief inspector?"

"That might be acceptable, provided this inspector had taken care of certain business problems and was no longer married."

"I do not believe you will have to worry about either one of those conditions much longer, Janine. And if you will allow me to come in, I shall explain why."

"Oh, forgive me, Jacky." She reached up and kissed him fully on the mouth. "Please, come in. What would you like to drink?"

LeClerc removed the bottle of champagne from the plastic bag he had been discreetly holding behind his back and presented it for her inspection.

"This has been chilling in my office refrigerator for the last two hours, 'just in case'."

"You have a dirty mind, Inspector LeClerc, and I adore it, almost as much as something else you have." She reached down and squeezed his crotch playfully, though not all that gently. "Make yourself comfortable while I get the glasses."

LeClerc removed his overcoat, suit coat and tie and tossed them all carelessly on a chair. He unbuttoned the top two buttons of his shirt and settled into the deep folds of the massive sofa that had previously served his amorous purposes so well, though not as well as he hoped it would tonight. Janine returned carrying an ice bucket and two crystal flutes. In opening the champagne, LeClerc made a small show of popping the cork. His dramatics caused him to over-pour both their glasses.

"We have a lively one here, Janine. What do you think?"

"I think, perhaps, that we may have two lively ones." She dipped her fingers in the spilt champagne and dapped a little behind each ear. "You had better put some of that champagne behind your ears as well, Jacky. At the moment, we need all the luck we can get."

"Really, Janine, you surprise me, believing in such old wives' tales. We make our own luck. Spilt wine is like spilt milk: it does no good to cry over it."

"That may be true. Still, I believe in luck, the more, the better. So tell me, have we had any since you put ears on Jean-Claude's telephone?"

"You do come to the point, Janine. No sense wasting good champagne on a little romance."

"I believe in business before pleasure, Jacky. You know that. And the better the business, the greater the pleasure afterwards. Tonight, I really hope you have good business news." She paused, stretched out on the couch and adjusted the sarong so that one naked leg was visible almost to the hip. "Because I am certainly in the mood for some pleasure. I hope you are."

"What do you think?"

"What do I think? I think we are wasting time. What have you found out?"

"Well, first of all, your hunch was right. Duchon is holding back information. Important information."

"It concerns the girl, doesn't it?"

"Sometimes you amaze me, Janine. Are you sure you do not have a tap on the telephone too?"

"I do not need a telephone tap, mon cher, to understand human nature. I have my intuition. When I heard that the girl had gone missing, I suspected she was being used, poor thing, to get to Jean-Claude. Who has her? That journalist? What is his name?"

"Ellis. Peter Ellis."

"Ah yes, Ellis. So, he has taken young Chantal and is trying to use her to get to Jean-Claude."

"I fear your intuition is wrong this time, Janine."

"Who has her then? The old one, that former inspector, Claverie-LaPorte?"

"Not him either. It is much better than that: Chantal has been kidnapped by our brilliant partner, Jojo."

"You are kidding? Really? That is very strange. I was sure the journalist had taken her. It would make more sense."

"It might make more sense but it would be impossible. That bastard, Ellis, has apparently gone to Paris."

"Paris? Are you sure?"

"Almost positive. He left me a message this afternoon at the office. I've checked at the hotel. His car is gone and the cleaning girl I talked to said she thought monsieur had gone to Paris. She is a simple girl, not the kind of girl who would try to lie to a police inspector."

"Paris? What could he be doing in Paris?"

"I don't know, but I don't like it. I'm going to teach him a lesson when he returns, the same one I'm going to teach your little friend, Duchon, when I get my hands on him tomorrow. When I tell someone to do something, I expect them to do it. Especially a little weasel like Duchon. Who does he think he is, disobeying my orders?"

"Easy, Jacky, easy. Remember, we need Jean-Claude."

"But he has been lying to us."

"You must not blame him too much. When it comes to Chantal, he does not think straight. Just like someone else I know when it comes to certain things." She reached down and, with spread fingers, outlined the cleft mound beneath the silky thin black fabric. "Is that not so?"

"That is not fair, Janine. Please, do not compare me to Duchon."

"Don't be stupid, Jacky. Of course I'm not comparing you to Jean-Claude. I'm just trying to make you understand his behavior. I did not say I was happy with it. But we need him and, in the end, we can trust him. You will see."

"Trust him? He's meeting with Jojo tomorrow morning! That's what else I discovered from the telephone tap."

"What did they talk about?"

"Nothing, except that he was to keep the meeting secret. Otherwise, Jojo told him, he would not get the girl back. Jojo is going to call him at a cafe in Negresse early in the morning and give him directions. He told Duchon he would be watched to make sure no one followed him."

"That is interesting. Very, very interesting. So, what do you plan to do?"

"To follow him, of course. And, don't worry, I won't be spotted. My guess is that Jojo will send Carlos to meet Duchon and bring him to wherever they are hiding. When Carlos shows up, I'll grab him. Once I have Carlos, Jojo will have no choice but to leave town or be indicted with Carlos for the murder of the American kid."

"And what if Jojo himself shows up? What then?"

"Do you think he would be that stupid?"

"You have to ask me that? After what he has done recently."

"I suppose you are right. It is possible."

"And if Jojo does come himself, how do you propose we find Carlos?"

"While Jojo is meeting with Duchon, I will put a small tracking device on his car to find out where they have been hiding. When Jojo comes into town to meet with you about the buyout, I'll go out there and pick up Carlos. I hope Jojo does come himself just to see the look on his face when I show up with Carlos in handcuffs. It would be amusing, don't you think?"

"It would be amusing and very stupid. My God, Jacky, use your head. It is no longer enough for Jojo to leave town. If he leaves town, he can still talk. And talk he will, you may be sure. You know what a big mouth he has. No, Jacky, he must be silenced, once and for all. It is the only solution."

"What are you saying, Janine? That you want me to kill him?"

"No. I am saying that I want him dead."

"Bravo! So tell me, how is he going to get dead if I don't kill him?"

"Use your imagination. Carlos would certainly do it if he had a motive. Jean-Claude might even do it if it was properly arranged."

"Duchon? Kill Jojo? You must be joking, Janine."

"Not at all. If Jojo did anything harmful to Chantal, Jean-Claude would have a strong motive. And he must have a gun."

"Come on, Janine, get serious. Duchon wouldn't know how to load a gun, much less fire one."

"Well then, you think of something. And it better include keeping this journalist, Ellis, quiet as well."

"You want me to kill the journalist, too? Are you crazy?"

"No, I am not crazy, just careful. I did not say that I wanted you to kill the journalist, Jacky. You are not listening to me. I said I wanted the journalist kept quiet. By that I mean that I do not want him writing about our affairs."

"And you think that I do? Don't worry about the journalist. He won't be causing us any problems. That I guarantee."

"And Jojo?"

"Don't worry about him either. I'll take care of Jojo, one way or another. Now please, Janine, let's not talk about it any more. I've had a day from hell. Tomorrow I will take care of everything. I promise."

"I'm sorry, Jacky. Don't be mad with me. I'm just worried to death about everything right now. Would you like some more champagne?"

"Sure, but I'll get it." The inspector started to get up. Janine quickly extended a leg and stopped him by placing her foot firmly against his crotch.

"No, I will get the champagne. You get undressed. I have other plans for you."

In one lazy, feline movement, Janine slipped her legs from the folds of the couch, stood up and stretched, arching her back slowly and deliberately. As she did this, she fixed her eyes on the inspector and began to run her hands suggestively over her nipples, teasing them into an erectness easily visible beneath the thin, silky material stretched tight across her chest. Satisfied that she had his full attention, she bent over the wide black marble coffee table, removed the beaded champagne bottle from the silver ice bucket and filled both their glasses. LeClerc, his mouth slightly open, watched her every movement while his thick fingers fumbled with the small white shirt buttons. Janine replaced the bottle then walked around the coffee table so that she was standing directly in front of him. LeClerc had succeeded in removing his shirt, though not without popping the two bottom buttons. He was now squirming against the deep couch cushions, trying to work his way out of his trousers.

"Take it easy, Jacky. There is no need to hurry. I'm not going anywhere." She paused and ran her tongue over her lips. "Watch me while I get ready for you."

Saying this, she untied the pareo and let it slip to the carpet. With her right hand, she reached into the ice bucket and removed a cube of ice. Then, with theatrical deliberation, she began to massage herself with the dripping piece of ice.

"You see, Jacky, I am so hot for you I must cool myself down."

Although his trousers were still around his ankles, LeClerc made a move toward her. "Oh, Janine, let me help you."

"No, Jacky. Sit and watch me. Watch me and touch yourself. I want to see how you touch yourself. Show me how you like it."

LeClerc finished undressing and did as he was told. He took care not to get himself too excited. But, staring at the rose-handled dagger and the wet, rosy flesh beneath it, he found the challenge daunting. He began to wonder whether he, too, might need a little ice to cool himself down. First, though, what he needed was some champagne. His mouth had suddenly become extremely dry. Janine, apparently, felt a similar sudden thirst. She tossed what little remained of the ice cube back into the bucket and reached for her glass. LeClerc started to speak but his private dancer quickly put a forefinger to her lips. She waved her hand at him in a gesture that said: 'Go on, drink up'. He raised his glass to her in a mute toast and took a large gulp of the sparkling wine. She acknowledged his toast with a slight tip of her glass, took a mouthful of wine and swallowed. Then she took another mouthful which she did not swallow. In one motion, she replaced her glass on the coffee table and knelt on the carpet next to the couch where LeClerc sat, nude and erect. She leaned over and deftly took him in her champagne-filled mouth, clamping her lips tightly around him so as not to spill any of the wine. LeClerc lay on the sofa moaning, crying out her name every time she pressed her teeth against him. As he lay there, in a mingled, surreal state of disbelief and shock, he could barely feel Janine's fingernails as they clawed deep, red gashes in the soft, white flesh of his ass.

CHAPTER THIRTY

Jean-Claude Duchon arrived at the little cafe near the La Negresse train station a full half hour before the time Gambia was to contact him. He had slept poorly and it was no wonder. Janine had called shortly after midnight, just as he was, finally, starting to fall asleep. She was obviously quite drunk and greeted him in a slurred voice trying to sound sly and coquettish. After several lewd, joking questions concerning his private parts and his abuses of them, she matter-of-factly informed him that she knew all about his early morning meeting with Gambia and Chantal. Not only did she know about it, she did not disapprove of it! She did, however, have certain concerns for both his and Chantal's safety and wellbeing. It was for this reason that, in spite of the late hour, she had decided to call and offer some friendly advice. She would have called earlier but a friend had dropped by with a bottle of champagne and, well, he understood. Duchon had assured her that he understood perfectly.

Now, as he stared blindly into his second bowl of cafe au lait, he realized that he understood nothing. Her so-called 'friendly' advice had been both vague and portentous. Especially disconcerting had been her advice about how he should prepare himself for the meeting. It was as though she knew something unexpected was going to happen. But how could she? He was certain she had not spoken with Jojo; Gambia had been adamant that neither she nor LeClerc be informed of their morning rendez-vous. Could Chantal somehow have contacted her? He thought it highly unlikely, even though Janine, during the call, had spoken at length about her concerns for Chantal's safety. He felt physically sick with worry. All the uncertainty, all the threats, implied and, in Jojo's case, baldly stated, all the intrigue and mistrust among the former partners, it was all, finally, too much. He longed for things to be the way they had been before that damned American kid had come on the scene and stolen Chantal from him. That had started it all. He was certain of it. He took a large gulp of coffee. He thought about the first time he had seen Chantal and Kevin Duffy together. It had turned his stomach. He still could not believe she had left him for the American kid. What could he possibly have given her that he, Duchon, had not? He certainly had known nothing of local customs and tastes. How could he have? He was an American, for God's sake! And now another American, that bastard of a journalist, was also trying to ruin his life. It was too much! He would never trust an American again. Let them have their McDonald's hamburgers and their Disneyland and Mickey Mouse. What would their hamburgers be without the <u>frites</u>? And where did <u>frites</u> come from, after all? From France, that's where! They were just one more thing the Americans had stolen!

Duchon's rambling, anti-American reverie was interrupted by the sudden ringing of the telephone. The sound immediately started his heart pounding. The hatchet-faced barman, who was sitting at the other end of the bar reading the morning newspaper, answered on the second ring, listened for several seconds, his face a mask of resigned ennui, then grunted a non-committal 'Oui'. This was followed, three seconds later, by an equally enthusiastic 'Just a moment'. Telephone in hand, the barman motioned for Duchon to come over and then placed the receiver on the counter and went back to reading the newspaper. Duchon jumped up and hurried down to the end of the bar and nervously put the handset to his ear.

"Hello?"

"You are quite the early bird, Jean-Claude."

"I had to get out of the house, Jojo. My wife kept asking me why I was leaving so early."

"What did you tell her?"

"Nothing. I mean I told her I had an early appointment with a client. That's all. Still, she did not believe me."

"Why not?"

"I don't know. She's a bitch. She always thinks I'm up to something."

"And, I imagine, she is usually right. You are not up to something now are you, Jean-Claude? You have not whispered to anyone about our little rendez-vous, have you?"

"Of course not! Do you think I'm crazy?"

"I certainly hope you are not, Jean-Claude. Now, listen to me. I want you to go over to the Au Haou bar. Drive slowly. Park around the corner on the rue Peyroloubilh and walk to the bar. Wait there for my call. If you have been followed, you will never see Chantal again."

The line went dead. Duchon placed the receiver on the bar and asked for his check. With a show of obvious impatience, the bartender put down his newspaper and slowly walked over to the cash register. He rang in the two coffees and waited for the register to spit out the little white chit. When it appeared, he put it on a brown plastic saucer and placed it in front of Duchon. All of this he did without saying a word. Duchon, suddenly feeling very ill at ease in the bar, fumbled three coins from his pocket and deposited them on the saucer. The barman gave him a barely perceptible nod, tore the chit to confirm payment and abruptly turned his back on his first client of the morning. Duchon hurried out of the cafe into the brisk autumn morning. He felt as if he had just been released from a prison, which is not to say he felt particularly good, just tremendously relieved to have escaped the confines of the small, depressing cafe and the unnerving gaze of its creepily taciturn barman.

During the short drive to the Au Haou bar, Duchon constantly checked his rear-view mirror. If someone was following him, he was unable to detect them. And if he could not spot anyone then, presumably, neither could Jojo or Carlos or whoever else was tracking his movements. He entered the familiar confines of the Au Haou bar. He greeted the owners and ordered an espresso that he didn't really want or need. Even at this early hour, the bar was half filled with regulars hunched over racing tip sheets studying the day's fields. Duchon knew several of the horse players. As he sat at the bar unwrapping a sugar cube for his coffee, he looked around the small room at the various faces, almost all wreathed in cigarette smoke. He wondered whether one of the group was secretly working for Jojo. There were at least two among the crowd whom he had never particularly liked. Still, if anyone there was working for Jojo, he would need to communicate with him somehow and, so far, no one in the room had budged from his chair. Maybe Jojo's spy had some sort of beeper or walkie-talkie hidden in his coat pocket. Duchon nervously patted his own overcoat pocket for Janine's gift, which she had suggested during their telephone conversation the previous evening that he bring with him.

Duchon's paranoid reflections were interrupted by the muffled ring of the telephone next to the betting kiosk at the end of the room. As Duchon watched, the owner answered and spent several minutes seemingly exchanging pleasantries with the caller. Just when Duchon had concluded that the call must not be the one he was expecting, indeed hoping for, the owner waved him over. He passed Duchon the receiver with a knowing smile.

"Hello?"

"Have you picked out any winners in the races today, Jean-Claude?"

"No, Jojo, I just arrived."

"I know, Jean-Claude. I saw you arrive. I congratulate you on following my directions so carefully. You will soon be rewarded. Here is what I want you to do."

***

Like Jean-Claude Duchon, Peter Ellis had hardly slept during the night just ended; his insomnia, however, unlike that of the food salesman, had not been caused by a mysterious late telephone call. Instead, it was the result of recurring visions of Anya, stripped naked, being fondled or worse by the punk, Carlos. Strangely, Peter Ellis did not picture Joseph Gambia in the same room with her, only Carlos. For some inexplicable reason, Peter Ellis believed, at least for the time being, that Gambia could be trusted not to harm Anya. Carlos, however, unattended and left to his own sick devices, was an entirely different matter. There was no telling what he might do, given the temptation of Anya's body. With such vivid thoughts making sleep, finally, impossible, Peter Ellis rose at a little before 5:00, showered and shaved and fixed himself a small pot of coffee. While he drank the coffee and waited, he tried to prepare himself mentally for his meeting with the obviously desperate mafia boss. When the buzzer to the front door of the old apartment house sounded at just after 7:00, it was with a sense of both relief and anticipation that he descended the stairs to meet his mystery morning caller.

Although Peter Ellis had figured Duchon to be still in Joseph Gambia's employ, he was nonetheless surprised to see the ferret-faced food salesman standing there on his front stoop, hands thrust in his overcoat pockets.

"So, M. Duchon, I see you are still working for M. Gambia. I should have known."

"I am not working for M. Gambia. I am only here because he is forcing me to be here, as you are well aware. He has kidnapped my friend, Chantal. So, please do not insult me. You have no right."

"M. Gambia has also taken a friend of mine, M. Duchon. If anything happens to her, I shall do much more than insult you. You understand? Now, tell me what's going on. Where are we meeting with M. Gambia?"

"I do not know. You are to come with me. M. Gambia will contact us when he is sure that it is safe. That is all I know."

"So where are we going now?"

"To the Perspective park in front of here. He said for me to take you to the overlook where the American kid had his accident."

"What? Are you kidding me, Duchon? We are to go to where your pal, Carlos, forced Kevin Duffy to jump to his death?"

"I assure you, monsieur, I am not kidding. It is not <u>my</u> idea. It is what Jojo instructed me to do: to take you to the overlook and wait. I assure you also, monsieur, that this Carlos is no 'pal' of mine. I detest him. He has ruined my life."

"Ruined <u>your</u> life? You are unbelievable, M. Duchon. Ruined <u>your</u> life? What about the life of Kevin Duffy? Carlos did more than <u>ruin</u> his life, he <u>robbed</u> him of his life. And you, M. Duchon, assisted in the robbery."

"It was an accident! I had nothing to do with it!"

"You had everything to do with it, M. Duchon. I just hope, for your sake, that you had nothing to do with the kidnapping of my friend, Anya."

"I had nothing to do with it, I swear to you, on the grave of my mother. It was all Jojo's doing."

"Well, we will see about that later. Let's get going and see what your buddy, Jojo, wants. You had better pray that no harm comes to my friend. I shall hold you personally responsible. Now let's get going."

They walked out through the enclosed courtyard to the rue Million and past the grey shuttered windows of the old apartment house. They crossed the rue Perspective and started along the macadam path that zig-zagged down the face of the cliffside park. After three switchbacks, they reached the elevated entrance to the overlook. Below them, the semi-circular structure jutted from the buttressed cliffside like a crenellated tower on the ramparts of a castle. Set back at even intervals from the waist-high, gap-toothed stone wall at the top were three green wooden benches. Growing directly behind the three benches, in an echoing semi-circle, were six wind-stunted cedar trees that had recently been trimmed. Their few, truncated branches sprouted short sprays of wispy needles. From where Peter Ellis was standing with Duchon, the branches looked like nubby arms raised to the sky in wailing, green-fingered supplication.

"So, M. Duchon, what are we to do now?"

"Jojo said to stand at the right edge of the lookout and to pay attention. He said that as soon as he was certain we had not been followed, he would give us some kind of sign. That is all he told me."

Peter Ellis and Duchon walked down the two short sets of steps that led down to the paved floor of the overlook. He took up a position next to the parapet wall in front of the right corner of the right-facing bench. Duchon stood at the other end of the bench a little farther back from the edge. Peter Ellis glanced over at him. The food salesman appeared nervous and distinctly uneasy with the situation. He was grasping the back of the bench as if for support.

"What's wrong, M. Duchon? Are you afraid to stand close to the edge?"

"Yes, a little."

"Why? Because of what happened to Kevin Duffy?"

"No, it has nothing to do with that."

"Don't tell me. You are afraid of heights."

"Yes. I don't know why."

"Well, I think it is time you overcame that fear. Go on. Get close to the edge. Look down. Maybe you can still see the blood stains on the sidewalk. I promise to catch you if you start to fall. Don't worry."

"Please! It is not possible for me."

"M. Duchon, you are truly pathetic. What did a lovely girl like Chantal ever see in you? God knows, she can surely do much better."

"That is enough, monsieur! Do not talk about Chantal like that. She loves me. That is why I am here. To save her. That is the only reason I am here. It is not for you."

"God help me, you know I think I almost believe you. Just remember, if and when we see Gambia, that he is holding my friend, Anya, hostage. Please don't do anything stupid in your passionate quest to 'save' Chantal."

"Do not worry, monsieur. I am totally under control."

"I hope so, for everyone's sake."

Peter Ellis turned from Duchon and looked down at the vast expanse of gently undulating, green-blue water. It appeared to be almost high tide and what little surf there was broke harmlessly and almost noiselessly against the tumble of large boulders that served as a breakwater for the Côtes des Basques beach road. With his gaze, he followed the road as it curved around the inside elbow of the promontory and out to the rocky point and the Villa Belza. In the misty distance, the legendary villa, with its cantilevered banks of mullioned windows and its single slender turret, seemed to grow out of the brown, angular rocks like some miniature fairytale castle. All of a sudden, he thought of Anya. It was as though the sight of the enchanting villa reminded him of the lovers' fairytale he and she had been living. It had all ended yesterday, however, when the thoroughly contemporary incarnation of a black prince had stolen upon the scene and spirited his Dutch princess away. If the Villa Belza could be said to represent the lovers' dream he had been experiencing, the abandoned Nazi artillery bunkers that honey-combed the south-facing promontory overlooking it were a chilling reminder and apt illustration for the nightmare in which he now found himself living. If anything happened to Anya, he knew he would never forgive himself. Carlos and Gambia's culpability notwithstanding, it was he, Peter Ellis, the clever, deep-digging, celebrated investigative journalist who was ultimately to blame for landing Anya in her present dire predicament.

Where was Gambia? He must talk to him and talk to him immediately. Whatever the gangster wanted him to do, however outrageous, he would do and do gladly if it allowed Anya to be released unharmed. He began in earnest to scan the terraced landscape of the promontory. Cut into the top of the cliff, just below where the Perspective road began its descent to the Villa Belza, was a series of grottos whose arched openings grew smaller in proportion to the road's incline. They faced south and provided an ideal place to hide and observe, unnoticed, the entire west-facing half of the cliffside park. Peter Ellis tried to penetrate their dark recesses, searching for some sudden flash of reflected light, some miniscule orange dot that would indicate the burning tip of a cigarette, some vague shadowed movement. He strained his eyes in vain: the gaping black apertures stared blindly back at him, showing no signs of hidden life. Peter

Ellis's attention was suddenly diverted by the approach, from the south, of a large displacement motorcycle, its high r.p.m. whine cutting through the morning stillness like a chainsaw. As it came closer, its driver geared down quickly and the whine diminished to a throaty rumble then disappeared altogether. The driver evidently had turned into one of the alleys that led to the rue Dalbarade and down into town. The hushed murmur of the slumbering ocean once again enveloped the hazy morning.

Peter Ellis returned to his close observation of the terraced park, scanning the paths immediately below him and to his right then moving his gaze beyond to the sweep of curving headland. The entire area was lined with switch-backing macadam paths and punctuated with jutting, walled structures, one of which was an exact, though smaller, replica of the turret-like overlook where he and Duchon were now standing. He studied each of these structures in turn then returned to the row of dark enigmatic grottos. Just above them, to the right, was the northern-most entrance to the park. It was located just across from the sentier des Corsaires, a road which descended in a long, sweeping curve down to the Port-Vieux section of Biarritz. He somehow felt certain that Gambia, if he was coming at all, would arrive from that corner of the park. Suddenly his heart leapt. A man had just become visible on the sidewalk running along the top of the cliff. He was coming from the direction of the Villa Belza, taking the hill slowly and, Peter Ellis thought to himself, cautiously. His interest in the man ceased, however, within a matter of seconds. Closer inspection revealed that the man walked with the aid of a cane and that he held a folded newspaper in his left hand. Also, he was bundled up as though a winter gale were blowing, a black scarf wrapped around his neck and lower face and a large black beret pulled low over his forehead. The man was obviously an old pensioner out for his morning paper and constitutional. He was evidently a careful man and had prepared for any sudden change in the weather. As if to prove Peter Ellis's supposition, the shuffling, stooped figure stopped at a bench next to the coin-operated telescope midway up the hill and sat down, appearing to open his newspaper as he did so.

Joseph Gambia did not show himself for another ten minutes, by which time Peter Ellis had nearly despaired of his coming at all. Twice during this time he had turned to ask Duchon point blank just where in the hell Gambia was hiding. Both times he held his tongue after seeing that the food salesman was evidently as depressed, as on edge and as genuinely frustrated as he himself was. As it turned out, he and Duchon spotted Joseph Gambia at virtually the same instant, for as soon as he recognized the gangster he heard the food salesman let out a little yip of excitement, much like a dog who suddenly becomes aware of the presence of his master. Seeming to appear from nowhere, Gambia and Chantal were suddenly standing at the front edge of the other, smaller, turret-like overlook. Duchon immediately waved at them and Gambia responded with a gesture for the two men to come over and join them. Duchon tried to rush past Peter Ellis, only to find his way blocked.

"What are you doing? Jojo's over there, waiting for us. With Chantal. Let's go!"

"Take it easy, Duchon. We waited for him, he can wait for us."

"What? Are you crazy?"

"No, not at all. And I don't want you to be crazy either. I want you to remember what I said earlier. Gambia is holding my friend, Anya. He has come to talk with <u>me</u>. I don't know what he wants or what he plans to do. Whatever it is, do not try to interfere. I will make sure nothing happens to Chantal. Understood?"

"You do not have to talk to me like a child. Show some respect for my position."

"I show respect where it is earned, M. Duchon. See if you can earn some today. Now, let's go."

The overlook where Joseph Gambia was waiting for them was barely a hundred yards down and to the right of its bigger twin. Four sloping lateral paths gave access to it, two from the south and two from the north. The higher and lower southern paths converged at a short set of stone steps at the edge of the semi-circular, crenellated overlook. The two northern paths ran parallel to each other as they approached the overlook and were separated by a thick cedar hedge.

They were twice as wide as the normal paths in the park and were lined, at intervals, with green benches that offered a more sheltered and discreet place to sit and take in the sea air.

Peter Ellis, with Duchon at his heels, reached the overlook by way of the lower of the southern paths. He found Joseph Gambia standing next to Chantal, lightly clutching her right forearm with his left hand. The girl wore a downcast, almost embarrassed expression. Gambia, on the other hand, was smiling broadly as he greeted them. In his right hand he held a short-barreled, black automatic pistol.

"Good-morning, Jean-Claude. Good-morning, Pierre. I may still call you Pierre, yes?"

"Whatever pleases you, Gambia. It is all the same to me."

"Très bien. There is no need for us to be formal. This is, after all, a friendly meeting."

"I suppose, then, you were just being friendly when you kidnapped Chantal and my friend, Anya, from the farm?"

"I do apologize for having to borrow your friend, Pierre. You must believe me. I am truly sorry. But I had to be certain you would agree to meet with me, just as I had to be certain that Jean-Claude here would cooperate with my plan. That is why I was forced to borrow Chantal as well. As you can see, she has not been mistreated. Nor has your beautiful friend, I assure you."

"Is this true, Chantal?"

The girl nodded meekly. "Yes, M. Pierre. We have not been treated badly."

"You see, Chantal, I have come for you." Duchon could contain himself no longer. "I will take care of you, I promise. Everything will be good, like before."

"That's enough, Jean-Claude. You and Chantal will have plenty of time to work out your situation when our meeting is over. At that time, I will leave her with you as promised. That is, if you have held up your end of the deal and kept our rendez-vous secret."

"I swear to you, Jojo, I have not spoken to a soul about our meeting. You have my word, on my mother's grave. If anyone knows about it, the information came from someone else, not me. Someone like Carlos."

"Carlos knows nothing specific about our meeting this morning. And even if he did, there is no reason to worry about him, Jean-Claude. I have Carlos firmly under my thumb and under control. At the moment, he is a very happy fellow. I have him babysitting Pierre's lovely Dutch friend. I must say, he seems quite taken with Mlle. Anya."

"You have left Anya alone with that sick punk?" Peter Ellis found himself almost screaming.

"Calm yourself, Pierre. We do not want everyone in Biarritz to know we're here. Nothing will happen to your friend, I guarantee it. Provided you cooperate."

"And just how can you guarantee he will not do anything to her? Carlos is not rational. We both know that from experience."

"I can guarantee it because I hold the fate of Carlos in my hands and he knows it. I have made sure of that. I have promised to take care of his little problem with Inspector LeClerc. I have also promised to set him up with some old friends who have a very successful nightclub in Belgium near the French border. I have taken care of him up until now, so he has no reason to believe I am lying. I feel absolutely certain he will do nothing to jeopardize our arrangement. It is his only way out of the mess he has created for himself."

"You had better pray that is true, Gambia. Should anything happen to Anya, you will pay dearly for it. That is a promise."

"There is no need to threaten me, Pierre. Carlos has certainly proved himself an imbecile, but I am not one, as I think you must realize by now. I am well aware that a good working relationship with you depends upon your friend being treated well. Is this not so?"

"You know it is."

"Exactly. So rest assured, Pierre. I have given Carlos strict instructions. He is not to touch your friend, much less harm her. Unless, of course, I do not return to my little country house by noon today. Or at least contact him by that time and give him a certain password. Should something happen to me, should I not be able to see or talk with him by noon today, he is on his own. Which means he is free to do whatever he wants with your friend. And I have a pretty good idea what he wants to do with her."

"You bastard!"

"I may be a bastard, monsieur, but I am also a businessman. Businessmen need insurance. Your Dutch friend is my insurance, nothing more, nothing less. As soon as our business is satisfactorily completed, I shall release her to you. I think that is a fair arrangement."

"How long will it take to complete this so-called 'business'?"

"That depends more upon you than upon me. You should be able to tell me how long it will take after I have told you what I need."

"I am listening, Gambia. Tell me what you need. I just hope it is something I can provide."

"I am sure you can, Pierre. Who knows? It may even be something you will enjoy doing. I hope so, anyway."

"Like I said, I'm listening."

"I want you to write an article, and not just any article. But before we talk about the nature of this article, I think we should walk over there by those benches where we are not in plain view of anyone who decides to take a morning stroll. One never knows who might happen to show up in a place like this on such a beautiful morning."

Gambia directed the small group down the lower of the two northern walkways past a green bench and around a slight bend to a protected area under a wind-deformed cedar tree. The curvature of the path shielded them from sight by anyone on the overlook while the high cedar hedge separating the two wide walkways kept anyone from above or to the north from seeing them. In front of them, facing the ocean, was a sheer drop of at least twenty feet. It was, as Peter Ellis quickly surmised, a well-chosen spot for a discreet meeting. He doubted it was the first time Gambia had used it.

"Please excuse me, Pierre, but before I begin my little story I must ask that you allow me to search you."

"What? You think I brought a gun?"

"No, not at all. But you may have brought a little machine to record our conversation. It would be a normal thing for a journalist to do, would it not? I realize it would be easier for you to write my article if you had a tape recording of our conversation; however, I do not want what I am about to tell you recorded. I have found that tape recordings have a bad habit of falling into the wrong hands. This will only take a minute. Jean-Claude, will you and Chantal please just stay where you are?"

Gambia began patting down Peter Ellis. He took his time, making sure nothing was taped either to his body or his clothes. During the search, he continued to talk.

"So, Pierre, I am surprised you did not comment on my choice of location for our little meeting?"

"I just thought it was your idea of a sick joke."

"Au contraire. One of the things I want to discuss this morning is precisely how the unfortunate accident that took the life of Chantal's friend occurred. I want her to understand how it was neither my fault nor Jean-Claude's. I thought it would be easier to explain here where it happened, easier to see exactly how it could happen."

"M. Gambia, your chivalry astounds me."

"There is no need to use such a tone. I am sincere in what I say."

"You want me to believe that the only reason we are meeting here is so you can illustrate for Chantal how the death of her friend was just an accident? I find that very hard to believe."

"I did not say it was the only reason, Pierre. Nor did I say there was no one to blame for the accident."

"So what was your other reason for choosing this unfortunate place to meet? You will excuse me for saying so, but such a public place seems like a very peculiar choice for a secret meeting. Do you not agree?"

"I appreciate the point you are making, but you overlook at least two important facts."

"Which are?"

"First, that very few people come here early in the morning. And the ones that do are almost exclusively from the immediate neighborhood. Their habits and faces are well-known to me. I would immediately spot an unfamiliar visitor here. Secondly, you have evidently forgotten that I have an apartment in the building overlooking this park next to the old house where you are staying. From my apartment, I have a bird's eye view of the entire park and most of the streets leading to it. Before I came down here, I made sure no one was tailing either you or Jean-Claude. That was why you were forced to wait."

"You really think I would jeopardize the safety of my friend by having someone follow me?"

"Not at all, Pierre. Nor do I think, knowing how Jean-Claude feels for Chantal, that he would put her in any danger by telling someone about our meeting. It is just that I have recently been betrayed by certain associates. I find myself, alas, at a critical crossroads. I can't afford any more mistakes."

"So your partners have turned on you and you want to repay the favor. That is really what this meeting is all about."

"Très bien, Pierre. I see I have not underestimated you."

"How do you think I can help you? Why don't you deal with them directly? Violence has never bothered you in the past according to my friend, Maurice."

"Ah, my old nemesis, Claverie-LaPorte. You know, I have come to develop a grudging admiration for the old bulldog. I think it would surprise him to discover how much I have learned from him. In fact, this meeting reflects one of those lessons."

"And what lesson is that?"

"How does the expression go? 'The pen is more puissant than the sword'. It is, no doubt, a verity you understand better than most, given your profession. Let us all hope you can put it to work effectively to resolve the present crisis."

"I can't work miracles, Gambia. I can only write the truth and hope something good comes from it. There are no guarantees."

"I realize that, Pierre, and I have every confidence that if you do your best, everything will work out nicely for all of us. A happy ending, if you will."

"Happy endings only happen in fairy tales, M. Gambia. We are not living in a fairy tale. So why don't you tell me exactly what you want me to do and I shall tell you whether it is possible."

"Oh, it is possible, Pierre, I am certain of it. When you hear what I have to tell you, you will see what I mean. Now, if you will just move over there next to Chantal, I shall tell you a very interesting little story."

While Joseph Gambia had been meticulously patting down Peter Ellis, Chantal had been left standing in the middle of the wide walkway off to the gangster's right, where the path curved slightly toward the northern exit. Duchon, on Gambia's orders, had taken up a position at the other end of the path, a position that enabled him to keep an eye on the approach from the overlook just around the corner. Now, as Gambia backed against the high cedar hedge separating the upper and lower walkways, the little group took on the rough outline of an isosceles triangle. The gangster tucked the gun into the band of his pants and covered the handle with the flap of his leather motorcycle jacket. He coughed, as if to clear his throat.

"Before I begin with what I have to tell you, Pierre, I want to explain something to Chantal. A few weeks ago, a terrible accident occurred not very far from where we are presently standing. Unfortunately, I am unable to undo what happened that tragic day. If only I could, I certainly would." Looking at Chantal he made an imploring gesture with his hands, spreading the palms out. "What I hope I can do, Mlle. Chantal, is try to make you understand how easily such a terrible accident could have happened and make you see how it was not in any way the fault of your friend here, Jean-Claude."

"See Chantal? It is as I told you. I had nothing to do with the death of your friend. Listen to Jojo!"

"Please, Jean-Claude. Allow me to continue."

"Forgive me, Jojo. Please continue."

"Thank-you, Jean-Claude. Now Mlle. Chantal, I must say that, in one small way, the accident was possibly my fault. Not legally my fault, you understand, but my fault in the sense of trying to help a friend without first seeking his approval. You see your friend here,

Jean-Claude—who is also my friend, I might add—was so miserable when you began seeing that young American that I thought he might try to kill himself. Although the affair was none of my business, I decided to try to help my friend, hating to see him suffer and worrying about what he might try to do to himself. I also thought, and you must forgive me for saying so for I now know I was being very egotistical, I thought you were making a grave mistake in leaving Jean-Claude for that American young man. Of course, it was none of my business and I have certainly learned my lesson. Anyway, I took it upon myself to have your friend questioned as to his intentions regarding you, to see whether or not they were honorable. To this end, I asked some young associates of mine to meet with him. I knew he came here in the morning to look at the ocean. I often saw him from my apartment window in Nadaillac. As I have already mentioned, my apartment has a bird's eye view of the park and the beach. I told them exactly what to do and what questions to ask. I even waited on a bench by the entrance to the park while they followed him, just to make sure nothing went wrong."

"But something did go wrong, M. Gambia. Something went murderously wrong and someone must pay for it. It is called justice, though little good it will do Chantal or young Kevin Duffy."

At the mention of the young man's name, Peter Ellis heard Chantal give a quick gasp and immediately regretted opening his mouth. The whole ordeal had been hard enough on her already without the misguided venting of his own anger.

"Please, Pierre, I realize Carlos must pay for his mistake and pay he will, I assure you, but all in good time. I just want Chantal to understand that he acted entirely on his own that morning. I told him specifically that I did not want the young man hurt in any way. You may ask the others who were with him. They will verify the instructions I gave. It was all a terrible mistake and I beg you, Mlle. Chantal, to accept my profound apology. If there is anything I can do to help you recover from this tragic accident, I am at your service. Do you understand?"

"Yes, M. Gambia."

"And you will not hesitate to call me or have Jean-Claude let me know what I can do to help you?"

"No, M. Gambia."

"One more thing." He gave the girl his best sincere smile. "If we are to be friends, and I certainly hope we will be, there is no need to be so formal with me. Okay?"

The girl nodded her head. Peter Ellis feared that she was going to begin sobbing at any moment.

"M. Gambia, I think you have made your point. Let us get on with our business. It can't be easy for Chantal to be in this place. The sooner we can leave, the better for all of us. Don't you agree?"

"Absolutely, Pierre. I just wanted you and Chantal to know the true story concerning her firend's death. As I said earlier, you may verify everything with Carlos's two associates."

"I intend to, M. Gambia. Now, please tell me what I must do to free my friend, Anya."

"All you must do is write an article about some things I am now going to reveal to you and have this article published in a major magazine or newspaper. As soon as I see it in print, I shall release your friend."

"Getting an article published could take days."

"You must see that it does not. You have connections. You must use them. It is critical that your article appear as soon as possible."

"Nothing had better happen to Anya in the meantime. You hear me?"

"I have given you my word. As soon as I see the article, I shall deliver her to you personally."

"So what exactly do you want me to write about? I trust it is something important enough to be published immediately."

"Important enough? Hah! Pierre, it is a bombshell. It is a story that should win you a prize. It has everything: Prostitutes and politicians, crooked policemen, drugs, you name it."

"And you can prove it all."

Gambia laughed smugly. "Prove it? That should not be difficult. It is about my partners."

"Your partners? Who are you in partnership with beside Janine Destin?"

"You don't know? I'm surprised. I thought old Claverie-LaPorte had figured it out."

"You mean Inspector LeClerc is actually a partner and not just on the take?"

"That is how it began. It was Janine's idea to make him a full partner. Now I am beginning to understand why."

"So, your partners are trying to force you out and you don't like the terms. Let me guess: They are trying to blackmail you with Carlos. That is why you have him hiding out and why you are pretending to be his protector and promising to help him. You are keeping his trust and temporary fidelity by tempting him with my friend, Anya. When you have compromised your partners with the revelations in my article, Carlos will mysteriously disappear. His young associates will implicate him in the death of Kevin Duffy. There will be some difficulties for you, you will have to forge some new alliances, but in the end you will be the one left standing. How is that for a scenario, M. Gambia? Am I close?"

Peter Ellis looked over at Gambia for a reply but the gangster just stood there transfixed, staring past him in the direction of the overlook. He turned to see what had rendered Gambia suddenly mute. What Peter Ellis saw froze him instantly: Chief Inspector Jacques LeClerc was slowly walking toward them, his gloved right hand thrust forward. In it was Peter Ellis's large black Colt .45 Mark IV automatic. It was pointed directly at Joseph Gambia.

"Permit me to answer your question, M. Ellis. I believe my friend, Jojo, has temporarily lost not only his mind but also his voice. And if he makes a move for the gun I am sure he is carrying, he will most certainly lose his life."

"What are you doing here, LeClerc? Is this some kind of a joke? I thought we had agreed to settle our differences like businessmen."

"That is what I thought too, Jojo. Imagine my surprise when I heard about this meeting from Jean-Claude here."

"That's a lie! I said nothing to anyone about this meeting, Jojo. I swear!"

"Take it easy, Jean-Claude. Why are you worried about what Jojo thinks? He can't help you now. Only Janine and I can help you now. For my part, I do not understand why she <u>wants</u> to help you but she does."

Joseph Gambia spit emphatically. "So, Jean-Claude, you are a traitor after all. I should have known not to trust a worm like you."

"Jojo, I swear! On my mother's grave! I told no one. Janine knew about the meeting but I didn't tell her. You have to believe me."

"Shut up, Duchon! You really are an imbecile. Your buddy, Jojo, is finished, or can't you see that?" The inspector waved the gun at Duchon. "If you want to go down with him, that's fine with me. Think about it."

LeClerc had moved to a spot directly in front of Joseph Gambia, midway between Duchon to his right and Peter Ellis and Chantal to his left. He motioned to Gambia with the barrel of the gun, three short vertical jerks. "Jojo, it would please me if you put your hands on top of your head. I must have a few words with our esteemed journalist here to see where we stand. If you move even a centimeter, I will not hesitate to shoot you. You understand?"

"Yes!" Gambia spit again, the small wad of saliva landing midway between him and LeClerc. "You bastard!"

"Good." LeClerc paused briefly. "Now M. Ellis, I must ask you something. Why have you disobeyed my orders once again? You are beginning to make me lose patience."

"I had no choice, Inspector. Your partner here, M. Gambia, kidnapped a friend of mine at the same time he kidnapped Chantal. He is holding her someplace out in the country. She is there with Carlos."

"I wonder where that might be, Jojo? I'll bet I can guess."

"That is where you are wrong, Jacky. It is my little secret. You will never find it. Or Carlos. That is, unless I tell you. Since you need to find Carlos to arrest him for the death of the American kid, maybe we can make a deal."

"Who said I needed Carlos? I have you. I think you will do very nicely for the death of the American kid. It was you, after all, who sent Carlos after him."

"You can never pin that on me, Jacky, and you know it. There were witnesses. They were with Carlos."

"Who says I have to pin anything on you? Dead men can't defend themselves in court. I'm sure I could find more than one person to say you were the one responsible once you are dead."

"Wait a minute, LeClerc! Gambia is the only person who knows where my friend, Anya, is being kept. If he does not contact Carlos by noon, she will be at his mercy. If that sick punk does anything to her, I will hold you personally responsible, Inspector."

"Is that so? That sounds like a threat. I don't like threats, M. Ellis. I also don't like reporters poking their noses into my affairs. You have been a pain in the ass long enough. I should have taken care of you long before now. Then again, there is no time like the present."

"I thought Gambia was stupid, but you make him look like a genius, LeClerc. You actually think you can kill me and get away with it?"

"Not at all. I have no reason for killing you. However Jojo here certainly might."

"The only person I might want to kill, if I got the chance, is you, Jacky."

"That is a big 'if', Jojo. You seem to be forgetting that I have the gun." He waved the weapon as if to display it. "And not just any gun. Is that not so, M. Ellis?"

Peter Ellis said nothing. Joseph Gambia looked at the gun, evidently perplexed. LeClerc gave a short grunt of laughter.

"Mon pauvre Jojo. For a clever man, you can be so slow at times. It is all very simple. Let me explain: This big nasty weapon belongs to none other than M. Ellis here. It has his fingerprints all over it. I was forced to take it from him yesterday morning after you sent Carlos and the other two clowns up to his apartment—another brilliant move on your part, I might add. No one knows I have his gun except us. Now, let's suppose M. Ellis had this gun with him this morning when he came to meet you. It would be a normal precaution, I dare say, after what you have already done to him. He is very upset, and who could blame him? You have kidnapped his girlfriend. He tries to bargain for her release but you refuse. Suddenly things get out of hand. Guns are drawn. Shots are fired. On a tip, I happen to be close by. I hear the shots and rush to the scene. Alas, I am too late. It is a double murder. How do you like my little story so far, M. Ellis? It is brilliant, no?"

"Except for one small detail, Inspector."

"And what might that be?"

"M. Duchon and Mlle. Chantal. You have just revealed what you plan to do. They will know the truth of what happened here. How do you intend to keep them quiet? Kill them too? Four accidental deaths might look a little suspicious even to your crooked superiors."

"M. Ellis, I have no intention of harming Jean-Claude or his lovely friend, Chantal. Why would I want to harm my new partner, especially after he has helped me dispose of my old one? Like I said earlier, Janine has a great fondness for Jean-Claude. She is determined to help him and his friend, Chantal, provided he helps us."

"And what about Chantal? How can you be so sure she will keep quiet?"

"Mlle. Chantal is a smart girl. Janine feels like a mother to her. I can't believe she would do or say anything that might incriminate either Janine or Jean-Claude. She is sure to recognize the benefits of silence, both to herself and to her friends."

"And if she does not?"

"Like I said, M. Ellis, Mlle. Chantal is a smart girl. I'm sure she will be discreet. In any event, what does it matter to you? You will no longer be on the scene. But enough small talk. Jean-Claude, it is time you and I get to work. It's getting late." LeClerc checked his watch. "Before long, the old farts will start arriving with their dogs."

"I can't do it, Inspector. I am not a violent man. I am not a murderer. Please! I can not do what you are asking."

"Yes you can, Jean-Claude. So come on. Stop acting like such an innocent all of a sudden. You had no problem asking Jojo to take care of Chantal's young American boyfriend. It's time you started doing your own dirty work. If you want to work with me and Janine, it will be necessary to get your hands dirty from time to time. You can't always trust other people to do your dirty work. Just ask Jojo. Look at the predicament he is in thanks to Carlos."

"But I did not ask Jojo to kill the American kid! You know that, Inspector. I just asked Jojo to talk to him for me."

"Please, Jean-Claude, just shut up and do as I say. I don't care to hear any more of your pathetic excuses. You forget. I have heard them all before. Now, let's go. If you value the life of your little friend, Chantal, you will do as I tell you. First, go over and get Jojo's gun. And don't try anything stupid. I don't want to have to shoot both of you. Go on!" LeClerc abruptly turned his head toward Peter Ellis and Chantal. "Mademoiselle, please step over here." He indicated a spot to his right close to the hedge.

Peter Ellis took LeClerc's last order as his cue to act. Ever since the inspector had unexpectedly arrived on the scene and made his intentions clear, Peter Ellis had been considering how he might manage to escape. It had not taken him long to conclude that his best, indeed only, option was to jump over the low cement railing that ran along the outside edge of the overlook and walkway. It was a long drop, to be sure, but he didn't see that he had any other choice. He hoped that, in the confusion, Gambia would be able to get to his gun. He prayed that the gangster was a good shot. There was just one problem with his desperate plan and the problem was Chantal. The girl was standing next to him and would be in LeClerc's line of fire if Peter Ellis attempted to escape. It was one thing to risk his own life but quite another to risk that of an innocent girl. He doubted LeClerc was prepared for the powerful kick of the combat model Colt. He could easily imagine Chantal being hit by an errant bullet. But now, as if by a miracle, the inspector had removed the problem by commanding the girl to move away from him and over by the hedge. Peter Ellis stood poised on the balls of his feet and waited for Chantal to move. But the girl just stood there, stood there as though she were rooted to the ground. Peter Ellis was about to say something by way of prodding her when LeClerc repeated his request, this time in the form of a command. His voice had suddenly taken on a strange, almost feral quality.

"Do you hear me, Chantal? Come over here! Come over here right now!"

"Don't make me do it again. Oh please! Not again! I can not do it again."

Peter Ellis could believe neither his ears nor his eyes. It was as though the girl had just seen a ghost, a very real and malevolent ghost. There was a palpable anguish and desperation in her voice. She was trembling violently and her face was a mask of fright.

"What is wrong with you, you little fool? Do as I say. Come here! Now!"

"No-o-o-o-o-o! Not again. Never again. I would rather die!"

"What in God's name are you talking about, girl? Have you suddenly lost your mind?"

"You! It was you! That night at the party. Behind the mask. Your voice like a wild beast. It was you who attacked me."

"Shut up, you little fool. You have lost your mind. You are talking nonsense. You leave me no choice." LeClerc took a step toward her. The girl's terrified scream rent the morning irrevocably asunder.

With cat-like quickness, Chantal leaped past Peter Ellis toward the guard railing. She was halfway over it when he managed to latch onto her trailing arm. At that instant, two, almost simultaneous, deafening explosions sounded close behind him. He pulled Chantal to the ground and covered her with his body. He waited for the first searing flash of pain. Instead, another explosion echoed in his ringing ears. Or was it two? He couldn't tell. He suddenly became aware of a high-pitched, animal-like sound. He cautiously raised his head and looked back over his shoulder for its source. He could barely believe what he saw: Over by the three steps leading up to the overlook, Jean-Claude Duchon stood doubled over clutching his right arm. He was squealing like a stuck pig. At his feet was a small caliber, shiny silver automatic pistol. On the ground midway between him and Duchon, Inspector Jacques LeClerc lay on his side, curled up in a fetal position, his hands buried in his groin. In the gravel, four feet from his bunched-up knees, was Peter Ellis's large black Colt .45. The deadly eye of the barrel stared at the groaning inspector like a dark wish. Beyond LeClerc, slumped against the low rock wall beneath the cedar privacy hedge, Joseph Gambia sat holding his stomach, his hands awash in liquid crimson.

It took several seconds for Peter Ellis to appreciate the significance of the bloody tableau. He immediately jumped up and retrieved his pistol. LeClerc followed his movement and tried to focus his cloudy, dying eyes.

"You must call for help. I have a radio here in my coat. You must call at once. I am dying."

Covering him with the Colt, Peter Ellis rolled LeClerc onto his back with his foot. The inspector screamed in pain. Peter Ellis carefully reached inside LeClerc's coat and removed his police revolver from a shoulder holster. The gun was sticky with warm blood.

"Call for help yourself, LeClerc."

"You bastard! Help me. You must help me."

"Go to hell."

Peter Ellis moved quickly over to Gambia. He bent over him and felt his pulse. "Jojo, can you hear me?"

Gambia seemed to nod his head.

"Jojo, where is my friend, Anya? I promise to call for help. But first, please tell me where you are hiding my friend. I beg you. Please. Tell me where she is."

The dying gangster tried to speak. He opened his mouth and a sickening, gurgling noise came from his throat. The effort took all of his waning energy. His face a rictus of agony, he made a vomiting sound that was meant to be a word. To Peter Ellis it sounded like the English word, 'black'.

"'Black'? What do you mean, Jojo? What are you trying to say? What is black? I beg you, Jojo. Please. Tell me where my friend is."

Joseph Gambia made one more blood-coughing attempt to speak. This time what came out was merely the sound 'ack'. Then he was dead.

"No-o-o! Jojo, talk to me. Where are you hiding Anya?" Peter Ellis lay down his gun and began to shake the body of Joseph Gambia. "Tell me, goddamnit! Do you hear me? Tell me where Anya is." He felt someone touch his back. He whirled around with his fists clenched, ready to lash out. An image of Duchon flashed through his mind. But it was not Duchon who was standing over him. It was Maurice's friend, Inspector Rectoran.

"Easy, M. Ellis, easy. It is me. Rectoran. Are you alright? Have you been wounded?"

"No. I'm fine. But Gambia is dead. The bastard has died without telling me where Anya is. She is there with Carlos. What are we going to do? The bastard is dead!"

Rectoran moved past Peter Ellis and bent over Joseph Gambia and checked for a pulse. He shook his head then turned and gently took Peter Ellis by the arm and helped him to his feet.

"M. Ellis, are you certain you have not been wounded? You are covered in blood."

"I'm fine. Have you checked on LeClerc?"

"Yes. I don't give him much of a chance. He was shot in the gut. He has lost a great deal of blood."

"What about Duchon?" He indicated the food salesman, who had moved over to a green bench next to the dividing wall and hedge. He sat hunched over holding his right arm. He was whimpering like a puppy. Chantal sat next to him, stroking his cheek, talking softly to him.

"Duchon will be alright. A bullet apparently grazed his arm. It looks worse than it is."

Peter Ellis became aware of voices and running feet. Small groups of men, some in blue uniforms, began to arrive. Rectoran huddled with each group briefly, giving them instructions. Two men immediately began attending to LeClerc while two others went over to work on Duchon. Rectoran returned to Peter Ellis's side.

"Now, my friend, can you tell me what exactly happened here?"

"Yes, Inspector, but first I must talk with Chantal. I must find out if she has any idea of where Gambia took her and Anya. Please. Then I will tell you everything."

Chantal had moved aside so that Rectoran's men could attend to Duchon's wound. Peter Ellis walked over and gently put his arm around the girl's shoulders.

"How are you doing, Chantal? Are you okay?"

"Yes, M. Pierre. But Jean-Claude has been shot. He is bleeding. It is terrible."

"Inspector Rectoran says it is not serious. It is just a slight wound with a lot of blood. Don't worry. He will be fine. He is in no danger. But my friend, Anya, is in great danger. You must help me find her, Chantal, before Carlos does anything to her. Will you help me?"

"I will try, monsieur. But what can I do?"

"Try to remember anything about yesterday when they took you to that house. Anything. Any clues. Please, Chantal, think. Did you see anything?"

"We were blindfolded until we reached the little farmhouse of M. Gambia. I saw nothing. I am sorry."

"How long did it take you to get to this little farmhouse from LaBorde."

"I am not sure. We stopped three times on the way. Maybe an hour."

"Did you hear anything during the trip? Anything unusual?"

"No, monsieur."

"What about once you were in their farmhouse?"

"Only chickens. And cows. They were very close. Next door, I think."

"What could you see from the farmhouse?"

"Nothing. The windows were all shuttered."

"Shit!"

"No, wait! I remember one thing, M. Pierre. It was last night. I was in the bathroom. There was a little hole in the shutter. I tried to look out. It was very small, but I saw a fire in the sky. It was like a single flame burning in the sky on top of a pole. It was very strange."

Peter Ellis clapped his hands. "Lacq! Le gaz de Lacq! You saw one of the tall chimneys that burn off the excess gas. You were staying close to Lacq. That's what Gambia was trying to tell me. But where?"

"Ask Janine. She will know. She knows everything."

It was Duchon who spoke. Peter Ellis immediately turned to face him.

"Janine? You mean Janine Destin?"

"Yes. She knows everything. She knew about the meeting this morning. She called me last night and told me to bring the gun. It was a present from her. She must have known I would need it to protect Chantal."

"Duchon, you may have just saved your ass. Where can I find Mme. Destin?"

"At her apartment. I was to take Chantal straight there after the meeting in the park. She wanted to make sure Jojo had not hurt her."

"Inspector Rectoran, we must go to Janine Destin's apartment at once. It is our only chance. We had better take Chantal with us. She may remember something else important. On the way, I'll tell you everything that happened here this morning."

"What about me?" Duchon looked imploringly at Peter Ellis. "Janine is expecting me. I must explain to her about Inspector LeClerc."

"What do you think, Inspector Rectoran? It may not be a bad idea to bring him with us. Mme. Destin may want someone to verify what happened here. Also, M. Duchon may give us some leverage if she becomes difficult."

"Yes. I think I see what you mean. The paramedics should be here any minute. When they have finished dressing M. Duchon's wound, we can go."

"One more thing, Inspector."

"Yes, Pierre?"

Peter Ellis indicated that he wanted to speak with him in private. The two men walked over to the overlook out of earshot.

"Yes, Pierre, what is it?"

"Before we leave, will you check and see if Inspector LeClerc was shot twice? I think I know the answer, but I must be sure."

"Certainly. Do you think both Gambia and Duchon shot him?"

"No. But it may be a good thing if someone else thought so."

Inspector Rectoran arched his eyebrows and rubbed an invisible speck from his chin. "I see."

***

When Janine Destin opened the door, Peter Ellis had the strange feeling that she had been expecting him, even though she failed to acknowledge him.

"Chantal! Thank God! You are safe and sound. Jean-Claude, what happened to your arm? Look at all the blood on your shirt. Are you badly injured?"

"I'm fine, Janine. It is nothing. I was very lucky."

"Mon Dieu! What happened? Jean-Claude, you must tell me at once."

"Inspector LeClerc tried to kill me. If I had not had your gun, I would probably be dead."

"Why in the world would Jacky try to kill you? It is incredible! It is too much!"

Peter Ellis decided he had heard enough of Janine Destin's little charade.

"It is not so incredible as you pretend, madame. Your friend, or should I say partner, tried to kill me as well. But then, you know all about what Inspector LeClerc was planning to do this morning if I am not mistaken."

Janine Destin turned toward him, as though just becoming aware of his presence. "You are the famous journalist, Peter Ellis, are you not? We met some days ago at my nightclub, though I believe at that time you were using a different name. This gentleman, however," she nodded toward Rectoran, "is unknown to me by name, though I believe I know him by occupation."

"My name is Inspector Rectoran, Mme. Destin. I worked with your friend, Inspector LeClerc. It is very important that we talk with you. We need your help. May we come in? Don't worry, I am not here in an official capacity."

"In that case, please, come in. You must forgive the mess. I had a little party last night with a friend. My maid does not come until after lunch. I often sleep late and do not like to be disturbed in the morning." She showed them in, taking Chantal by the hand and leading her and Duchon over to the big white couch. In passing, she waved her free hand dismissively at the cluttered marble coffee table. On it were two empty champagne bottles, two crystal flutes, a silver ice bucket filled with water and a half-filled coffee cup. "As you can see, my friend and I did some celebrating. I hope he feels as bad as I do. May I get you and M. Ellis something to drink, Inspector? I have some fresh coffee made."

"No thank-you, Mme. Destin. We do not have much time."

Sitting on the sofa next to Chantal, Janine Destin reached over and retrieved her coffee cup. She took a slow, meditative sip. "Now then, Inspector, what is all this nonsense about Jacky trying to kill people? I saw him only yesterday and he did not seem to be in a particularly murderous mood."

"I think it would be best if M. Ellis told you about it. He was there. Unfortunately, I arrived on the scene too late to prevent Inspector LeClerc's death."

"Jacky is dead? Surely you are joking, Inspector Rectoran."

"I fear I am not, madame. Death is not something I joke about. Joseph Gambia, who I understand is an associate of yours, is dead also. Inspector LeClerc apparently killed him before he himself was shot."

"Mon Dieu! Unbelievable! What in the world happened? Please, M. Ellis, you must tell me what happened. And why were my dear Chantal and Jean-Claude there to witness this shocking accident? I just can't believe what you are saying. It is all too much!" She flung up her hands to indicate incomprehension. "I fear I understand nothing."

"I find that fact difficult to believe, Mme. Destin."

"M. Ellis, please do not insult me in my own house. Especially if you have come here seeking my help."

"Excuse me, Mme. Destin. I did not mean to insult you. I am not myself right now. Forgive me. It is just that I have a friend who, at this very moment, is in mortal danger because of what happened this morning in the Perspective park. You may be the only one who can save her. If I was rude it is because I am so upset. Once again, please forgive me."

"I accept your apology, M. Ellis. Now please, tell me exactly what happened this morning. Leave out no details. Then you can tell me how I may be of assistance in the matter of your friend. Understand, however, I promise nothing."

Peter Ellis quickly recounted the events of the morning and what had led up to them. In describing LeClerc's mortal wounding, he led Janine Destin to believe that it was Jean-Claude Duchon who had fired the fatal shot. He finished by asking her if she knew the location of Gambia's secret hideaway close to the gas refinery at Lacq.

Janine Destin turned to face Chantal and took her hand in both of hers. "My dear, is all of this true? Were you and this Dutch woman kidnapped by Jojo and that salaud, Carlos?"

"Yes, Mme. Janine. It was terrible. You must help M. Pierre find Mlle. Anya before Carlos hurts her. Please, Mme. Janine, I know what he will do."

"I will do what I can, my dear. Do not worry. But first, M. Ellis and I must come to a little understanding. I have heard from some friends in Paris that he is a man of his word, so I will not require anything in writing. It will be a private agreement between me and M. Ellis. Will you agree to such an arrangement, M. Ellis?"

"Yes, Mme. Destin. I will do whatever is necessary to save my friend."

"You are, as I suspected, a sensible man. And since you are, I believe I can help you. I do know of a house, a little rundown farm-house, near Lacq that Jojo often used for secret assignations. I learned about it from one of his former lovers who had become disenchanted with him. I shall tell you its exact location as soon as we have conclud-ed our private agreement. Will you follow me please, M. Ellis? We will do our business in my bedroom. It is, I fear, what I use for an office."

CHAPTER THIRTY-ONE

Before going to meet Janine Destin, Peter Ellis had called Maurice and briefed him on what had happened in the park. He had told him he would call back after his meeting with Gambia's surviving partner to let him know how they were going to proceed. This he had done from a small cafe across from the formidable woman's apartment building. Now, as he rode with Inspector Rectoran to pick up his car, he outlined the plan he had hastily formulated to rescue Anya. Inspector Rectoran listened attentively, voiced his guarded general approval and then, with self-effacing tact, suggested what he called 'some little precautions'. Listening to them, Peter Ellis recalled what Maurice had said about the inspector's background. Rectoran had obviously attempted this sort of rescue more than once. Peter Ellis quickly realized that, his diplomatic disclaimers notwithstanding, Inspector Rectoran was preparing for the worst possible scenario. The realization made his stomach tighten.

Two of Rectoran's men were waiting with Maurice when they arrived in the alley behind Les Flots Bleus. After a short briefing, the five men departed for Joseph Gambia's not-so-secret former love nest in a caravan of three cars: an unmarked police Renault with Rectoran and his two men, Maurice's venerable old Citroen, and Peter Ellis's white Porsche 911. The farmhouse was near Mourenx, on the outskirts of the tiny village of Sauvelade. They arrived in the village just after eleven and parked on a side street. Maurice and Peter Ellis joined the policemen in the Renault and the whole group proceeded out to survey their target. Janine Destin had given them exceptionally specific directions and they had no trouble identifying the farm-house. They drove slowly by it twice. It was an old one-story stone structure typical of the Béarn region. It stood to the left of a fair-sized gravel yard overgrown with weeds and across from a decrepit two-story barn. All of the doors and shutters on both barn and house were closed. The property was fronted by a low stone wall and gave every appearance of being abandoned. Next to it and to the right was a much more substantial farmhouse with a big barn and several out-buildings, all situated around a large stone-paved yard. At the back of the yard, a short man in blue work clothes and a black beret was tinkering with the engine of an ancient red tractor. The scene clearly bespoke a working agricultural enterprise.

On their way back to Sauvelade, it was immediately decided that Inspector Rectoran should go and secure the old farmer's coopera-tion, if not his assistance. As it turned out, the farmer was eager to help them, having long since concluded that anyone who let a farm fall into such a sorry state must be up to no good. By 11:45, everyone was in place for the rescue operation Peter Ellis had devised.

It was a simple, straight-forward plan involving a minimum of risk: Maurice, who was unknown to Carlos, would drive into the farmyard and park next to the barn, as far away from the house as possible so as not to spook him. In plain sight, Maurice would walk to the house and knock on the door, posing as a real estate agent. When Carlos came to the door, Maurice would tell him that he had a client interested in buying the property. He would attempt to have Carlos step outside and talk. Once out of the house and away from Anya, Rectoran would take over, shooting Carlos if necessary. It seemed a feasible plan, provided Carlos took the bait and followed Maurice outside. But not only did Carlos not take the bait, the little thug did not even come to the door.

Peter Ellis, stationed next door at the farm with Rectoran and his men, immediately began to panic, voicing his fears to the inspector: What if it was not the right house? Janine Destin had certainly given them extremely specific directions but what if she had misled them? Rectoran pointed out what a stupid thing that would be to do and Peter Ellis had to agree that it would be entirely out-of-character for Janine Destin to do anything stupid. Then it hit him like an unforeseen blow to the stomach: What if Carlos had not come to the door because he was engaged in some unspeakable act inside? He told Rectoran he was going in right away. He had to know if Anya was there and if she was safe. He would let Carlos take him hostage if necessary. The inspector would just have to do everything in his power to see that Anya came away unharmed. His own safety was not to be taken into account. Rectoran reluctantly agreed to this request.

"You are sure you want to do this, Pierre?" Maurice touched his arm.

"I have no other choice, Maurice. I must know if Anya is in there and if she is alright. I got her into this. I must get her out of it, whatever the cost."

"I understand. Just be careful, my friend. Remember, that boy, Carlos, is sick."

"Yes, I know."

***

Anya was in the end of the old farmhouse that served as both kitchen and dining room. She was seated in a rustic wooden chair, her ankles tied to its legs, her wrists lashed loosely to its thick oak arms. She had been sitting there since 4:30 that morning when Gambia had left with Chantal. It was Gambia who had tied her to the chair. He had made a point of being both gentle and polite with her. Before he left, he had instructed his short, creepy underling, the one called Carlos, to keep his hands off of her. He seemed to make a point of doing this in front of her. He had said that he would be back before noon and that, provided his business in Biarritz went according to plan, she would be freed on the following day or, at worst, the day after. Then he had gone with Carlos into a bedroom where he had evidently given him further instructions. Before leaving, he had returned to the kitchen and apologized for having to hold her in such a way and for having to tie her to the chair, which he said was for her own protection. Then he had said goodbye. It had all been very surreal. It was as though he were trying to make her like him, in spite of all that he had done. And then there was that last remark. Her French was not excellent but it was better than average. She was virtually positive that he had said he had tied her to the chair for her own protection. She had no idea what he meant.

At first, Carlos had pretty much obeyed Gambia's instructions. After Gambia had left, he had napped in a tattered armchair by the massive old fireplace. At around eight, he had gotten up and made a pot of coffee. With a leering gesture, he offered her a cup. She shook her head 'no' and tried not to make eye contact with him. He evidently did not get her intended message. He talked incessantly. Although he used a lot of slang, she understood most of what he said from the gestures, almost exclusively lewd, that he used to illustrate his words. So as not to have to look at him, she decided to feign sleep. The nightmare began at 11:35 according to the old clock on the mantle.

First, Anya felt his hand on her cheek. She bucked violently against her lashings. He was standing behind her. He grasped her by the shoulders to stop her from moving. He moved closer to her and she felt his crotch press against the back of her head. She bent her head as far forward as the ropes binding her wrists allowed. He leaned forward over the back of the chair. Suddenly she threw her head backward into his genitals. He screamed something at her and slapped her hard on the side of the head. He then ripped away the two blankets that Gambia had wrapped around her against the cold. Beneath them, she wore only her bikini. She turned around and spit in his face.

"So, you want to play rough. Very good. Carlos likes to play rough. If Jojo does not return by noon, you will see just how rough."

He went over to the sideboard and retrieved the length of sheet that had been used as a gag during their ride to the farmhouse. He tied it tightly so that it cut into the sides of Anya's mouth.

"There now. How does that feel? Is it tight enough?"

Anya sat perfectly still. Her ears were ringing from the sharp slap to the side of her head. She stared straight ahead. She tried to show absolutely no emotion.

"I think it is time I told you about my arrangement with Jojo. He told me that if he did not return or call me by noon, it meant something had gone wrong in Biarritz. He told me I was free to do anything I want with you. It is almost11:45. If I were you, I would start trying to be nice to me. That way, maybe I'll decide to be nice to you later. What do you say?"

Anya did not move a muscle. She continued to stare straight ahead, focusing on nothing, Carlos grunted. It was meant to be a laugh. He walked around and stood in front of her. He was grinning.

"I can't hear you. You say you want to do something to prove you are sorry for trying to hurt me? You say you want to show me your nice tits and your pretty pink nipples? Well now, that would be a start. Let's see. I have an idea. Let's play a little game. It's called 'You show me yours and I'll show you mine'. You know how to play? You do? Excellent. What? I can't hear you. Oh, you say you want to show me your tits but you need help. You are having trouble removing your top. Well then, permit me to help you."

Carlos walked behind her and untied the neck and back spaghetti straps holding her bikini top in place. The small top fell into her lap. He reached down and retrieved it. As he did so he let his fingers linger on her crotch. Anya visibly tensed but did not move.

"Relax, cherie, we are just beginning our game. It is much more enjoyable if you are relaxed. Now, you have shown me yours so I must show you mine. I must warn you though, he is a very big fellow and I think he wants to show off for you. He is telling me that your tits excite him."

Carlos unfastened his belt and unzipped his pants, revealing his erection. Holding his penis with thumb and forefinger, he raised the head and pretended to talk with it.

"Oh yes! He is showing off for you. You bad boy! What do you have to say for yourself? What? You say you want to do your favorite trick for the pretty Dutch lady but you must first see how she feels.

Well, well!" Carlos looked over at Anya and shook his head. "He is very demanding today but, alas, there is nothing I can do about it. He is totally spoiled. He always gets his way." Carlos moved close to Anya's side and brushed her left breast with the tip of his penis. "There now. Is that better, mon vieux?"

At that moment, he heard the car pull into the gravel courtyard. He quickly backed away and pulled his pants up over his dying erection, swearing as he did so. He carefully fastened the zipper and notched his belt. He took his switchblade from the table and moved over to one of the windows next to the front door. He peered through a small peephole in the shutter. Within seconds, there was a loud knocking on the door. The knocking was accompanied by a Béarn-accented voice asking if anyone was home and identifying the speaker as a real estate agent. The knocking was repeated several times. The old man was nothing if not insistent. Finally, though, he gave up, returned to his old Citroen and puttered away toward Sauvelade. Carlos returned to the kitchen and replaced his knife on the table. He walked over next to Anya and reached down and fondled her breasts.

"Sorry about the interruption, cherie. Some old fart wanted to sell me some real estate. It looks like we must start over." He pinched one of her nipples and then the other. "I'll bet you thought someone had come to rescue you. There is just one little problem: no one knows where you are. Still, I'll bet you got wet thinking about it. Tell me the truth. Did you get wet thinking your old American friend had come to rescue you?" He ran his middle finger between her legs. "You know, I think it did make you wet. Or were you thinking about my big fellow? But of course! He always has that effect on the little girls. I'll bet you were wondering when he was coming out again to play. Well, you are in luck. He will be ready to play again as soon as he takes care of a little business. So sit tight and I'll be right back."

Carlos went into the bathroom. Soon Anya heard him singing. Then she heard something else and her heart leapt wildly. It was the sound of an engine, that distinctive sound made by the engine of Peter's white Porsche. It grew louder then suddenly died. She wondered if Carlos had also heard the engine. She did not have to wonder for very long. As if on cue, her captor returned from the bathroom. He was whistling. He wore nothing save an idiotic, leering grin and a sleeveless white undershirt.

"Look who I brought to play. When he heard you were wet for him, he really became excited. But you can certainly see that for yourself."

The three knocks sounded like three shots fired into the door. They were quickly followed by the sound of Peter Ellis's screaming voice.

"Carlos! Do you hear me? I know you are in there. Open the door. I need to talk to you immediately. Jojo has sent me with a message for you. It is very important. Open the door!"

"Merde! I don't believe this." Carlos rushed back into the bathroom. He was only gone a matter of seconds, but in that short time Peter Ellis repeated his knocking and message twice, the second time as Carlos emerged from the bathroom tucking in his shirt. He rushed to the window, peered through the peephole then began screaming.

"Get away from the door! Go where I can see you. Put your hands on your head. I warn you, don't try anything stupid. I have your friend here. Go on! Do as I say. Now!"

Peter Ellis stepped back ten feet from the door.

"Get back farther, twice as far. Now wait and do not move."

Peter Ellis did as he was told. Carlos quickly went to where Anya was sitting and replaced her bikini top. Then he snatched his switchblade from the table and snapped it open. He put the point under Anya's chin.

"Listen to me. This is not the way Jojo planned it. I don't know what kind of game your friend is playing but if he tries anything stupid, I will use this." He pressed the dull side of the blade against her chin. "You understand?"

Anya nodded her head.

"And you will do everything I tell you?"

Again she nodded.

"Okay, let's go talk with your friend. He better have something good to say."

Carlos bent down and untied the lashings from Anya's ankles and wrists and motioned for her to stand. He then bound her wrists behind her back and led her, at knifepoint, to the door. Keeping the knife firmly pressed against her back, he leaned over and surveyed the courtyard through the peephole. It was empty, save for the white Porsche and Peter Ellis, who was standing midway between the car and the house with his hands on his head. Carlos opened the door and pushed Anya just over the threshold. Holding her firmly by her bound wrists, he flashed his switchblade at Peter Ellis.

"You remember this, I believe."

"Yes. It is hard to forget."

"Good. Don't make me use it on your friend. It would be a shame to spoil such a beautiful face."

"If you put one mark on her, you are a dead man, Carlos. Remember what Jojo told you. He told you to keep her safe. It does not look like you are doing your job. You have taken her clothes. She is obviously freezing. Jojo will not be happy."

"Shut up! You talk too much. I'm in charge here. Remember?" He held up the switchblade again. "And I think you need to answer some questions. Like why you are here instead of Jojo."

"He sent me here to get you. He was forced to change his plans."

"So why has he not called me?"

"I don't know. Maybe there is something wrong with the telephone. Have you tried it recently?"

Peter Ellis knew the telephone line was dead. Rectoran's men had cut it before Maurice had been sent to the house.

"No. I'll try it in a minute. You had better hope it is not working."

"Maybe Jojo did not have the opportunity to call. He was in a big hurry to leave the country."

"Leave the country? You are kidding, right? Leave the country? That was not part of our deal."

"I know. But the police were closing in. He left for Spain two hours ago. That's where he wants me to take you. We are going to meet him in a restaurant in Irun."

"What about her?"

"Anya stays here. I will come back for her after I have taken you to Jojo. It is very important that we hurry. Jojo thinks the police might be on their way here. Apparently his friend, Inspector LeClerc, and his partner, Janine Destin, have both turned on him. He thinks Janine might know how to find this place."

"Shit! Wait where you are. Do not move. I'll be right back."

Carlos pulled Anya back inside the doorway and, shielding himself with her body, reached around her and closed the heavy oak door and locked it. He led her back to the chair.

"Sit here and do not move."

He went back to the shuttered window and looked through the peephole. The American journalist stood in the middle of the court-yard with his hands on his head. Carlos moved quickly from the window to the massive sideboard and reached for the telephone. The line was dead. He slammed down the receiver and stood thinking for several minutes. He realized he did not have many choices. He wished Jojo had left him one of the guns. Then he could just shoot the American bastard if he tried anything. Hell, he might just shoot him later anyway. He had taken a great dislike to the American. He thought he was so smart. He would show him how smart he was, just wait. If the bastard of a journalist out there thought he could tell him what to do, he was making a big mistake. And if this change of plan was Jojo's way of trying to frame him for the American kid's death, that was also a mistake. Two could play that game. He was tired of everyone telling him what to do. From now on, he was going to be his own boss.

Carlos went over to Anya and grabbed her by the arm, led her brusquely into the bedroom and sat her down on the bed.

"Behave yourself and everything will be fine. If you try anything stupid, I won't be responsible for what happens. We are going on a little trip. But don't worry. I will bring your blankets. I don't want those nice tits of yours to get cold."

Carlos hurriedly threw some clothes and a toilet kit into a small canvas bag. From a peg by the door, he retrieved a black leather jacket. He gave the room one last, cursory look then led Anya back to the kitchen where he picked up her blankets from the floor next to her chair. He hastily wrapped them around her so that they also served as a hindrance to free movement. He led her over to the window and did a final survey of the courtyard. Everything was as before. The American bastard was standing in the same spot, midway between the house and his car, hands on his head. At least he could take orders. Hopefully, he would continue to do so. Of course, it could be a trap but Carlos didn't think so. He didn't think that the American would be so foolish as to risk the life of his beautiful girlfriend. That's why Carlos had decided to take her to Spain with him. If Jojo objected, tant pis. He was the one who had complicated everything with his stupid idea of kidnapping the two women so he could make a deal with this American bastard of a journalist. What could this journalist do for them anyway? Carlos had told Jojo they should just kill the son of a bitch and be done with it. Now he was forced to take things into his own hands. Well, so much the better.

Carlos opened the door slowly and pushed Anya out ahead of him. He reached around her and threw his bag next to the stoop. He would retrieve it when he had things under control.

"Monsieur, I have thought about what you have said. The situation with Jojo may be as you say but there is one detail that bothers me."

"What is that?"

"The old man. The one who came here just before you arrived. I want to know who he was."

"What old man? I don't know who you are talking about. I came here by myself, as you can see. Look around if you like."

"So you did not see an old man in an old Citroen on your way here?"

"No. I saw no one."

"Please, monsieur, think about it. He left just before you arrived. I think it is too much of a coincidence, both of you coming at almost the same time. No one ever comes to this place. I think you sent the old man to trap me. That is what I think. I think you sent him to get me outside the house so that you could somehow try to rescue your friend."

"You're crazy, Carlos."

"Yes, monsieur, I am a little crazy. That is why you better not try anything stupid. It might make me do something crazy to your pretty friend here. Anyway, crazy or not, I am making a little change in the plan."

"A change? What kind of change? Jojo will not be happy. He said you were to come with me. He and I made a deal."

"Good for you. But I have made no deal with you. If Jojo is unhappy, too bad. He is the one who has changed our arrangement. He will have to live with the consequences."

"So what is your change of plan?"

"You will see. Now shut up and do as I say. If you are a good boy, no one will get hurt. Understand?"

"Yes."

"Good. First, I want you to remove your car keys from your pocket very slowly. Throw them on the ground over there." He pointed to a place between Peter Ellis and the car.

Peter Ellis did as he was told.

"Very good. Now I want you to tell me the name of the restaurant in Irun where you are to meet Jojo. I am going to go there with your pretty friend here. If everything is as you say, I will leave her there. If I should be followed or get stopped on the way by the police or anyone else, your friend will not be so pretty when you next see her. She may not even be alive. Her fate is in your hands."

Peter Ellis locked eyes with Anya. "Darling, please forgive me."

"Shut up!" He jerked Anya by her bound wrists. She winced and let out a little cry. "I told you. Speak only when I tell you. I have asked you a question. What is the name of the restaurant?"

Peter Ellis gave the name of the only restaurant he could remember in Irun. His only hope now was that Carlos would actually go there in search of Gambia and that Rectoran and his men would find a way to rescue Anya.

"Monsieur, you had better hope Jojo is waiting there for me at that restaurant. Otherwise, I am going to have to play a little rough with your pretty friend. But who knows, maybe she will come to like it. Most girls do after they've tried it." He nudged Anya forward then suddenly pulled her to a halt. He pointed his knife toward Peter Ellis. "Monsieur, you must not blame me if I ruin your friend for you and every other man. I can't help it. It is a gift I have." He grinned a smug, gap-toothed grin. "Shall we be going, cherie?"

Peter Ellis, hands on his head, stood trembling in the middle of the courtyard, feeling helpless, angry and incredibly stupid. He watched as the smirking psychopath led Anya to where his car keys lay in the gravel not far from his car. When Carlos came to where they lay, he stopped and again pointed his knife at Peter Ellis.

"Thank-you for your car. I have always wanted a Porsche."

He bent down and reached for the keys with his left hand, momentarily releasing his hold on Anya's bound wrists. As soon as he did so, she lurched forward and tried to run. The tightly-wrapped blankets immediately caught her legs and sent her sprawling to the ground. As she fell, Carlos leapt toward her, slashing with his switch-blade. In that instant, two rifle shots sounded in quick succession. The bullets ripped into Carlos's bent-over body, lifting it sideways and then backwards. He was dead before he hit the ground.

Anya screamed and writhed violently against the confining folds of the blankets. Peter Ellis was already running to her. People were shouting at him but he paid them no attention. The switchblade Carlos had been pointing at him only moments earlier lay on the gravel several inches from Anya's feet. Peter Ellis reached down, picked it up and threw it as far as he could. Then he bent to his knees and, ever so gently, gathered Anya up into his trembling arms. As he did so, he felt the wet sticky warmth of blood.

CHAPTER THIRTY-TWO

O ver the next several days, Peter Ellis saw very little of Anya. He paid brief, daily visits to LaBorde where he inevitably found her working alone in the studio. He would drink a beer and watch her sketch. They spoke very little and, when they did, their conversation was limited and inconsequential. Before he left, he would huddle with Olga in the kitchen and receive an update on Anya's progress. Luckily, the knife wound to Anya's thigh, though ugly, had not been as bad as first feared and only required stitches. The emotional wounds she suffered, however, were a different matter. Peter Ellis and Olga had mutually agreed that Anya would need space as well as time to recover from these deeper, psychic injuries.

When he wasn't visiting LaBorde, Peter Ellis spent his time either walking on the beach or working on his article about the connected deaths of Joseph Gambia, Inspector Jacques LeClerc, the punk, Carlos, and Kevin Duffy, whose reported 'accidental' death had put the whole fatal train in motion. True to his word, he left any mention of Janine Destin out of the article, except to say that she owned 'Le Gentleman' nightclub in partnership with Joseph Gambia.

On the second day after Anya's rescue, Maurice invited Peter Ellis to lunch at one of the beachfront restaurants at Chambre d'Amour. At the end of the meal, over espresso and snifters of Armagnac, their conversation turned to Chantal Clairac.

"So, Maurice, how is our poor beauty doing? Have you seen her?"

"I saw her just this morning. She is back at work at Dodin's."

"The girl is a trooper, I'll say that for her."

"It is true. But she is very unlucky."

"Yes. She has certainly been visited with more than her fair share of tragedy and suffering these last few months."

"And I fear will continue to be, my friend."

"What do you mean, Maurice? You don't mean to say that she is back with Duchon?"

"That is exactly what I mean to say."

"After all that he has done to her? Don't you think you should try to talk to her about him, about what he is really like?"

"Alas, I have already tried. At the moment, it is of no use. She will not listen to anything and I do not want to force the issue. All she can think of now is that 'poor Jean-Claude' got shot trying to save her. He is her hero and she feels responsible for his wounding."

"You're kidding! It was Duchon more than anyone who is responsible for almost everything that happened. Not her rape, of course, although even that, it could be argued, would not have happened had he not introduced her into Gambia's circle."

"We both know that, Pierre, and maybe I can make her see the truth about him one day. But that day is not today. Not with Duchon walking around with his arm in a sling and Janine Destin championing his cause. As you yourself have witnessed, Mme. Destin can be a very persuasive woman."

"That is another thing I do not understand. Why is she so concerned that Duchon and Chantal get back together? If I am not very much mistaken, she is the kind of woman who only does things that contribute to her own best interests."

"Oh, my friend, in that you are not mistaken. The woman has the killer instinct of the shark and the intelligence of the porpoise. I can only speculate why she is playing matchmaker for Duchon and Chantal, but I feel certain it has to do with control. She wants Duchon permanently under her thumb."

"But why? He is an imbecile. How can he possibly help her?"

"Under her expert guidance, he can be a great help to her. I believe Mme. Destin has big plans for our favorite food salesman. With Gambia out of the way, Duchon will become her front man and procurer. And unlike M. Gambia, he will be totally loyal to her. The girl is Mme. Destin's insurance that he will remain so."

"Yes, I guess you are right. But tell me one other thing. Why, in God's name, did Janine Destin give Duchon that little pistol? Did she actually expect or want him to shoot someone? And, if so, who?"

"That is a good question, my friend. My guess is that she hoped Duchon would shoot Gambia over his treatment of the girl. Or, perhaps, shoot Carlos for the same reason. Then again, maybe she is even smarter than we think. Maybe she set up the whole thing. Maybe she wanted to get rid of LeClerc as well. Whatever she did or did not do, it all worked out perfectly for her. She bagged not two but three birds with the help of one little pistol."

"And my help. That's the great irony." Peter Ellis shook his head then took a sip of Armagnac. For several seconds he looked pensively at the dark amber liquid in the snifter. Then he looked up at his old friend. "You know, Maurice, it is a shame LeClerc showed up so soon in the park. Gambia was just about to identify Janine Destin's high-profile political associates and backers. Exposing them would have made for an explosive story."

"Which you would certainly be sued for writing."

"Why? If the facts were true?"

"I have a pretty good idea, from my investigation of Gambia, who most of these political figures are. If they are who I think they are, then they are virtually untouchable. To get at them, you would have to obtain photographs of them having sex with farm animals. And even then, it would be a hard sell. They would probably use the defense that they were merely trying to protect the peasant's farm subsidies."

"So, Janine Destin will continue with her business as if nothing had happened?"

"Oh, she will take certain precautions to protect herself, should you, for example, decide not to keep your word. And my guess is that she will disassociate herself from Gambia's drug contacts. She was never very enthusiastic about that side of the business, though she willingly accepted the profits it generated. Now that she has total control of the gambling and prostitution operations in this corner of France, she should be able to make more than enough money to keep her supplied with champagne and young men."

"You will not try to go after her?"

"My God, no! With Gambia and LeClerc dead, my work is finished. Unlike them, Mme. Destin is not inclined to violence. She does not inspire the sort of holy passion in me that they did. Anyway, I'm too old to undertake another major investigation. Let some eager junior agent try to ensnare Mme. Destin. One thing is certain: Whoever goes after her will have his hands full."

"So, what are you going to do with yourself, Maurice? I can't believe you are just going to sit around and do nothing."

"I think I may get a dog, a smart dog I can train. Something small with short hair and a good nose. I have always admired that English breed of terrier called Jacques Russell."

"You are pulling my leg, Maurice. You? Get a dog?"

"Not at all, mon ami. I have been thinking about it for some time. A man of my age needs a companion. And a good dog becomes an old man."

***

On the third morning after the farmhouse rescue of Anya, Peter Ellis woke to thin bars of bright sunshine slanting through his darkened bedroom. There was no sound of the wind that rattled the old wooden windows in their frames the previous evening. He quickly dressed in jeans, t-shirt and sweatshirt and went over to the window and threw open the shutters. Sunlight streamed into the chilly bedroom. Outside, the corrugated surface of the glistening green ocean stretched to the horizon.

He hurried down the stairs, crossed the rue La Perspective and started down the path to the fateful overlook that had figured so prominently in the recent deaths of four people. Like the Duffy boy several weeks before, Peter Ellis was walking down to that jutting, crenellated overlook to have a better view of the surf. Once there, however, he found it hard to concentrate on the green, glassy waves breaking one after another in long lateral lines across the bay. He stood there several minutes staring at the peeling waves while thinking of the deadly events of the recent past. He was startled by a high-pitched bark seeming to come from just behind his heels. He turned, looked down and was greeted by the apprehensive, bewhiskered face of a panting grey schnauzer. The timing of the dog's arrival was downright eerie. For an instant, he half-expected to see some ghostly twin of Carlos poke his head around the corner of the cedar hedge bordering the path. Instead, Peter Ellis's gaze fell on the shuffling figure of the pensioner, Haraout, who, with his alert canine companion, had discovered the body of Kevin Duffy. The old man, his head bent and his eyes shaded by the lip of his large black beret, did not at first see Peter Ellis. It was only after the dog barked a second greeting, or perhaps warning, that the pensioner looked up and saw him.

"Marcel! What are you doing?" He glanced apologetically at Peter Ellis. "Excuse me, monsieur. Marcel! Arrête!" The dog tentatively approached Peter Ellis and began sniffing at his shoes. "Marcel! If you please! Do not bother the gentleman. Come here. Come over here at once."

"It is no problem, M. Haraout. Your Marcel is not bothering me." He reached down and scratched the panting dog behind the ears. Marcel immediately began wagging his bobbed tail.

"He is impossible, the little rascal. He has a mind of his own. He never listens to me anymore."

"He has a spirited and intelligent face, M. Haraout. You should be very proud of him."

"Thank-you, monsieur. You are very kind."

"I speak only the truth."

"You are M. Ellis, are you not, the journalist from Paris? I spoke with you several days ago about the death of the poor young American here."

"I see that your memory is as good as ever, M. Haraout. It is a pleasure to see you again."

"What a story, the other morning! Inspector LeClerc and that gangster, Joseph Gambia, from the building up there," he waved a hand in the direction of the concrete monolith looming over the cliff, "both shot dead. It has made me start thinking of taking Marcel elsewhere for his morning walk. This place seems to have become cursed."

"Oh, I think you and Marcel will be safe here from now on, M. Haraout. I doubt there will be any more violent deaths in this lovely park during our lifetime."

"I hope you are right, monsieur. But tell me. The newspaper said the deaths of the inspector and the gangster appeared to be accidental. It is incredible, no? Three accidental deaths in the same place within a month."

"Indeed it is, M. Haraout. But you should not believe everything you read in the papers. And that goes even for some of the things I myself write."

"You are going to write about what happened here?"

"Actually, I just completed my article about this strange business last night. It is scheduled to appear next weekend. And I have you to thank for some important information concerning the death of the young man, Kevin Duffy."

"It was not really an accident, was it?"

"No, not really."

"And the others?"

"You must read the article, M. Haraout. Just remember what I said: Do not believe everything you read."

"I shall look forward to reading your article next weekend, M. Ellis. Then I shall tell Marcel all about it. You know, he is a very curious animal."

"That is evident. In that regard, I believe he resembles his master. It has been a pleasure meeting you, M. Haraout. I hope you and Marcel enjoy this beautiful morning."

"And you as well, M. Ellis." He gave a slight tip of his black beret. "Come, Marcel! We must be going. Remember, you still have your business to do."

After saying his goodbyes to Marcel and M. Haraout, Peter Ellis retraced his steps up the park's switch-backing macadam path, crossed the coast road to Les Flots Bleus and ordered a cafe au lait and a croissant. While he was waiting for his coffee, he used the telephone at the reception desk to call Marc Dufau. His friend picked up on the fourth ring and answered 'Hello' in an obviously hurried voice.

"What are you doing, Marc? You sound like you've been running."

"I was on my way out to check the waves."

"I'll save you the trip. I was just down at the overlook checking out the break at Côtes des Basques."

"How does it look? It is good, no?"

"No, it is not good, it is incredible. You must come over right away. It's glassy and almost head high and, so far, nobody is out. Stop by Les Flots Bleus. I'll be waiting for you."

"I'll see you in fifteen minutes."

They parked midway down the beach access road at the base of the elbow formed by the south face of the Pointe Atalaye. Two other surfers had just arrived and were preparing to paddle out. Marc recognized them and waved, shouting a greeting.

"Wait until you see those two surf, Peter. It's a good sign that they're here. It means they have checked out the other breaks and that this looks the best to them."

"Well, it's hard to imagine anywhere else being better."

"So, let's go!"

They paddled out in the natural channel along the arm of the promontory next to the rock breakwater fronting the beach road. The water was extremely cold and Peter Ellis thought as he stroked alongside Marc that this might just be his last surf session until the spring, unless he was able to manage a trip to some warmer locale during the winter. Maybe he could convince Anya to go somewhere with him. He had always wanted to visit Costa Rica and he had heard that the waves there were fabulous. And the water was always warm.

He was still shivering when he reached the line-up. It took him several waves to figure out the take-off. He misjudged his first two waves and started paddling too late. On the third wave, he made the opposite mistake, dropped in as the wave was breaking and had to grab the rail of his board to keep from being washed off by the exploding whitewater. As he was paddling back out after this near wipeout, one of Marc's friends took off to his immediate left. He was perfectly positioned in the middle of a small peak and caught the wave after four or five quick strokes. Once up, he made a clean, hard bottom turn and raced up the face of the wave, snapping off a 180 degree turn at the top that sent up a rooster-tail of sea-spray glistening in the bright morning sunlight. For as far as Peter Ellis could follow him on the wave, he repeated this jerky maneuver several times, the last time managing to launch himself above the lip of the wave and make the turn in mid-air. He was evidently a member of the new radical school of surfing, what Peter Ellis thought of as the skateboard school of surfing, where 'getting air' and snapping off sharp, vertical turns took precedence over horizontal fluidity and grace. Although Peter Ellis respected these radical surfers for their obvious skill and power, he himself preferred the relatively old, 'carving' school of surfing, what he liked to think of as the porpoise school where the surfer tried to become one with the wave while taking what it gave him.

Suddenly it occurred to him that thinking about such petty things on such a beautiful, surf-perfect morning was ridiculous. The day was too magnificent for such judgmental ruminations. It was a day to be savored, a magical day carved from lambent green crystal, feathered with icy kaleidoscopes of sea-spray, pulsing with pure liquid energy. Peter Ellis let his eyes wander over the scene surrounding him: the Villa Belza, its elegant single turret and cantilevered banks of mullioned windows bathed in radiant sunlight, seemed to rise with renewed vigor from its ancient rocky perch and to impart a mute blessing on the sea-play taking place in its watery backyard; the two semi-circular, gap-toothed overlooks, seen from his transforming ocean perspective, now seemed to smile good-naturedly from the green shadows of the cliffside park; even the rows of decrepit abandoned Nazi artillery bunkers honeycombing the steep southern face of the promontory seemed to speak of a renewal of hope as they, one by one, began to catch the cleansing morning sunlight.

It was a magical morning of surf as well. There were even extended moments when Peter Ellis was not even aware of the foot-numbing, ice cream headache-giving cold, moments when he was slicing clean, unconscious bottom turns just ahead of the crashing water wall, getting into perfect trim midway up the sparkling green wave face and racing with heart-pounding exhilaration ahead of the collapsing lip, moments when he was immersed entirely in the present of the wave, the past merely a disappearing white foam gash, the future a swelling promise of emerald energy. It was both a transforming reality out of time and a fluid reality representing time's very essence.

Unfortunately, the frigid water was also a reality, one that could not be long forgotten or ignored. Just as Peter Ellis was beginning to succumb to the bone chilling, deadening effects of prolonged exposure to the water, a set of large waves began to take shape, their evanescent green backs rising in rapid succession out of the icy depths. As soon as he became aware of the size of the approaching set, he screamed 'outside' and began to paddle furiously. As the third wave of the set began to wall up, he swung his board around and angled it into the wave, his arms digging hard as the tail of the surfboard rose up and its nose, barely an inch above the surface, began its critical descent. His hands were so numb from the cold water that he nearly lost his grip on the rails as he grabbed them and sprung to his feet. At the instant that his feet made contact with the nubby waxed deck of his board, he momentarily broke loose from the wave and freefell to the bottom of the trough. Thanks to his angle of take-off and the forgiving shape of his board, he managed immediately to regain control, though the contorted way he did so was more comical than controlled. After his jerky recovery, however, his ride was almost flawless: a speed-building, arching run up the wave face, a sweeping cutback into the curl, a brief, exhilarating cover-up in the wind-hollowed tube, another power drive ahead of the collapsing lip to the crest of the wave where, for an instant, he rode its curved, breaking back prior to making a floating re-entry. Instead of kicking out of the wave, he straightened his board in the direction of the beach and rode it prone all the way to the sand. It had been not just a wave to end the day on, but a wave to cap the season.

After changing out of his wetsuit into jeans, two t-shirts and a hooded sweatshirt, he walked over to the cafe on the ground floor of the apartment building overlooking the beach. He ordered a bottle of sparkling mineral water, a bowl of cafe au lait and a sandwich of jambon de Bayonne. He sat by the large picture window, totally content, and watched Marc and his two friends take turns carving up the sparkling green, Côtes des Basques waves thundering in from the Bay of Biscay.

Marc stayed out for another forty-five minutes. When he finally arrived in the cafe, he was shivering but smiling broadly.

"Not bad, our little waves here in the Pays Basque, eh Pierre?"

"They are magnificent. My last wave was a classic. I decided I did not want to catch anything else that might mar the memory of the ride. Also, I was nearly frozen to death."

"Yes, I saw that wave. At first, I thought it must be someone else riding it."

"Thanks a lot."

"Then I remembered that day two years ago up in Oleron when you were surfing like Wayne Lynch and I realized it had to be you."

"I hardly looked like Wayne Lynch, though I appreciate the compliment. He is still one of my all-time favorite surfers. You know, I saw a film with him and Tom Curren recently. He is still an incredible surfer."

"Yes, I think I know the film, though I have forgotten the name. M. Lynch was indeed quite impressive in it."

The waiter arrived and Marc ordered a mug of hot chocolate and a croque madame.

"So, Pierre, how much longer are you staying with us?"

"I'm not sure, Marc, at least a week or so. I've decided, after all, to write an article on the surf scene here. Give the history and describe how it has changed over the years. I want to try to find some of the original guys and talk with them. How long I stay depends a little on Anya as well."

"How is she doing?"

"I'm not sure. It was a very traumatic experience for her, as you can imagine. Not exactly the way to spend a vacation. I feel entirely responsible for what happened to her. I fear it may have ruined things for us."

"Come on, Pierre. It was not your fault. How could you or anyone know that Gambia would be able to discover where Chantal and Anya were staying. It was just bad luck. As for you and Anya, my feeling is that there is something special between you two. She just needs some time. Don't worry."

"I hope you are right."

"I am right. Tell me, though, what's going to happen to that bastard, Duchon?"

"Nothing."

"Nothing?"

"Not for the time being. Unless he does something really stupid, which I don't think he will, not with Janine Destin looking after him. It seems he was telling the truth about not raping Chantal at the party. It was the good Chief Inspector LeClerc who raped her."

"You are kidding?"

"Not at all. Which leads me to believe Duchon when he says he did not participate in the rape of your friend, Madeline Delay. This is not to say he does not share in the guilt for bringing her to the party with Gambia and his friends. But he swears he left the party before things got out of hand and, as much as I hate to admit it, I believe him."

"What about his part in the death of Kevin Duffy?"

"With Gambia and Carlos dead, it would be impossible to make any charges against him stick. He will say they acted on their own."

"And it's true that he is really back with Chantal Clairac?"

"Apparently. He is playing up his gunshot wound for all it's worth."

"Incredible!"

"Yes, it is. I feel sorry for the girl but she is, after all, an adult."

"In years, maybe. She is so naive in other ways. I wish there was some way I could help her."

"She is too old for adoption, Marc. If you want to do something, just go by Dodin's and check on her from time to time. She knows you now, knows you are my friend. You will be able at least to tell if anything is bothering her. She's not very good at hiding her feelings."

"And there really is nothing you can do about Duchon?"

"I shall talk with him before I leave. I intend to remind him I still have Kevin Duffy's diary which recounts in detail how he threatened the boy."

"You really have his diary?"

"No. But Duchon does not know that. As Chantal can attest, Kevin <u>did</u> keep a diary. Who's to say I did not get my hands on it?"

"Indeed. I forget, sometimes, what you do for a living."

"I may not be doing it much longer. Not if I lose Anya over this business."

"You will not lose her, Pierre. At least not over what happened here. When are you seeing her next?"

"I'm not sure. I'm calling her as soon as I return to my apartment."

"In that case, I had better be getting you back. We must have dinner, all of us, before Anya leaves. That is, if she feels up to it."

"I'll find out and let you know. Are you ready?"

"Yes. It was a good morning, was it not?"

"Superb. It was just what I needed. Now I can put my surfboard away for the winter without regret and just dream about that last wave."

***

When Peter Ellis checked in at the hotel, there was a message from Anya for him to call her immediately. In a panic, wondering what else could possibly have happened, he quickly dialed the number at LaBorde. Anya answered on the second ring. She sounded slightly breathless.

"Hello?"

"Anya? I just received your message. I'm sorry to be so late getting back to you. I was out surfing with Marc. What's happened?"

"What do you mean, my dear?"

"Your message. It sounded urgent. Is something wrong?"

"No. Something is right. I woke up this morning, saw what a beautiful day it was and decided it was time to start living again. In spite of everything that has happened, I realized that I have been, after all, very lucky. I thought that if you were free and not fed up with me, we might go to Sauveterre for lunch. I am well aware I have been somewhat anti-social the last few days. I want you to know my behavior had nothing to do with you. So what do you say, my love? My treat."

"I think it's a wonderful idea, except for the last part. It is I who will treat. After everything that has happened, I owe you not only lunch but a lot more."

"Peter, all you owe me is your undying love and devotion. When can you be here? I'm starving."

"I'm getting in the car right now."

"Peter Ellis made the drive to Olga's in record time, skidding to a stop in front of the familiar farmhouse. Even before he had turned off the car engine, Anya was running out to meet him. Her physical change from the day before was close to miraculous. Yesterday, she had sat almost lifeless in her somber studio, rarely speaking and drawing as if by rote. Today, as she ran towards him smiling in the bright midday sunshine, she was a vision of radiant vitality. Peter Ellis was barely out of the car when she flung herself into his arms. And then she did something totally unexpected: She began sobbing and laughing at the same time.

"Oh, Anya! I have missed you."

"Yes, I know, I know."

She buried her head in the crook of his neck. He held her close for several seconds until the emotional heaving that racked her shoulders and chest had subsided. Then he kissed her on the lips, took her by the hand and led her into the house. Olga was waiting for them in the kitchen. Anya immediately excused herself so that she might go and collect her things.

"So, Olga, how do you find the patient?"

"Peter, it is like a miracle. Last night I was having serious concerns about her. I'd even thought of calling the doctor back. Did she say anything to you?"

"No, not really. Only that she woke this morning feeling like a changed person and that she wanted to go to Sauveterre for lunch. I'm sure we will talk more this afternoon."

"Well, let me know if I can do anything for her. I have felt quite helpless these last few days."

"You did what needed to be done. What else could you do? At least she seems to be over the worst of it."

"Or is trying to make us think so. Though it's a good sign that she wants to go back to Sauveterre. Maybe you can convince her to take a little trip with you. Perhaps go to Spain for a couple of days. A change of scene will help to distance her from what happened, help her to forget."

"It's a good idea, Olga. I'll talk with her about it."

"You know she does not have many days of vacation left?"

"Yes, I know."

"You are really in love with her, aren't you?"

"Yes I am."

"May I give you some advice, then? As a friend of you both."

"Of course."

"Take it easy with her, Peter. And don't worry. Unless I am much mistaken, she is also very much in love with you."

"You really think so, Olga? After everything that has happened?"

"She called you, didn't she? She obviously wants to see you."

"It could be she just wants to tell me she is no longer interested in continuing. After all that I have involved her in, I can't say I could blame her if she felt that way."

"That is certainly a possibility but it would surprise me very much. She has been standing by that window for the last thirty minutes waiting for you to arrive."

"I have done no such thing!" Both Peter Ellis and Olga turned at the sudden sound of her voice. "I'm surprised at you, Olga, telling Peter such stories. I had better get him away from here before you start giving him other ideas. Are you ready, monsieur?"

"Oui, mademoiselle. For you, I shall always be ready."

"See what you have done, Olga? He has already started."

Olga walked them to the door and waited there, talking with Anya while Peter Ellis packed her painting things in the trunk. Before sending Anya on her way, Olga whispered something that caused her to smile broadly. Peter Ellis started the engine and Olga waved to them.

"Goodbye you two. Have a nice afternoon."

Peter Ellis waved and eased the car out of the driveway. When he reached the main highway and settled the car into a cruising speed, Anya reached over, took his right hand and began tracing sensual little messages with her slender, articulate fingers. Every so often, she removed her hand to point out some unusual feature of a farmhouse or pleasing aspect of the Béarn landscape, only to return, with a dreamy smile, to her eloquently mute, tactile discourse.

Peter Ellis drove directly to the Hostellerie du Chateau and parked in the leaf-strewn gravel parking lot under an enormous beech tree next to the dilapidated ancient wall of the town's old fortified tower. M. Camy, the proprietor, greeted them at the door as though they were old friends. He led them to a table and informed them he had a special Menu Chasse that day. It featured seasonal vegetables and several sorts of wild game. He said he hoped they were hungry.

They ate a gargantuan meal: potage paysan, a vegetable rich variation of the Béarn's most celebrated soup, garbure; roasted wild pigeons with cepe mushrooms a la Bordelaise and a large dish of pommes au four; a delicious simple lettuce salad; a thick slice of fromage de montagne with a small serving of homemade fig preserves.

They washed down the feast with a half bottle of pale, dry Jurançon followed by a bottle of Chateau de la Motte Madiran, a purple-crimson wine with a peppery, grapey taste and a wonderfully clean finish. In view of the glorious fall weather, they decided to take their coffee and digestives at one of the tables scattered on the lawn outside.

During the meal, Anya had asked Peter Ellis to tell her everything that had happened between the time she and Chantal had been kidnapped and the morning of her rescue. Peter Ellis said he would recount the whole story as soon as they had finished eating. So it was, sitting on the sun-drenched terrace of the old hotel, high above the shallow, rushing green water of the Gave de Oloron that Peter Ellis told Anya everything that had happened: told her about his morning meeting with Joseph Gambia in the Perspective park; told her of Gambia's scheme to ruin his two partners; told her how Inspector LeClerc had surprised them and revealed his murderous plan; told how Chantal Clairac had suddenly recognized the inspector's voice as that of the masked man who had raped her at the party and how the girl had tried to leap over the parapet; told her how Jean-Claude Duchon had pulled out the little gun that ultimately (he had to admit) had probably saved his life; told her about his panicked meeting with Janine Destin and about the deal he had struck with her in return for her revealing to them the location of Gambia's hideout; told her about their initial plan to rescue her by having Maurice pose as a real estate agent; told her how the sharp-shooting Inspector Rectoran and his men had seized the moment and killed Carlos; and, finally, told how he had taken her, delirious, to the hospital in Pau where a doctor had treated her for shock and the knife wound.

"It's incredible, Peter. I remember almost nothing of the day after that horrible creature, Carlos, was shot and I was crawling on the ground. I vaguely remember you taking me in your arms and riding with you in the car. Then nothing until I woke up the next day, which is when all of the terrible experiences of that morning came rushing back to me. I felt so incredibly dirty. I didn't think I would ever be able to wash away the filth from the places he touched me."

"I'm so sorry about everything, Anya. It is all my fault."

"That is what I thought as well when I woke up. Of course I was just looking for someone to blame. Now I know better. But tell me, how did Gambia find out that Chantal and I were at Olga's farm? Did Chantal manage to telephone someone while she was there?"

"No, though that is what I first suspected. So I asked her. She vehemently denied calling anyone. It remained a mystery to me until last night. I was having a late drink with Philippe, the bartender at Player's. He asked me if my friend had found me. I asked which friend he meant. When he described the so-called 'friend' to me, I immediately realized he was referring to Joseph Gambia. You see, Philippe knew about my friendship with Olga. Once, in the course of discussing the traditional method of making foie gras, I had told him about the old woman who raises geese on the farm next to LaBorde. He had asked for directions to the farm so he could speak with her about buying some of her goose liver. It was Philippe who, wholly inadvertently, told Gambia where Olga lived and how you were staying with her. From there, it was only a question of making the connection. It was a total accident but I still must accept the responsibility for what happened. Will you ever be able to forgive me?"

"Only if you take a walk with me right now down by that beautiful green river. Also, I believe you promised me a surprise."

"Indeed I did. It is a special place in Laas, a few kilometers down the river from here."

"We can go there after our walk then?"

"That would be perfect."

***

Olga did not seem surprised when they stopped by the farm and announced that they had decided to spend the night in Biarritz. While waiting for Anya to pack an overnight bag, Peter Ellis told her about their afternoon. Uncharacteristically, Olga said very little; but Peter Ellis noticed that she was wearing a kind of Cheshire cat smile that seemed to say 'I told you so'.

He and Anya arrived at the apartment on the rue Million almost an hour after sunset. The mountains of the northern Spanish coast were a dark purple outline against the dying light. They showered and changed then walked down the rue Gambetta to a little restaurant across from Les Halles. Still feeling the effects of their gargantuan midday feast, they ordered only appetizers and wine. Anya, having had time to reflect on everything Peter Ellis had told her on the terrace in Sauveterre, asked many questions regarding the specific details of the whole affair. She was especially curious about what had happened to Chantal the night of the fateful party.

"So they drugged her and then raped her? What bastards!"

"It seems that LeClerc was the only one who actually raped her."

"What a pig! And he the one charged to prevent such crimes. That, I think, is worse than the crime itself, if that is possible. When you can not trust those charged with your protection. It is like not being able to trust your parents. It is what causes you to lose respect for all authority. And with some justification, I think."

"Yes, it is like when lawyers bend the law to prevent justice. Only it is worse, much worse. And innocents like Chantal and Madeline Delay are the perfect victims for such people, for the Duchons, the Gambias and the LeClercs of the world."

"Did Inspector LeClerc rape Madeline Delay as well?"

"Oh yes, although he was not the only one."

"Oh my God! That poor girl. What exactly happened?"

"It seems LeClerc showed up late, after she had passed out. That is why she didn't remember him. Inspector Rectoran has been talking with her as well as the other girls who worked for Gambia. The pieces are starting to fall into place. Chantal and Madeline Delay were far from LeClerc's only victims. By all accounts, rough sex was the good inspector's big weakness."

"And LeClerc's wife suspected nothing the whole time?"

"She was aware of his 'little affairs', as she described them to Rectoran, but apparently was not bothered by them. It seems that her primary interest in life is possessing the latest fashions from Paris and New York before anyone else in her peer group. So long as LeClerc provided her money to indulge this passion—or sickness depending on your point of view—she pretty much let him do what he wanted, provided he was discreet about it."

"Amazing. I will never understand women like that."

"Nor will I."

"Well, my dear, you certainly need not worry about me in that regard. If anything, my taste in clothes tends to be anti-fashionable."

"When you have style, you don't have to worry about fashion."

"Not bad, my dear. Who originally said that?"

"I did. But you inspired it."

"Watch out. You are going to start making me think you are after something."

"I am."

"And what might that be?"

"Your heart."

"Just my heart? And not my body?"

"Only if that comes with it."

"It does. Sometimes." Anya paused and seemed to reflect on something. "Peter, do you think we might walk by the ocean on our way home?"

"Of course. I was going to suggest it myself."

They walked down to the Grand Plage, where they strolled along the boardwalk before starting their climb up the coast road bordering the rocky Pointe Atalaye. When they reached the Port Vieux, they decided to have a nightcap at the Santa Maria. It was a windy, though relatively warm evening. They sat outside on the bar's little terrace overlooking the tiny tongue of sandy beach. The beach was protected, like the small natural harbor it had usurped over the last few centuries, by enveloping rocky cliffs. Below them, waves crashed continuously against the concrete diving platform that jutted out into the miniscule bay. Above them, visible in the glare of the resort town's bright nocturnal lights, large clumps of cloud drifted slowly in from the Bay of Biscay.

"Peter, there is something I must tell you. I apologize for doing it at such a time, on such a lovely night, in such a lovely place. I hope it will not completely ruin the evening."

"Don't worry, Anya. I was expecting something like this to happen. I felt it coming."

"You did?"

"Yes. I even mentioned it to Marc this morning after our surf session."

"What in the world are you talking about, my dear? I am sure you have misunderstood me."

"No, I don't think so. Nor can I blame you after everything that has happened."

"Blame me for what?"

"For not wanting to continue seeing me, of course."

Anya, to his utter surprise, burst into laughter.

"What is so funny all of a sudden?"

"You are, my sweet, crazy man."

"What do you mean?"

"I mean that the last thing in the world I want is to stop seeing you, you silly goose."

"Then what is it you want to tell me that might ruin the evening?"

"I'm not sure I can tell you now. It will sound so, I don't know, so melodramatic." She paused and sipped from her snifter of Armagnac. "All I wanted to say, my dear—and I suddenly realize that it is absolutely unnecessary—is that as much as I want to make love with you tonight, I am not sure I am ready yet. See, now I'm the one being silly."

"Yes, you are. And you should know better."

"I do, now." She quickly leaned over and kissed him. "I certainly do."

***

During the night, Peter Ellis woke to find Anya shivering, holding him in a death grip. Her face was flushed and wet with tears.

"Anya, what's wrong? Are you alright?"

"Yes, I think so. I just had a dream. In it, you were dead. I was in a big bed, naked. There were no covers. I could not move, as much as I tried. They were all there: Gambia, LeClerc, that monster, Carlos.

They were arguing about who should have me first. It was so real. It was terrible. Please, hold me close. I'll be fine in a minute."

Peter Ellis lay awake long after Anya fell back to sleep, thinking of all that had happened and all the mistakes he had made. He had come far too close to ruining at least two lives, not counting his own. His behavior had been far too reckless. He wondered whether it might not be time to change the kind of work he was doing. Maybe Burke had been right. Maybe it was impossible for someone to remain with him as long as he continued putting himself and others in compromising and dangerous situations. He felt Anya's breathing on his neck, her heart beating gently against his chest. He could not begin to think about losing her, to think about being alone again. He kissed her softly on the temple. When he finally drifted into sleep, it was to the sound of the wind beating against the heavy wooden shutters.

He awoke to find Anya sitting up in bed sketching on a large pad propped against her raised knees.

"The artist is working early today."

"Oh, I'm sorry, Peter. Did I wake you? I couldn't sleep so I decided to make a little sketch of our first bedroom. Something to remind me of you when I'm alone in my cold Amsterdam bed."

"How much more do you have to do?"

"Why do you ask, sir? Do you have something else in mind besides art?"

"Only a sudden urge to curl up with you for a few minutes before getting out of this lovely warm bed. But if you want to finish your drawing, I can read."

"I'm sure you can but I like your first idea better."

She leaned over the side of the bed and dropped her drawing pad on the floor. She moved close and Peter Ellis took her in his arms. It started with a few light kisses and flickering tongue play. Then came a long, deep, sex-mimicking kiss. Soon she was moving down his body, taking him gently, all soft lips, caressing tongue, hardening pressure. And just before loss of control, his insistence on a sweet delving, fluttering tongue-tip reciprocation. The sudden, wild, inevitable joining, the wet electric entry, tension building with slow-rocking rhythm, flexing inner muscles gripping until a world explodes in shuddering, moaning, ecstatic release. Then breathlessness, deflation, heart-pounding silence. And in the soaked-sheet, energy-spent afterglow, purged memory, the glorious void.

***

During coffee and croissants at Cafe Au Haou, Anya reminded Peter Ellis of his promise, the previous evening, to take her to see Chantal Clairac. So, as soon as they had finished, he accompanied her down to the Patisserie Dodin to arrange a rendezvous with the girl.

Chantal had not seen either of them since the morning of the shootout in La Perspective park. When they greeted her, she seemed almost embarrassed at their presence in the shop. But Anya soon had her smiling and easily convinced her to meet for lunch, even though she now had a standing midday engagement with Duchon. Peter Ellis promised her that he would take it upon himself to entertain M. Duchon.

Duchon, when he finally arrived at 1:00 to pick up Chantal, was evidently not thrilled with the change of plan. But he readily agreed to it when he saw that he had no other option. The meeting took place at the nearby Cafe Royalty and was a relatively civilized, amicable affair. Peter Ellis insisted on paying for the drinks, citing the gesture as a small repayment for Duchon's potentilly life-saving actions in the park. He made polite inquiries about Duchon's new job and was quickly assured that it was much more suitable than his former employ. Duchon added, somewhat smugly, that the increased income would finally allow him, before long, to divorce his wife and marry Chantal. Of course, if there was a scandal, his wife would certainly try to bleed him dry. She was already dubious about his new position and the hours it required. Luckily, she respected Janine Destin and had great confidence in her good judgment. Peter Ellis assured him there would be no scandal over his part in the death of Kevin Duffy, provided he did not mistreat Chantal in any way or try to keep her from leaving should she, for whatever reason, decide she no longer desired his attentions. Deeming that eventually highly unlikely, Duchon, nevertheless, gave Peter Ellis his 'word as a gentleman' that, even if Chantal was foolish enough one day to make the same mistake she had made with the young American surfer, he, Jean-Claude Duchon, would continue to treat her with 'the respect and love of a good father'. Peter Ellis left the meeting feeling depressed, frustrated and, ultimately, sad.

On their drive back to Olga's farm, Peter Ellis discovered that Anya had come away from her lunch with Chantal with similar feelings of futility and sadness. By the time they reached LaBorde, they had mutually concluded that Chantal's situation, however seemingly hopeless, was beyond their control. Unless she asked for help, they could do no more except to stay in touch with her and maybe say the occasional prayer.

In the few days remaining before her return to Amsterdam, Peter Ellis took Anya to some of his favorite places in the Béarn and Pays Basque. One day they drove to Sare for lunch then up into the mountains to the ancient border town, St. Jean-Pied-de-Port. On another, they went to a nouvelle cuisine restaurant in Salies-de-Béarn that Peter Ellis had always wanted to visit and then passed the afternoon walking around the medieval fortifications of Orthez. One chilly, overcast day, they journeyed into Spain down to the coastal town of Mundaca and watched a handful of hearty surfers brave the drizzle and cold, dreary conditions in order to experience the celebrated long, left-breaking wave that peeled, with mechanical precision, across the wide river mouth.

On the last day before Anya's departure, they drove down to the venerable Basque fishing village of Guètary. It was a warm, windless, hazy day, the sunlight muted as though filtered through gauze. Mist hung over the silver-green ocean in the lee of the cliffs bordering the old harbor. Several hundred yards out to sea, fifteen-to-twenty surfers sat in the line-up, waiting for the sets of glassy, double-head high waves to rise majestically out of the deep water. From the vantage point of a cliff-top park, Peter Ellis watched the surfers for almost an hour while Anya made a sketch of the port below. Later, at a small restaurant overlooking the miniscule harbor, they had an excellent lunch of crab farcie, mixed salad and a Peyresol Rosé de Béarn. Afterwards, they walked around the harbor's breakwater and down the shingle beach, stopping for a few moments to watch a large Spanish family raking pungent, black-vermilion seaweed into piles and then loading it into a decrepit truck. In response to Peter Ellis's inquiry, a smiling, leather-faced woman told them that the seaweed was used to make skin cream. To make sure they understood, she illustrated her explanation by rubbing some imaginary cream on her grinning, weather-beaten face. Before leaving Guètary, they walked out to the end of the narrow concrete breakwater and, hand-in-hand, stood for several minutes staring at Biarritz in the hazy distance. Shrouded in mist, the fashionable and recently fatal resort town seemed to belong to another world.

For their last evening together, Peter Ellis organized a surprise farewell dinner party for Anya at Les Flots Bleus, inviting Olga, Maurice, Marc and Christine. It was a gay, warm, friendly affair, the conversation lively and humorous. They feasted on moules marinières, gigot d'agneau in garlic sauce and, for dessert, a delicious homemade gateau Basque. Not once during the meal were the names of Joseph Gambia, Jacques LeClerc, Jean-Claude Duchon or Janine Destin mentioned.

The following morning, Peter Ellis took Anya to the La Negresse train station, arriving late so that he barely had time to kiss her good-bye. And before he knew it, she was gone and he was standing alone on the platform.

He spent the next three days interviewing old local surfers and making detailed notes on all the surf breaks of the region. On the day before he left for Paris, his article about Gambia and LeClerc's involvement in the death of Kevin Duffy and its cover-up appeared as an exclusive in a national newspaper. With great difficulty and not a little self-loathing, he had managed to keep Janine Destin and Jean-Claude Duchon out of it, as well as the integral part played by Le Gentleman Club. On the morning of his departure, he found a heavily-perfumed note slipped under his apartment door. It thanked him for his discretion and wished him <u>bon voyage</u>. It was not signed.

On his drive back to Paris, it started raining on the outskirts of Bordeaux and continued all the way to the capital. By the time he finally climbed the narrow stairs to his cold apartment, he was bone-tired. He deposited his bags in the bedroom, turned on the heat and went down to L'Ecluse to have a glass of wine and collect his mail. Anya's postcard was near the top of the stack. It showed two bicycles, one mauve, one saffron-yellow, leaning against a flower-entwined, black iron fence. Peter Ellis turned the card over and read the short message:

"Dear Peter,
I have your bicycle ready. When are you coming to ride with me? I miss you terribly.
Love,
Anya"

Peter Ellis turned the card back over and looked again at the two bicycles. It occurred to him that he had never been to Amsterdam in November.

Made in United States
North Haven, CT
02 February 2022